**In loving memory of my wonderful
parents, Joy and Theo Baynton**

Copyright © 2025 Martin Baynton

ISBN 978-0-473-73531-9 (paperback)
ISBN 978-0-473-73532-6 (epub)
ISBN 978-0-473-73533-3 (Kindle)

Any references to historical events, real people, or real places are used fictitiously. Some names, characters, and places referred to are from the works of Lewis Carroll, their use is gratefully acknowledged by the author. All other names, characters and places are products of the author's imagination.

12 11 10 9 8 7 6 5 4 3 2 1   5 6 7 8 9 / 2

Cover art by Martin Baynton
Book design: Smartwork Creative, www.smartworkcreative.co.nz
Printed in New Zealand by Yourbooks

www.takingwonderland.com

TAKING
WONDERLAND

Truth and Transformation

BOOK TWO

Martin Baynton

REVIEWS FOR THE FIRST BOOK
IN THE TAKING WONDERLAND SERIES

In 'The Secret of Safe Passage', Martin Baynton breathes new life into the beloved Wonderland universe ... an enthralling read that has left me desperate for the next book. Baynton masterfully blends elements of fantasy, mystery, and adventure... his ability to write a fresh and exciting narrative while still honouring the original is outstanding. Many have tried and failed to fully recreate the mood and whimsy of Wonderland. I am very happy to say that Baynton is one of the very few successes. The Secret of Safe Passage is a must-read for all fans of Wonderland and Portal Fantasy.

- Sarah (Wondermajica). Goodreads

An enthralling adventure that kept me on the edge of my seat from start to finish. The story follows Ali, a witty science-loving teenager, who finds herself in Wonderland. ... I was drawn to Ali's resilient character and found myself rooting for her at every turn ... a must-read for anyone seeking a thrilling and magical journey.

- Abigail L. Goodreads

This was an intriguing take on the Alice In Wonderland story and is a good mix of fantasy, science fiction, and mystery... so if this type of thing is your cup of tea, you should definitely check it out. For my part, I can't wait for the next two books in this trilogy!

- E Thiessen. Amazon

Imagine fairy tales on steroids, but with a dash of scientific curiosity and a strong no-nonsense attitude. I couldn't put this book down... it's like someone mixed Alice in Wonderland with a pinch of Nancy Drew and a generous sprinkle of mystery. If you're up for an adventure that will make your heart race and your mind whirl, dive into this book and get ready for the unexpected – it's a wild ride worth taking!

- Su. Goodreads

Martin Baynton did an amazing job reimagining wonderland. The little girl I was and the woman I am now came together to scream over a story. I was captivated by the storytelling and I truly enjoyed every single page of this book. The beginning of every single chapter sucked me in and I fell in love with Ali, Aunt Martha and the delightful Uncle Bertie. I am anxiously awaiting for book two and the opportunity to continue following Ali on this journey

- Savannah Jo. Goodreads

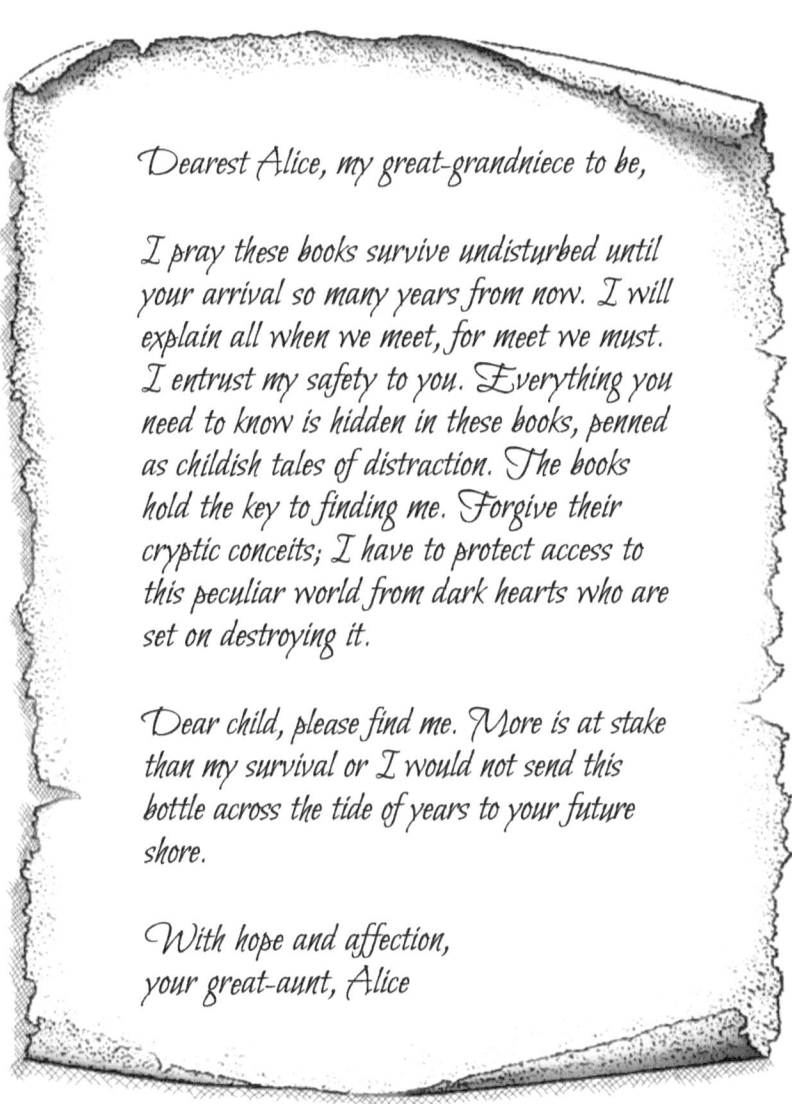

Dearest Alice, my great-grandniece to be,

I pray these books survive undisturbed until your arrival so many years from now. I will explain all when we meet, for meet we must. I entrust my safety to you. Everything you need to know is hidden in these books, penned as childish tales of distraction. The books hold the key to finding me. Forgive their cryptic conceits; I have to protect access to this peculiar world from dark hearts who are set on destroying it.

Dear child, please find me. More is at stake than my survival or I would not send this bottle across the tide of years to your future shore.

With hope and affection,
your great-aunt, Alice

CONTENTS

CHAPTER 1

FAMILY FIRST

The journey to the next village went without incident. Lord Grey drove as carefully as he could, keeping below the speed limit, conscious that every bend in the road would be a challenge for Ali curled up in the boot. From time to time, he shook a little, unable to suppress the image of Potts rising from the debris of their dining room like a bloodied demon from a Goya painting.

'Potts!' It was all he could think to say.

'I know, dear.' His wife, Martha, rested a gloved hand on his elbow. They had called for an ambulance as soon as they were clear of the village, keeping the information brief, giving just the location of the accident and the extent of the injury before ending the call when they were pressed for more details.

'Can you believe this? What in God's name have we done?' He reached down and squeezed her hand.

'What we had to. No time for regrets.' She paused. 'What time we do have will be in service to that girl. We will rescue her father. Everything else is just so much flotsam on the beach.'

They arrived at the next village and found a quiet street on the outskirts where tall hedgerows lined a municipal park.

'This will do,' said Martha. They parked. Lord Grey climbed out, checked that no one was about, opened the car boot – and felt his old heart clamp tight in his chest. The boot was empty, except for a note.

'Oh Ali,' he sighed. 'What now?' He took the note, slammed the boot lid, and climbed back into the car. He didn't say a word, but Martha had read his expression the moment he'd opened the door.

'She's gone, hasn't she?'

'She has, my dear.' He took a deep breath, unfolded the note, and they read it together.

Thank you for making me fall in love with you. Please keep driving and don't be angry. I know where the secret is, and I know how to keep it from them. When Dad gets hold of you – and he will, I'm sure of it – tell him I found Jackie and I'll take care of her for Mum. Tell him I love him with all my heart and I'm sorry I was so angry all the time. It was never him. Never.

Now keep driving, and don't stop till you get safely to London.

They sat in silence, holding hands, their cheeks wet. Then without a word between them, Lord Grey turned the car around. Ali was family, and family stuck together, no matter what.

They stopped once, when Martha said she needed a restroom. She didn't, it was for her husband, but she knew he'd never say and would press on whatever his discomfort. They pulled into the courtyard of a country pub, parking as close to the main door as possible.

'This will do us.' Lord Grey got out, stepped round the car and helped his wife out in a well-practised ritual. He lowered his head and lent down towards her so she could put her hands behind his neck and lock her fingers together.

'May I have this dance?' he said as he straightened his back, pulling her gently to her feet. Then, with his hands on her hips, he took her waist to support her as they walked slowly into the pub, him forwards, her backwards, as if they were dancing to music no one else could hear.

'We used to come here, Bertie ... years ago. Do you remember?'

'I do. Sadly, you won't know the interior. Some colour-blind delinquent was let loose on the place, all cash and no class. Be warned.'

'Oh, and how do you know this?'

'Rotary. Can't have all our meetings in one pub. Must spread the love.'

They carried on through the lounge, their slow-step hardly registering on the only other customers – three workers in orange safety vests. They were sitting together at a corner table, two men and a woman, their eyes fixed on a TV behind the bar.

The toilets were small, clean and tidy. The washbasins were in a shared space outside the cubicles. They stood side by side washing their hands, and caught sight of their reflections in the mirror.

'We need a brandy,' said Lord Grey, and to his surprise, his wife agreed. They eased their way back into the lounge, Martha holding to her husband's arm with one hand, the other taking hold of whatever support she could find on the short journey: the top of an old radiator, a side table. They sat, perching on bar stools like exhausted pigeons recovering from a long flight.

'What in God's name does she hope to do?' Lord Grey stared at his drink.

'I doubt she knows. The dear child is doing exactly what we are.'

'Which is what, exactly?'

'Thinking with her heart.'

'Yes.' He reached out and placed a hand on her arm. 'Well, it has served us well enough.'

Across at the corner table, the workers in their orange safety vests got to their feet, their phones all pinging some call to action. They left their drinks and hurried from the lounge. Lord and Lady Grey finished their brandies and followed at a more sedate pace.

'My toiletries please, Bertie,' said Martha. She lifted her arms clear of the seat belt her husband was struggling to place across her tiny frame. 'In the top of the travel bag I think.'

Lord Grey reached over onto the back seat and opened their bag. Tucked into the top beside the bag of toiletries was Ali's journal.

'For us, I suppose?' He pulled it out and handed it straight to Martha. She glanced at it, briefly closed her eyes as if gathering strength, then took her reading glasses from her purse.

'I'll read, you drive.' She opened the journal, and Bertie drove the Bentley out onto the road. Inside the cover was a note.

If all goes to plan, you'll be safely in London unpacking your bags when you read this. There's so much I have to tell you, and no time left. So read this, keep it safe, and give it to Dad when you find him. It's just bullet points – what I saw over there, and what I think is going on. And you were never crazy, Auntie, your bluebell clearing among the silver birch trees is a real place, but it's good your family sent you away, or you might be lost over there like our Great Aunt Alice … AND … you would have never married the best uncle on the planet.

Stay in London and stay safe. I don't think these people will touch you there, not with me gone, they don't need you as leverage anymore and they don't like attention, so just find Dad – but that's all. PLEASE don't kick the hornet's nest, Uncle Bertie, we really don't know what's in there.

Forgive me,

Ali XXX

Neither made comment. Lord Grey kept driving and listened intently as Martha read through the journal. He shook his head from time to time but kept his eyes on the road ahead, flexing his hands and fingers from time to time to ease the cramp in his knuckles.

'You're speeding, Bertie.'

'Yes.' He glanced across at his wife, realised her comment was a statement, not a reprimand, and kept his foot down. They were almost home when they hit traffic.

'What the blazes!' Lord Grey stared at the line of cars up ahead. In all the years they'd lived here, neither had ever seen any congestion in the village.

'Can we get around it?' Martha was watching the scene outside. It was far more than a simple traffic jam. The pavements were crowded with locals hurrying on foot towards the main green. She cursed quietly. Whatever this was, she'd bet it involved Ali. How could it not?

'We could try the service road behind the shops,' said Lord Grey. A siren drowned him out as two fire engines came weaving their way through the cars behind them.

'Something's not right,' whispered Martha.

'Obviously, my dear.'

'Not the traffic – the skyline.' She leaned forward and stared through the windscreen. 'Something ... what is it ...?'

At first, she couldn't place it. Then it struck her like a blow to the stomach. 'Oh, dear God! The church spire – it's gone!'

They pulled over to let the fire engines through. All the cars were stationary now, their drivers getting out, everyone reaching for their phones and setting off on foot.

'Follow them!' said Martha. She saw her husband's hesitation, the concern clouding his eyes. 'I'll be fine. Go!'

He did, joining the surge of people heading toward the green. In minutes he had a clear view of the church.

'Bloody hell!' Lord Grey had been a teenager in London during the Blitz and had experienced its depressing aftermath, the demolition of so many damaged and unstable buildings. Now, here in front of him was his own parish church, its steeple gone and much of the roof. Not that he cared in that moment; all that mattered was the girl who might be under all that rubble.

He pushed his way towards the yellow tape of a police cordon where locals were badgering a young officer. The young woman looked fresh out of college.

'Was it the builders?' asked a teenager with green hair. 'Are the builders buried under that lot?'

'I don't know.'

'Anyone hurt?'

'No word yet.' The officer raised her voice, responding to the moment as best she could with lines borrowed from some TV show. 'Can everyone please stay behind the tape. Let everyone do their jobs, okay?'

'There was a girl ...' A mother holding a small baby waved a finger at the church. 'She was climbing the scaffold. I called you. I called the police.'

Lord Grey pushed his way towards the woman but felt his knees giving way so leaned on the nearest shoulder to steady himself. He needed to sit down. He needed another brandy.

An ambulance pulled out from behind the church, it's blue light flicking into life as it found a path around the scattered bricks.

'Ali!' Lord Grey pushed his way back to his car as the ambulance weaved a slow passage through the chaos around him. Martha said nothing as her husband climbed in beside her; she'd seen the ambulance and their next move needed no discussion.

'Damn it!' Lord Grey executed a clumsy five-point turn, clipping the bumper of a Toyota van and toppling a parked motorbike. He graunched gears and turned the air blue with expletives. They followed the ambulance a few short blocks to the medical clinic.

Lord Grey pulled up, climbed out, and was heading for the rear doors of the ambulance when a police car came racing in from the other direction. The back of the ambulance swung open and a medic stepped out. He was pink with dust. On the gurney behind him, a body lay beneath a green sheet.

'What are you doing here?'

Lord Grey turned. Superintendent Dovecot was standing behind him. She too, was pink with dust.'

'Who's this?' he asked, ignoring her question.

'We don't know.'

'Thank God!' Lord Grey's relief was so transparent, Dovecot couldn't fail to notice it.

'You thought it was Alice.'

'Nonsense!' He almost barked the response.

'Yes, you did. Plain as day. You think Ali was in that church?'

'All right, yes.' Lord Grey tried to gather his wits. 'The thought had occurred to me. She ran out on us, you see. Gone to find her father. Hitching her way down to London as we speak.' He could feel the officer's gaze scanning him like a laser, dissecting his performance.

'But you're not a hundred percent sure.' She said it softly, guiding him to trust her.

'No …' he said, appearing to drop all pretence. 'London was her plan, but did she really leave? How can we know? When that young lady has her mind set on something, I think the fates must take great care to step out of her way.'

'Yes. Bit of a hothead, that one. We must talk, Lord Grey. I'll be in touch.'

CHAPTER 2

THROUGH AND THROUGH

Waxstaff coughed again. No specks of blood this time. Was that good or bad? Ali didn't know and felt helpless. None of this had been planned. She was running on instinct. So, what now? Hold Waxstaff's hand till she died?

They were side by side in the bluebell clearing; Waxstaff lying on her back, Ali sitting beside her. The sun was behind them, hovering low in the sky, a ball of vermilion flame behind the trees. In front of them, a giant moon hung in a sky of deepest turquoise.

'Dawn or dusk?' Ali wondered aloud. 'Hard to tell.' She had been tracking the shadow cast by a blade of grass near her feet. It seemed to be getting shorter.

'Dawn,' said Waxstaff. 'Dawn would be best.'

'Yes. Not keen on spending a night in the open.' They fell silent again. Ali watched a swarm of butterflies lifting from the bluebells on the far side of the clearing. It rose above the treeline, a shimmering cloud of beating wings. 'Strangers in a strange land.' Ali said it quietly; something to say.

'That's us.' Waxstaff paused. Another cough. 'Your aunt has a copy.'

'I know.' Ali's aunt liked science fiction. The shelves in her bedroom were an A to Z of the classics, Asimov to Wells. 'Maybe it was her way of making sense of this place. It was easier for me. Dad was always going on about the multiverse. He made it sound normal.'

'Till you see it.'

'Yeah.' Ali chuckled. 'Who knew bluebells could be this blue?'

'Lots more to see.' Waxstaff coughed again. 'You need to be on your way.'

'No!' Ali almost barked the word, like a child refusing to go to bed. She was not going to leave Waxstaff to die alone. Instead, she concentrated on the shadow cast by the blade of grass. Was it getting shorter, or had she moved her head and stuffed up the observation? 'Relativity,' she whispered.

'What is?'

'I've been watching a shadow getting shorter. So, either the sun's climbing, or my head moved. With an observer in the experiment, any measurement is relative to the position of the person doing the measuring.'

'Your beloved Einstein, I presume?'

'Yes.'

'Did he stop to smell the bluebells, even once?'

'Roger that.' Ali stretched out beside her mother's friend; two visitors on a sea of bluebells, content for the moment just to be there, staring into a turquoise sky few people had ever seen.

'I did the right thing, didn't I?' Ali said quietly. 'Bringing us through?'

'For me. Not for you.' Waxstaff paused. 'I imagine King will come after you.'

'I guess so.'

'Those papers you found in the church,' another long pause. 'Does King think the secret to safe passage is among them?'

'Yes.' Ali watched as a line of geese came honking across the sky, their feathers glowing pink.

'Then she'll come.'

'And she'll be trapped here. Aunt Martha and Uncle Bertie will be safe. So will Dad.'

They fell into silence again, watching the bluebells turn to purple as the sun cleared the treeline and washed the ground in red light.

'Tell me about Potts,' said Waxstaff.

'Tell you what exactly?'

A large bee came humming across the bluebells towards them. It paused in the air just inches from Ali's face, big as a fist, its wings vibrating like a chainsaw. Ali sat still, holding her breath until the bee lost interest and buzzed away.

'She burst into the barn,' said Waxstaff, 'just before we came through.'

'I thought you were spaced out from all the painkillers.'

'She was soaked in blood.'

'Yes,' Ali said softly, her voice barely a whisper. Images she'd been pushing away began tumbling back into focus – a horror show, raw and uncensored. The Bentley crashing into the dining room. The shattered window frame falling onto Nurse Potts, pinning her with daggers of glass. The giant nurse rising from the debris like a harpooned whale, her white uniform blooming with red stains, blood pooling like treacle at her feet, enough to fill a bath.

'I just wanted to stop her. Not kill her.'

'You don't know she's dead.' Waxstaff reached for Ali's hand. 'That woman is tough. I would gladly put her down like a sick animal for what she did, but I don't want you bearing the guilt of it.'

'Aunt Martha promised she'd call an ambulance when we were clear of the village, but Potts was still trapped when I came back for you.' Ali wondered if her aunt had even made the call. 'Maybe the emergency number was too busy.'

'Busy with what?'

'I brought the church spire down on top of King. I buried her.'

'What?!' Waxstaff rolled her head to the side and stared at Ali. 'Tell me everything.'

Ali did, leaving nothing out. Waxstaff listened quietly. No comments, no interruptions.

'Now I should write it down,' Ali pulled a blank writing pad from her pack. It was a small spiralbound notebook that she'd found in Potts' medical bag.

'Why?' Waxstaff's eyes were closed.

'We're explorers,' said Ali. She glanced at her mother's old friend. Waxstaff's breathing had eased, and there was a softness around the eyes, as if her pain was easing. 'And we need to keep the memories fresh. Alice warned about it, how you forget yourself over here if you don't keep notes.'

'She does? I missed that.'

'Second book, first chapter,' Ali reached into the backpack and pulled out her two Wonderland books. 'So, Alice has just arrived through the mirror, and she picks up two chess pieces lying in the hearth; a King and a Queen.' Ali flicked to the right page and began reading:

"The horror of that moment," the King went on, "I shall never, never forget!" "You will, though," the Queen said, "if you don't make a memorandum of it." Alice looked on with great interest as the King took an enormous memorandum-book out of his pocket and began writing.'

'Well, well,' said Waxstaff, her eyes still closed.

'Everything important is hidden in these books. Everything. The identity of the two boys, the secret of safe passage.'

'King thinks so too," said Waxstaff. 'She has a whole team sifting through every page. If the secret for going back safely is in there, they would have found it by now.'

Ali didn't reply. Anything she said would sound boastful or just plain stupid. How could she decode a secret that King's experts had all missed? And yet she knew with an absolute certainty that she would. Her great-aunt Alice had been younger than her when she'd written the two books and made up all the riddles. Some of those secrets were hidden in plain sight.

'I think King must be overthinking it, treating everything in the book as if it's been written by an academic, when some of the facts are just dressed up as silly stories. No riddles, she just tells it like it is.'

'Such as?'

'Okay, there's a simple one in the first book. Alice takes the crying baby from the Duchess.' Ali found the page, cleared her throat, and started reading:

The baby grunted again, and Alice looked anxiously into its face to see what was the matter. There could be no doubt that it had a VERY turn-up nose, much more like a snout than a real nose; also, its eyes were getting extremely small for a baby. "If you're going to turn into a pig, my dear, I shall have nothing more to do with you." The baby grunted again, so violently, that she looked down into its face in some alarm. This time there could be NO mistake about it: it was neither more nor less than a pig.'

'You think your Alice really saw a baby turn into a pig?'

'Yes.'

'You? The girl who loves science and rational thinking?'

'Yes,' Ali laughed. 'The same girl who talked to a giant rabbit last time I was over here.'

CHAPTER 3

LITTLE WHITE LIES

―――――――――

There was no sign of Nurse Potts when Lord and Lady Grey arrived back at the house. There was blood, a great deal of it, mostly in the dining room where Ali had crashed the car and trapped Potts beneath the shattered French doors.

'Obviously the wretched woman's not dead,' growled Lord Grey. 'Is that good or bad, do you suppose?'

They had driven onto the main lawn and were staring out through the car windscreen at the mess.

'I'm having trouble registering this, Bertie.'

'Well, of course you are. This entire day has been a massive kettle of fish! But there it is. No Potts! At least we won't have to deal with her dead carcass.'

'Bertie! That's not worthy of you.'

'No time for niceties. Our single focus must be to keep that barn safe so Ali can find her way back to us. Agreed?'

'Yes, dear.' Martha stared through the windscreen at the shattered windows. 'So ... what happened here? We called the ambulance, so either it came here and took her to hospital, or the wretched woman dragged herself away.'

'I believe she did exactly that – look at the patio.' Bertie pointed to a set of bloody footprints leading out onto the lawn. He climbed from the Bentley, pulled the wheelchair from the back seat, and helped his wife settle into it.

'Best bring your walking stick, Bertie. Potts may be injured, but I won't have you playing the hero.' They followed the trail of blood across the lawn, Lord Grey growling under his breath at the strain of pushing the wheelchair across the grass.

'Enough of this malarkey.' He turned the wheelchair around and began dragging it backwards. 'Sorry for the indignity, my dear!'

'Shouting an apology doesn't make it more sincere,' said Martha. 'Keep your voice down.' The door to the barn lay broken on the floor. Lord Grey made ready to enter, but his wife reached up and took his elbow.

'She's not in there, Bertie. The prints come back out again.'

Lord Grey bent forward. His wife was right, two sets of bloody prints. One in, one out. 'So, what do we do?'

'We go to the house, lock ourselves inside and call Superintendent Dovecot. Then we make a large pot of tea, catch our breath and plan how to explain all this when the police arrive.'

'Fair enough. Tea and brandy it is.'

'Just tea.' Martha looked at her husband and smiled. 'The brandy can wait. That policewoman is sharp as a tack, so you will need your wits about you.'

'Yes. Which brandy will provide.'

'No, dear. Now ... before you drag me up to the house, you must check the tunnel. In her note, Ali said she would try to take Waxstaff through with her. If she failed, then the poor woman is still alive down there and suffering.'

'Indeed.' Lord Grey tilted the chair a little, pushed his wife across the fallen door and surveyed the mess. The floor was littered with the contents of Potts' medical bag. The bag itself lay upturned on the bed. The dust sheets that had covered the furniture had been torn into strips, and smears of blood were on everything.

'God in thunder, what a bloody mess!'

'Yes. Push me into the middle and park me up, Bertie. I'll try to make sense of all this while you check the tunnel. I've seen enough police dramas to know we shouldn't disturb anything but in this case that's rather the point. Our task is to confuse the picture as best we can and print our own narrative on it.'

'Right you are.' Lord Grey did as instructed. The trapdoor stood open, and he lowered himself down into the tunnel. He emerged a few minutes later, his white hair adorned with a veil of cobwebs. 'No sign of Waxstaff.'

They spent the next hour in the kitchen, drinking tea, and getting the basics of their story straight, which boiled down to: Ali had lost her temper and gone off to London to find her father.

'And Waxstaff?' asked Martha.

'More difficult.' Bertie scratched at his white beard. 'Perhaps she followed, volunteering to bring her back?'

'No, dear.' Martha topped up her cup of tea. 'If Waxstaff had volunteered, you would most certainly have taken her in the car. Keep it simple; the woman has gone, and we have no idea why.'

'Fair enough.' Lord Grey helped himself to a gingernut biscuit.

'Potts is our real problem,' said Martha.

'Yes, the elephant in our room!'

'Don't be cheap, dear. All the damage and all the blood? How on earth can we explain all that?'

'Yes indeed ...' Lord Grey was silent for a long time, his storytelling brain in overdrive. Then he thumped the table and grinned. 'We tell the truth about Potts. We must spin an entire castle of white lies around Ali and Waxstaff, but with Potts, we tell the basic truth of it. The woman got completely plastered on my precious port, then took the car for a very expensive joy ride.'

His wife agreed, and they spent the next hour rehearsing their story.

'Good, I think we have it,' Lord Grey stood up and stretched his back. 'Oh, wait here, one small detail to attend to.'

'Do share.'

'I need to take the car for a spin on the lawn. Trash the grass a bit.'

'No. If you're spotted, our whole story comes apart. I'm surprised that police officer's not here already.'

'With that mess in the village, and a body under the church rubble? Paying us a visit will be a long way down her list. We must call them as soon as I've messed up the lawn.' Lord Grey went out and spent five minutes destroying a lawn that had been tended with love and care for hundreds of years.

Then his wife placed the call, and two hours later they were telling their version of events to Superintendent Dovecot.

'No idea what got into her,' said Bertie. 'She was out on the lawn, driving the Bentley all over the grass – my beautiful lawn! – drunk as the proverbial skunk, ripping the turf to shreds.' He paused and looked thoughtful. 'That's it for croquet this summer.'

'What prompted it? Had you fired her?' Dovecot was standing in the door to the dining room, surveying the wreckage within. The Greys were behind her in the long hallway.

'Heavens no,' said Martha. 'I've come to depend on her.'

'No hint of any this madness,' her husband gestured into the room. 'One minute the woman is sane as a sandwich, the next she's a bulldozer.'

'You saw the whole thing? Both of you?'

'We did! She drove onto the patio and in through the French doors! Then the damn fool got out and started dancing through the wreckage. Cut herself to ribbons. Blood everywhere! Enough to paint the house.'

'We called the ambulance,' said Martha. 'It never came. Far too busy at the church, I imagine.'

'No doubt.' Dovecot turned from the wreckage to face them. 'This really has been quite the day. So, where's Nurse Potts now?'

'Aye, there's the rub,' said Bertie.

'Disappeared,' said Martha.

'Another one? Please say you're kidding me.'

'No trace of her, just her bloody footprints out to the barn.' Bertie paused as if recalling the details. 'Her medical bag is lying on an old bed, vials of medication scattered all about the place.'

'She tore an old bed sheet into strips,' said Martha. 'For bandages I assume. Then there are more footprints out across the lawn.'

'And you know all this – how? By trampling across all the evidence?'

'Well, we had to try and find the poor woman,' said Martha. 'Now, can we please move this discussion to the kitchen? I need a cup of tea.'

'Me too.' Lord Grey set off down the hall, pushing his wife in her chair, his mind racing. That damned policewoman wasn't buying any of it!

'Here we are.' He settled Martha at the kitchen table and put the kettle on the stove. 'How do you take your tea?'

'Strong with milk.' Dovecot sat down, pulled her phone from her pocket and put it on the table in front of her. 'I use this for my notes, do you mind?'

'No, please go ahead.' Martha was careful not to glance up at her husband.

'So, let me recap this madness. Your nurse, dependable up until now, gets blind drunk for no reason that you're aware of. She takes your car and drives into the dining room where she gets out and begins prancing around on broken glass.'

'Exactly!' said Lord Grey. 'Biscuit?'

'No, thank you. And instead of calling the police, you follow a trail of blood to your barn, trampling and contaminating the crime scene.'

'Crime scene?!' Lord Grey did his best to act bewildered. 'What crime? One of our staff was running about bleeding like a fountain. Our only duty was to her! There was no crime, unless we choose to press charges for wanton vandalism.'

'So, you called for an ambulance.'

'Yes.'

'When? What time was the call?'

'Here,' Lord Grey took out his phone, pulled up the call history and showed Dovecot the screen.

'Then we drove to the clinic,' said Martha. 'We hoped to find Potts there. That's when Bertie saw you.'

'Yes.' The inspector looked Lord Grey straight in the eye. 'You said nothing to me about any of this.'

'You did have rather a lot on your plate.'

'No … this is all wrong.' Dovecot scanned both their faces. 'Wait here please.' She stepped out into the garden and placed a call, watching them both through the window as she spoke.

'This is not going well,' whispered Martha.

'Okay,' Dovecot said as she came back inside. 'Your house and the grounds are now a crime scene. A forensic team is on its way here. You will be instructed on where you can go, and where you cannot. Do you understand?'

'Not really, no.'

'The blood, Lord Grey, as you put it yourself – "enough to paint a house". So, no arguments or you'll be out of here and lodging at the pub.'

'We will not,' said Martha. 'Bertie would prop the bar up all day.'

'Not with their scotch list. Not a decent single malt in sight!'

'Oh, do stop it, both of you,' sighed Dovecot. 'You need to take this very seriously. I have a dead body at the church, and the real possibility of another body curled up under a tree here at your estate. Now ... tell me about Alice.'

'Why?' Lord Grey took a sip of tea. 'What has any of this to do with her?'

'Seriously? Is that how you want to do this?' Dovecot remained standing but picked up her tea and sipped it. 'Lord Grey, I saw your face at the clinic when they brought the body from the church. You weren't there looking for Potts. You were looking for Alice. You were terrified it was her body on that stretcher.'

Lord Grey said nothing and kept his eyes on his teacup.

'So, here's my problem. Your niece was sent here by her school. Suspended. And why was she suspended? For assaulting another student. Then, yesterday, she assaulted your housekeeper.'

'You're drawing a very long bow,' said Martha.

'Enough. You can help me or hinder me, but here's my problem. One of my officers at the church has a statement from a witness who saw a young lady climb the scaffolding up to the church spire just before it collapsed. A man died under that rubble. How long a bow do I need?' Dovecot stared at the old couple, daring them to argue the point. They didn't.

'Good. I shall bring a forensic team here as soon as I can assemble one. In the meantime, I suggest you contact young Alice, because right at this moment, like it or not, she is my prime suspect.'

'That's ridiculous!'

'Is it? Then find her,' the inspector sat down again. 'I will have that biscuit now, thank you.'

'Gingernuts!' said Lord Grey, scrambling to his feet, glad of the excuse to break eye contact with Dovecot. Damn she was good!

'I'm sure we'll discover young Alice safely in London,' said Martha.

'I hope so, Lady Grey, because apart from being a prime suspect, I must list her as a missing person, of which I now have four! How is that even possible in one small village. Potts, Waxstaff, Alice and a woman who helps at the church, a Mrs King.' She counted the names on her fingers, tapping each in turn, a mother counting on a child's hand: four little piggies going to market. Lord Grey thought it amusing to point this out. Dovecot wasn't impressed.

'Stay here in the kitchen, both of you. I only brought the one constable with me. He'll do a thorough search of the house and grounds for Potts, please stay tight in here till he comes back. He will set yellow tape around the dining room and barn and remain here for the night. Can you organize a meal and bedding for the young man?'

'Perhaps,' Lord Grey raised an eyebrow. 'Is he house-trained?'

Martha shot him a look. 'We can,' she said, 'for tonight at least. Tomorrow we can hire someone from the village.'

'Good.' Dovecot rose from the table. 'And please stay out of the dining room and the barn. I'll try to have forensics come out first thing tomorrow. Now, if you'll excuse me, I can see myself out.'

'Nonsense,' Lord Grey got to his feet. 'This is a big house, and we could lose you. One more missing person on your list.'

'Poor taste, Bertie,' said Martha as her husband led their guest into the hall. He was back a moment later and spread his arms in mock defeat. 'She doesn't believe a word of it, Martha. Not one word.'

'No, but some cards have fallen in our favour.'

'Not from where I'm sitting.'

'The police are taping off the barn, Bertie. No one will be going in or out. A young police constable will be standing guard all night, and tomorrow the house will be crawling with forensics.'

'How is that to our advantage?'

'Because the only thing that matters is keeping that barn safe for Ali, how much safer can it get?'

'I suppose you're right.' Lord Grey crossed to the kitchen window and stared out at the grounds. 'When that constable gets back, we'll go to the parlour for that brandy.'

'Yes, dear.' She watched her husband for a moment, then sighed. 'And what aren't you telling me? You're sparing me something. I can always tell. What is it?'

'Maybe nothing. But that was the last packet of biscuits. Waxstaff always kept a decent stock. Saw them myself ... I come pilfering most nights.'

'We know, dear, that's why she kept so many packets.'

'Well, they're gone. Every last one.' He crossed to the sideboard and opened the bread bin. That was empty too.

'You think it's Potts?'

'Who else. The damned woman patched herself up in the barn, then came to grab rations. She's gone to ground, hiding out somewhere here in the house.'

CHAPTER 4

RIBBONS AND RHYME

———————————

A flicker of light caught Ali's eye, a rainbow of scattered colours dancing across the white bark of the tree above them.

'What's making that?' She pointed it out to Waxstaff as she scanned the branches for the cause. A crystal pendant, the size of her thumb, was hanging from the branches. There was a ribbon tied beside it, weather-torn and faded.

'I remember those.' Waxstaff smiled. 'There used to be more. I thought they were markers left by others – to show the right tree. Mark the way home.'

'Maybe ...' Ali got to her feet and climbed the tree. She reached the pendant easily enough, untied it and brought it down. 'I think there's more to it than that.'

'Like what?'

'Just an idea.' Ali polished the grime from the small crystal. Could reflected light play a role in this? A mirror in the barn, a crystal in the tree? 'Half an idea, anyway. I need time to think it through.'

'You do that.' Waxstaff tried lifting her head, and let out a groan. 'But right now, it's time you set off on an errand.'

'Not going to happen.' Ali started to climb back up the tree. 'Somebody will come by. The Hatter or that white rabbit.'

'Or King,' said Waxstaff. It was statement, not a question.

'Yes. But she's got to get out from under the rubble first. We have time.'

'She's had time. Half a day at least. Maybe a day. Time moves a lot faster over there, remember?'

'It would be good to know how fast.' Ali tied the crystal back on the branch and started down. 'I'd need two clocks. Take one of them with me and check the time difference when I got back.'

'Good, now fetch me some water. I'm thirsty as hell.'

'I'll pop to the nearest store, shall I?'

'I'm serious, Ali. My mouth is so dry it hurts.' Waxstaff lifted a hand and pointed off to their left. 'The ground drops away behind that treeline over there. There's a gully with a stream at the bottom. It was a long time ago, but I was stuck here for weeks, remember. Foraging to survive. Camping near this tree waiting for your mother to come back for me.'

'This isn't a trick? Like in the movies, sending me off on some dumb errand so you can quietly drop dead on me.'

'No.' Waxstaff managed a grin. 'And don't make me laugh, it hurts.'

'Okay, I'll get water, but you stay put. No crawling off into the bushes.'

'I won't.' Waxstaff paused as a fit of coughing took hold. 'How odd that I can remember where that stream is. So much else has faded.'

'Which is why we must both write in the notepad,' said Ali. 'We'll make notes and read them together at the end of every day.'

'Not me, dear, I plan to forget.' Waxstaff paused for breath and caught sight of Ali's expression. 'You don't approve?'

'No, I get it. What you went through. Forgetting might be good. I understand.'

'But?'

'Nothing. It makes sense.' Ali started putting the books and notepad into her backpack. 'I'll go look for that stream.'

'Oh god, of course!' Waxstaff closed her eyes and let her head rest back on the grass. 'How cruel of me. I wasn't thinking. I have memories of your mother.'

'Of when she was young, yes. Before I knew her. Before Dad knew her. That will all be lost if you forget everything.'

'Then we make a deal.' Waxstaff's breath still rattled, liquid bubbling deep in the lungs. 'When you get back, I'll dictate what I can remember of your mother.'

'And in return?'

'You agree to move on without me.'

'No deal.' Ali bent down, kissed her mother's friend on the cheek and set off to find the stream. She crossed the bluebell clearing and moved into the copse of trees Waxstaff had pointed to. The ground sloped away gently under the canopy of trees. The undergrowth was a deep emerald green. Nettles, ferns and ground-creeping vines formed a dense, tangled carpet.

There was a path. It was narrow, no wider than Ali's foot. A deer path? She started along it, working her way down the side of a shallow gully. Soon the silver birch trees gave way to giant ferns. Ali had seen fern trees at the botanic gardens in Hyde Park but never such a dense forest of them. Overhead, their spreading fronds grew from the tops of the trunks like vast umbrellas.

Ali heard the water before she saw it. The stream itself was concealed by fern trees. The ground became steeper, and she needed to move from trunk to trunk, aiming at each and grabbing it to control her momentum. Then she saw the Hatter.

He was standing in the creek, the water cooling his bare feet, his boots hanging from his neck by their laces.

'Hello,' Ali stepped out from behind a tree.

'Ah. There you are.' The Hatter didn't seem surprised to see her. He was fanning his face with his hat, and Ali could see his hair properly for the first time. It was jet black and braided like rope, each braid waist-long and tied with small ribbons, dozens to each braid, hundreds in total.

'What are you doing?' asked Ali.

'Looking for you.'

'In a stream?'

'Why would I do that?' asked the Hatter.

'That's my point.'

'Then your question could have been better phrased, don't you think? Something along the lines of – what am I doing in the stream whilst I am looking for you?'

'And your answer is?'

'Cooling my feet,' the Hatter pointed to his bare feet. 'I do my best thinking with both feet in water. I think my blood rushes to my head to escape the cold.'

'That's the shunts in your blood vessels,' said Ali. 'Cold water gets them working overtime.'

'Interesting,' he tipped his head on one side and stared at Ali as if studying an unusual butterfly. 'Theodore said you were prone to talk like this on occasion.'

'Like what?'

'Like a scholar, strings of words nobody understands. Are you a scholar?'

'If you mean a student, then, yes, I am a scholar.'

'A girl scholar! Ha, imagine that!' The Hatter laughed and kicked the water. 'Wonderful. There will be fireworks when we get you to the palace. Tell me more about these shunts.'

'They act like valves and send the blood where it's needed. They want to stop you losing body heat, so they're directing blood away from your feet.'

'To my head. Exactly as I said. To make me think more clearly.'

'Just get out of the water before your toes fall off.'

'Duly noted. Enough thinking for one day.' The Hatter gave Ali a mock bow and made his way to the bank.

'Can I borrow your hat?'

'My hat? Gracious, no. Far too big for you.'

'Not to wear. To carry water back to the clearing. Someone came through with me. I think she's dying.' The Hatter said nothing for a moment. He stared down at the water, then nodded, dipped his hat into the steam, and stepped up onto the bank.

'How badly is she dying?' he asked.

'How badly? She's in a lot of pain, is that what you mean?'

'No, not at all.' The Hatter leaned in and studied her face. 'Something new to learn, young scholar. A bad death here can be painful, certainly, but very rare and very complicated.'

'Explain.'

'Briefly then, not the full lecture. Dying is very difficult to manage over here. Her body will do its very best to repair itself, to mend. What form that mending will take, that depends on her.'

'What form?' Ali grabbed his elbow. 'Can a baby turn into a pig over here?'

'Yes.'

'And are you saying that it's damage that triggers a transformation? You get badly hurt and your body starts adapting to save you?'

'Exactly so.' The Hatter passed the hat of water to Ali, then sat on the bank to pull his boots on. 'Our bodies do everything in their power to mend. And I mean everything, young lady. But don't press me for details. None of the palace scholars can agree on the subject, except for one detail – do NOT get badly injured.'

'So, that white rabbit I met last time, Theodore. He was badly hurt?'

'Badly does not come close. The poor chap was in a very sorry state when he stumbled through,' the Hatter leveled his gaze at Ali. 'You must promise not to discuss any of this with him. It was traumatizing and he chose to forget all about it. Now that he has forgotten it all, he yearns to remember, to know his history. That is a shared dilemma. Who can choose to have sweet oblivion from our past traumas, and replace them with a single trauma, the desire to fill the vacuum of your past and remember it all again.'

'How come you remember all this?

'It takes diligence, and in my case, a great many ribbons,' the Hatter shook his dreadlocks, setting his ribbons to dance like butterflies.

'They're your notes.' Ali could see that each ribbon had writing on it.

'Yes indeed. This was the Queen's idea. I remember nothing of my life before meeting her. But I remember everything from that day forward on account of my ribbons. You are on here somewhere, a yellow ribbon, I think. The full memory of a day returns with the reading a single note; we all do it. Theodore prefers verse to ribbons.

He writes a new verse every day and recites it every night. To himself, thankfully, the ballad is rather long now and far from entertaining.'

'Does it include what happened when he first arrived?'

'No, he chose to forget his painful arrival, so best we don't remind him.'

'Okay. I'd never hurt him.'

'Never?' the Hatter shook his head. 'He might test you on that score; I want to slap his ears most days. As to what happened to Theodore, he was a hunter, a poacher of rabbit and deer. His last and defining memory of that life was of being torn to pieces by dogs and left for dead.'

'Bloody hell!'

'Quite so, very bloody and very hellish. I know, since I was the one who came across the poor fellow when he appeared. He was dying badly. Choices had to be made, watch and tend as best I could, or bring the affair to a tidy conclusion.'

'Go on.'

'All right, disturbing as this is, it's best you know the truth of it, since this will apply when we return to your colleague,' the Hatter resumed, pulling on his boots. 'There is no change without pain, but unfortunately, there can be a great deal of pain without change. So, you must prepare yourself.'

'I have to get back to her.'

'Yes, and quickly. We don't want the others finding her.'

'Others? You mean the disgusting beetle thing?'

'The Jabberwocky, yes. And his nasty little pack rats. They come and go through here, but Theodore is close at hand, sniffing for any sign of them.'

'They're looking for me, aren't they? They want their histories.'

'They do indeed,' the Hatter jumped up, boot laces tied. 'As do we all.'

CHAPTER 5

AN AXE OF KINDNESS

———————

They set off at a steady lope. Ali wanted to run, but she was carrying the hat of water like a bowl, and a fast, loping walk was all she could manage.

'So, did you find them? The histories?' The Hatter made the question sound casual but Ali had spent too many hours in therapy to miss a needy and loaded question when she heard one.

'My great-aunt Alice went to a lot of trouble hiding them. Why was that?'

'It's complicated.'

'Most things are.'

'Yes, indeed.' The Hatter turned and started walking backwards, his eyes scanning her face as if he were looking for something specific. 'I think Alice had two reasons for hiding them. The first concerns our sanity; we can discuss that later. It is the second reason that occupied her the most.'

'Which is?'

'No one can return safely back to your world without first remembering their former life over there. It's one ingredient of what Alice called "The Secret of Safe Passage." We talked of it on your last visit. You believed eating mushrooms was part of the secret.'

'I thought mushrooms would stop me throwing my guts up.'

'Gut-throwing?'

'Vomiting.'

'Ah! How distressingly expressive.' The Hatter skipped back round to walk forwards again. 'And yes, you are right in part. The palace scholars are of a similar mind. Mushrooms can help with the stomach, but not with the dying. They believe there is formula, a combination of elements that allows for safe passage, and that Alice discovered it and employed it to go back and forth. Knowing the details of your previous life over there appears to be one of them.'

'She never shared the secret with anyone here?'

'No. Most accept that Alice held tightly to the secret for good reason, to stop the corrupted, like the Jabberwocky, from returning back to the other world.'

'I hope to find her.'

'Good, I hope you do. Alice was a law unto herself and never announced her intentions unless it served her plans. She was a constant source of irritation to the Queen, who for all that still loves her dearly.'

They were climbing the steady rise from the river. Ali stumbled, almost dropping the hat but saving it and the water by dropping to her knees.

'Question,' she said. 'If that disgusting beetle creature is so keen to get his hands on the histories, why hasn't he set up camp in the bluebell clearing?'

'Not possible, thankfully. It would be a torture for them.' The Hatter reached down and cradled his hat while Ali got to her feet. 'Lingering this close to the palace seems to hasten their corruption.'

'Is that their name for the transformation?'

'We don't know; perhaps it is some odd extension of it. It's nothing we can see, and nothing any of the palace folk have endured. But for the Fringe dwellers, it seems distressingly real. They pass through these parts at a run, screaming their hearts out. The scholars believe this yelping and hullabaloo is a distraction from their pain. So you see they cannot linger here, they race through and race back to the fringes to lick their wounds.'

They emerged out of the trees, and Ali could see Waxstaff on the far side of the clearing. She wasn't alone. The white rabbit was standing over her holding a very large axe.

'Look at this,' Waxstaff said, as she turned and grinned at Ali hurrying towards her. 'Death comes in many forms. But an axe-wielding rabbit who insists I call him Theodore?'

'Insisting has little to do with it,' said Theodore. 'My name is my name.'

'Put it down, my dear fellow.' The Hatter stepped past him and gave Waxstaff a short and rather theatrical bow. 'Hello again, I can see it's been rather a long time for you. But you are our Jackie, yes?'

'Yes, it's been many years,' said Waxstaff. 'Though not for you, clearly.'

'Indeed.' He turned to Theodore. 'Are any of the critters close by?'

'Yes and no.' The rabbit dipped his head towards Waxstaff. 'No whiff of Jabber and his rat-pack, just from our new arrival here.'

'Good.' The Hatter put a hand on Theodore's shoulder. 'So stop swinging the axe like a woodsman, it's a little intimidating, don't you think?'

'Yes, I do. That's rather the point.' Theodore lowered the axe. 'Mend it or end it. You know the rules.'

'Firstly, it is a custom not a rule,' said the Hatter. 'And secondly, have you explained the logic of this to our guest?'

'Oh, indeed!' Waxstaff laughed. 'Your pet rabbit painted the full picture.'

'Pet rabbit!' Theodore hefted the axe up again. 'Come, Hatter, we need a moment alone to discuss this.' He swung the axe over his shoulder, stuck his pink nose in the air and marched a short distance away across the clearing.

'Forgive him. He can be a stickler for protocol.' The Hatter gave Waxstaff an apologetic shrug and went to talk to Theodore.

'Cute bunny,' said Waxstaff.

'You didn't meet him when you were here before?' Ali knelt and held the hat of water across Waxstaff's lap like a basin.

'Not that I can remember but perhaps I did. I remember meeting the Hatter, but not axe bunny.' Waxstaff dipped her hands, took a drink, then splashed her face. Her hair fell free of her neck and Ali saw a purple boil starting to emerge. Waxstaff caught her expression.

'Yes, disgusting and very sore. It appears my body has started this rather colourful repair business.' Waxstaff dipped her hands again, changed her mind, lifted the full hat of water and dumped it over her head. 'Whoa! That was good!'

'You certainly sound better – no rattle in your lungs.'

'I know. A few minutes ago, I was ready to die. In my mind at least. Now my body seems hellbent on repairing itself. It defies all logic.'

'So does talking to an angry rabbit.'

'Yes, and we've both seen King's disgusting bat wings.' Waxstaff closed her eyes and sighed. 'Life at any cost ... I don't think so, do you?' She opened her eyes again and leveled her gaze at Ali. 'So, what do I do? Do I wait and see, or do invite the rabbit to put a stop to it now?'

'Remember what King said? How we become an expression of how we think of ourselves.'

'She said we become a manifestation of our self-esteem. And that coming from the mouth of a very real blind old bat! How is that even possible?'

'How is *any* of this possible?' Ali paused. 'What matters right now is the other thing King said. Do you remember?'

'Be careful what you wish for?'

'Exactly. You have to control your thoughts. Take charge of the process. Picture what you want to become.'

'That would be a mistake!' yelled Theodore. The rabbit and the Hatter were heading back towards them.

'Good ears, rabbit. I must remember to whisper.'

'I did not *choose* to have large ears and good hearing. Choosing is not a good option and I strongly counsel against it.'

'Why?'

'Your body has already begun the process,' said the Hatter. 'If you try to fight it by imagining something else, you might get stuck with a mix of the two.'

'Like the unfortunate Mister Prendergast,' said Theodore. 'You will see him at the palace. Half lion, half eagle, and a touch of snake for good measure. The poor man was in a world of pain throughout and still suffers greatly. I hold to the view that we should have axed him.'

'Chopped off his head?'

'Precisely. I thought I made that perfectly clear,' Theodore spun the axe for effect. 'It's the only way to be sure. Anything else and the body still tries to mend, even with bits missing. It's a funny old world. This one anyway.'

'Remind me to laugh,' said Waxstaff.

'Nothing about this is remotely funny,' said the Hatter. He slapped his hat a few times to scatter the last of the water, then he put it on, taking care to tuck in his braids with all their handwritten memories. 'Now, it's time to go.'

'In a moment.' Ali got to her feet and started climbing the tree.

'What are you doing?' asked Theodore. 'There are no apples up there,'

'Smart rabbit,' said Ali. 'I just need to test a hypothesis.'

'Which is ... what?' Theodore stepped up to the tree. 'That you are more agile than a rabbit? Comparison noted, now come down.'

'Soon.' Ali kept climbing. 'See that crystal up in the branches?'

'What of it?'

'Frequency entrainment. Do you know what that is?'

'No, I do not, nor do I care to know!' Theodore turned and looked back at Waxstaff. 'She's doing it again, she's talking piffle. She's forever talking piffle!'

'Definitely a scholar,' said the Hatter.

'Enough!' The rabbit hefted his axe from one hand to the other. 'Young lady, come down right now or you and that tree are coming down together!'

'Not yet. Did you see how the crystal started swinging on its thread when I began to climb the tree?'

'Well of course it did, you're shaking the tree. Let's see how much shaking we need to bring you out of it, shall we?'

'Shaking causes a transfer of energy from me to the tree, then to the crystal. Everything does that. Everything wants to be energy efficient. Energy flows like water till it finds a balance. If you put two grandfather clocks on the same wall—'

'I wouldn't!' The rabbit folded his arms. 'What sort of dolt would put two clocks on the same wall?'

'A scientist studying energy transfer, that's who. If you set the pendulums swinging at different times, and in opposite directions, what would you see if you came back a few days later?'

'I wouldn't see anything because I wouldn't go back!' Theodore hefted his axe again. 'Why would I set foot in a room that was so ridiculously furnished as to boast two clocks on one wall.'

'You would find the pendulums swinging in concert together. The clocks are connected by their contact with the wall. The movement of both pendulums gets transmitted through every atom of that wall and after a time they swing together. It's more efficient.'

'And the point of your scholar waffle is what, exactly?'

'Light will try to do the same.' Ali pulled herself up one more branch until her eye was level with the crystal. 'I think the mirror in the barn and the crystal in this tree bounce light back and forth between them. Entrainment is energy efficiency.'

'You are as irritating as Alice.' Theodore threw the axe on the ground, then threw himself down beside it. 'She was forever lecturing us like this!'

'Yes, she was.' the Hatter sat down beside his friend and began scratching him between the ears. 'Yet you miss her dreadfully, and chastise yourself every day for not paying her more attention. In short, less mouth and more ears please.'

'Very well! And if you insist on scratching me, put more effort into it.'

'Young lady,' the Hatter said, gesturing up to Ali, 'you think light has some part to play in keeping the gateway open?'

'Yes, and I think Alice thought so too. In the book she finds a key that will open a door to a beautiful garden. Do you remember what that key's made of?'

'Glass.'

'Yes, and so is the table the glass key sits on.'

'The scholars all agree on a quite different interpretation,' said Theodore. 'They hold to the idea that the glass represents clarity of vision. They suggest that to pass through, you must picture the other world very clearly in your mind.'

'Equally plausible,' said Ali. She untied the crystal, polished it on the front of her shirt, then hung it back on the branch.

'Let me guess,' said Waxstaff. 'You clean the crystal. It reflects the light more brightly and makes it easier for someone to come through?'

'I hope so. And if I ask them to clean the mirror back in the barn it could make it even easier.'

'No!' Waxstaff almost barked the word, the effort setting off another fit of coughing. 'You can't go back till you know how to do it safely. It will kill you.'

'I don't think so. Not if I don't stay there. I'll drop a note and then bounce right back.'

'Too dangerous,' said Waxstaff, 'but you're going to do it anyway so I shall save my breath.

'Popping back to deliver a note will convince her I really do have the secret to safe passage. She'll come through and the others will all be safe from her.'

'Let me understand this,' Theodore sat up and slapped the Hatter's hand away. 'You want to assist someone to come through, someone dangerous?'

'Yes,' Ali started climbing back down. 'A woman called King wants to come back here so she can finish her transformation. She's half bat and she's in a lot of pain. I think you can help her with that problem.' Ali pointed to the axe lying in the grass beside Theodore.

'My dear child ...' The rabbit closed his eyes and took a deep breath. When he looked up, his eyes were open again and rimmed with tears. 'Never make light of such a deed. Taking a life is terrible thing, no matter the circumstances.'

'I'm sorry.'

'Good. We will discuss your experiment with the Queen once we get you safely to the palace. She instructed us to bring you there should you return.'

'Yes, Theodore.' The Hatter patted his friend on the shoulder. 'She did, and we know why she did, don't we?' He turned to Ali as she jumped down onto the grass. 'Please sit a moment, Miss Ali, we all need to be of one mind on this.'

'Never been one for committees,' said Ali. But she sat anyway.

'Theodore is correct,' the Hatter picked a slender bluebell and rolled the stem between his fingers. 'The focus of everyone's need, the Queen's included, is to find out who we are, how we got here, and how to go back safely. No one has managed to do what you have done. No one except Alice. Going back and forth as you do *and* remembering life on the other side. That is a powerful currency here, a wealth which must be shared openly. The Queen wants you to tell everything you know, not just to her but to everyone, from the scholars to the scullery maids. A banquet will be organised, and you will address the room. Everyone there will be transfixed, you may count on it.'

'We are agreed then, we set off for the palace,' Theodore started to rise. The Hatter shook his head.

'Hold still, my friend. If our young visitor is correct, if she can indeed go back and deliver a note, if she can instruct friends on the other side to clean the glass there and make the transition more certain, what might the Queen say to us if she was sitting here?'

'She would say a great deal about a great many things ...' Theodore reached for the axe and used it to push himself to his feet, 'at the end of which we would agree to whatever she asked of us. Which, I must allow, would include supporting Ali's ill-considered experiment.' He swung the axe over his shoulder and started walking off. 'So best you be about it.'

'Good,' said Ali. 'And where are you going?'

'We left the boys watching the fork in the road for any sign of the Pack.'

'The boys? Ricky and Ted? They're here?'

'Indeed, they are. While you undertake your experiment, we will pass the time fashioning a carrier for our injured companion.'

Ali opened her pack, pulled out her journal and turned to a blank page. With any luck, Aunt Martha and Uncle Bertie was safely in London by now, so she addressed the note to the only other person who knew what was happening. Peter, the young man from the village who'd tried to help. Would he still want to help after everything that had happened?

CHAPTER 6

THE PROBLEM WITH POTTS

―――――――――

'We're prisoners in our own bloody house,' growled Lord Grey as he helped himself to his second scotch of the afternoon. 'I can't keep this charade up for much longer.'

'You must. We have no choice.' It had been two days since their return and Lady Grey was exhausted. The physical work had been hard enough, taking care of themselves without Potts or Waxstaff to assist, but it was the mental effort she found the most draining. Her husband was a master of weaving tall tales but even he was struggling to remember every floor in the tower of lies they had constructed. Complete truth was not an option.

Dovecot had brought in the forensic team and the Greys were now banned from key areas of the house: the dining room, the library (which Ali had used as her room), the bedrooms of Waxstaff and Potts, and the barn itself. The police had also requisitioned the parlour, turning it into an incident room. One entire wall was now a pinboard.

'Why here?' Lord Grey indicated the room with a sweep of his whisky glass. 'Why not down at the station? Seems poor form to have the whole narrative up there on our own wall! It's like we're on her team, instead of prime suspects.'

'Because, my dear Bertie, she is smart. The superintendent knows we're spinning her a web of nonsense. Every time she pins something on the board she watches our reaction. I'm sure there's a very different board at the police station with our faces pinned at the very centre of it.'

'I dare say there is,' he stared at his glass. He preferred his scotch with a single ice cube bobbing around in it, but it wasn't worth the effort of going all the way to the kitchen. 'I almost feel sorry for the poor woman. There's no way she can get a proper handle on any of this, no matter how good she is. I mean, I've read Ali's journal, and I struggle to believe some of it. That King woman! A bat? The forensics can pop that in their pipe and smoke it.'

He strode out into the hallway and stared at the lines of yellow police tape that cross-hatched the open door to the dining room. He began plucking on them like harp strings. 'Didn't even bother to tune the damn things!'

The front door opened, and a young constable stepped into the house. He had been billeted with them for two days now, a lean young man with gentle eyes and a wicked sense of humour. The Greys had warmed to him instantly.

'Hello, Jeremy, what news?' Lord Grey insisted on using the constable's first name. 'Have you driven the Potts woman out of hiding yet?'

'No, sorry. Still no sign of her.'

'Stay alert. She'll surface when her gingernuts run out.'

'I should carry a packet with me. Shake it like dog biscuits.'

'That's the spirit.' Lord Grey led the way back into the parlour and beamed at his wife. 'We have a visitor.'

'Good afternoon, Jeremy.' Lady Grey put down her book and gestured for the constable to sit. He did, stretching out his long legs and staring down at his feet, as if surprised to see them there.

'My Super just called in. She's on her way with one of the forensics and your local GP.'

'Doctor Cherabics?'

'That's the one. I was told to put the kettle on. She doesn't want you running around the house waiting on us.'

'Running!' snorted Lord Grey. 'Happy days. A few sit-ups on a bar stool and I'm spent. So ... any heads up on what she wants?'

'No.' Jeremy turned at the sound of wheels on gravel outside. 'And here she is. I'll get the tea sorted.'

Five minutes later, everyone but Jeremy was sitting at the kitchen table. Dovecot had given him a mug of tea and sent from the room.

'What's happened?' asked Lord Grey. Something had changed. He'd seen it the moment Dovecot had stepped from her car. More smiles and much less eye contact. She was nervous and doing her best to mask it.

'Just a few more questions,' said Dovecot.

'Nonsense. My wife and I didn't survive into our dotage by accident. We got here by watching life's stage very closely and its players more closely still. Your manner has changed since we saw you earlier today. Therefore, I ask you again: What has happened?'

'Here's the thing,' the man from forensics said, smiling at Lord Grey. 'We've been analyzing the blood. Most has come from one person; we assume from Nurse Potts. We have no medical records for her, so we can't do a match.'

'How did she get the job?' asked Dovecot. 'Was she from an agency?'

'No.' Martha smiled; a thin smile, self-deprecating. 'We should have, but I was in no fit state. I had taken a fall and we needed a nurse urgently. Miss Waxstaff took care of it. I dare say you'll find the paperwork among her things.'

'We've checked. There's nothing,' said Dovecot. 'No contract, no invoices, nothing at all regarding Potts. Which is odd, don't you think?'

'Very,' said Lord Grey. 'But I don't think Potts' pedigree is the reason for your visit. You said most of the blood was hers. Which means other folk were splashing their plasma about as well.'

'Hardly splashing,' Brooks looked mildly offended, 'but yes, we found traces from two other people. Which is why Doctor Cherabics is here. I need samples from both of you, and a sample from your great niece.'

'Ali is in London.'

'You've heard from her?' asked Dovecot.

'Not yet.'

'Well, we need to match the blood traces, and I understand that a few days ago you took Ali to see Doctor Cherabics.'

'Yes, I did.' Lady Grey hesitated. 'Oh, I see. You want our permission to see the results of her blood test?'

'Yes please,' Doctor Cherabics took a sip from his tea and smiled. 'That was quite a night, wasn't it? The truth is, Lady Grey, the police have been thorough.'

'I would expect nothing less.'

'Quite so, and I should tell you I've been questioned at length about the demeanour of your niece that evening – and the nature of the emergency.'

'Why?' Lord Grey tried to keep his composure. 'What the hell has that to do with any of this?' He turned to Dovecot. 'Why all this focus on Ali? She came to you for help to find her father. You should be searching London for them both.'

'A noble display of outrage, Lord Grey.' Dovecot returned his gaze and held it. 'Ali attacked Waxstaff, your housekeeper. I was there, and Potts held her down till her tantrum subsided. Clearly there was a great deal going on between them and I need to make sense of it. If they came to blows in the barn, if any of the blood matches hers, then Ali has more to worry about than a missing father.'

'Are you even attempting to find the poor man?' asked Martha.

'My colleagues down in London are. With no luck I'm afraid. And, because he is missing, you two are her legal guardians, which is why I need your permission to see her lab results.'

'How very unfortunate for you,' said Martha, her voice soft and even. 'Rather a Catch-22 for you, isn't it?'

'I don't understand.'

'You understand perfectly well,' Martha continued. 'Ali reported her father missing, yes, but you refused to assign that status to the investigation.'

'Not exactly.'

'Your colleagues in London went so far as to suggest he was having a secret tryst with his secretary. Despite all Ali's protestations to the contrary.'

'That's not my investigation. He went missing in London, not here.'

'Then you have a problem. Until he's declared missing, we aren't Ali's guardians and can't give permission for the doctor to release her records.'

'Hear, hear!' Lord Grey beamed at his wife, his eyes shining with admiration.

'The situation can be swiftly remedied,' Martha continued. 'You can officially declare her father missing and start an investigation into his whereabouts.'

'I shall do my best,' sighed Dovecot. 'In the meantime, we do have a match for the third blood type.'

'Oh? Do tell.'

'A cold case,' said Brook. 'A young girl who went missing over thirty years from this house.'

'Jackie!' For all his skills at play-acting, Lord Grey couldn't hide the surprise on his face. 'The little play friend of Ali's mother?'

'Yes,' Dovecot studied their faces. 'No foul play was recorded at the time – she simply went missing. The child disappeared from the face of the earth.'

'Yes,' Martha did her best to keep her voice steady, 'we remember it all too vividly. Her poor parents. The investigation went on for weeks. Are you saying you have found traces of blood from all those years ago?'

'No,' Brook tapped his notes. 'They were fresh, days old at most.'

Lord Grey stared at his wife; his eyes wide in alarm. Lady Grey closed hers and dropped her head. Dovecot tried to read their expressions. The news about Jackie had obviously stunned them. Were they in shock? In pain, perhaps?

'My very own cold case, back from the dead.' Dovecot pushed herself up from the kitchen table. 'On top of everything else. Aren't I the lucky one? Lady Grey, I need some fresh air, would you care to join me?'

'Air would be good.' Martha opened her eyes as Dovecot took the handles of the wheelchair. 'Look after these two gentlemen, Bertie.'

Outside, there was a refreshing chill in the air, an early hint that autumn was on the way. The copper beeches that lined the sides of the drive were losing their purple. As a child, Lady Grey had always loved the autumn. Not anymore. Now the season heralded a slow descent into rugs, chilblains and hot water bottles.

'Tell me about Jackie,' said Dovecot.

'No.'

'Why?'

'Because I need to tell my poor husband first. Your little bombshell has dealt him a very painful blow. Now, you didn't bring me outside for my health. Maybe for yours. Potts said pushing my chair down this drive was a decent workout.'

'And a noisy one, the wheels make a racket on this surface. And that's why we're out here. I want you to listen. Please don't show any reaction to what I say.'

'How dreadfully melodramatic.' Lady Grey tried to keep her voice light and playful. What game was Dovecot playing here? Separate the key witnesses and prod their stories for inconsistencies? It's what they did in all the police dramas she used to devour when TV had been such a novelty.

'Your house is bugged, Lady Grey, every room. Multiple devices, all very sophisticated. Constable Glover came across the first one by accident.'

'Young Jeremy?'

'Yes, he had the presence of mind to leave it alone. He's a bit nerdy, loves tech and gadgets and asked if he should put a box of tricks together and scan the house.'

'Is that allowed?' Lady Grey glanced at the thin strip of woodland that ran round the property, a band of green planted long ago to hide the perimeter wall. What else was it hiding? Cameras? Is that why Dovecot told her not to react?

'Allowed? Yes, but I will need to make an application, much like a search warrant, show due cause or get your permission. Then wait days for a tech team to fit us into their schedule.'

'You went ahead on your own?'

'Yes. The last twenty-four hours have been pure frustration. I'm being stone-walled by my Chief Constable. Everything in this case must go through him, but he won't tell me why.'

'You think Ali's fears for her father might be legitimate?'

'I don't know. But if he has been kidnapped, and if Ali was taken from her school and sequestered here to make sure he played along, it would explain the surveillance. Potts could have been supplying Ali's father with proof-of-life video footage of his daughter.'

'So, what do we do?' Martha tried to sound non-committal. This could all be a change of tack, a way to loosen her up.

'I don't know, Lady Grey. Whatever is going on is above my paygrade, so I'm being kept out of the loop. That body we recovered from the church, it was taken from the morgue yesterday, one hour before the coroner was due to examine it.'

'How very cloak and dagger.'

'Very. My Chief Constable said it was taken to London by the Met. I asked to see the paperwork and I was blown off. I have no idea who to trust.'

'But you trust young Jeremy.'

'I must start somewhere. Jumping at shadows is not in my nature. I have built my career on hard graft and good process. If I'm to resolve this, I need facts, and I need you to trust me. Tell me about Jackie. Your husband was shocked, but not you.'

'Jackie is Waxstaff. The blood you found in the barn must come from her. Jackie turned up on our doorstep a few years ago. I recognised her immediately and promised to keep her return here a secret.'

'She blackmailed you?'

'Heavens no. The poor woman was a broken shell, and we needed help around the house.'

'So why all that negative chemistry towards your niece?'

'Waxstaff didn't want her here.' Martha paused. How close to the truth could she go? Now that she'd read Ali's journal, she knew exactly why Waxstaff had behaved so appallingly – the poor woman had been trying to push Ali to leave, to get her away from King and her manipulation of the girl. But not in open defiance of King for fear of the evil woman's response. How on earth had poor Waxstaff managed it for so long? Please God, let her be alive and recovering over there so that Ali's impulsive decision was worth the sacrifice.

'Lady Grey?'

'Sorry, yes, Waxstaff. She made her dislike for the girl very clear from the beginning. And Ali didn't do herself any favours, you saw for yourself how volatile their chemistry was.'

'Which brings me to Potts. Waxstaff found her and gave her the position.'

'That's right.'

'And now both women at the centre of this are missing. Four women if we include your niece and the blind woman from the village, King.'

'Yes.'

'Clearly it's all part of a much bigger investigation that I'm not privy to, and given the work Ali's father was engaged in, and his disappearance, all this has to be tied together somehow.'

'Then we are all of the same mind?'

'For the moment. Especially given what I've discovered about Potts.' Dovecot turned the wheelchair and set off back to the house. 'Yesterday, Constable Glover found out something that points to a rather disturbing conclusion.'

'Go on.'

'Potts doesn't exist. Not on any official data base, or not under that name. Young Jeremy took it upon himself to do some digging on the dark web, and don't ask me how that works. The boy revels in conspiracy theories and seems to have a small network of like-minded nerds.'

'A new generation with new toys.'

'Yes, and he found a match for Potts' age and profile. There was a photo.' Dovecot pulled out her phone and searched for the picture. The image was old, but it was Potts.

'Oh yes, that's her,' said Martha. 'And who is she really?'

'Quite the character. She made the Olympic shotput trials during college. Gained a medical degree – she's a fully qualified doctor – then she trained to be a surgeon but jumped sideways into medical electronics. Then she was recruited by the army for MASH field training. She only served for six months before leaving to work for a militia group operating out of Iraq. She was recruited two years later by a special operations unit in Beirut. Then she disappeared off the radar for a very long time.'

'Until?'

'Until she was killed three years ago.'

'That doesn't make sense.'

'It might. You don't get more under-the-radar than a corpse.' They were almost back to the house when Jeremy came sprinting across the lawn towards them. He looked confused.

'What is it constable?'

'I'm not sure, ma'am. I think I saw a ghost. Well, no, not a ghost, I mean of course not. But she appeared and then vanished, like a ghost. Except ghosts don't hand you notes, do they?'

'Constable Glover, sit down before you fall. You're white as a sheet.' Jeremy sat, and Dovecot sat down beside him. 'Head between your knees, take a deep breath and hold it.' She put a hand on the back of his head and pushed, easing his head down.

'Was it her?' asked Lady Grey, trying to keep the excitement from her voice, and failing. 'You've seen her photographs, was it young Ali?'

'Yes,' his voice was muffled, his face pressed between his knees. He sat up, pushing back against Dovecot's hand. He looked at the two women in turn. His open face said it all. The boy was white as a sheet and clearly in shock. 'I thought she was a ghost, I really did. One minute she was there, the next she was gone. She must have set the whole thing up like a magician, maybe used the trap door.' Jeremy seemed to be thinking aloud, reprogramming what he'd just seen, forcing it to make some kind of sense. He looked up at his boss. 'So – not a ghost. A clever deception. Because ghosts don't hand you notes, do they?'

'She gave you a note? Where is it?'

'In the barn, I dropped it, sorry ma'am, I ran out like a little kid! I'm not born for this job.'

'No one is born for police work.' Dovecot stood up and helped Jeremy to his feet. 'I'll go to the barn; you escort our host back to the house.'

'By escort, she means push,' said Martha. Jeremy nodded and got behind her wheelchair and they set off in Dovecot's wake.

'So, a note?' Martha's head was spinning. Ali had made it across safely, and she was letting them know. 'Did she say anything?'

'No.'

'Of course she did, that girl had verbal diarrhea. She handed you a note and then said what?'

'It's kind of embarrassing.'

'It's important. I know her. Tell me what she said, word for word.'

'She said. . .' Jeremy gave a short, embarrassed laugh. 'Well, she said "Oh, you're cute. Give this to Peter."'

'Ha! Oh yes, that would have been Ali. No doubt at all.' Lady Grey kept her face to the front so Jeremy wouldn't see her tears. The relief was so intense she wanted to leap from the chair like a child. She wanted to run to dear Bertie and hold his face and see the joy light up his eyes.

Ali was alive, and she could find her way back. Their job – their only job – was to keep that barn secure from King and her people.

CHAPTER 7

TO THE PALACE

———————

'Bloody hell!' Ali took a deep breath, collapsed onto the bluebells and lay there panting. 'That was a rush!'

What had just happened? It had been so easy this time. Could cleaning the crystal have made such a big difference? Or had something else changed?

The Hatter reached down to support her. She waved him away.

'Give me a second. I need to process this.'

The transition had been more gradual, more fluid than before and with no loss of consciousness, each moment remaining clear in her head. It had been like stepping through jelly, as if the air had a dense film to it like the surface tension on water.

She had written instructions to Peter on a page torn from the notebook. Then she had stood on the spot in the clearing where she'd come through each time, and asked the Hatter to slap her on the cheek. He had, too softly.

'Harder!' She glared at him, and he slapped again. It was still too soft, yet the pain was enough to trigger an adrenaline response because the barn came into view; a ghostly impression, superimposing itself on the bluebell clearing.

She'd seen the young policeman staring at her. He was transfixed, his mouth and eyes wide open. She had bent forward, taking care to hold her breath; there had been an odd pulsing in her ears as her face pushed through the film of surface tension. She was in the barn ... or her head was. She had kept holding her breath as she pushed a hand through and dropped the note for the young man.

'I had more control.' She lifted her head and looked up at the Hatter. 'I had no pain, no vomiting. I held my breath, pushed my head through and watched.'

'Let me see your eyes,' said Waxstaff.

'I'm fine, really,' Ali insisted. Then immediately vomited.

'Go fetch some water,' Waxstaff instructed the Hatter. He set off and crossed paths with Theodore who was heading back with the two boys.

'She's back,' said the Hatter. 'Did you collect some mushrooms?'

'I did.' Theodore broke into a bouncing run, calling over his shoulder to the two boys. Ricky and Ted were carrying a makeshift stretcher, a blanket strung between two poles of willow.

'We made it ourselves,' said Ricky, as the Hatter hurried past them.

'Well done. Good work.'

'All by ourselves. No help!' said Ted. The boys caught up with Theodore who was standing over Ali.

'Are you sick, Miss Ali?' asked Ted.

'We can carry you on our stretcher,' said Ricky. 'We're very strong,'

'I can walk.' Ali rolled onto her knees and smiled up at the boys. 'It's good to see you again.'

'Your stretcher is for our guest,' said Theodore. 'Come and meet Miss Jackie. She is repairing, so she is in a great deal of discomfort and too weak to walk.'

'We knew a Jackie once.' Ricky set the stretcher down beside Waxstaff and pointed to a new boil on her forehead. 'You're changing. We don't change.'

'We never change, we always stay the same,' said Ted.

'Clearly.' Waxstaff let the boys help her onto the stretcher. 'I remember you two, now that I see you. I'm the same Jackie you met before.'

'The lost girl by the campfire?' Ted bent and peered at her face. 'I don't think so. She was very young and very pretty.'

'Yes,' Waxstaff chuckled. 'Yes, she was. Many years ago.'

'No. Months ago,' Ricky corrected her. 'Which means you can't be campfire Jackie.' Then Ted caught a glimpse of the silver pendant Waxstaff was wearing, it slipped into view as she eased herself onto the stretcher.

'Where did get that?' he demanded. 'It belongs to Jackie. Did you steal it?'

'No, my dear child, I did not. Time moves more slowly here in this world.'

'Coming through!' Everyone turned as the Hatter came racing back, his hat cradled out in front of him. He lowered the hat to Ali, and she took a long drink.

'Thank you. I needed that.' She looked round at all the worried faces. 'I don't feel bad, not like before. I held my breath, and I was only there for a few seconds. Thirty or so.'

'You never left,' said Waxstaff. 'We didn't take our eyes off you. You took a step, then you flickered … that's all, just for a moment.'

'Like a candle flame,' said the Hatter. 'But you never flickered out altogether. Seconds might have passed over there but only a heartbeat here.'

'I don't think I went through completely. All my senses were there, but it was like watching through a film of water … and then *BAM!* I bounced straight back, like I was being pulled by a tight bungee cord.'

'All very interesting.' Theodore handed her the mushrooms. 'Now chew on these as we walk, we have quite the journey ahead of us.'

'You said the palace was close by.'

'As the crows fly, yes, but the safe road is a great deal longer.'

They set off at a gentle pace, the two boys bearing Waxstaff between them on the makeshift stretcher, Theodore bouncing along at the front, the axe over his shoulder, the Hatter and Ali following behind. The pace was set by the two boys, not because Waxstaff was heavy but because she winced with every bump of the stretcher, so the boys stepped carefully, matching their strides like soldiers.

Moving slowly suited Ali. The mushrooms were helping, but she still felt a little nauseous. Cleaning the crystal had made a difference, one slap in her face, one small hit of adrenaline was all it had taken.

Up ahead, Theodore started sniffing the air, turning as he sniffed, small samples from every direction. *Sniff, sniff, sniff* in a complete circle, spinning like a ballerina. *Sniff, sniff, sniff.*

'What's with all the sniffing?' Ali called out.

'Mushrooms,' said Theodore. He turned to face Ali and started walking backwards, his bouncing gait giving him the air of an excited child.

'Thanks, but I feel okay, I don't think I need them.'

'Good. But they are not for you. They are for me.' Theodore tapped the bridge of his nose. 'For my head, my map.' He spun back around and bounced off ahead of the party, ending the conversation.

'Okay. . .' Ali turned to the Hatter beside her. 'What was that about?'

'He charts our path with mushrooms,' said the Hatter.

'Explain.'

'Best to ask him directly, I barely understand it myself. Ah! Look through there. That's our destination.'

They were following a track along the side of a hill. Large fern trees lined the route on either side, obscuring views of the distance, but one had fallen, providing a glimpse of the palace.

'It's so close!' Ali stared through the gap.

'Yes and no.'

'It is! Half an hour at most,' Ali estimated. It stood in the near distance on a rise of ground; a ridge running parallel to the one they were walking. The valley between was hidden from view. Ali tried to describe it to Waxstaff who was too low to see over the fallen tree. 'There are formal gardens, flower beds. Paths everywhere. Just one building. Could be others down the slope behind the trees ... the one I can see is a stone tower, four stories – maybe five. There are battlements and corner turrets. It's like a kid's drawing of an old castle. There's a castle wall ... and maybe a moat. Hard to tell from here ... could be a gravel track going round the wall.'

'Good,' sighed Waxstaff. 'How far.'

'Just a couple of miles,' said Ali. 'We'll be there in no time.'

'No, it's several hours yet,' said Theodore, who had hurried back to see why the party had stopped. 'Let's keep moving.'

'A few hours?' Ali looked from the rabbit to the palace. 'I could run there in twenty minutes if there's a track through the valley.'

'No,' Theodore took Ali's hand, pulling her from the view. 'Appearances can be deceptive. There is a track, but it could take us many days, perhaps weeks. We go a different way. We follow my nose.'

They set off again, the rabbit up ahead, the Hatter and Ali walking beside the stretcher, ready to take a turn if the boys started to tire.

'We must trust his nose,' said the Hatter. 'Alice had her own way of doing things, she could be very direct. But sometimes it's best proven to do things the old way, from the time before Alice.'

'She made that much difference?'

'Most certainly she did. She turned this world on its head. With her in the lead we could have taken that path, but without her? No.'

'Where is she?'

'No one knows. We keep on looking. The Queen most of all. Those two were very close.'

'And you?'

'Me?' The Hatter looked away for a moment, then turned back and nodded. 'I miss her terribly.' His voice cracked mid-sentence, and he dropped his eyes to the ground. Ali said nothing. The raw emotion in the Hatter's voice had slipped through her defenses. She remembered reading about a war correspondent, a woman who kept her camera to her face when the shelling started. She used it as her force field, a way to keep the emotional impact at arm's length, allowing her to maintain an impossible calm in the midst of such a brutal storm.

Ali knew she was doing something like that, holding herself together by an intense and narrow focus; not as a war correspondent but as a scientist dropped onto some foreign shore to record every exotic detail. But this was not a science experiment. This was a world of real people with all their grief, all their hopes and heartache.

'Excuse me,' Ricky said, turning to Ali, 'are you being sad?'

'A little, maybe.'

'I can always tell. It means you need friends. What name do you want to be called? If you don't remember your real name, we can make one up for you.'

'I remember my name very well, It's Alice.'

'You can't have that name,' said Ted. 'We already have a friend called that.'

'You look a bit like her and you're very rude and demanding like her. But you can't have the same name.'

'My friends call me Ali.'

'Can *we* call you Ali?' asked Ricky.

'Are you my friends?'

'Yes,' said Ted.

'Definitely,' agreed his brother. 'We've been watching out for you for weeks and weeks, haven't we, Mister Hatter?'

'You have indeed.'

'And we're carrying *your* friend.' Ricky smiled up at Ali. 'We are sharing your burden – that's what friends do.'

'Sharing,' said Ted, nodding hard in agreement. 'So now you can share something with us because we're your friends.'

'I see where this is going,' said the Hatter. 'The answer is no.'

'We only want Miss Ali to share a story with us as we walk.'

'I know.' The Hatter grinned across at Ali. 'They want you to read to them.'

'A story,' Ted said, beaming up at Ali. 'We want you to read us a story.'

'Our story,' said Ricky.

'I said no,' the Hatter said firmly, reaching forward and squeezing Ted's shoulder. 'It's hard to be patient, hard for all of us, but the rules were made for a reason: no one reads their true history unless they're safe and sound inside the palace.'

'Rules?' asked Ali.

'Not rules exactly ...' The Hatter slowed and beckoned Ali to do the same. They dropped back to walk a few paces behind the others. 'Precautions more than rules. Experience has made us cautious. The first time Alice uncovered someone's history and read it to them, they went mad. All their memories came back in a rush, a forgotten past of children, of parents, all their friends, every single memory pouring back in a flood. Yet, in that very same moment, they understood that all these loved ones were long dead. Imagine it, an overwhelming torment of bittersweet memories and no arms outstretched to welcome you home. Dead. All of them.'

Ali tried to imagine it. A scene from the first Wonderland book came back to her – the story of the tea party. 'I think Alice warned about this ... was the March Hare the one who went mad?'

'Yes. His name was Daniel Chaser, rather a celebrity in his day. Alice was able to discover his true history because the unfortunate Daniel Chaser retained one persistent memory from his life. It turns out that some powerful memories of grief or trauma remain like scars, and poor Daniel could clearly remember falling from his horse and being trampled. He told Alice this, and back in your world she came across a newspaper headline in her own village archives.'

'He was a local?'

'He was. Daniel was Master of the Hounds. His disappearance had caused a stir and there had been no end of speculation within your village. Alice brought the article back with her. Daniel read it and every detail of his life came flooding back. The fellow retreated into madness. A sobering lesson for us all.'

'How frigging awful.' Ali tried to imagine it – *really* imagine it – but couldn't. Then she looked at Waxstaff on the stretcher ahead of them. 'Poor Jackie had forgotten everything when she was whisked back to our world. She fell into her campfire over here, the pain and shock were enough to send her back through. She found herself in the barn with her clothes on fire and serious burns to her hands and chest.'

'Ah, we wondered how she'd left.'

'She had no idea who she was. She'd forgotten everything. Four or five years had passed back home, and the burns to her face meant no one recognised her. She was found whimpering in the village church.'

'Poor Jackie.' The Hatter took a deep breath.

'She was taken to a hospital – well, a series of hospitals, burns units. From what she's told me, everyone did their best. But then, when a few memories of this place started coming back, she was locked up on a psych ward.'

'A what?'

'Another kind of a hospital,' Ali searched for the right word. 'I think they were called asylums back then.'

'Ah, yes! There's an asylum at the palace. We use sleep narcotics for the most part, till all is forgotten again.'

'Do people try to go back?'

'Sometimes. Folk like you, the ones who keep records of their past and read them every day to remember. They endlessly plot their return. If they succeed, we never see them again. Your Mrs King must be such a person. Bat wings, you said?'

'Yes.' Ali did her best to describe her. The glass eyes and the bat wings. How she seemed to be stuck partway through her transformation. 'You said she might have lived out in the fringes with the Jabberwocky.'

'It's possible. You must give a full account to the scholars when we reach the palace. But be prepared for disbelief and objection. Many hold to the opinion that it's impossible for the transformed to go back, as talking animals would not be tolerated over there.'

'You hear stories', said Ali. 'Every country has a fable about talking animals, yetis, mermaids, talking unicorns. Talking owls are popular. And cats. Anyone who arrived back as an animal would soon learn to keep their mouth shut.'

Up ahead the two brothers were starting to slow. Their shoulders had slumped and, though neither complained, it was clear they were starting to tire.

'Our turn to carry, I believe,' said the Hatter. He strode forward and took the handles from Ricky. Ali took over at the back and looked down at Waxstaff. She was awake again, her eyes open. She seemed more at peace, her face softer, the lines of pain receding.

'How are you feeling?'

'Odd,' Waxstaff whispered. 'Everything hurts, but the pain is distant, like it's happening to someone else. This must be the start of it, my body repairing itself.'

'Are you scared?'

'Not yet, it doesn't seem real. And I'm too exhausted to care.' She stretched out a leg and tapped the Hatter's back with her foot. 'How long will this take?'

'Our journey or your transformation?'

'Don't be a smartarse – call it my recovery, it sounds less dramatic.'

'I prefer we leave the explanations to the scholars.'

'I prefer we don't,' said Waxstaff, and she kicked him again, harder this time.

'I could drop this stretcher!'

'Are we talking weeks or years?'

'Never years and never days.' The Hatter looked back over his shoulder at her, his eyes troubled and compassionate.

'Face the front! You'll stumble and drop me.'

'Yes, I could most certainly drop you.' He turned to face the path ahead. 'In most cases the process takes a number of weeks.'

'Weeks?'

'Yes. The main changes can occur within two weeks. But appendages, tails or fins and the like, these can take longer.' He was interrupted by Theodore, who came bounding back along the path.

'Good news! Set the stretcher down. I smell lavender – bushels of it, all in flower.'

'Not before time!' sighed Ricky.

'We needed it a dozen furlongs past,' said Ted.

'I cannot simply conjure it up,' said Theodore. 'It grows where it grows, and this is the first patch we've come upon.'

'We can gather bushels and bushels,' said Ricky. 'It will make a comfortable mattress for you, Miss Jackie.'

'Very kind,' said Waxstaff. 'But don't delay on my account.'

'It is on our account, not yours.' Theodore handed his axe to the Hatter. 'You stay here with our guest, the rest of us will collect as much as we can carry.'

'If I must.' The Hatter held the axe as if it were a sleeping snake. 'Quick as you can. I'm poorly equipped for this.'

'Needs must,' said the rabbit. 'Please join us, Miss Ali – we must gather as much of the lavender as we can, and as swiftly as we can.' He bounced away through the undergrowth with the two boys skipping along behind him. Ali turned to the Hatter and held out her hand.

'I'm not leaving you here with that. Give it to me.'

'Nothing would please me more,' said the Hatter, 'but rules are rules.'

'Set by whom?'

'The Queen, though it's not a rule as such, more a consensus view, but it seems to keep society ticking along, like shaking hands.'

'Chopping someone's head off is not like shaking hands.' She clicked her fingers at him impatiently. 'Give the axe to me.'

'You are worse than the Queen,' said the Hatter.

'Is that good or bad?

'I'm not sure.' Reluctantly, he handed her the axe. 'One thing is for certain. I intend keeping my distance when first you meet her.'

CHAPTER 8

THE TROUBLE WITH TRUST

———————

Dovecot's team had left for the day. It was 6pm, and the garden outside the parlour window was shining after a brief summer shower. The lawn sparkled in the late afternoon sun as if the shower had dropped a million sequins. The house was still an active crime scene, but forensics had finished their investigations.

One constable remained: Jeremy Glover, the slender young man billeted there as a precaution. He was out patrolling the gardens and the Greys were celebrating the peace and quiet with a glass of scotch in the front parlour.

'There he goes.' Lord Grey was standing by the window watching Jeremy. 'He's crossing the lawn like a cat! Why the deuce does he pick his feet up like that? Grass isn't going to bite the silly fellow.'

'It's still wet from the rain, Bertie. He's trying to keep his boots dry.'

'He's a police officer. What if Potts turns up? She'll brush him aside with her little finger. Look at him – you've got more meat on you than that boy. He's all wire and no whiskers.'

'Don't be rude.' Lady Grey wheeled her chair to the window and stared out. Her husband was right though, the young man would be no match for Potts. He was tall and thin with delicate features and the long slender fingers of a pianist.

A soft creak came from the other end of the house. They both heard it and turned to face the door. Every squeaking floorboard had its own signature. Lord Grey grabbed his walking stick and made for the door.

'Bertie! No!'

'The devil with it! I've had enough of skulking around in my own damned house!' Lord Grey hoisted his stick like a club and marched off down the hall. He paused briefly at the kitchen door, then thrust it open.

'You!' He recognised Peter immediately.

'Hi.' Ali's young friend was emerging from the pantry with a tin of peaches.

'Are you thieving food?'

'This?' Peter held the tin up. 'I suppose I am. May I open it?'

'You foolish, foolish, old man!' Lady Grey wheeled herself into the kitchen. 'Hello Peter, it's good to see you. Bertie, you are beyond stupid! That was an act of whisky courage, and you will never do that again. Promise me.'

'I'm sick and tired of—'

'Promise me!'

'Very well.' Lord Grey didn't have time to complete the apology. The door leading out to the garden opened and Constable Glover came in.

'Pete! What the hell! Good to see you, man.' Jeremy strode across and gave Peter a bear hug. 'Where the hell have you been? My boss wants to talk to you.'

'Keeping my head down.' Peter put the peaches on the table.

'Understatement. I'll need to report seeing you.'

'Why?'

'Kind of goes with the job, Pete.' Jeremy pulled out a notebook and scribbled a message: *House bugged. Make small talk till we get some noise going.*

'Can I pull a meal together, do you think?' said Peter. 'Been a long day. I could cook something for the four of us maybe?'

'Capital idea!' Lord Grey took the cue and started rattling through cupboards and opening drawers. Then he turned on the tap for good measure.

'How do you two boys know each other?' he asked. 'Not school, there must be a few years between you.'

'We're cousins.' Jeremy replied, rattling through a drawer for a tin opener.

'And gamers,' said Peter. 'E-sports mostly. Fortnight, a bit of Dungeons and Dragons. All the usual, you know.'

'Assume we don't,' said Martha. She smiled across at her husband who sat down beside her, and they listened quietly to an enthusiastic summary of gaming as the boys made a simple meal.

Everyone kept up the charade as they cooked, ate and washed up. Then Jeremy suggested he walk Peter to the gate.

'Not arresting me then?'

'There's no warrant for you. You're just a person of interest, a witness my boss wants to question.' As he spoke, he scribbled: *That's bullshit, of course, better to keep your head down. We can talk on the drive. Now say something about going to see Ali in London.*

'Thanks for the meal,' Peter got up from the table. 'I'd better scoot, I'm heading back to London tomorrow.'

'That's where you've been hiding?'

'Someone has to help Ali look for her dad, and your bunch are doing bugger all about it. Why is that?'

'Not my call. You can ask my boss tomorrow. Let's walk.' Jeremy pointed to all their scribbled notes and mimed setting them alight as Peter and the Greys said loud goodbyes to each other.

When the young men had left, Martha slumped down even further into her wheelchair. Ever since Dovecot had told them about the surveillance equipment, every aspect of their lives had become exhausting, one charade on top of another. Outwardly they kept to one narrative, while privately they had to exchange notes about all the things they really needed to talk about. Taking long walks down the drive each day was the one respite they had, but pushing the wheelchair was taking its toll on her husband.

Martha lifted her head and saw him smiling at her, his eyes moist. Lost in the same thoughts, no doubt. She drew a big heart in the air with a fingertip. He nodded, blew a kiss back, then collected up their scribbled notes and dropped them into the wood-burning stove.

'Okay, what's going on?' They were halfway down the drive when Peter stopped and confronted Jeremy.

'You tell me, Pete. I can't help if I'm in the dark. Or you could tell my boss. Seriously, she's not out to get you, she's not out to get Ali or that amazing old couple back there.'

'What is this, good cop, bad cop?' Peter grabbed Jeremy's elbow. 'Just how stupid do you think I am? That charade back there, sucking the Greys in so they feel safe with you. I've watched you work your charm online, remember. You took my whole team out by taking *me* in.'

'Two years ago!' Jeremy shook pulled his arm free. 'It was a game, Pete, get over it! I needed the prize money.'

'And I didn't?'

'No! You bloody didn't. You were still at school, I was grafting my way through college – law degree, remember.'

'Which you dropped out of! Hero to zero in one day!'

'Fuck you, too!' Jeremy paused and held up a hand. 'Look, enough with this. I dropped out because I couldn't keep up with the fees!'

'Oh. My dad never said.'

'He didn't know, because my parents didn't know. Happy?' Jeremy took a deep breath and shook his head. 'I couldn't tell them. They would have gone and found the fees somehow, another mortgage on their house, whatever. How could I do that to them? You know how tough it was when Dad lost his job.'

'Could have told me though. I thought we were tight as.'

'We were, Pete. Still are from my end! Doesn't mean we have to share every piece of shit that happens to us.'

'But a cop?'

'Yes, I figured five years, then I can apply for a police grant police to study law. Bit of a long road to get there, but it's working.'

'Good to know.' Peter studied his cousin's face. How much of this was true, and how much was bullshit? Jeremy had always out-ma-noeuvered and outplayed him in their game lives. 'Well, if you want to get in good with your boss, then solve this mystery. And that starts with finding the King woman!'

'The blind lady who works for your dad?'

'Not works, she's a volunteer.'

'She's listed as a missing person. What's she got to do with this?'

'Everything ...' Peter hesitated, he wanted to trust his cousin, but the truth was too bizarre. Jeremy needed to see it for himself. 'Go and find her, but watch out. She's not a sweet old lady.'

'You've got to give me more than that.'

'All right,' Peter tried to find an angle that would intrigue Jeremy without giving too much away. A little white lie that could become an itch his cousin would need to scratch. The guy was a big tech nerd. He was the IT trouble shooter in their Fortnite team, so any new tech was his soft spot. 'Mrs King's not blind.'

'Bullshit. She's got glass eyes.'

'I think they're fancy cameras. Have you ever seen her without that big scarf thing on her head?'

'No, but ...' Jeremy paused. 'You think it's hiding something?'

'I know it is.'

'A headset computer? Transposing the camera data into ... what? Sound cues?'

'Find her and see for yourself. Then ask my dad about the guys in expensive black suits who come and keep tabs on her.'

'Okay. So maybe she's signed up for a medical trial? That doesn't explain this mess.'

'Just find her. Ask her. And take a look under her fucking scarf.'

'And you? What are you going to do?'

'I think I really will go to London and find Ali.' He tried not to blink as Jeremy stared him down, searching for the lie. 'I thought she'd be here. Hiding out. Looks like I was wrong. She really has gone to London to look for her dad.'

'No, she hasn't. You're right, Pete. Ali's hiding out here, I saw her.'

'Bullshit!' Peter couldn't disguise his reaction. He tried, but he knew the surge of hope must have shone from his eyes like flash bulbs.

'She was in the barn and played some panto trick on me with the trapdoor and lights. She dropped a note and told me to give it to you.'

'What the fuck! Let me see it.'

'I never picked it up.' Jeremy tipped his head back and laughed, reliving the embarrassment. 'God, I was an idiot. I thought she was a ghost. I mean, just for a second. So, I panicked like a stupid kid and ran out. Dovecot went to the barn and found the note, but she's kept it out of her report. I asked her what it said but she wouldn't tell me. Just said it was gibberish.'

'Find it. Take a photo and flick me a screenshot.'

'Go through her desk?' Jeremy shook his head. 'I'd lose my job. Best way is to ask her yourself. Turn up at the station and give your witness account. Then ask to see the note.'

'Okay. One condition. You come with me right now to King's teashop and we ask to see her.'

'Ask who? She's not there. Dovecot's already had the place checked. And I can't leave them.' Jeremy pointed back at the house. 'This place isn't safe with that Potts woman still missing.'

'She's not here. Trust me. I've been hiding out in the house since all this went down. She's gone. I think King's people took her.'

'The guys in the fancy suits?'

'Yes. Come and check out her tea shop. It'll take us twenty minutes, tops. Nothing will happen to the Greys in twenty minutes.'

'Apart from indigestion. That was a pretty crap meal we made.' Jeremy grinned at Peter and they set off for the village green at a steady jog.

'What is it with this girl?' asked Jeremy. 'Got the hots for her?'

'She's different. Bit of an emotional train wreck who thinks the whole world's out to mess with her. Aside from that, yeah, she's okay.'

There were a few locals about when they got to the village green. The cousins had grown up in the village, so everyone recognised them immediately.

'This was a dumb idea,' said Peter.

'What did you expect?' Jeremy eyeballed a dog walker who was changing direction to meet them, her expression a mix of surprise and concern. Jeremy held up his hand like a traffic officer signalling a vehicle to wait and called out.

'He's fine, Mrs Williams, thank you.'

They picked up their pace and veered away across the green. The centre of the village was a group of shops clustered around the church. A safety barrier had been erected around the churchyard and hazard warnings were everywhere. The neighbouring shops had escaped damage. The church spire had collapsed inward onto its own footprint. Only the scaffolding tower that had been built to service the spire's repairs had toppled outwards, but even that had landed safely in the graveyard.

The teashop was two stores along and had a CLOSED sign in the window. They peered inside. Both cousins knew the place, it had changed little over the years and was so familiar to them, it was almost invisible. Everything was as they remembered it, from the tablecloths to the net curtains.

'Can't see anyone in there,' said Jeremy. 'It's been closed since the collapse.'

'Can I help you, gentlemen?' A tall man in a dark suit appeared behind them. He had a lapel pin: a white enamel rose.

'I don't know,' said Jeremy. 'What help are you offering?'

'It was a figure of speech,' said the Suit. 'I have absolutely no intention of helping you.' The man turned to Peter. 'But this young man can help me, I think? Can't you, Peter?'

'Why would I want to do that?'

'Let me think,' the man cocked his head. 'Civic duty perhaps. Remorse? No, wait, what is it you Christian folk seek so desperately? Oh yes, forgiveness and absolution for your sins. I can help you with that. I believe stealing is held to be a sin by your community. You have something which doesn't belong to you, and I think its real owner would be inclined to forgive and forget this whole unfortunate business if that package was returned.'

'Your boss knows I don't have it. She knows where it is because she knows who I gave it to. She saw it all before she disappeared under a ton of slate!'

'Care to fill me in?' said Jeremy. 'Maybe introduce yourself?'

'I'll pass, thank you.' The Suit tapped Jeremy lightly on the chest. 'You want to question me, Constable Glover, go ask your Chief Constable for his approval.' The man turned away and started to leave. Peter pulled out his phone and tapped open the camera app.

'Excuse me, about that package ...' he said. The Suit spun round, Peter took a quick-fire series of photos and stepped back as the man's hand shot out to grab the phone. Jeremy stepped in the way.

'No, I don't think so,' he said quietly, his voice calm and measured.

'Delete it!' ordered the Suit. 'I haven't given you permission to film me.'

'None required,' said Jeremy. 'This is a public place. Anyone can take any pictures they want.'

'Your phone. Now!' The Suit held out his hand to Peter. 'I won't ask again.'

'Not going to happen,' said Jeremy. 'Leave before I arrest you. So far, I've got intimidation with menace. Want to add assaulting a police officer?'

'Tell you what,' Peter held up both hands to the Suit, 'I'll make you a deal. You get me a face-to-face meeting with Mrs King and I'll tell her where the package is, what was in it, and I'll delete your mugshots from my phone.'

'One meeting?'

'Yes, with the two of us and Detective Inspector Dovecot.'

CHAPTER 9

ON TAKING A LIFE

―――――――――――

It didn't take Ali long to catch up with Theodore and the two boys. They were wading through a sea of blue lavender. Dozens of bushes grew waist high along a narrow clearing, a corridor of open ground framed on either side by stunted elm trees. Lavender filled the clearing, mound after purple mound of them, the scent overpowering, a sweet, pungent odour that hung in the air like a dense blanket.

The boys were standing with their arms outstretched as Theodore loaded them up with vast bundles of the herb.

'Here she is.' Ted was first to spot her. 'Come and help, it's not heavy.'

'I'm trying,' said Ali. It was hard work pushing her way through the bushes, the movement releasing more of the overpowering fragrance. 'You can have too much of a good thing. I can hardly breathe.'

'It's a lovely smell,' said Ricky.

'A healthy smell,' added Ted, 'much better than our friend Jackie. We'll pack it all round her. She'll sleep all the way after this.'

'Enough talking.' Theodore dropped another load into their arms. 'And you, young lady, you can help to pick. Getting the whole flower is best, leaves, buds and stems too. We can—' He stopped mid-sentence and stared at Ali. 'You have the axe.'

'Yes, I do. No one is chopping Jackie's head off today.'

'Oh dear, oh dear, we have to get back.' He beckoned to the boys. 'Bring what you have, quickly now. And you, foolish girl – give me the axe!'

'No.' Ali planted it on the ground. 'The axe stays with me.'

'Very well, I don't have time for your theatrics.' He bounced off, leaping from bush to bush as if they were small trampolines. 'I hope you know how to use it.' The boys followed, shaking their heads at Ali as they pushed past her.

'What?' She lifted the axe and fell in behind them.

'You do everything wrong,' said Ted.

'Then tell me!'

'Mister Hatter needed the axe to keep the flies off our friend Jackie.'

'What?'

'She's starting to smell of rotten meat,' shouted Ricky who was forging ahead. 'It's not her fault, everyone smells of rotting meat when they start the mending and flies love rotting meat.'

Ali didn't reply, she was thinking about King and her disgusting boils, how Potts had to squeeze them, the pus oozing out like cords of grey cream. Then Ali heard multiple chainsaws, and Waxstaff screaming obscenities.

'Hold on!' Ali roared, as she covered the last hundred yards and burst from the undergrowth. There were no chainsaws, just flies, six of them the size of chickens, all buzzing around Waxstaff who was up on her knees swiping at them with both hands. One settled on the back of her neck. The Hatter slapped it away and the fly tumbled to the ground. It lay there buzzing on its back, it's wings and body vibrating so quickly it was difficult to see it properly, the thing was just a shivering patch of grey. Then Ali buried the axe in it.

'Next!' Theodore had struck a second, stunning it. The fly began stumbling about on the ground, shaking its head, sunlight glittering from the mirrored facets of its compound eyes. Ali pulled her axe from the body of the first fly, strode over to the second and raised the axe again. Then the fly looked up at her.

Ali saw dozens of reflected images of herself, every image the same – a girl with an axe against a clear blue sky. An angel of death.

Ali froze, unable to strike. Then the fly burst into a mess of grey as Theodore clubbed it with a branch.

'Don't stare at them, child, kill them!'

More flies were arriving, making straight for Jackie, three landed on her face, choking her screams. Ali dropped the axe and ran to her, grabbing at one fly. A wing tore off in her hand. The fly fell to the ground, and tried to crawl away, its one wing still buzzing. Ali jumped on it, then fell off as the fly spun under her foot in a frantic death throw.

Still more flies kept arriving. Ali pulled Waxstaff to the ground and started piling the discarded lavender on top of her, burying her as if they were children playing in a mound of leaves. A picture rose behind her eyes, her mother laughing as Ali and her father buried her under red and golden leaves.

The boys joined in, picking up the scattered lavender and throwing it on to Waxstaff. Within moments she was covered. The flies circled for a moment, lost interest, and departed. One settled to drink from the burst carcass of another but took off when Ricky hurled a stick at it.

Silence. The yelling and buzzing was over. Everyone dropped to the ground to catch their breath. Waxstaff reached up from under her shroud of lavender and cleared them from her face.

'Thank you all,' she said. The boys were the first to sit up.

'Enough resting,' said Ted.

'We have to get our friend Jackie to the palace,' said Ricky. They grabbed the Hatter by two of his dreadlocks and began pulling him to his feet.

'Ow!' The Hatter jerked his head back, pulling the boys over. They sprang up and went to Ali.

'Please Miss Ali,' said Ted, 'Mister Hatter says we can't read our histories till we get to the palace, so – let's get to the palace!'

Ali lifted her head from the grass as the boys reached down to take her arms. She looked over at Waxstaff, who nodded. 'Time to tell them, Ali, they deserve the truth, don't you think? The effort they're going to.'

'I guess so,' Ali groaned as she sat up.

'Tell us what?' asked Ricky.

'The truth,' sighed Ali. This was going to be hard, the boys were so eager, so desperate, and there was no way to do this gently. 'I do have some of the true histories Alice discovered. The identities of some of the people trapped here. But not yours. Your story isn't among them. I'm very sorry.'

For a moment the news didn't seem to register. The two boys continued to stare with the same eager expressions on their faces. Then slowly their eyes filled with tears, and they started crying silently, their heads buried in each other's shoulders.

Theodore and the Hatter pulled themselves up and gathered the boys in their arms, consoling them as best they could with soft words and the promise of jam tarts when they reached the palace.

'Alice said she knew our true story,' Ted spluttered between sobs.

'She lied to us,' said Ricky. 'She said we were special.'

'Very, *very* special!' sniffed Ted. 'But she didn't find out anything about us.'

'I think she did.' Ali tried to read their faces, but the boys pushed their heads deeper into each other's shoulders. 'I think you're the reason Alice tried so hard to keep this place safe. I think you're *more* than special, much more.'

The boys kept their heads buried, but their sobbing stopped. They were listening.

'I think Alice found out who you are. She didn't want to break her promise, but something frightened her, so she's kept your true identities a secret. I think she's buried them inside a riddle in one of her storybooks.'

'Why?'

'To keep you safe.'

'Come along,' said the Hatter. 'We will discuss this with the Queen, but first we must get there. Pack the stretcher with lavender and let us be on our way.'

Ali remained where she was, staring down at the grass.

'What is it?' Theodore came over and stood beside her.

'Nothing. I'm fine.'

'Not so. You're upset to have disappointed the boys, but I don't believe that's what troubles you. I venture to suggest you're thinking about the fly you killed.'

'Yes. It's not easy killing something the size of poodle. It felt more personal than squishing a bug.'

'Steel yourself. There will be many more confrontations before this is over.' He laid his paw on Ali's shoulder. 'Ask me the question that troubles you.'

'I killed the first fly. Chopped it with the axe. But then – the second one – it stared at me. I mean, really stared at me.'

'And you hesitated. I say again, ask the question that troubles you. You would be a dark soul if the thought had *not* stayed your hand.'

'Okay!' Ali looked up and met his eyes. 'Were they babies once? Were the flies human babies that have transformed?'

'No.'

'They can't have been adults, you didn't shrink down to rabbit size when you transformed. The disgusting King woman didn't shrink down to the size of a bat! Where would all that material even go? I'm guessing that when people transform, its only their shape, not their size.'

'True ... in part. However, if limbs are severed in whatever accident compels the transformation, then the body will do its best with whatever is left.'

'Like the creatures who run with the Jabberwocky?'

'Exactly so, he calls them his children, but they were adults when they came through. They lost bits, whole limbs some of them.'

'So, the fly I killed, that was never a human baby?'

'No. All the scholars agree on this point, the insects and plants that thrive here came though during the early evolution of this place; a barren world made fertile by the flotsam and jetsam falling through from our own. Every kind of grub and bug and animal has wandered through over time. Not every creature you'll meet will be a trans-formed human like me.'

'So how do I know for sure that fly was just a fly.'

'Because it didn't beg for its life.'

'Good point.' Ali was surprised how relieved she felt. 'So I'm not a killer.'

'Not yet. Unhappily, this world may yet require it of you.'

They had been walking steadily for a while, Ali was finding it hard to judge the passing of time. The boys had insisted on carrying Waxstaff, relenting only once when the Hatter had forced them to take a short break. The boys had pulled faces, feigned sickness, and threatened to recite poetry until the Hatter relented and handed the duty back to them.

'How long have we been walking?' Ali was at the rear again, the Hatter keeping pace beside her. 'My sense of time doesn't seem to work over here.'

'Yes, it's vexing, but we learn to live with it. Except for Alice, she became very intent on understanding it.'

'She must have figured it out.'

'How so?'

'All the references to time in the books. No reason to put them in there, except for safe keeping. One of them must be an equation, how much faster time flows over there. Waxstaff was stuck here for months that first time. Years had gone by in the other world when she made it back, but what's the ratio? Twice as fast? Ten times?'

'It's confusing, I'll grant you.'

'It's been over two hundred years since Alice first came through. How old did she look when you last saw her?'

'Your age. A little older, perhaps.'

'According to Aunt Martha—'

'Another aunt?'

'Yes. According to her, Alice was twelve when she disappeared. If she's two years older than me, say seventeen, then five years have passed here and two hundred years have passed back in my world. But that's a guess. What's the real ratio?'

'Why does it matter?'

'Why? I have a father back there. I want to go back while he's still alive.'

'Of course. Yes, silly of me. The time differences defy reason, but look at Theodore hopping along ahead of us. Reason is in short supply over here.'

'If you met Alice when she first arrived, that means you've been stuck here for two hundred years at least. And you look twenty at most!'

'Why thank you.' The Hatter puffed out his chest and gave an elaborate bow. 'Good food and clean living do their part.'

Ali laughed. What was his history? She was planning to read the journals before handing them over. Was that rude? To know more about these people than they did? Bad manners might be a small price to pay given what was at stake.

'Why does everyone call you the Hatter?'

'Does it matter?'

'Yes, if Alice gave it to you. Did she?'

'Why would you suppose that? I know it's what she calls me in her books, but it might have been my name already' – he pointed at his head – 'given the hat.'

'But she did, right?'

'Yes, she did, and what made you think so?'

'Lucky guess,' said Ali. But it wasn't. Everything in the books was there for a reason, and Ali had a hunch for why her aunt had given him that name. It was a simple anagram. Shuffle the letters of HATTER, and you got THREAT.

'Ah, look!' The Hatter stopped and pointed to a peculiar, bottle-shaped tree up ahead. 'We are in luck!'

A vine of blackberry climbed the trunk on the tree like threads on a spool of cotton. Waxstaff was asleep on her cot of lavender, and didn't stir when the boys set her down in the shade. It was an odd-looking tree: squat, with a wide orange trunk and a tuft of branches sprouting from the top. Ali thought it looked more like a gigantic carrot than a tree.

Then Theodore took a bite.

'Bloody hell!' Ali looked closer. 'It *is* a carrot!'

'A very delicious carrot,' said Theodore.

Ali started gathering and eating the blackberries. They were small, but their flavour was intense. She only managed a handful before the sugars kicked in.

'Whoa! Energy drink! I'll need some water to drown this.'

'And carrot,' said Theodore. 'Lots of carrot – you can chew it as we walk. It's very nourishing, I can assure you.'

'Very disgusting, you mean,' said Ricky, his face and hands stained purple from the berries.

Ali looked at her own fingers. Purple! 'I hope this washes off.'

'Not easily,' the Hatter replied, grinning at her, his own chin dark with the juice. 'Our crime will be written on our faces for some time unless we can find gong leaves. Which we will, I'm sure. They grow in fortunate abundance, given their main use.' He set off into the scrubby undergrowth beside the path.

Ali followed. 'Main use?'

'When you feel the call of nature and need to retreat into the bushes.'

'Ohhh, toilet paper! Good to know.'

'Here.' The Hatter pointed to a patch of blue nettles. The leaves were huge.

'Stinging nettles!' Ali stared at them. 'You can't seriously expect me to wipe my hands or anywhere else with stinging nettles!'

'They don't sting. These are gong nettles, scrunch them a little as you pick them, they work better that way.' The Hatter picked a few, scrunched them in his fists and rubbed his chin with them. Ali was impressed with the result and set to work cleaning her face. Scrunching the leaves released a white sap that smelt of tar, and in a few minutes her hands were clean. They picked more nettles for the others, returned to the tree, and handed the leaves around. Waxstaff was awake, propped up, her back to the carrot tree. She was eating blackberries.

'These are good, I remember them from last time.'

'How are you feeling?' Ali tried not to focus on a large grey boil that was growing on her forehead.

'I'm not sure.' Waxstaff popped another blackberry in her mouth. 'These taste good, but I'm not drawn to eating them. I want meat.'

'Hunger's a good sign.'

'Raw meat.' Waxstaff chuckled. 'I always liked my steaks well done, now all I can picture is a slab of anything red and runny.'

'I will be sure to sleep with my eyes open,' said Ali. If Waxstaff wanted to keep it light with black humour, then Ali would play along. She sat down beside her. 'How close should I sit?'

'I think I'd eat the rabbit first,' said Waxstaff.

'I heard that!' Theodore scampered round from behind the tree. 'I've got an axe, remember? Your hunger cravings are no indication of your coming form. You will get bursts of insane hunger for all kinds of food, then long stretches when you can't stomach anything.'

'Right now, all I crave is sleep.' said Waxstaff. 'How much longer till we get to the palace?'

'Uncertain,' said the Hatter.

'We don't have the map,' said Ricky.

'A map!' Waxstaff shouted. 'Why the hell do you need a map? You live here! You must know every path backwards by now.'

'We do,' said Ted, 'but Alice knew the quickest paths to take.'

'Yes,' said Ricky. 'She made a map. But then she hid it from everybody. We try to remember the best paths.'

'Stop!' Ali held up her hand. 'Why didn't you tell me this last time? There are all kinds of maps in the boxes back at the barn. I could have looked for it.'

'Oh dear.' Ricky looked at Theodore for support. 'Was it a secret? I didn't know it was a secret.'

'We didn't know,' echoed his brother.

'Yes, you did,' sighed the Hatter. 'You were both in the Great Hall when the Queen made her request. Everyone wrote it down; it was required reading for your morning memory recitals.' He turned to Ali and shrugged. 'This is a precaution. We can't share everything with you until we can be certain of your intentions.'

'My intentions?'

'You don't have to explain yourself to me. But try to have your thoughts in order when you meet the Queen.'

'I don't understand my intentions. I'm running on instinct. At first it was just curiosity, then curiosity turned to a kind of obsession, even though going back might kill me.'

'And yet it didn't.' Theodore spat a lump of chewed carrot from his mouth. 'You came back, despite the risk to life and limb. Why is that, I wonder?'

'For me.' Waxstaff threw a blackberry at the rabbit. 'The girl did it for me. I was dying; all I wanted was to see this place one last time. Now leave her alone.'

'No!' Theodore's ears folded back on his head. His eyes narrowed. 'Back at the clearing you made it easier for someone to follow you through. You are a very troubling young lady who does very troubling things.'

'What ... like this?' Ali dived full-length at the rabbit, bowling him over and knocking the axe from his paws. The two boys yelped and ran for cover behind the carrot tree as Ali jumped up, grabbed the axe and stood over Theodore.

'Please, stop!' The Hatter stepped forward. 'Theodore is a gentle soul, he's not built for a fight.'

'Nor is this interloper!' Theodore scoffed. 'This is the girl who wouldn't hurt a fly, remember.' He cocked his head to one side and glared up at Ali. 'Or can you? Prove me wrong!'

'Stop! Both of you.' The Hatter held out his hand for the axe.

'You can't blame them, Ali,' sighed Waxstaff. 'I wouldn't trust us. Not yet.'

'But *we* are trusting *them*.' Ali could feel her face flushing, the pulse of blood in her ears. Another temper was brewing. 'This bunny has been demanding I follow him to the palace ever since I arrived. How do we know the Queen won't chop my head off?'

'She won't.' The Hatter shrank back a little. 'But I know a hothead when I see one, and I'm looking at one right now. The Queen had the very same look when Alice hid the map from us. Are you going to hit me?'

'No.'

'I can read the signs.'

'No hitting. Look.' Ali dropped the axe onto the grass and made a display of uncurling her fists. Then she folded her arms behind her back.

'How do you do that?'

'Keep my temper?'

'No. That! Fold your arms behind your back – it's unnatural.' The Hatter tried to do it himself and failed. Ricky and Ted came out from behind the tree and gave it a try. Soon all three were stumbling around in contortions, trying to copy Ali.

'Enough!' Waxstaff dropped her head back on her stretcher. 'I don't have the strength for this. Can we get moving? Ali, pull Theodore up and apologise to him. You behaved like a common bully. Pick on a rabbit your own size in future.'

CHAPTER 10

NEFARIOUS NERDS

Dovecot stared at the wall. None of it made sense. None of it! She was in her office at the station, one entire wall of which was a chaotic brain map of the investigation. She had been moving the pieces around for weeks now, trying to find one key element to put in the centre, one incident or person around which the madness might coalesce. Her photograph of Ali, provided by the school, kept gravitating back to that position.

'This bloody girl.' Dovecot could draw direct lines from this London teen to all the other events, to every person on the board. Even to their one corpse, the body of the man buried under the rubble. A witness had seen a teenage girl climbing the church scaffolding just minutes before the collapse.

She pushed herself from her chair and went to the kitchen at the far end of the building. It was early, half seven, and she was the first person there besides the duty sergeant manning the front desk.

'Coffee?' she called out.

'No, I'm good thanks, ma'am. Gives me the shakes.'

'Very wise.' Dovecot fixed her own, her second of the morning. She knew she had to cut down. One day. But it was her only vice, so to hell with it. She'd fought for the station to have a decent espresso machine and loved the model they'd been given. It even had a glass hopper on the top for the beans. Every cup a fresh grind.

She was heading back to her office when Jeremy came backing in through the front doors, a large cardboard box cradled to his chest.

'Morning, ma'am.'

'Yes, it is. You're not on duty till this afternoon.'

'I know.' He crossed the open office to a small desk in the corner and set the box down. 'I want to do something on my own time this morning. Just wanted to get your approval first.'

'Oh dear. Come. My office.' She led the way and parked herself behind her desk. Jeremy hovered, waiting for permission to sit. 'Okay, what are you up to now? If it's more dark web intel, I can't hear about it in here.'

'It's not. Well, some related discussions are, but we can cover that later if you like.'

'I don't know ... will I like?'

'Probably, it's all connected.' He grinned. It was a shy and disarming grin. Dovecot wondered if the boy was conscious of using it. It would help him in this job. Witnesses and suspects would open up to him, spilling every last detail.

'Here's the thing, ma'am. I have a bunch of small cameras in that box on my desk. They're from my gaming room. I was doing some multi-cam selfies to wrap on an avatar of I made of me, like old school texture mapping but with cameras. Photo telemetry. You need about six to ten images to get a decent three-sixty degree coverage.'

'Should I nod my head like I understand any of that? What do you want – and no geek speak.'

'The gaming group I'm with, they want somewhere to set up an arena, full VR with a 360 environment. One of them suggested the barn. It would be perfect.'

'Let me guess. By one of them, you mean your cousin Peter.'

'Well, yes, and—'

'The young man who's on my missing person list. The same Peter you went strolling in the village with during your afternoon shift yesterday?'

'It'll be in my report. I started on it last night.'

'And I heard all about it from the Chief Constable. I should have heard it from you before you went off duty.'

'I'm sorry.'

'Sorry doesn't cut it in our job. All information pertinent to an inquiry gets passed up the line as soon as possible. In some cases, lives can depend on it. We are the police force. We work as a team.'

'So why is London blocking us from investigating Ali's father?

'Because it's not part of our investigation.'

'But it is. You *know* that and that's why you're not happy about it.'

'Constable!' Dovecot did her best to look aggrieved and failed. Jeremy was right of course; she was furious at being kept out of the loop. Something much bigger was going on. 'Sit down and close the door.'

'I knew it,' Jeremy punched the air, closed the door and sat down.

'Clearly you don't! So let me remind you. Am I frustrated by our colleagues in the Met? Yes, I am, but I also know why there are fire-walls. We have undercover cops out there who spend years getting close to serious felons, only to have their work thrown away and their safety compromised by well-intentioned cops like us who stick their noses in at the wrong time. If our superior officers tell us to back off something, we back off.'

'Right. Sorry ma'am. I get that, I really do. But if you can show your case is connected to the other one, at some point they must bring you in.'

'Or take me off the case altogether.' She paused. 'What do you have?'

'The prime suspect,' he pointed at the incident wall. 'I think you have the wrong face in the middle of this board.'

'And?'

'It's not the girl, Ali. She's caught up in it. But it's not her.'

'Impress me.' Dovecot sat back and sipped of her coffee. She had a soft spot for Constable Glover. He was smart, he could think outside the box and he enjoyed the hunt.

'It should be her dad.' Jeremy took the photograph of Ali's father from the corner of the wall and pinned it in the middle. 'I think he's done a runner with a load of government money, and matching funds from the private sector.'

'Okay. I'll play along. Enlighten me.'

'Ali's dad is a big deal in the research of quantum gravity.'

'Which is what?'

'Some theory to unite quantum physics with Einstein's relativity. But what it is doesn't matter. What matters is that Ali's dad got a massive government grant for his research proposal.

'Good for him.'

'Three million pounds, but it was "matched funding". Which means he had to have another three million from private investors to unlock the grant.'

'All this from the dark web?'

'Yes. But wait for the kicker ... the private venture fund that put the matching three million in has one main investor, and guess who that is? Another from your missing person list. Mrs King.'

Dovecot didn't say anything at first, she simply stared at her constable. What she really wanted to say was: *You are fucking kidding me!* But she tried her best never to swear, it was a point of pride as well as a point of difference in a profession where her male colleagues could hardly say 'good morning' without swearing.

'That's not all,' said Jeremy.

'There's more?' Dovecot had found nothing of interest about King. In fact, almost nothing at all. A few parish records of her work at the church, two council letters regarding the late payments of local rates and the social security number King used for receiving her pension. Aside from that – nothing. Not even a birth certificate. No registered will or indications of family. Now here was Jeremy, the new face of policing, a digital native completely at home on the dark web who had uncovered more information in one evening than she had in four days.

'Surprise me,' she said. Jeremy came around the desk and leaned in close, dropping his voice to a whisper.

'The Greys let me use their library. Did you know their ancestors built the village? I mean built it *and* owned it. Owned the church, the first houses, the first shops. Everyone was a tenant.'

'I did know that, yes.'

'Well, they still have all the historical books and ledgers in their library. The original cost of the buildings, maintenance records, the names of the tenants over the years, and once cameras were a thing, they collected pictures of the village over the years.'

'And?'

'And they have a picture of Mrs King when she first became a tenant. She's much younger. No glass eyes. She's carrying a white stick though, and you can tell it's her – same face, same hair. She's not called King though, her real name is Kate Butcher, and that's the name she uses now for all her investments.'

'Thank you,' Dovecot put down her coffee mug and smiled at her young constable. 'Good job. For this I might overlook your lack of judgment yesterday.'

'Not sure you should be thanking me. I might have made your investigation a lot more complicated.'

'More complicated?' Dovecot laughed. 'That would take some doing!'

'It's the photograph of King. It's very formal. Taken in the teashop. Lord Grey is presenting her with the keys to the shop.'

'Why is that a complication?'

'Because the Lord Grey in the photo is Martha Grey's grandfather. The picture was taken in 1892. If Mrs King was in her twenties in the picture, that makes her at least a hundred and fifty years old.'

CHAPTER 11

WALNUTS AND WATER

———————

Since leaving the lavender patch, the party had been walking through an open woodland of oak trees, the ground on either side of the track a thick sprawl of heavily scented bushes. Over the last mile, that had changed. The trees were now tall conifers, the ground a soft carpet of yellow pine needles.

Then, quite suddenly, they emerged from the pine forest, and a green valley stretched out in front of them, lush and damp, a patchwork of wetland and marsh.

'Oh dear.' Theodore stopped and pointed to a clump of thorn bushes a dozen yards in front of them. 'We might have a problem.'

'We can get around that,' said Ali.

'That one, certainly.' Theodore turned to the Hatter. 'The blight smells quite recent. Two days at most.'

'Blight?' Ali turned to the Hatter. 'Like an infection?'

'Quite so, an infection of the ground. Thorn bushes spring up wherever the Jabberwocky and his pack linger.'

'The longer they stay, the bigger the thorn bushes,' said Theodore. 'I'll see what's growing further on.' He eased himself past the first thorn bush and was back in moments. 'Blocked. Far bigger clumps further on.'

'Then we must take the river,' said the Hatter. 'All rivers flow to the palace lake, and there are no thorn bushes on the water.' He stepped off the path onto a clump of reeds. 'Follow me, stay on the reeds. Don't step on any nests.'

'Nests?' Ali scanned the marshes for wading birds. 'Herons, ducks? Not swans, I hope, they can be aggressive.'

'No. Alligators.'

'What?!'

'One pair. Perfectly friendly so long as you don't step on their nest.' The Hatter set off, picking his way from clump to clump, the others following in line, showing no concern at all.

'Right. Okay then.' Ali took a deep breath and tagged onto the back of the line, taking care to step only where the others had stepped before. Ted was in front of her, holding the rear of the stretcher.

'Are there boats on the river?' asked Ali.

'No, just walnuts.' Ted didn't look round as he spoke. 'We like riding in the walnuts, you can spin and do jousting.'

'Jousting,' laughed Ricky. 'I love jousting in walnuts.'

'Not today,' said Theodore. They arrived at the riverbank and everywhere Ali looked, walnuts were bobbing about on the water, as huge as boulders. Most were still whole, but some had split in half, their interiors eaten out, the shells bobbing about like bathtubs, each large enough for a single passenger.

Under Theodore's directions, the boys selected six of the half-shells and roped them together with lengths of vine taken from the stretcher. They placed the lavender into one shell, lifted Waxstaff into it, then urged Ali to get into hers.

'They don't tip,' said Ricky, and he climbed into his shell and rocked it furiously to prove the point.

Ali was impressed. She took off her backpack and climbed into one. The shell was small, and she had to sit with her knees up, her arms hugging her pack to her chest. Her weight pushed the shell down into the water, stabilising it.

'Pretty comfy.' Ali tapped the rim. 'How do we move without paddles?'

'Our hands are enough to steer a course,' the Hatter told her. 'The river flows to the palace lake. We just need to keep to the middle of the stream and stay clear of the banks.'

They set off, pushing themselves free of the reeds, and were soon gathered up by the gentle current.

'So, tell me about the map.' Ali's shell was strapped in front of Theodore's, so she didn't try turning to face him, she just lay back, talking over her shoulder, arms dangling over the side, hands in the water. 'What did it look like?'

'Alice called it a chart,' said Theodore. 'No one could read it but her; nothing but lines. Dozens of squiggly lines, side by side and round and round, the sort of thing a child might doodle on a rainy day. She was very secretive about it – with good reason, of course.'

'To keep it from the Jabberwocky.'

'Quite so. Alice hid the map when she wasn't using it, and left clues in the storybook for finding it – clues to herself, if she started forgetting. She was very thorough in such matters, relentlessly so.'

Ali leaned back on the rim of her walnut shell and stared up at the sky. It was so like lying in a small, round bath that she felt oddly at peace, as if she might wake up in her own bathroom ... wake to hear her father calling out for her to hurry up or she'd be late for school. She closed her eyes. He was her priority now; she had to get back and find him. Waxstaff was safe and in good hands. So were the Greys if King had indeed come through, chasing Ali for the secret of safe passage, believing it was in the documents she had brought with her.

'Look, we're getting close,' cried Ricky. 'Here are the golden woods, they grow just a few miles from the palace.'

Ali opened her eyes and lifted her head to scan the riverbank ahead. Golden dandelion flowers grew there, as tall as trees, their tops like giant yellow umbrellas. Ali was lost for words; the view was so bizarre and unexpected.

Then something struck the underside of her walnut boat.

'Critters!' yelled the Hatter, pointing to the bank on their right. There were seven of them. They emerged from behind the trunks of the dandelion trees and began whooping and jeering.

'Paddle!' screamed Ali. She rolled onto her knees, stretched her arms over the side and paddled the shell like it was a surfboard, pulling at the water with cupped hands.

The others copied her, the water churning from their efforts. Then Ali's shell tipped to one side, rocked by something in the water. She leaned the other way to try and keep the boat stable, but over-corrected and toppled headlong into the river.

To her surprise, the water was shallow, only chest deep. She got to her feet, grabbed her floating backpack and lifted it above her head to keep the books and journals dry.

'Ali! Ali!' The attack had woken Waxstaff who was screaming at her as the other boats drifted on. 'Behind you!'

'Hello, pretty thing.'

A face surfaced behind her, a disfigured face covered in scars. Exactly what kind of creature it was, Ali couldn't tell, all she could focus on was its sharp, yellow teeth. She let go of her backpack with one hand, and punched down as hard as she could, connecting with the creature's nose.

'Naaaaa!'

The creature screamed, then lunged at her, fastening its teeth on her hip. Ali felt the bite pierce the denim of her jeans, tiny thorns puncturing her skin. She brought the point of her elbow down on the creature's skull and heard the bone between its eyes crack.

The creature drifted away, a trail of blood leaking from its nose. Ali finally saw it for what it was: a large, disfigured water vole. She held her bag above her head and made for the opposite bank, the side without the yelping critters. Giant lily pads the size of dinner plates lined the shallows of the bank. Ali pulled herself through them and dropped down on a wide strip of river sand.

The others would come back for her, she was certain of it, as soon as they could steer their shells to the same bank. She scanned both sides of the river for any sign of more critters. Nothing. They must be chasing along the bank after the boats. Ali unzipped her pack and checked the books and histories for damage. Some covers were damp, but nothing was soaked. It was a good backpack; she had chosen it for a school camp a year ago, strong, sturdy and rainproof. Her dad had insisted they get a good one.

'Wet clothes on a camp?' He'd shaken his head. 'No fun in that.'

'No fun carrying a heavy pack, either. I want a super-light one.' She'd picked up one that took her fancy.

'Sturdy and light can be expensive,' her dad said, checking the label. 'Bloody hell! This one is *very* expensive!'

'That's okay,' she laughed. 'Nothing but the best for your daughter.'

The memory came back like a punch to her stomach, a rush of such deep sadness that for a moment she could hardly breathe.

'Enough!' She blinked away the tears and started spreading out the books and journals on the dry sand. The covers were all a little damp, but it was nothing the sun couldn't dry if she had enough time.

She didn't.

A second group of critters scuttled out from the high grass above her. There were a dozen at least. There was no shrieking or wailing; they moved forward with a quiet malevolence, yellow eyes locked on hers, lips curled back.

One, a hedgehog the size of a full-grown pig, jostled to the front, its spines twitching. Ali looked around for a weapon. The sand was covered in flood debris. She grabbed a branch the size of a cricket bat and swung it from side to side.

Not one spoke. Ali could tell they were weak from their suffering. She could see pain in the tight lines around their eyes. If they tried to attack her one at a time, they would be no match for her. But as a pack?

The critters circled, then one lunged forward, testing her. It was as big as a bulldog, and its nose was invisible under thick folds of grey skin. it looked like a gigantic mole and tried to creep under the arc of Ali's swinging club. It failed, took the impact of the blow on its shoulder then scurried off, shrieking in anger.

'Next!' screamed Ali, swinging the driftwood from side to side. 'The rabbit's going to be here any second with his axe.'

'Who, Theodore?' the pig-sized hedgehog edged forward. 'My dear young lady, no rabbit comes to the rescue this day.'

'He'll come.' Ali swung the bat wildly. The hedgehog stepped clear.

'Not until this unpleasantness is over. We have instructions to hurt you – lots of damage, force you to transform.' The hedgehog waved for his colleagues to come forward and surround her.

'Not so,' spoke a huge stoat, stepping up beside the hedgehog. 'I must correct you on that point, Mister Spikes. The instruction was to bring her back as she is so he can do the damaging himself.' The stoat grinned at Ali. 'The Wocky is an expert at damaging, an artist in his own way. He likes to remove a good half, likes cutting you down to size. We were full-grown folk when we arrived. The Wocky doesn't like full-grown; he calls us his children, his little family.'

Ali was surprised at how calm she felt, how unreal everything seemed. Was it shock, this odd serenity? An otter to her left moved in, staying low, lunging for one of the journals lying on the sand. Ali kicked out and struck it on the nose, but the kick threw her off balance, and the other creatures charged.

Where the black dog came from, Ali didn't see. Her attention was locked on the hedgehog. It leapt at her face; its claws extended. Ali dropped to the ground and the hedgehog flew over her head. She rolled, sprang to her feet, and braced for the next attack. It was only then that she saw the dog. It had the otter, screeching, in its mouth.

The hedgehog launched itself at Ali again, grabbing one of the journals that lay drying in the sun. Ali brought her club down on its paw. The creature yelped, but held on to his prize, and scrambled clear. The others backed away, uncertain about the huge black dog, then they turned and fled into the trees.

Ali turned to face the dog. It was ripping the otter, tearing at its throat. Ali took a step back as the dog looked up at her, the otter's body hanging from its jaws, the severed head on the ground.

'Time to go,' said the dog, its voice a bass growl. It dug a hole in the beach, buried the otter's body parts, and padded over to Ali where it sniffed her face. Shreds of fat and tissue were stuck between its teeth and around its muzzle.

'You're the newcomer, yes?'

'And you're a messy eater,' Ali replied, her false bravado undermined by the tremor in her voice. The dog raised one eyebrow, walked to the river, jumped in and sluiced water round in its mouth. It strolled back, stood next to Ali, and shook itself.

'Better now?' asked the dog.

'Better and wetter,' said Ali.

'One forgets these things, the pleasantries.'

'I won't forget this,' said Ali. 'You saved my life. Obviously.'

'I saved the histories. Gather them up and follow me.'

The light beneath the dandelion canopy made it hard to see. Sunlight pierced through, but in narrow beams. Ali felt as if she was walking through a nightclub, her eyes struggling to adjust as she stepped from blinding glare into deep shadow and back again every few steps.

'Can you slow down?' she yelled.

The dog was a long way ahead and neither slowed down nor replied, leaving Ali to stumble on as best she could. The zip on her backpack had broken, which didn't help matters. Everything stayed in, but it was more like shouldering a basket than a backpack.

Ali heard the knight before she saw him. Partly it was the clanking of his armour, mostly it was his swearing. The man was sitting on the trunk of a fallen dandelion tree and appeared to be lecturing his horse.

'It's not a matter of bloody choice,' the knight exclaimed. 'This is a matter of duty, and our duty is crystal bloody clear.'

'Duty without discussion is blind servitude,' replied the horse.

'Nothing of the goddamn sort,' said the knight.

'Everything of the sort. I'm a horse. Do I ask *you* to carry *me*? No, I do not. Becoming a horse forces a level of introspection you are ill-equipped to endure.'

'The simple fact is this. This duty we carry is not a duty to each other, it is to a common cause.' Then the knight spotted Ali and the dog. 'And now that cause approaches. You found her! Excellent, excellent.'

'I did, and barely in time,' the dog growled. 'What delayed you?'

'Henry threw a shoe,' said the knight.

'And Stoke threw a tantrum,' said the horse. 'What of the critters?'

'There were a dozen. I took the head from one. They will regroup and try again, so we must go now. Shoe or no shoe.'

'Yes, indeed.' The knight turned to Ali and dipped his head. 'Greetings.'

'Yes.' It was all she had the energy to say.

'Where are your companions?'

'We were separated,' said Ali. 'We need to find them.'

'Find them we will, once we have you safely to the palace. With luck our paths might cross en route.' The knight gestured to Ali's hip. 'Is that your blood?'

'Yes. One of the creatures latched on to me.'

'Then you must ride the rest of the way. Henry will carry you.'

'There!' said the horse. 'That casual offer of my service is the real measure of how gallant he is. A true knight would have dropped to his knees and offered you his own back.'

'Then I thank you both,' said Ali, and swung herself up into the saddle.

'You've ridden before,' said the dog. 'Good, we'll make good progress. No stopping until the palace, not for anything.' Then it loped off ahead of them.

Ali shuffled in the saddle, shifting her weight to find a comfortable position, but it was like sitting on a log of wood.

'Kindly stop fidgeting,' said the horse. 'I have bruises on bruises from this dreadful saddle.'

'Sorry, Henry. That's your name, yes?'

'It is.'

'Well, Henry, you need a thicker saddle cloth,' said Ali. 'The one under this extremely uncomfortable saddle looks as thin as a handkerchief.'

'You noticed, how very kind. Some people do not! Even when the matter is brought to their attention.' The horse rolled its eyes to glare at the knight who was keeping pace beside them.

'That bloody saddle cloth is plenty good enough when you take the bloody Queen out for a gallop,' said the old knight.

'She is half your size, half your weight and twice your good company.'

Ali listened to their arguments for as long as she could, but they quickly faded to become a background noise, like distant surf. The sense of being wide awake inside a vivid dream returned. Yet no dream could deliver so much detail: the rust and dents in the armour of the man walking beside her, the motes of dust drifting in the funnels of sunlight that pierced the forest canopy, the discomfort she was feeling from the saddle and from the bite on her hip. Could a fevered mind come up with this much detail? Could she be lying in a coma on a hospital bed, or dying under the rubble of the church spire? Both explanations made more sense than this – riding on a talking horse through a forest of giant dandelions!

And yet, with every passing minute, Ali could feel herself buying into it. This really was a small universe stuck like a barnacle to the keel of her own.

'Question,' said Ali. 'Did either of you think this place was a dream when you first came through?'

'Many do,' said the knight. 'Sadly, I have no memories of my life before, or of my early days here. There are scholars at the palace who debate this very point. They go to great lengths to pull holes in the reality of this world, as does this very cynical horse you are blessed to be riding.'

'Asking our opinion has no merit,' said Henry.

'Why not?'

'If this is your dream, then we are players in your dream, conjured up by you. So, our opinion would be your opinion. We would merely be puppets you created to express them.'

'Good point,' said Ali.

'And one further observation, if I may,' said Henry. 'If this was your dream, then you are a mean-spirited little god responsible for a great deal of brutality and suffering.'

'I can't argue with that,' Ali adjusted her position again. 'And I'd be a stupid god too, dreaming up such a shitty saddle for myself.' The dandelion forest was less imposing now, it was thinning out. 'Tell me about Alice.'

'Why?' the knight looked up. 'Is she your sister? There is a family likeness.'

'She is my great-great aunt.'

'Not possible,' said the horse. 'You appear much the same age.'

'Yes, I know. It's hard to explain.'

'Not hard at all,' said the knight. 'Life gallops headlong in the other world, Henry, you know this. Whole generations pass over there while we sit marveling at a few sunsets.'

'I know the theory well enough,' snorted the horse.

'So, back to my request: tell me about Alice.'

'Alice is challenging,' said the knight, 'and resourceful and courageous.'

'Challenging? Definitely,' agreed the horse, 'and opinionated, headstrong and stubborn. She is calculating and intense. She is systematic in all she does, unsparing of herself and others, and worse yet, relentlessly smart and knows it.'

'I like the sound of her,' laughed Ali.

'Liking her is beside the point.' Henry flared his nostrils and snorted. 'What matters is finding her.'

'She has gone to ground,' said the knight, 'For reasons of her own. Reasons she has not shared with the rest of us, despite everything.'

'Not even with Stoke here,' said Henry, 'and she held him in the highest regard. Exactly why is a mystery to me.'

'Stoke? Is that your name?' Ali asked the knight.

'I have no bloody memory of my previous life, but my name was stitched into the hem of the rather fine waistcoat I was wearing when I arrived here, plus the name of the town of my birth. I am Sir Stoke of Trent.'

'Sir Stoke of Trent?'

'Exactly so. One damned word was threadbare, but clearly, I must have been a gentleman to have my name and my birth town stitched into my waistcoat.'

'Alice wrote a version of you in the books, you're obviously the white knight.'

'Yes. Her parody of me is bloody vexing, but Alice always had her reasons, obscure as they often were to the rest of us.'

CHAPTER 12

THE PALACE

————————

They were clear of the dandelion trees now, walking a path of gravel and beaten clay. For the first time, Ali saw fields. They were small, defined by low stone walls, and they stretched out on either side, acre upon acre of them, a vast patchwork, more urban allotment than country farm. Much of it was taken up with orchards. There were apples, pears and plums, all at different stages of fruiting. Some trees were covered in spring pollen, others heavy with autumn fruit. Ali had many questions but decided to shelve them, contenting herself with taking in as much detail as she could.

There were no dwellings, just sheds of stone and wood that squatted like buttresses against the field walls. Men, women and children were at work, and some creatures too. Ali watched a large monkey scampering up a pear tree to collect fruit.

'No livestock.'

It was an observation not a question, spoken softly to herself, but Henry heard and snorted loudly.

'You put a lot of attitude into your snorting,' said Ali.

'Yes, he does,' said the knight. 'I believe that snort signified derision.'

'It did,' said the horse. 'Our guest made the observation that there is no livestock here. Any reasonable student of life would have seen this observation to be unworthy, even before it left their lips.'

'Why?'

'Because we have no appetite for eating our companions.'

'Theodore told me there were real animals over here as well, not just the transformed. Animals that stumbled through from our world?'

'There are. Many of the transformed, like the dog who scouts our road ahead, like to hunt for wild meat in the forests. But farming creatures here, in our fields? No, we do not fatten them for our table.'

The monkey Ali had seen, now saw her. It scampered down the tree, calling out to others and pointing at Ali.

'Prepare for a great deal of irritating attention,' said Henry.

'Yes,' said the knight. 'Your safe arrival has been looked to since word came of your first appearance.'

They were walking up a steady rise towards a ridge line. The locals gathering in their wake formed themselves into a respectful retinue.

Ali saw the turrets of the palace first as she approached the crest of the hill. The palace was a square tower, five or six storeys of white stone. It looked new – a filmset depiction of a castle keep. There was none of the wear Ali was used to seeing on historic buildings in London, no erosion from centuries of wind and rain, no caustic decay from a century of industrial pollution.

The tower looked practical, built for strength, not aesthetics. The effect was both majestic and reassuring. The building was also strangely familiar. Ali had seen one just like it before but couldn't place the memory. It stood alone, a single building amid gardens and sweeping lawns. To Alice it looked more like a stately, ancestral home than a royal palace, its gardens dropping away to a large lake. A fortress wall encircled everything, the outer face a vertical cliff, the inner face buttressing out like the base of a pyramid. A path ran along the top of the wall and Ali could see figures there. Guards, perhaps?

With the growing procession of followers behind them, the party passed into the palace grounds through pillared gates topped by stone griffins bearing roses. The surrounding grounds were beautiful: pathways of white pebbles running beneath archways of climbing roses. White pagodas and marble statues dotted the lawns, and beds of exotic flowers curved away on every side.

'Home, such as it is,' said Henry. He stopped and dipped his head. 'If you wouldn't mind dismounting, my long-suffering back would be most appreciative.'

'Of course.' Ali slid from the saddle and stretched. Every single muscle felt cramped and sore. All she wanted right now was to soak in a steaming hot bath. Did such a thing exist here? If not, the lake looked inviting.

'Come along,' said Stoke, as if reading her mind. 'First order of business is to get your wound cleaned in the infirmary.'

He turned and held up his hands to the small crowd who had followed them into the palace grounds. 'Allow our guest some room,' he said.

The group ignored him completely and pressed forward, fanning out to form a circle around the three of them. Ali tried to read their faces. They seemed eager, yet apprehensive. For what? For their stories? If so, most of them would be disappointed.

'You look a bit like Alice,' said a small woman with an open face and bright eyes. 'A bit taller, I think.'

'We're related,' said Ali.

'You've come to help us,' said a small gorilla, no bigger than child. It was a statement, not a question. Ali held the creature's gaze as she tried to come up with a response. Help them? No. If anything, she was going to make their lives more dangerous by stranding King on this side of the gateway.

She was spared by the blare of trumpets and everyone turned to look at the white tower. A tall woman stepped out into the late afternoon sun. She wore a blue gown, elegant and simple, and carried a white parasol.

'The Queen,' said Henry.

The woman started down the steps, a small entourage of courtiers in her wake. There was a handmaiden, several guards and – stretched out on a pallet of cushions – a massive caterpillar.

'Bloody hell,' Ali whispered softly. Four elderly courtiers, all men dressed in black gowns, bore the pallet on their shoulders. The Queen beamed at Ali and held out her hands as she strode across the lawn to greet her.

'Safe, all of you. Wonderful.' She rubbed Henry on the nose and embraced the knight, all without taking her eyes off Ali. The men carrying the caterpillar stood quietly, bearing their load with a quiet dignity, but they were watching Ali too, their eyes bright with excitement. Ali tried her best not to stare at the giant grub. Its face was still partly human and sported a well-groomed moustache. His body was mostly caterpillar, except for dozens of small hands. These made him look more like a centipede, the hands protruding from his sides like tiny pairs of feet from chest to tail.

'May I introduce Plato,' said the Queen, 'our most eminent scholar – in fact, our Chief Scholar.'

'Plato?' said Ali. 'Not the original ...'

'Correct.' The caterpillar had an odd voice, as if the air was climbing its way up from a deep and very damp well through layers of mucus or slime. 'Not the original. Like most of us here, I have no idea of my history. However, I have a passion for learning and philosophy, so I chose a name I could identify with.'

'If you've forgotten your old life, how do you know about Plato?'

'Books, my child. We are blessed to have an extensive library. Many of the unlucky folk who have stumbled through here have come laden with all manner of treasures, books included. People of different trades, vendors, schoolteachers, even doctors with their medical encyclopedias. Over time we have amassed quite a library in this way. Then of course, Alice arrived, and everything changed.'

'Changed how?'

'She came bearing books with every new visit. Boxes and boxes of them.'

'More on that later,' said the Queen. 'My goodness, young lady, our two boys are quite right. You do bear some small resemblance to Alice.' She took hold of Ali's hands, clasping them between her own. 'Now, you must answer me three things. Have you brought some histories through with you? Is your memory still with you? And, most importantly, do you have the secret of safe passage?'

Ali weighed up the moment, conscious of all the faces studying her, then chose her words carefully,

'Not one for small talk, are you?'

'Ha!' The Queen clapped her hands and laughed. 'You share more than just looks with Alice. There will certainly be a great deal of small talk. We are starved of both news and distractions and hope to get both from you.'

'Jackie and the others,' said Ali. 'Did they make it back here?'

'Your friend Jackie did, as did the boys. The Hatter and Theodore doubled back in search of you. They are yet to return. Now to my questions ...'

'Your questions, yes.' Ali held up three fingers, folding them in turn as she gave her answers. 'One – yes, I do remember myself. Two – yes, I do have a few of the histories here with me. And three – no, I don't have the secret to safe passage.'

'Oh!' The Queen's smile faltered a little.

'Disappointing,' said Plato. 'Did Alice not share it with you?'

'How could she, I've never met her.'

'Interesting,' the caterpillar studied her face. 'According to the boys, this is your third visit.'

'Yes, it is.'

'And yet, like Alice, returning to your world hasn't killed you?'

'Clearly,' said Ali. 'It came close, but no gold medal.'

'Medal?' The giant caterpillar looked confused.

'Just an expression.'

'Later,' said the Queen. 'We can discuss all this later. No further questions, Plato, our young guest needs to refresh after such a journey. Come, Ali, a room has been made ready for you.'

'Thank you. First, I'd like to see Waxstaff, I mean Jackie.'

'Why, of course.' The Queen took a step back and smiled. 'I forget myself in my eagerness, forgive me. My dear Stoke, will you be so good as to escort our guest to the infirmary?'

CHAPTER 13

THE INFIRMARY

———————

'That was interesting.' The elderly knight glanced at Ali as he escorted her across the lawns and down to the lake. 'The Queen has grown accustomed to having her way in most things. She assumes compliance.'

'Why? Did you all elect her?'

'No. Leadership is instinctive to her; she wears the mantel with ease.' They came to the lake, a wide band of clear water with a central island.

'Instinctive?' said Ali. 'Did she wake up one day and think, you know what? I'll make a great Queen. And just started ... queening?'

'Exactly so.'

'And everyone else rolled over like good little puppies?' They headed down a gravel pathway that skirted the lake.

'By accepting her guidance, we effectively gifted authority to her.'

'Why would you do that?'

'She unites us by our common purpose.'

'Keeping you safe?'

'No. I can manage that for myself. The purpose that binds everyone here is the pursuit of knowledge. The palace is a great centre of learning, a university.'

'A university with a castle wall?' The grounds were in a shallow dish of land, the castle wall visible on every side like a crust of pastry on the rim of the dish.

'Indeed. And guards too. Knowledge is power; it is also a threat to cherished beliefs and a challenge to those who profit from perspectives born of deceit.'

'Nicely put.' Ali couldn't argue with that. It was why she loved science. It was pure, unsullied by doctrine. It was why she was so irritated by any religious group that claimed to have the last word on fundamental truths. 'Does the Jabberwocky control his little flock with his own take on reality?'

'He does. And there are others like him. But here in this place of learning, we thirst for the answers to three simple questions. Who are we? Where are we? And how do we get home? We are all accidental explorers here, shipwrecked on a foreign shore. Thus, our common purpose is to understand this place in order to escape from it.'

They had circled half the lake, making their way round to an iron bridge that arched over to the island in a single span. Ali now had a clear view into a grove of trees on the island. It was the setting for a large building of glass and iron.

'Bloody hell!' Ali couldn't believe her eyes. It was huge, the size of several sports fields at least, and she recognised it at once. Her knees almost buckled, and she grabbed the handrail of the bridge to steady herself.

'Are you all right, child?'

'Yes, just tired.' But she wasn't all right. Far from it. The impact of seeing this particular building was an emotional punch in her stomach. The original had been built in Hyde Park, a massive engineering feat created for the Great Exhibition in the reign of Queen Victoria. The whole place, every iron girder and pane of glass, had been taken down a few years later and reassembled halfway across London.

'This is the Crystal Palace,' said Ali. 'My parents took me to the site when I was small. The building's been demolished, but there's a park and a museum.'

'And why did they take you?'

'It was where Mum proposed to my dad.' She took a deep breath to steady herself. 'That's what she said, anyway.' She turned away from the knight so he wouldn't see her tears welling up. She couldn't show weakness to anyone here. There was no one she could completely trust except Waxstaff.

'You have turned remarkably pale, child,' said Stoke, his voice soft and deep. 'We should consider the possibility of infection. A bite can be a very dirty wound. There are scholars in this building who can clean it and administer a poultice.'

'Okay.' Ali looked up at the building as they crossed the bridge. Thousands of panes of glass shimmered in the late sun like facets in a massive kaleidoscope, the burning disc fracturing and repeating in every pane. Stoke dismissed himself with a low bow as they reached the main entrance.

'I shall leave you here. I'm told your colleague lies at the far end.'

'You're not coming inside?'

'No!' He paused, searching for the right words. 'To linger here is to admit to a morbid fascination with suffering. That is not my disposition.'

'Morbid?' It was a moment before Ali understood him. 'Oh! It's bad?'

'It can be confronting. I shall see you out here when you're finished. Please have your wound attended to.' Ali promised she would and stepped inside.

The most immediate impact, and the most overwhelming, was the smell of lavender. The plants were growing everywhere; they hung from girders in woven planter baskets like an armada of purple airships. They were at the foot of each bed, line after line of them, all in terracotta pots.

The similarity to the Crystal Palace was striking, Ali could remember the photographs from the museum. The most striking difference was the endless rows of hospital beds, each occupant recovering from whatever accident had befallen them, each enduring the torment of transformation.

Ali tried not to look as she walked down the central aisle to the other end of the building, but a mix of compassion and curiosity made that impossible. Faces looked up at her as she passed. She saw fear on some, pain and bewilderment on others, but mostly she saw resignation. There was a young man with the eyes of a cat, his skin soft with new fur. A woman with a vastly extended jaw was adjusting pillows to take its weight. Every bed was the stage for a different personal drama. Then Ali noticed iron rails set into the floorboards. She was walking a train track! Inside a building. What was that about?

She found Waxstaff easily enough. The two boys were there, sitting at the end of her bed like loyal dogs perched on the prow of some Viking funeral ship. Except Waxstaff wasn't dead, that much was clear the moment Ali reached her bed. The transformation was accelerating, however. The boys looked up and put fingers to their lips like librarians. What was it with these two and Waxstaff?

'Shh! She's sleeping,' whispered Ricky.

'Am not.' Waxstaff opened one eye. It opened slowly, two lids peeling back like skin from a grape. The cornea was a translucent green, the iris a vertical slit. It was the eye of a reptile. Despite this, the gaze was kind – warm even.

'How am I looking?'

'You want a mirror?'

'Hell no, are you mad? Describe me. I chose lizard, right?'

'Not sure yet. Your eyes and skin look reptile and there's a row of small bumps down the centre of your head. Maybe a crocodile?'

'Oh.' Waxstaff patted the bed cover beside her. 'I guess I will be what I will be.' Ali sat and took her hand. The skin had scales now, but it felt warm.

'How come we aren't completely freaked out by all this?' Ali tried her best to look into Waxstaff's reptilian eyes. 'My mother's best friend is turning into a lizard, and I'm holding her hand like it's the most normal thing in the world.'

'It is. In this world. Our capacity to adapt is extraordinary.'

'I guess so.' Ali forced herself to appear calm and casual. 'It's warm. Your hand. Are you still in pain?'

'It's all pain. Every cell … but distant, like it's happening to someone else.'

'Do you need anything?'

'Snails,' Waxstaff said it immediately, without thinking. 'Interesting, I really would like a plate of raw snails.'

'I'll see what I can find, must be some out in all these gardens.' Ali stroked the back of Waxstaff's hand with her fingertips. The scales were soft as leather.

'What next?' asked Waxstaff. 'Any word of King yet?'

'No. I didn't think it through, did I? Any of it.'

'Actually, I think you did. Not consciously, but your brain was crunching options like a computer – it spat out the best of a bad bunch.'

'I wanted King to come after me so Dad and everyone else would be free of her. That was as far as any thinking went.

'Perhaps.'

'And even that was selfish. I wanted so badly to come back here, I think everything else was an excuse to do it.' Ali realised she was squeezing down on Waxstaff's hand. She let go. 'Sorry.'

'It's fine. Look Ali, your sense of responsibility for this borders on vanity. This world, whatever it is, existed long before you were born. Let things unfold around you for once.'

'They think I've come here to help them. They crowded round me when I arrived. Great help I'll turn out to be if I've lured King to come across?'

'Perhaps you can help them. Perhaps you can't. Stop taking it upon yourself to fix everything.'

'I can't stop.'

'You mean you won't.'

'No, I can't, because I know what I need to do for them.'

'A plan?' Waxstaff laughed, 'Another one? Surprise me.'

'I need more time with the books … lots of ideas came to me today, popping into my head one after the other.'

'Such as?'

'Alice talks about maps and geography in both the books. She's left clues to finding the time map the Hatter was being so secretive about' – Ali leaned in and whispered so the two boys wouldn't hear – 'and I know where she hid it.'

'Be very careful,' Waxstaff whispered back. Then she sighed and closed her eyes again. 'Promise me you won't trust any of these people. Not yet. Alice hid all these things for a reason and so must you.'

'I know.'

'Do you? I doubt that.' One of Waxstaff's eyes peeled open again. 'Then tell me, where have you hidden your journal?'

'I keep it with me.' Ali took it from her bag and waved it like a fan in front of her face. 'I'll add to it every day.'

'This was exactly your great-aunt's dilemma. Alice had to record everything, and she had to read it daily to remember herself. So will you. Which means that everything you discover – all your thoughts, all your theories, all your explanations – they will all be vulnerable, all written down for anyone to read.'

'I guess so.'

'You know so. Therefore, lesson number one is *do not* keep your journal with you. Hide it and, if possible, encrypt everything.'

Ali raised her head and smiled. She had come to the same conclusion. The books weren't encoded messages for others to read. They were notes Alice had written to herself. Her great-aunt must have discovered the problem of memory loss very early in her travels here. Her enigmatic stories were memory joggers. If Alice read the passage she'd written about the March Hare, it would trigger all her memories associated with it, everything she had discovered about transformation. She had created similar stories for every piece of information she knew would be important to her.

'I'm sure you're right,' whispered Ali. 'The stories were her memory joggers, for the most part, anyway. I think some things she buried more deeply with her riddles. Another layer of protection.'

'Yes, I think so too.'

'Okay, you sleep,' Ali got up from the bed. 'I'll be back later tonight. You have a promise to keep.'

'I haven't forgotten.' Waxstaff reached out a foot and prodded Ted. 'I've made the boys see to that, haven't I, Teddy?'

'Yes,' Teddy nodded.

'Every time Jackie wakes up,' said Ricky, 'we ask her to tell us stories of when she was a girl, so she can remember and keep her promise to you.'

'Some people keep their promises,' added Teddy, doing his best to look as cross as possible.

'Tonight then, I'll dictate everything I can remember of your mother.' Waxstaff rolled over onto her side. 'Then you must release me from this, let me slip into forgetting.' She waved her hand for Ali to leave and drifted back to sleep.

Ali found Stoke waiting for her outside. He was asleep, sitting with his back against a tree, the setting sun glowing pink on his amour. He looked exhausted. Ali hesitated for a moment, then decided she could find the Queen on her own and set off across the bridge without him.

'Hold on!' The knight got to his feet. 'I was just resting my eyes.'

'You were snoring.'

'I never snore.'

'Your armour was rattling. Either you were snoring or you were trembling in fear from a bad dream.'

'I never dream. Did you have someone dress your wound?'

'Yes,' Ali lied. She didn't trust anyone yet. Far safer to check it herself later. They reached the palace and Stoke conducted her to a side entrance where a narrow spiral staircase led up to a balcony. Plato, the large caterpillar, was there. He was lounging on a chaise longue and puffing on a water pipe. He said nothing, gestured for them to sit, then proceeded to ignore them completely.

Ali hardly minded; she needed some time with her own thoughts. She stared at the extraordinary view, at the brilliant red of the setting sun and the long blue shadows it was casting over the gardens below. Everything had a serene magic to it. Several minutes passed before a young woman came and set the table with a light supper.

Ali stared at the food. There was hardly enough for one! She glanced across at Stoke and saw the same disappointment on his face. Then the Queen arrived.

'How is your friend?' The Queen played host, pouring tea for everyone.

'She's frightened. Trying to hide it from me.'

'Good for her. I think we will get on. We are a small family here, thrust together by happenstance, so we need to get along, but how more pleasant it is to be among true colleagues.' She handed Ali a cup of tea. 'I hope to find this with you.'

'Then I hope you like someone with a short temper and a big appetite.'

'Indeed.' The Queen surveyed the table. 'Forgive me, this is rather a dismal offering after a journey such as yours.'

'Not our finest welcome,' agreed the knight.

'Aphelia!' The Queen beckoned to the young woman who had set the table. 'Go and say sweet things to Cook and have her prepare more of everything.' The attendant dipped her head and left. The Queen gestured for Ali to help herself to a slice of cake.

'It's good,' Ali said, her mouth still full from her first bite. 'Very good.' In fact, it was delicious. Like the vivid sunset colours lighting the sky overhead, the cake had such a mix of intense flavours that Ali felt her taste buds being overwhelmed. Further conversation was impossible, what was going on in her mouth was far too distracting. She could taste all the ingredients at once: the sugar and the butter, the milk and the eggs, the flour and the baking powder. Yet she could taste the cake too, just as cake, a creamy symphony of all the other notes.

'Not another word,' said the Queen, and she turned to the Chief Scholar. 'Do you remember that, Plato? The assault on your senses when you first arrived.'

'I do,' The huge caterpillar nodded slowly. 'We forget facts but not feelings. I have never understood this. We remember a wasp to be a wasp, we remember our language. But our personal history? That we lose. No doubt this is a mystery we will resolve one day.'

'Perhaps Alice has solved it already,' said the Queen. 'Solved it, and buried the answer as another riddle in one of her books.'

'I agree,' said Ali, finding her voice at last. 'I think the secret to getting back safely is hidden in there too. Bundled up inside a riddle.'

'Pah!' snorted the caterpillar.

'Our learned colleague disagrees.' The Queen turned to Plato. 'The scholars have failed to find it in either book, despite many years of effort.'

'Because the secret is not hidden in there.' The caterpillar let out a sigh as if explaining the obvious to children. 'If it were, I would have found it.'

'I'll find it,' Ali kept her voice level. 'I just need more time with the books.'

'Your Majesty,' Plato continued as if Ali hadn't spoken. 'We must accept the uncomfortable truth that Alice buried that secret back in the other world.'

'She did not,' said Ali.

The Chief Scholar didn't seem to hear her. He drew on his pipe, blew a smoke ring and started telling the Queen of the discussion he had been chairing that morning. 'We have come upon a new approach for solving the riddle of the raven. The difference between a raven and a writing desk might well be the silent w.'

'It's not', said Ali.

The caterpillar continued to ignore her and began telling the Queen how they were also working on a new theory concerning the meaning of treacle in the story told by the Dormouse at the tea party. 'We think treacle is a metaphor for how sticky some areas are here-abouts. Those places in the woods where you seem to be walking through treacle.'

Ali leaned forward and put a hand over the air intake of Plato's water-pipe. The Chief Scholar drew on his mouthpiece, frowned, then slowly registered the fact that Ali was covering the vent.

'Good, do I have you attention?'

'Are you sure you want my attention, young lady?'

'Perhaps not. Someone who thinks himself into becoming a grub must have serious self-esteem issues.'

'Young lady!' The old knight almost barked his disapproval. 'No one ventures an opinion regarding another's appearance. Not here. Not ever.'

'Sorry,' said Ali, 'I was overreacting. It felt like I'd been transformed myself, into an invisible person. Mister Plato, the discussion you were chairing about the treacle story — it's Alice's way of reminding herself about all the small gravitational anomalies that exist over here. That's what those are, the places where it feels like you're walking in treacle.

Gravitational anomalies. Alice didn't know what they were, she just knew what they felt like.' Ali reached into her pack set at the foot of the table beside her. She took the books out, found the passage and read it aloud:

'I should see the garden far better,' said Alice to herself, 'if I could get to the top of that hill: and here's a path that leads straight to it – no, it doesn't! This goes straight back to the house! Well then, I'll try it the other way.' And so she did: wandering up and down, and trying turn after turn, but always coming back to the house. She set out once more down the path, determined to keep straight on till she got to the hill. For a few minutes all went on well, when the path gave a sudden twist and the next moment, she found herself walking in at the door.

'You are mistaken.' The caterpillar lifted his head slightly and tried to focus on Ali, his hooded eyes rimmed with water; the smoke seemed to be a constant irritant to them. 'That pull she describes there is her desire to return home, a pull we all feel, child. It has nothing to do with gravity.'

'Then I shall test it.'

'Do as you please, but retain an open mind. After all, your great-aunt goes on to describe much the same pull towards these Palace Gardens, a transfer of longing if you will, she becomes drawn to them by their seductive beauty.'

'No, she is describing changes in gravitational density. Which means they can be measured and mapped as anomalies in the speed of the passage of time.' Ali saw her words strike home. Plato looked at her properly for the first time.

'How very intriguing,' he said. 'Debate is to be encouraged of course, but so are contemplation and humility.'

'Let us table this discussion for later.' The Queen leaned forward and fixed Ali with a hard stare. 'A note regarding Sir Stoke's commentary on etiquette. No one here ever makes disparaging remarks about another's appearance. It diminishes both parties.'

Ali's apology was interrupted by the return of Aphelia, who arrived bearing plates of bread and honey.

'Good,' said the Queen. 'Now, can we discuss the histories?'

'Sure.' Ali lifted her backpack from the floor and pulled out the journals Peter had unearthed from the herb garden.

'Six journals. There were seven of them,' explained Ali, 'but a hedgehog grabbed one when they attacked me at the river. It was story of the Hatter.'

'My fault entirely,' said Stoke. 'If I had found her sooner, she would never have been attacked.'

'You all did your best,' said the Queen. 'Yet the loss is very distressing news. If they take that history to the Jabberwocky, he will use it to his advantage. He will barter for the Hatter's allegiance.'

'It's my fault,' said Ali. 'I should go and get it back.'

'I appreciate the impulse. Alice has the same streak and takes everything very personally. I think our suffering has become unbearable for her.'

'You think she's dead?'

'No, death is hard to come by over here, but where she is or what she has become, no one knows. What interests me is why you have come to find her.'

'She is my aunt. Actually, she's my mother's great-aunt.'

'That explains the *who* but not the *why* of it.' The Queen gazed out across the lawns. 'We will discuss Alice in more detail when trust has been established between us. Tell me, did the Hatter know his history was among the papers?'

'No. He didn't ask, and he wouldn't let anyone else see them till we were safely here at the palace.'

'Good. I've come to depend on the Hatter, but if he learns his story has been taken, who can say what he might do.'

'I can.' Stoke got to his feet. 'The Wocky will play him like a damned fiddle. Best I set off and find him before he learns of it.'

'He won't learn of it, Stoke. Unless Ali tells him. I suggest you get a good night's sleep, you must be exhausted. Aphelia will see you both to your rooms.'

CHAPTER 14

PORTRAITS AND PEPPER

'I'm sure you'll be most pleased with the room.' Aphelia was almost skipping as she led Ali through the palace.

'How old are you?' asked Ali.

'That is a matter of great discussion amongst the kitchen staff. They put it at somewhere between fourteen and sixteen. I have no idea, of course, as I have no memory of my past life. But I feel neither old, nor young, so I have settled upon the middle year – fifteen.'

'Same as me, then,' said Ali. 'And did you choose your name too?'

'The Queen chose it. I don't altogether care for it, but then no one chooses their name at birth, do they? I dare say my real name was a mouthful too.'

They arrived at a wooden door at the end of a long corridor. It had a stout frame and ornately carved panels depicting a forest scene.

'Here we are.' Aphelia opened the door and ushered Ali inside. The room reminded Ali of a hotel she'd stayed in many years ago when her mother was still alive, an old castle that had been converted into a holiday lodge.

'I love it.' Ali dropped her pack on the bed and looked around. The outer wall was made of blocks of stone with narrow windows over-looking the grounds. The internal walls were wooden, their oak panels draped in tapestries. The ceiling was high and vaulted, its beams carved with depictions of fruit, and there were potted plants every-where, tall as young trees.

Ali registered it all in one sweeping glance, her attention coming to rest on a painting facing the windows. A portrait of the Hatter and Theodore. 'They don't look happy.'

The pair were standing shoulder to shoulder in front of a towering oak adorned with lanterns. A picnic lay on the grass in front of them. The general impression was of two friends pausing for a photograph, but Ali knew immediately this was more than a simple portrait. There was too much detail: the whole painting screamed with subtext, from the choice of clothes to the various items spread out across the picnic blanket.

'It's a little odd, don't you think?' Aphelia came and stood beside her. 'We were all surprised when Alice requested it. She never asked anything for herself, certainly nothing grand like this.'

'This was her room? Alice lived in here?'

'It is still her room. We keep it ready for when she comes back. We all think she will, you know.' Aphelia hesitated, doubt passing like a shadow over her face. 'I believe it. I do. She made a promise. Anyway, no one else is allowed to use this room, but the Queen says you are family, so it's only right and proper you should sleep here.'

'How well did you know her?'

'In truth, though I attended to her a great deal, I hardly know her. She is very secretive, very guarded. But I like her very much.' The girl's face lit up and she giggled. 'She calls me Custard.'

'Custard?'

'It started as a joke. She was longing for some custard, a taste of home she said, and I asked our cook to make her some. The name stuck and now everyone calls me Custard except for the Queen.'

'Okay. Custard it is.' Ali crossed to one of the windows. A water jug and a bowl stood on the sill. 'Is this for washing?'

'Yes, there are towels on the chair beside it.'

'A sparrow couldn't wash in this! Is there a bath somewhere in the palace?'

'No, sorry,' the girl dropped her head and stepped backwards, as if she had been chastised. Then she brightened as an idea came to her. 'Sir Stoke of Trent will sometimes soak in a horse trough when he comes back from patrol.'

'That might work,' Ali grabbed the towel off the back of the chair. 'Can we get hot water there?'

'Not in the stables. Just in the kitchens.'

'Then we go to the kitchens.' Ali turned back to the portrait. 'Custard, this tree in the background. Is it growing here in the palace grounds?'

'No, I don't think so, I'm sure I would have noticed.'

'And what do you think of the portrait? Do you like it?'

'No,' Custard stepped closer to the picture. 'No, I don't. Not that I'm any judge of such things.

'What don't you like?'

'Their expressions. People should be happy on a picnic. Theodore doesn't look happy ... his nose is turned up and he's squinting. He's going to shout at us.'

'Oh yes.' Ali had to agree. The rabbit's shoulders were raised, his mouth open, his lips pulled back. 'He's about to scream.'

'And the Hatter looks very upset. Maybe he's cross at all the clutter on the picnic blanket. Look at that treacle tin. Who takes treacle to a picnic? And why is there a needle and thread? And look at all the pepper pots – there are three of them, and no salt shakers, just three pepper pots.'

'I can only see two.' Ali scanned the picnic blanket. 'One here by a teapot, and one lying on its side near the bowl of fruit.'

'There,' Custard pointed at the Hatter's jacket. Neatly embroidered on one sleeve, was a very small black pepper pot.'

'Oh, yes. I see it. How very odd.'

'The Queen thought it might be a clue for how to go back without dying. That secret of safe passage you were talking about. She asked the scholars to sprinkle rings of pepper on the ground, like they do with salt in the gardens.'

'Rings of salt?'

'To keep snails off the lettuces.'

'I'm surprised the portrait's kept in this room. It's clearly full of clues. Don't the scholars want it in their library?'

'They do. Very much. But they won't allow women in the library.'

'What! Seriously?'

'Yes. I can't read, but even so. Anyway, the Queen won't let them take it to the library unless they change that rule.'

'Good for her.'

'Yes, I know!' Custard's smile said it all; the girl was clearly smitten with the Queen. 'She doesn't hold to such ideas and makes the scholars come here if they want to study the painting.'

'Into my room?'

'Only with the Queen's approval. They won't walk in unannounced.'

'Good to know.'

The palace kitchen was straight out of a medieval movie. As she walked in, Ali had to remind herself she hadn't stepped onto a film set. The sense of theatre was heightened by beams of moonlight that slanted like spotlights from windows set high in one wall. Smoke from a fireplace coiled up through the moonbeams, the motes of ash flickering silver as they danced their way in and out of the light.

Steps led down into the kitchen, their flagstones polished by time, and over on the far side, flanked by cutting benches and cast-iron shelving, stood a huge traction engine, venting steam.

Ali stared at it. 'You have a traction engine.' It was all she could think to say.

'Yes, isn't he magnificent?' Custard put her hands on her hips and smiled. 'He's like a mechanical dragon puffing out his steam. The scholar in charge calls him Thomas.'

'Thomas?'

'Yes.'

'Thomas the traction engine?'

'Yes. What's wrong with that? It's a perfectly good name. That's how we make our hot water. Alfred, he's the scholar who keeps it running, well, he can tell you all about Thomas, but be sure to have a good hour to spare – once Alfred starts talking it's hard to turn him off, a bit like the engine, it goes night and day. The heartbeat of the palace, Hatter calls it.'

'I feed his boiler.' A young boy with flaming red hair and a mass of freckles spotted them. 'Are you her? The one just came through? Everyone's talking 'bout you. What are you doing down here? Should be up top. You're gentry. Can see that just by looking. Proper lady, right?'

'Catch your breath, Rupert,' an old woman yelled out from the far side of the kitchen. She was no taller than a child herself, but she had strong arms and was using them to good effect, pounding a mountain of dough.

Custard took Rupert by the shoulders and led him across the room. 'Evening, Cook. Can I borrow this young man? Our guest has requested a hot water bath.'

'A bath!' The cook laughed and gave her mound of dough a massive punch. 'In my kitchen? There's a novelty. Rupert, go fetch the big copper from the wash house, the one we use to scrub bed sheets. And slowly, there's no rush.'

The cook clapped flour from her hands. 'He's a good boy, hard-working, but he does everything at a gallop, then he gets the agitations and has to sit down.'

'Agitations?'

'That's right. Gets the trembles something terrible if he gets excited, and most anything does that. Hencewise, we'll need a screen for your modesty.'

'I'll fetch one down,' said Custard. She turned back towards the stairs and then hesitated. Ali guessed the reason.

'It's all right, I won't run away the moment you're gone. I'm sure the entire palace will be keeping an eye on me.'

'I'm to look after you, nothing more,' said Custard, and she set off up the stone steps to search the palace for a screen.

'It's heavy!' yelled a voice from the other end of the kitchen. A door inched open, and Rupert appeared. He was dragging a large copper tub.

'Perfect.' Ali went over to lend him a hand. The tub looked more like a huge saucepan, but it was deep. Together they pulled it across the floor, Ali steering them to a gap on the far wall between two cupboards. Both the cupboards looked heavy, their open shelves stacked with plates and bowls, their sides bearing pots which hung on nails like copper fruit.

'It's warmer over there by the fire, 'said Rupert. 'Why do you want it here?'

'No reason,' she lied. Together, they filled the copper tub with buckets of boiling water from the traction engine, the huge machine hissing and rumbling as valves opened to let fresh water into its boiler tank.

'Here we are,' said Custard, arriving with a screen, a large towel, and some news. 'Theodore and the Hatter are back safe. They're giving a full account to the Queen and then Theodore said he would come to see you.' They set the screen around the tub, Ali stepped behind it and began peeling off her clothes. As she pulled up her tee shirt, sand from the riverbank fell to the floor, together with brick dust from the collapsed church.'

'Do you need more hot water?' Rupert was hovering outside the screen.

'Not sure yet, it looks deep enough.'

'What our guest needs is a bit of privacy,' the cook called out. 'And what this kitchen needs is for you to get about your duties.'

Ali's skin was raw and chafed and it was painful to pull her jeans off. She inspected the wound on her hip. There were two rows of puncture wounds, and the surrounding skin was red and swollen. Infection? She lowered herself into the tub. It was wide enough to sit if she kept her knees pulled up. And the hot water was wonderful; it bit into every scratch and scuff but the pain was worth it, a fair exchange for the instant relaxation she felt in her muscles. Custard had given her a bar of laundry soap, it smelt like tar and didn't foam up, but it did the job.

'More hot water if you want,' Rupert called from across the kitchen.

'I'm good, thanks.' Ali closed her eyes and let the heat work its magic. The sting of the soap became a distant, background noise. She let her mind drift and placed one word into the centre of that stillness.

Time.

It was more a picture than a word: an old-fashioned pocket watch floating on its back, threads of associated ideas drifting in and out of the picture; references from the two Wonderland books; Einstein talking to her from a flickering cathode-ray tube; sand spilling through an hourglass.

'Don't you drown in there while I'm gone.' Custard's voice, half heard. Ali's ears were full of water and soap. 'I'm off to fetch a change of outfit for you. We'll make sure your clothes get a proper scrubbing in that tub later.'

'Thanks.' Ali waited, eyes closed. She heard Custard's footsteps padding up the stone steps. Then she peered over the side of the tub and scanned the gap under the two shelving units that stood beside the bath. Good. They looked deep enough to hide her journal.

'Are you quite done in there?' the cook called across the kitchen. 'Much longer and you'll be shriveled as a walnut. Not a pretty look for a young lady.'

'I like walnuts!' yelled Rupert.

'You'll like the back of my spoon, any more lip from you!'

'Nearly finished,' said Ali. 'I'll just give my hair a wash.'

'Not with that tar soap! You'll need coconut oil.'

'Too late.'

Images of pepper pots floated into Ali's head. Why all those references to pepper? It clearly was important. Perhaps the Queen was right and it was a key to the secret of safe passage. Alice had left herself enough references to it, the last one came at the end of the first book, just before Alice woke up and left Wonderland.

'Whoa!' Ali clapped a hand over her mouth.

'You all right?'

'Fine, thanks Rupert.' Ali closed her eyes to remember the scene. She had read the book so many times now, it was like looking at an old movie in her head. The Duchess and the Cook had come marching into the courtroom with a large box of pepper. Everyone knew who'd arrived because they heard sneezing from the people standing near the entrance door. Was that a simple reference to the door between the two worlds? And why all the sneezing? It served no function for the narrative.

'Are you falling asleep in there?' Custard tapped the outside of the screen.

'No.'

'Theodore's here. Do you want to dress, or shall I set a chair for him.'

'Chair please, still rinsing.'

'I'll bring one,' yelled Rupert. Ali heard a chair being dragged across the flagstones, then she heard the soft patter of Theodore's feet as he hop-skipped across the floor and parked himself on the chair.

'A bath! They told me, and now I believe them.'

'Hello, rabbit,' Ali dropped her head back on the rim of the tub and kept her eyes closed. 'Thank goodness you're safe.'

'Safe and insulted. I shall let it go, as I think you mean it kindly.'

'Theodore is a bit formal.'

'And rabbit is too informal by far.'

'Not for friends.'

'We are but colleagues-in-arms, young lady.'

'No. We're friends.' Ali smiled to herself, eyes still closed and waited.

'Very well.'

'So, friend Theodore, you need to tell me everything.'

'I need to do no such thing. I *choose* to tell you. When you fell from your boat, the Hatter told the boys to keep going to the palace. For ourselves, we tried to make it to the bank. Alas, those walnut shells have quite the mind of their own in a strong current.' He paused, snuffled, and let out a high-pitched sneeze.

'I was just thinking about sneezing,' said Ali.

'How nice for you. For me, it has not been a matter of choice, we had to tip the boats and wade to the bank. I bobbed like a cork, too much fur I think.'

'I'll fetch you a blanket,' said Custard.

'And I'll make you some soup,' said the cook. 'Nothing like hot soup when you've caught a chill.'

'Thank you both, that's very kind.' Theodore sneezed again. 'Where was I?'

'Bobbing like a cork.' Ali slid down, letting her legs hang over the far end of the tub so she could tip her head back into the water and rinse the soap from her hair. She scrubbed it with her fingers. Theodore's high-pitched voice was still audible, but sounded far off.

'. . . and we made it to the bank and back to the site of your skirmish. All that blood! We feared it was yours.'

'It would have been,' Ali said, lifting her hair clear of the water, 'but that gigantic black dog saved me.'

'I heard. Puddles, yes.'

'Puddles!' Ali laughed. 'That killer dog is called Puddles?'

'Alice gave him the name, he doesn't much care for it.'

'Why 'Puddles'?'

'He has a nervous bladder. The Queen won't tolerate him inside the palace. But I digress. Seeing the blood, we feared the critters had seized you and taken you to the Fringes.' Theodore paused as another round of sneezing overtook him.

'Bless you.'

'Thank you. Well, to make it short, we hastened back to organise a rescue party.' Theodore paused, then unleashed a volley of sneezes. 'Sorry about that, I find it hard to catch my breath after a bout of sneezing. It forces every ounce of wind out of me.''

'*What* did you say?' Ali sat up suddenly, splashing water onto the floor.

'I merely noted that ...'

'Can that be it?' Ali scrambled up out of the bath. 'How bloody obvious. I'm an idiot! Of course that's it!'

'What's wrong?' asked Theodore.

'Nothing.' Ali couldn't believe she'd missed something so simple. Even Aunt Martha had guessed a piece of it through her love of the tales of Captain Nimmo. The Queen too, with her idea of a pepper circle. If this was right, it was the secret to safe passage. She could go back and find her dad!

CHAPTER 15

MEMORIES AND MAPS

Custard passed a towel over the screen and Ali began to dry herself. The towel was crisp with starch, and it scoured her skin. It felt good, even though it scrubbed the tops off her scabs and scratches. To hell with it, if she really had the secret to safe passage she could go back and disinfect the bite wound herself.

The relief was so intense, she started to laugh. It sounded a little manic, so she forced herself to stop and take a deep breath. She could feel her mind fizzing with ideas, her exhaustion replaced by excitement. A memory rose up, her mother chiding her. *You won't sleep if you work yourself up like this!*

'You're bleeding all over the towel!' Not her mother's voice. Custard's. The girl was peering over the screen at her. 'Why are you laughing? Bleeding isn't funny, if you keep bleeding lots of blood, your body will try to mend you.'

'Oh, yes. That's not the least bit funny.' If she could go back and forth safely, it changed everything. She could find her father. She could lure King through and trap her here.

'Here you are – from the Queen's wardrobe.' Custard draped a change of clothes over the screen. 'I was told I could choose anything for you.'

'Thanks,' said Ali. 'Does the palace have dungeons?'

'Dungeons?'

'Yes, dark cellars where you can chain up bad people.'

'I'm sure I don't know, Miss Ali.'

'I do,' Theodore called from across the room. He was sitting near the fire enjoying a bowl of carrot and onion soup. 'We use it as a dry store. Grain, for the most part.'

'And wine,' added the cook. 'Not forgetting the occasional scholar should they need drying out.' She paused. 'Not in with the wine of course.'

The clothes were a good fit. There was a silk blouse, a linen tunic, knee length boots and brown leather breeches.

'Interesting ...' said Ali, 'and the Queen really wears these?'

'It's her riding outfit,' said Custard. 'She wears gentleman's breeches for riding, tailored to fit tight to her legs like yours.'

'Mine? Oh, my jeans. Right.' She thanked everyone for her bath, then let

Theodore escort her back to her room. As soon as they were inside, she closed the door and stood Theodore in front of the portrait.

'Tell me about this tree.'

'You are relentless! Can we not talk tomorrow?'

'These lanterns hanging in the branches, they're glass jars with candles in them. I've seen jars just like these over on the other side.'

'I'm sure every child in history has built such a lantern. Now let us all get some rest.'

'Not yet. Jackie is going to tell me all her memories of my mother.'

'Tonight?'

'Yes, it must be tonight. Jackie can feel the forgetting coming over her and she wants to welcome it in'.

'Then we must go there immediately.' He sighed and closed his eyes. 'We shall be sorry company at breakfast tomorrow. I have never been more tired.'

'Oh, I think you have.'

'No. Never.'

'Not even when Alice had you racing around with a pocket watch?'

'What?!' The rabbit perked up instantly and stared at her. 'How in the blazes do you know about that? It was a matter of complete confidence between the two of us. Not even the Queen knew.'

'I'll tell you later. But it's all in the books, my dear rabbit.'

They left the palace by the side stairwell and set off across the lawns. A lot of people were about, sitting on the grass in small groups, their faces lit by the rising moon. Ali turned and called up the slope. 'If you're going to shadow us this badly, we might as well walk together.'

Custard ran down the slope to catch up. 'Sorry. I'm not used to this.' She laughed. 'Are you going to visit your friend?'

'Yes, I am, come on.' Ali picked up the pace, striding down the hill to the track that circled the lake. Theodore kept up easily, but Custard started to struggle. She grabbed her skirts, lifting the hem clear of her feet. Ali laughed and started to run.

'Not easy to run in all those skirts, is it? Breeches are better.'

'Why would I want to? Running is for farm labourers.'

'And me,' laughed Ali. 'See you down there.' She sprinted off down the path to the bridge.

Waxstaff was sitting up when Ali arrived at her bedside. The boys were at the foot of the bed reciting a poem, their audience crying with laughter.

'My god, you look so much better.' Ali perched beside her. 'Not your colour, though, you're getting greener by the hour.'

'Thank you. And you look sickly-white with fatigue and slightly ridiculous in that outfit.' Waxstaff reached for Ali's hand and gave it a gentle squeeze. 'Oh, and Theodore too. Hello, my friend.'

'Hello, Miss Jackie. I see the boys are still intent on annoying you.'

'We were entertaining her,' Ricky corrected him.

'There's Custard,' said Ted. 'She's very kind.'

The girl had just arrived at the far end of the infirmary, her face flushed, her breathing ragged.

'And very slow,' said Ali.

'Off you go, boys,' said Waxstaff. 'Ali and I need time alone.'

'We'll stay here if it's all the same to you,' said Ricky.

'Clearly it's not the same,' said Waxstaff. 'How do you suppose being alone is the same as having you two perched like vultures ready to pick my bones?'

'We just want to keep you safe and look after you.'

'Then go and find more snails for me to eat. The bread and broth they gave me earlier barely filled my toes.'

'But the Queen said—'

'Snails! Now!' Waxstaff barked.

Theodore lent his support. He clapped his hands and took the boys by their elbows. 'Come along, we can all go. I will sniff out the snails for you.'

The boys set off at a slouch, their shoulders drooping in reproach.

Custard arrived and curtsied to Waxstaff. 'Hello, Miss Jackie. My name is Aphelia, but everyone calls me Custard.'

'Let me guess, you're here to keep Ali safe, is that right?'

'No, Miss Jackie, I'm very poor in matters of the sword. I'm here to serve Miss Ali, so if she wishes me to wait outside, then that's what I'll do.'

'That is exactly what she wishes.' Waxstaff dismissed her with a wave.

'I'll pick you up as I leave,' said Ali. Custard gave another curtsy and left.

'They don't trust us,' said Waxstaff.

'We wouldn't, would we?'

'Hell no, but it's irritating. Those boys stick like gum.' Waxstaff pushed herself further up on her bed. 'Now, tell me about the map?'

'Yes, the map. Push over and make room.' Ali snuggled up close, so their heads were touching. 'We whisper, okay.'

'Sure. But you're making rather a big deal of this, don't you think?'

'No, I don't.'

'Okay. So, the map?'

'Yes.' Ali wondered where to begin. 'When you returned from here that first time, back to our world, your parents were dead. Years had passed over there, but not for you. Only months had passed – you went back still a teenager.'

'I don't need reminding.'

'According to the old knight, Alice would go missing for hours from this world. We know she went back and forth investigating missing persons, trying to compile the true histories of everyone here. She was able to spend a lot of time over in our world doing that because so little time would pass here. But when she was back here, she needed to do everything as quickly as possible because of the different time streams.'

'Your point?'

'This map she made ... I think it was a time map.'

'Okay ...' Waxstaff fell silent, playing the idea through in her head. 'You came to this idea how?'

'The clues are in the second book, the chapter where Alice and the Red Queen are discussing speed. They both start running, just to stay in the same place, and in the middle of all this craziness, for no reason, the Red Queen says: *I could show you hills, in comparison with which you'd call that a valley.*'

'Why does she say that?'

'No narrative reason, she just says it. Then she announces she's going to make a grand survey of the country that will be, and I quote, *something very like learning geography.* Three ideas mashed up in one conversation.'

'You're losing me.'

'Okay,' Ali said, holding up three fingers. 'One: time goes at different speeds. Two: comparing hills to valleys. Three: making a survey of the country.'

'She thinks she made a topography map.'

'Yes, but instead of hills and valleys, she measured gradients of time.'

'How?' Waxstaff realised she was raising her voice. 'How in hell would a Victorian kid do that? Even THINK to do that?'

'She experienced how more time had passed in the real world, so it's a small jump to imagine she wanted to measure the difference with pocket watches. She gave one to Theodore and kept one herself. Compared the difference between them when she came back.'

'That's one fixed time difference.' Waxstaff was trying her best to whisper like Ali, but her transformation was messing with her vocal cords and her voice crackled between a whisper and nothing at all.

'Yes. I know and I need to know what that is. Then something over here made her think there were places where time moved more slowly. Perhaps she took a different path somewhere and found it took a lot longer; took Theodore into her confidence, and wandered around taking separate paths all over this area, and measuring every time difference.'

'I hope we get to meet her one day.' Waxstaff rolled her head to look at Ali.

'Me too.' Ali looked back into Waxstaff's eyes. She could see the slits of her reptilian pupils in stunning detail. 'If your eyes are any indication, you're going to be a beautiful lizard one day.'

'Ha!' Waxstaff reached up with an elegant green finger and pulled one of her bottom eyelids down. 'What about now?'

'Less beautiful.'

'So, the map. Where did she hide it? Have you worked that out?'

'I think so. In the second book, Alice talks about the world looking like a chessboard. Do you play chess?'

'I do,' said Waxstaff. 'Your mother taught me when we were kids.'

'Really? She taught me too.'

'Any good?'

'I think so – I was the best at my last college anyway. Does that count?'

'That depends on how many were in your chess club.'

'Not many,' Ali tried to picture their faces. 'Six, I think.'

'Then, no.'

'Thanks.' Ali poked her tongue out. 'So anyway, in the second book there's a conversation where the Red Queen tells Alice to get to square Q7, all the way across the board. And you know what happens when a pawn crosses the whole board, right?'

'It becomes a Queen.'

'Yes, and Queens can move in any direction on the board, instantly. The move takes the same time as a pawn creeping forward just one square. Having the time map gives you the power of speed, like being a Queen.'

'You think she's hidden it in a chessboard?'

'Just a guess, hidden under Q7.' Ali sat up. 'I'll look for a large board in the morning. Right now, you have a promise to keep.' She opened her journal and pulled out the picture of her mother with Waxstaff, two happy girls, their whole lives ahead of them.'Here you go.'

She handed the picture to Waxstaff, and spent the next hour writing down her recollections. At first the accounts were sketchy, mere snippets of memory; but the more Waxstaff talked, the more she seemed to remember. It was as if a dam into the past had been breached and it grew increasingly hard for Ali to keep up with her as memory after memory came pouring out. It was harder still when her tears began to fall.

When it was done, Waxstaff fell silent, clearly exhausted, and in less than a minute she was she fast asleep.

'Thank you,' Ali whispered. She turned to a fresh page and started writing again.

Dad. I think there are gravity wells over here, places where spacetime is pulled out of shape around pockets of dense gravity. Alice mapped them.

I think her map will look like a topography map, except the lines will be time gradients. I think Alice made her measurements the way NASA does. You know, the way they use atomic clocks to measure how fast time passes for their astronauts in space compared to everyone back on Earth. For them the differences are nanoseconds, but here they're bigger. I think Alice used a pair of pocket watches. She and a rabbit (yes, that's what I said) took different paths and compared watches when they met up again. She also measured the time difference between the two worlds. Maybe she told the rabbit what it was – if not, I'll need to measure it again. I'll leave a watch here with Theodore and take one with me.

There was more she wanted to record, so much more, but exhaustion overtook her. Ali closed the journal, used it for a pillow, and stretched out beside Waxstaff. Ten minutes, she told herself, she would close her eyes for just ten minutes then head back to her room in the palace. Sleep came so quickly that she didn't hear the boys return, or feel the warm blanket Theodore spread over her.

CHAPTER 16

GATEWAY

———————

Lord Grey stared at the new doors. The carpenters had done their best to match the originals, yet something was irritating him, and he couldn't put his finger on it. His wife could.

'They look new,' she said, simply.

'Dare say we'll get used to them.'

'I certainly won't,' Martha turned her chair and wheeled herself to the door. 'After what happened in here, I won't be troubling this room with my company for a very long time.'

'If we're even invited to use it. This whole situation is intolerable. We've been treated like prisoners in our own damned house!'

'Keep your temper and voice down.' Martha glanced back at her husband, and steered herself from the room. 'We keep up appearances. Now, come and push me to the barn. I'm delighted Peter and Jeremy are getting along, and I want to talk to them. It was a good idea to rent the barn to their gaming group. It will make it that much harder for King and her people to barge in and threaten us.'

They arrived at the barn just as Jeremy was connecting the last of the camera lights.

'Hello!' roared Lord Grey. 'This was a stroke of pure genius, Peter. Well done, very much appreciated.'

'The police are fine with this?' Martha looked up at Jeremy. 'Your forensics people have everything they need?

'Yes,' said Jeremy, 'and my boss, she sees the upside. I'll be here in my spare time so she gets an extended pair of eyes on you two for free.'

'And, breaking news …' said Peter, 'our friend King has turned up in a private clinic in Oxford.'

'You're very well informed.'

'The church keeps Dad in the loop. They're picking up King's medical tab.'

'Do the police know?'

'We do now,' said Jeremy. 'Peter called me as soon as he heard. My boss has requested an interview.'

'King has agreed?' Martha was surprised.

'Not yet.'

'No surprise there.' Lady Grey stared at all the lights. 'Well, Jeremy, we shall leave you to it. Peter, could you spare a minute in the kitchen? We haven't had a proper catch-up since you surfaced. I want to hear all about your adventures.'

Five minutes later, they were heading to the parlour with a tray of tea and biscuits, and for the next hour they exchanged everything they knew about King and about Ali.

Lord Grey poured himself another scotch, offered one to Peter and got a loud rebuke from his wife.

'Sorry my dear,' he said, 'just running on instinct. So, what do we do next?'

'We have to expose King,' said Peter.

'We can't tell Dovecot the truth about any of this.' Martha stared into her teacup, as if trying to read the leaves. 'I was locked away in a clinic the last time I tried that. We don't have a single piece of hard evidence.'

'We have her wings and ears,' said Peter. 'I'm going to rip off her headscarf in front of Dovecot.'

Martha shook her head. 'Too dangerous. That woman has played this game for a long time – she's too smart to meet anyone in front of the police.'

'Not if I'm the bait,' said Peter. 'I made the offer to one of her Suits. We know she wants to talk to me. She knows I dug up documents and gave them to Ali. So maybe I read them. Maybe I know this secret of safe passage Ali goes on about.'

'And do you?'

'No, but if King thinks I do ...'

'It's worth a shot.' Lord Grey looked across at his wife. 'Better than sitting here like rats in a sewer pipe waiting for King to make the next move.'

'No,' she replied. 'Even if we succeed, what will happen? King will be revealed as a freak of nature. A five-minute sensation. It doesn't make her a murderer, it makes her a victim, and we will be cast as bigots, or whatever the correct term is for anyone who fears deformity.'

'Aborationists?' suggested her husband.

'For heaven's sake, Bertie, I was being rhetorical, it's not a cross-word. My point is, even if we succeed, how will it help our cause? And before you venture an answer, think for a moment about the conse-quences. If what Ali has told us is correct, then King is quite happy to kill. She will stop at nothing to wrestle that secret out of you.'

'Well said, my dear.' Lord Grey raised his glass to his wife, saw it was empty and headed for the sideboard. 'My wife is right, of course. Always is, bless her. Young man, your father would not ask you do this. We cannot ask it of you, and I know for certain that young Ali wouldn't.'

'I know.' Peter stared down at his teacup. 'That's exactly why we have to do this. Look what *she's* done to keep all of *us* safe. We have to do something ... we have to get her back.'

They were interrupted by the arrival of a car pulling up on the drive outside.

'I'll see to them,' said Bertie. 'You carry on, but save a gingernut for me.'

Lord Grey stared at the paperwork, his mind in a turmoil. He didn't need to read it again to understand it. He needed a moment to think.

'The details won't change on a second reading.' A tall gentleman in a dapper Savile Row suit was sitting opposite him at the dining room table.

'It might!' snapped Lord Grey. All he could think of at that moment was how on earth he was going to tell Martha.

'I think you'll find it more than reasonable. The bank has no obligation to offer anything at all. This agreement covers a single bedroom in the retirement village and all your medical expenses until you, well ...'

'Drop dead.'

'Exactly, though I wouldn't have used such a colourful idiom.'

'I meant you! Drop dead!' Lord Grey held up the agreement and tried to show his contempt by ripping it in half. He couldn't, arthritis had robbed his thumbs and fingers of their strength. He groaned. What a depressingly accurate metaphor for his position right now. The weight of defeat threatened to overwhelm him. Losing their home like this was devastating enough. But losing control of the barn? That was a disaster – and all of his making.

'When?' He leaned back in his chair and stared at the man.

'One month. Enough time for you to find a buyer for all your furniture and fittings. I can ask the new owners if they wish to make an offer for it all.'

'Stop! New owner? There has been no sale, your bank is taking possession of this place. It was collateral for the loans. When you take it to market, I can still raise the funds to buy it back.'

'I'm sorry, Lord Grey.' The man held up a hand. 'The house will not be going on the open market. We were approached by a charitable trust. Their offer far exceeds market value and it was they who added the very generous terms for covering your fees in the retirement village.'

'What charitable trust?'

'I am under no obligation. . .'

'Their name! It will be on the deed of title soon enough, so tell me.'

'Very well, it is a non-profit business entity called Gateway.'

'Gateway?'

'Yes, an odd name, but we have done our due diligence of course, as required of any bank in these circumstances. I believe the name is their secular term for the end of life. They are not a religious group, but they wish to run a hospice that is devoid of such trappings.'

'A hospice? Here?'

'Yes, that is our best understanding of their plans, although they use a rather different, rather old-fashioned term for it. They have been calling it an infirmary.'

* * *

'I trust you slept well?' The Queen smiled across the table at Ali.

'Like a log.' Ali was taking breakfast with the Queen in a small, east facing room. It was sparely decorated: a few tapestries hung on the walls and the table was set with an odd collection of crockery, none of it matching. The main feature of the room was a huge stained-glass window through which the morning sun was pouring. The stained glass depicted a grove of giant sunflower trees.

Custard was in attendance. The girl had shaken Ali awake a short while before, and they had raced up the lawns to the palace, arriving in the room moments before the Queen.

'Will the Hatter and Theodore be joining us?' asked Ali.

'Shortly – together with Sir Trent.' The Queen waved a hand at the food.' Don't let that restrain your appetite, we can send for more. Our friends are debating the risks of mounting a party to track down the band who attacked you.'

'To get the journal?'

'Quite so.' The Queen refreshed her tea cup. 'To retrieve it before it gets back to the Jabberwocky.'

'Does the Hatter know it's his history?'

'No.' The Queen looked up from stirring milk into her tea. 'We debated this last night. I thought you agreed?'

'I don't remember a debate. More like a proclamation.'

'Now there's a big word.'

'Patronising. There's another one.'

'Touché!' The Queen laughed. 'So let us debate it now. Do you agree that it's the most important thing imaginable to him? Will you take a boiled egg?'

'Yes. And yes please.' Ali took two eggs, plus a slice of bread and cheese. 'You think he might place himself and the others in danger?'

'Quite the opposite. I think he would slip off on his own without telling us. He would hope to reach the thieves before they made it back to the Fringes.'

'And if he's too late?'

'If his history is already in the hands of that wretched creature, you mean?' The Queen threw up her hands. 'Who knows. Will he turn back? Will he go in alone, relying on his natural cunning to steal it back? Or will he barter for it?'

'I don't know him well enough to say.' Ali took a bite of her bread and cheese.

'None of us does. My heart tells me the Hatter is true and noble, but my head urges caution. All that is immaterial, since the decision will no doubt be yours.'

'Mine? How's that?'

'Must I do your thinking?' The Queen sliced the top from her egg. 'You know perfectly well. I shall enjoy my egg as you figure it out.'

'The Hatter is going to ask me.'

'That wasn't too hard, was it? Yes, of course he will ask you. When the Hatter joins us shortly for breakfast, he will level his ridiculously attractive black eyes on you and ask you that one very simple question. To put it bluntly, young Ali, his happiness is in your hands.'

'You mean, I decide?'

'Welcome to responsibility.'

'I'm not very strong on responsibility. Ask my dad.'

'Nonsense. You will take to it easily enough, given your heritage.'

'You mean Alice?'

'Of course.' The Queen waved a spoon at her egg. 'Enough talking, I need to eat this egg before it becomes a chicken.'

Ali was grateful for the silence as she was struggling to concentrate again. Everything was an assault on her senses. The intense flavours of the food. The sunlight shining through the gold and yellow glass of the window. The morning chorus of birdsong outside, and the distant heartbeat of the palace itself, the chuffing and puffing of Thomas down in the kitchens below.

'That was delicious.' The Queen dabbed the corners of her mouth with a serviette. 'Now, where were we?'

'My great-aunt Alice.'

'Yes. She shouldered a great many burdens. She had a fierce belief that she knew what was best for everyone. She took that upon herself'.

'You miss her.'

'Of course I miss her! She was extraordinary. She was no more than twelve years old when she first stumbled through. She aged of course, with each return there. She was a little older than you are now when last we saw her.'

'I hope I get to meet her.'

'Yes, I hope so too. She made incredible promises and, for the most part, she has kept them. Your relative has a pathological need to help, for whatever reason, and she did help. She spent hours with some of us, noting down any memories we might still have, however fractured they might be. Then she went back and did hours of tireless research matching those fragments to records of missing folk.'

'I read her note about the Walrus and the Carpenter.'

'Yes, the tragic story of Captain Hudson and his son. And there have been many more. She would find out the history of one of our citizens, then we would support them through their trauma of remembering and the brutal realisation that every single person they had ever loved would have died long ago.'

'Did some still want to return?'

'Yes, and Alice would take them. Others chose to stay and let their forgetting return, a blessed salve to remove the pain of such unimaginable loss.' The Queen paused, her eyes glistening with tears.

Ali said nothing. She watched and waited. The tears seemed genuine, but for what? Tears of rage or sadness? Tears of self-pity? Was she venting it all in front of the only person she could afford to show vulnerability to?

'This is our blessing and our burden, Ali. We are the only family any of us will have, ever again. And, like family, we try to take care of each other as best we can, to shoulder some degree of responsibility for our joint welfare. Alice did not flinch in this.'

'I have to take on my share of that burden, is that what you're saying?'

'No, I most certainly am *not* saying that, I am saying quite the opposite.' The Queen tapped the table to stress her point. 'You are blessed with choice. In fact, you are the only one here blessed with choice. You alone are free to leave, for only you can survive the journey home, though with some cost to your health. We cannot, so we work diligently at being a community of compassion and support for one another.'

'Bottom line ... I decide if I tell Hatter the truth or not?'

'Yes. Because he will ask you. My recommendation is not to tell him, but I cannot, and will not, instruct you on this.' She paused, watching Ali closely. 'Or perhaps we could scatter sacred bones and read tea leaves together?'

'Yes. Let's do that.'

'There! I knew we would get along. Now ... Theodore tells me you took a bath in the kitchens.'

'I did,' said Ali, happy to be changing the subject. 'It was wonderful.'

'And thus it goes.' The Queen took a bite of her bread, nodding as she chewed, as if maintaining the conversation in the interval of silence. Ali did the same. Thus it goes? What did that mean? She waited politely while the Queen swallowed and looked up.

'Your bath is but the latest, Ali. Everyone who arrives here brings the latest customs. We might forget who we are, but oddly, matters of habit, like language and behavior, stay with us. We do our best to adapt to every new fashion. I dare say the entire staff will now be demanding baths. Please eat.'

Ali did, and they sat in silence for a while, intent on their meals.

'I can hear them coming,' said Custard. 'I heard them arguing from halfway down the corridor. Shall I let them in?'

'Please do, Aphelia,' the Queen said, rising from her chair, 'and be so good as to bring some more items from the kitchen.'

'At once, ma'am.' Custard dipped her head, opened the door and waited as Stoke, Theodore and the Hatter came blustering in.

What happened next caught Ali by surprise. The Queen jumped up and ran across the room to greet them. She threw her arms around the Hatter, released him, pulled his head to hers and planted a kiss on his lips. Ali hid her surprise by stuffing a large wedge of bread and cheese into her mouth.

'Ali!' The Hatter released himself from the Queen's embrace, stepped to the table and knelt in front of Ali's chair. He took her hand, and for a dreadful moment Ali thought he was about to propose.

'You really are safe and well, how splendid.'

She was spared further embarrassment by Theodore, who plonked himself at the table and announced he was going to eat the table itself if more food didn't arrive soon. Custard hurried out to do her best, and Sir Trent and the Hatter sat down, scooping up what little was left and setting it on their plates. Ali watched, wondering what to say when the Hatter inevitably asked her whose history had been stolen. To her surprise, he didn't.

'So, gentlemen,' said the Queen. 'Have you come to a decision?'

'We have indeed.' Stoke wiped tea from his moustache, and Ali wondered why anyone would want that much hair constantly dipping into their food.

'They have had too great a head start,' said Theodore. 'Chasing after them would be a waste of time.'

'Easy for us to say,' the Hatter said, lifting his eyes to Ali's, 'a great deal harder for the subject of that history, whoever that might be.'

'Only if they knew it was their history,' said Ali.

'What if they were ninety percent sure?'

'Then that small doubt is a very precious thing.' Ali looked around the table. The Queen's eyes were on her, but Stoke and Theodore had become very focused on their food all of a sudden.

'Question,' said Ali. 'Everyone I've spoken to here speaks English. Why is that?'

'The doorways hereabouts,' said Theodore. 'They all access England.'

'Doorways – plural?'

'Three that we know of,' said Theodore. 'First is the doorway you and Alice came through in the bluebell woodland. On the other side there is a barn in the grounds of an old manor house, correct?'

'Yes, it's in the village where Alice grew up. Where are the other two?'

'Right here in the palace grounds,' said Theodore. 'Both sealed from the other side as far as we can understand it. One is in the dungeons below us, the other is in the infirmary.'

'Why are they sealed?'

'You tell, us my dear,' said the Queen. 'We all have made our guesses. Most of us have settled on the depressing notion that our return is unwelcome. Yet that begs other questions of course. Who has locked us out – and why? So in answer to your last question, most folk here speak English because they lived in the area hereabout, that is to say the south-east of England.'

'Quite so.' Stoke wiped egg yolk from his moustache. 'However, we are aware of one other enclave – Germanic – so we assume there might be others.'

'Aware, how?'

'There have been interactions over the years,' said Theodore. 'Strangers who have stumbled, more dead than alive, into our community.'

'Difficult to do.' Ali cut a slice of bread and covered it in plum jam. 'If each community has formed at a gateway, and each gateway has a steep gravity well like this one, then crossing to another would be almost impossible.'

Alice looked up from her plate and eyeballed the Queen. 'In some places time might seem to drag on forever and leave them stranded, moving a few inches a day at most.'

'What a curious notion.' The Queen cocked her head to one side, stared at Ali for a moment, then looked slowly at everyone else before settling back on Ali.

'Not at all.' Alice held her gaze. 'On the other side, this is a commonplace notion. A man called Einstein described it in his general theory of relativity.'

'Here we go again!' Theodore shrugged an apology to the Queen. 'More of the gobbledygook I warned you about.'

'Which is why my great-aunt Alice made her map,' said Ali.

'Oh dear.' Theodore studied his empty plate, as if the crumbs held a secret wisdom like tea leaves. 'I'm afraid she goes on like that rather a lot.'

'Goes on like what, Theodore? Like a scholar?' The Queen turned her scrutiny on the rabbit. 'Am I to understand you have broken with the arrangement?'

'Excuse me?' Theodore frowned at the Queen. 'I don't follow. I was speaking of our young visitor's propensity for using gobbledygook.'

'Did you break our agreement?'

'No one broke any agreements.' Ali took a bite of her bread and jam. The others waited patiently for her to continue. Ali mimed an apology, pointing to her full mouth, grinned and kept chewing.

'Young lady' – the Queen sat back in her chair – 'I said we try our best to adapt to the customs of new arrivals. But limits can be pushed.'

'Finished!' Ali took a deep breath as if surfacing from a dive. 'Great bread, I couldn't help myself. As to the map, I worked it out from the clues Alice left in both books. The map is obviously a time map.'

'And what else did you figure out?' Theodore leaned forward. 'Did you figure out where Alice hid this map?'

'Perhaps. Do you play chess, rabbit?'

'A change of subject. Hooray!' Theodore tapped the table with one paw. 'No finesse to it, but I applaud you all the same. Yes, young lady, I can play chess, but very poorly.'

At that moment Custard arrived with more eggs and toast.

'Hoorah!' said Stoke as he helped himself. 'Speaking of chess, the Hatter and I both play. As do the scholars.'

'We have a league,' said the Hatter.

'A chess club?'

'Club?' The Queen laughed. 'The scholars would rail if they heard you call it that! They have a champion's league. Writing the winner's name on the honours board is quite the ceremony.'

'It takes pride of place in the library,' said Theodore.

'Should I make a big thing of it when I go there? Will that tickle their egos?'

'What an expression!' The Queen helped herself to a slice of toast. 'And if by tickle you mean irritate, then yes, it would irritate them. I have broached the Head Scholar with your request to work in the library – he is quite set against it.'

'Why?'

'Well firstly, you hardly ingratiated yourself yesterday. Your manner was very confrontational. And secondly, and more to the point, ladies are not welcome in the library as they are ill-equipped for research. In his view.'

'So I heard.' Ali wondered how she should respond to this. If she blew up, she would be proving the scholars' point. Someone with a short fuse would be a pain in a quiet library. 'What do you think? Are men better equipped for study?'

'They are certainly more in need of it!' said the Queen. 'It is my experience that we have a native intelligence that most men lack, so they need to work that much harder to keep up with us.'

Ali clapped her hands together and laughed. At last, someone she could talk to!

'Don't mind the rest of us,' said Theodore. 'Assume us to be irritated and tickled in equal measure by this discussion.'

'I need to study in the library,' said Ali. 'Why can't you issue some kind of royal proclamation or whatever the right term is?'

'The scholars don't take instructions from me. The mantle of Queen carries no real authority here. We operate by a hard-won consensus. The library is the domain of the scholars who employ their own system of hierarchy, one that is completely obscure to me. Plato, the Chief Scholar who joined us for supper last night, has the last word on all such matters.'

'Is that right?' Ali thought about it for a moment. 'What happens if he's proved wrong in front of all the other scholars?'

'I have no idea ...' The Queen arched an eyebrow. 'What are you suggesting?'

'Set me a challenge, something you want to understand from the books, some mystery the scholars have failed to unravel.'

'I think not. Everyone is on edge as it is, your arrival has created a great deal of excitement and speculation. Your resemblance to your aunt is clear for all to see. The whole community is unsettled by it.'

'What's that compared to learning the secret of safe passage?'

'You're playing me rather well,' said the Queen. 'If the Chief Scholar believed you could unwrap that mystery, he would be obliged to place the library at your full disposal, and every scholar with it. But you have the two novels anyway, so you can undertake your studies without the distraction of being in the library.'

'No, I need other documents.' She looked thoughtful for a moment, then asked, 'What would happen if I challenged Plato to a game of chess?'

'Ha! Really?' The Queen turned to Theodore. 'Advise me how would this play out. It would be a delightful distraction.'

'They would welcome the opportunity to put our young guest firmly in her place. As would I.'

'I do believe they would.' The Queen rose from the table. 'Help yourself to more breakfast. This will require a deal of diplomacy on my part. Come, Aphelia, we shall go and do our best.'

'Let me come along,' said the Hatter. 'If he refuses, I can accept our guest's challenge. It might belittle him into doing so instead.'

They left the room. Custard followed, but glanced back and threw Ali a massive grin.

'That girl is enthralled by you,' said Stoke. 'Be careful not to place her in any trouble on your behalf.' He pulled himself to his feet and stretched. 'Now, after that delightful breakfast, I shall go and give Henry a brush. He will complain of course. He will lecture me on how demeaning it is, while simultaneously ordering me to put more effort into it.'

'So, we are alone,' said Theodore when Sir Trent had left the room.

'Yes, we are.'

'Tell me, young lady, what are your intentions? I have played my part and delivered you here to the Queen as she requested. I didn't axe your friend Jackie, and she seems to be repairing well enough. So I imagine you will be going back. Leaving us, as Alice has done.'

'You think she went back?'

'I do.' Theodore drummed his front paws on the table. 'And if you intend to do the same, can I ask one thing of you before you go?'

'It depends what it is.'

'You made a promise to the boys on the way here. You said the secret to their identities was hidden as a puzzle in the books, a puzzle you promised to solve for them. Was that an empty promise?'

'No, I think I've figured out who they are.'

'What?' Theodore almost bounced out of his chair. 'Really?'

'Yes, but if they are who I think they are, they could be in danger. Do I share that with the Queen? Will she use it to harm them?'

'Harm them?' Theodore stared at her. 'Gracious no! She has come to treat them as her own sons, and since they wish to know their own histories, if you can help, you are duty bound to do so – not to the Queen but to the boys themselves.'

'I agree. To the boys, anyway.' Ali took another bite; the toast was delicious, and very distracting. Which was irritating because something the Queen had said needed her full attention.

'Excuse me,' said Theodore. 'You have that look of being somewhere else. Your aunt did that to me – it's very disrespectful.'

'I'm sorry. Last night Plato said a great many people had come through over the years. It's how so much stuff came through. But how many people?'

'As far as our written records go,' Theodore said, scratching his head, 'it must be thousands.'

'Thousands?'

'Oh yes.' Theodore nodded vigorously. 'We would gather over in the bluebell clearing for the sheer entertainment of it, and to lend support of course. Several folk a day, at least, would come bumbling through. Some would gasp, drop their possessions in shock and disappear back to their world The shock retrieving them we believe.'

'Adrenaline, yes.'

'Others would fall to the grass, weeping in joy or confusion. Thomas the traction engine arrived that way, we thought it was some dragon come to kill us, till we saw the poor man driving the thing.'

'And then it stopped?'

'The engine?' Theodore frowned. 'Yes.'

'No. The people arriving. The Queen said it all stopped a few years ago. How many years ago?'

'Close to four, I believe. Anyway, there was a great deal of speculation about why, but no one knows the answer of course.'

'I do,' said Ali. 'A great big manor house was built there, surrounded by a large wall with iron gates to keep it people out.'

'Goodness! That would explain it then.'

'Before the house was built, the area was common land, open to everybody. My uncle has a history of the house with maps and plans and old photos.'

'And the upshot was no more arrivals, until your aunt Alice.'

'And then me.'

'No,' Theodore corrected her. 'Then the campfire girl – Jackie – then you.'

'Right.' Ali fell silent. She wanted some time to herself, a chance to write all this down as shorthand memory joggers, and to do some basic math. If she could find out the date the manor house was built, she could make an equation for how different the passage of time was between the two worlds.

'Tell me, Theodore, the bluebell clearing with my gateway ... how far is it from here if we take the direct route?'

'I don't believe I can discuss this.'

'Yes, you can. I saw this palace through the trees when we first set out from the clearing. The Hatter told me the direct route wasn't the quickest.'

'There you have it then. No need for further elaboration.' Theodore began folding up his table napkin.

'Alice always ran that path, didn't she? To save time. And she always took care to avoid one area like it was poison itself.'

'How can you know all this?' Theodore stared at her. 'Yes, there is a spot halfway along the path, an area strewn with elegant rocks sculpted by the wind. Everyone loved that spot; they would go there to sit and could be gone for days.'

'And apart from that one area with the rocks, Alice took a straight line from here to the bluebell clearing?'

'Yes. You intend to desert us?'

'No, I've worked out who the boys are, I think, but I need to check. I can write a full history over there and bring it back for them.'

'I knew it! Oh, my whiskers!' He pushed back his chair and began to pace the room. 'You do know the secret! You know the secret to safe passage!'

'I have a theory but I have to go back to test it. Will you tell the Queen?'

'Do you want me to tell the Queen?'

'Not yet. Alice hid the secret for a reason, hid it from everyone including the Queen. I have to find out why. The trust has to start now, Theodore. Who do you trust here, more than anyone?'

'The Hatter.' Theodore answered without hesitation.

'Really? Okay, why?'

'Trust is built over time.' Theodore tipped his head to one side, closed his eyes as if scouring his mind for the right answer. Then gave up. 'There's no one thing, but the actions not the words of someone are their true measure.'

'And who does the Hatter trust the most? Is it you?'

'No, it's your great-aunt,' said Theodore. 'He is determined to find her.'

CHAPTER 17

THE PROBLEM WITH TIME

'You two look thick as thieves,' the Queen remarked. She didn't take her seat but remained standing, fingertips resting on the edge of the breakfast table and smiling like a mother waiting for young children to confess to a squabble. 'Anything I should be aware of, Theodore?'

'Yes,' Theodore dropped his eyes. 'Our guest has asked a favour of me.'

'Then I trust you will oblige, if the request is reasonable.'

'It is.' Theodore glanced across at Ali, then dropped his gaze. 'Our guest has asked for my assistance in one of her investigations.'

'Regarding?'

'She believes she has uncovered the identity of Ted and Ricky.'

'My dear child!' The Queen stepped around the table, took Ali by her hands and pulled her to her feet. 'Is this true?'

'Yes. I'll need the rest of the day and Theodore to bounce ideas off, but yes, I think I know who they are.'

'Wonderful.' She turned to Custard, who had followed her into the room like a shadow. 'Aphelia, please ask Cook to prepare a picnic lunch for Theodore and our guest, and let it be known to everyone that they are not to be bothered.'

'Right away. And what of The Telling, will that be postponed?'

'Yes. That can happen after supper. Let everyone know, but not a word to anyone about the nature of Ali's studies.'

'Of course.' Custard's intelligent eyes flashed with indignation. 'If gossip about this reached the boys they would be agitated beyond measure, and then beside themselves with grief if the studies came to nothing.'

'Exactly so.' The Queen beamed at Aphelia, making clear her pride in the girl. 'Where are they, by the way? I've hardly set eyes on them since they came back.'

'They've been attending to the campfire girl,' said Custard. 'The boys have taken to her rather special.'

'Have they indeed?' The Queen sent Custard on her errand, and turned back to Ali. 'The Chief Scholar has agreed to your chess challenge.'

'Was he irritated?' asked Theodore.

'Very, and he wouldn't be held to a time.'

'What is The Telling?' asked Ali.

'A tradition. Every new arrival speaks to the community in the Great Hall. We are all thirsty for news from the other side.'

'Ha! My very own Ted Talk. I'll do my best.'

'Your best should not include any of your gobbledygook,' said Theodore.

'I'll try.' Ali turned to the Queen. 'Can I ask you a personal question?'

'If you must. But in private.' The Queen looked at Theodore, who dipped his head and left the room.

'Allow me to second guess your question ...' The Queen took an apple from the table and crossed to the window. 'Do I know my own history? Is that it?'

'Yes.' Ali was impressed. 'You don't mess about, do you?'

'I'm not sure what that means, so I will choose to take it as a compliment. And the answer to the question is no. I am not familiar with my own history.'

'But you want to know, right?' Ali joined her at the window. The view looked out across the lawns to the lake where the sanatorium was hidden by trees.

'Almost everyone here longs to know. Myself included. It is hard to map the future without guidance from the past. A few, when they do learn of their history, come to regret the new knowledge; the trauma can be completely overwhelming.'

'The Hatter told me about the March Hare.'

'Yes. It's deeply distressing.' She turned to Ali and smiled. 'Now ask the second part of your question.'

'Did Alice discover your identity,' said Ali, 'and did she keep it from you?'

'Why would she do that?'

'I don't know.' Ali studied the Queen's face. It was hard to read. There was no anger there. 'And neither do you. If you don't know your history, then you can't figure out why Alice would keep it from you, can you?

'Welcome to my dilemma,' the Queen took a bite from her apple. Ali watched the morning light reflect off the woman's teeth. They were beautiful, no sign of decay or staining, the kind of teeth only money and modern technology could provide. Yet the woman was not a recent arrival, she had been here when Ali's great-aunt first came through. Had she gone back and had modern dental work, or did teeth repair themselves here, along with everything else, the fillings pushed out by new enamel rebuilding and sculpting the teeth? Waxstaff's transformation was well underway, and Ali had noticed her teeth last night; they were small, razor sharp and perfect.

'I remember everything that has happened to me over here,' said the Queen. 'I keep a diary and read snippets each morning to hold those memories in place. I hope you are doing the same?'

'I am.' Ali wondered if this was genuine concern, or was the Queen making sure Ali was recording all her discoveries in a diary that could be confiscated.

'Good. Back to the issue of trust. If Alice learned of my history, and chose to keep it from me, then the question is, why? Correct?'

'Maybe she found out you were a terrible person?'

'Perhaps, but I don't believe so. If I had poisonous traits, I feel certain they would still be part of my nature. I invite you to ask anyone here for their honest opinion of me.'

'Already asking.'

'Of course you are. So what other reason could there be? Perhaps she was worried for my sanity. Did she uncover some brutal truth and thought to shield me from it? I don't believe so. She allowed others the freedom to learn of their true identities, however bitter. We have evolved a process of care and support for such revelations. I pose the question back to you, Ali. Why do *you* think she kept my history hidden, and why did she hide other histories back in the other world?'

'I don't know.' Ali sat back at the table, not to eat but to escape the Queen's penetrating gaze. Everything about the woman made Ali want to trust her. There was a directness that was refreshing. It was also disarming.

'Your Aunt Alice always had a good reason for everything she did.'

'Seems like it,' Ali agreed. 'Why don't we ask her?'

'Ah, you haven't worked this piece out yet, have you?' The Queen turned from the window and smiled at her. Ali couldn't read it. There was no smugness there. 'I would definitely ask her if she was here. She is not.'

'So where is she?'

'You know where. Come on, don't disappoint me.'

'She went back.'

'Yes, my dear. I escorted her to the gate myself, together with the Hatter and Theodore. There was something vital she had to retrieve. She refused to confide in us, but her urgency and distress was clear. She knew forces over there in the other world were desperate to intercept her. Yet she went anyway.'

Ali folded her arms on the table and dropped her head on them. A memory snapped into focus. An emotion. She was six or seven, doing a jigsaw puzzle on a small table; a tough puzzle for her age, each connection a tiny triumph. Parts of the picture were forming, two pieces making a hand over here, three revealing a dog over there. Small, disconnected windows into the bigger picture ... and then someone had knocked the table over. All sense of the complete picture was gone, nothing left but a mess of disconnected pieces.

'How long?' She looked up at the Queen. 'How long since she went back?'

'Why does that matter?' The Queen put a hand on Ali's shoulder. The touch was firm, too firm to be sympathy, almost a pinch, as if she was encouraging Ali to stay focused.

'I need to work out how much time has passed over there.'

'Again, I ask why?' The hand remained on her shoulder, the grip tighter now. and Ali knew she'd made a mistake. 'Let me answer that for you. You came here to find your great-aunt. If she's back in your world you will want to return as well. But you can't, can you? Not without the secret to safe passage. Correct?' Ali gave a small nod. 'A secret you hoped, even expected, your Alice would tell you.'

'Yes,' Ali lied.

'Now she is back on the other side and you are stuck here like the rest of us. You can try to go back, of course, but you may not survive the journey.'

'I know.'

'So here we are, child. We have reached an understanding. You don't trust me because you don't know me yet. I don't trust you, not because you are some agent of evil sent to harm us but because you are a heady mix of arrogance and intelligence. Your motives, naturally enough, are driven by self-interest. In time you might have compassion for everyone here, as your great-aunt Alice did, and your motives might align to ours. Until then, we will work together because we need each other, but there can be no trust until it has been hard won. Agreed?'

'Yes.' Alice found herself smiling. She did agree, completely. Why couldn't all adults be this clear, this open, this precise? 'We see it the same, I'd like to trust you, but I can't. Not yet.'

'So, let us make a small start, a narrow bridge in this divide. You tell me something I don't already know, something you have discovered and can share with me. I will do likewise. We can start there.'

'You go first.'

'To be expected.' The Queen laughed and drummed her fingertips together. 'What would you like to know?'

'What stops everyone from going back? Or at least trying to? Crossing back makes you really sick, it doesn't kill you.'

'But it can. You and Alice appear to be cushioned by some unique biology. Alice went back twice and it made her ill, but she survived. This was before she found the secret to doing it safely. Then she popped back and forth as if was nothing at all.'

'So when someone wants to go back, do you stop them?'

'That's two questions. No, we don't stop them. If their mind is set on it, then we assist as best we can. The histories help of course, because it means they can go back armed with some information. Most people here want to return, but fear is a barrier. Now it's your turn. Tell me something I don't know.'

'Glass helps the transition.'

'I know this already. There will be some piece of glass in your world, and a piece here. They exchange light at points where the skin of the worlds touch each other. Alice believed the glass reflected light through, one to the other. She put a reminder to herself in her first book, the glass key by the locked door. Tell me something I don't know.'

'Time passes at different speeds in our two worlds.'

'We know this.' The Queen waved a hand, dismissing her disappointment. 'Alice would be gone for a few days only, but she would be older on her return. Weeks or months had gone by in the other world.'

'But do you know what the time difference is?'

'No. If Alice discovered it, she didn't tell us.'

'She did, she put it down in the first book. I've worked it out.'

'Have you indeed?' The Queen's air of disappointment evaporated. 'This *is* valuable news. Go on, tell me.'

'The ratio is sixty to one. One hour here is sixty hours over there. One day here, sixty days over there. One year here, sixty years over there.'

'Sixty! God in heaven. Will you be offended if we go together and I ask the scholars to verify this? Will you show them the passages in the book that lead you to the figure?'

'Happy to,' Ali said, grinning. 'But only if we do it in their library.'

'Ha!' The Queen clapped her hands again. 'Yes, why not. Your arrogance must be encouraged if it leads to such discoveries. Let's go and present this right now, but don't expect them to obliging. Offended, yes.' The Queen laughed and opened the door. 'Come along, young lady, I may not quite trust you yet, but I rather enjoy the dynamic you've brought to our lives in a single day.'

'I will choose to take that as a compliment,' said Ali, echoing the Queen's own words as they set off through the palace.

'Touché! And Cook tells me you have an admirer in the kitchens.'

'The kitchen hand, Rupert? He's got a crush on me.'

Ali hurried along behind the Queen. Agreeing to see the scholars would eat up time she couldn't afford, but they were the closest thing the palace had to scientists, and getting them to take her seriously and confirm her findings would be like having a peer review. Which is exactly what she needed right now, because something about the math didn't fit. Either the sixty-to-one ratio was wrong, or else her assumptions about the boys' identity was wrong.

The library door was a humble affair. Bare wood, highly polished with no signs or symbols, just a hatch. A velvet rope hung to one side. The Queen pulled on it gently and a bell sounded in the room beyond, its chime soft and muted.

'Yes?' The small hatch opened, the kind Ali had seen in movies; spy hatches into cells or nightclubs. A face appeared in the opening. 'Another visit so soon.' The hatch closed, and the door opened.

'Come on in.' A bald man, extremely tall and sporting a magnificent black beard, welcomed them inside. He dipped his head and gestured towards a set of elegant chairs and a large coffee table to their right. 'Can we offer you tea?'

'Just advice please, Broadman. Our guest would like to discuss a theory regarding the passing of time in the two worlds.'

'Very well. Do sit down. Will reference books be required?'

'The first Wonderland book,' said Ali.

'I shall be back directly. The Chief Scholar is occupied, but I will do my best to debate with you, young lady.' He paused and bent towards her, his tall body curving like a banana, and dropped his voice, 'Please know that we are not all of one mind on matters of protocol. Tradition is to be applauded, a bedrock to hold us steady, but not if it becomes a barrier to knowledge. Blind adherence to form is the very antithesis of learning.'

'Interesting,' said the Queen as they took their seats and watched Broadman set off on his errand. 'You might have an advocate in that man, but tread carefully, the scholars are forever playing power politics amongst themselves.'

Ali nodded, but her attention was taken up studying the room. The entrance door was behind her and bench seats rose in front of her on three sides. She was, Ali realised, on the lecture floor of a small amphitheatre. The library itself seemed to occupy the high ground above the tiered bench. From where Ali sat it was hard to make out much in the way of detail. The far walls were lined with shelving and books, but there were tables, sideboards and dressers too. Many years ago, Ali had been on a school trip to the Natural History Museum. The storage and study rooms had looked like this – organised chaos. The scholar's library seemed part museum, part classroom and part charity shop. Books sat on the shelves, but the tables and sideboards were buried in all manner of objects, from microscopes to toy soldiers.

'Here we are,' Broadman announced as he returned with a manuscript and a music stand. 'We can use my own handwritten copy. Which chapter are we studying?'

'The tea party. You copied the whole book?'

'Certainly, we all make copies. Each one is checked for accuracy of course. So here we are – the tea party, where the famous discussion on time takes place. Needless to say, we have all studied it at length.'

'And your conclusions?'

'Nothing we can agree upon. Alice appears to be stating the obvious in her description of the watches, how we ascribe arbitrary units to time, chopping it up into units of convenience such as years, months and minutes. Beyond that, we are flummoxed.'

'Yes,' Ali agreed, 'she's being really clear about measuring time on different scales. Like this bit.' Ali pointed to the text and read aloud. *'What a funny watch! It tells the day of the month, and doesn't tell what o'clock it is!'*

'We could see no hidden message in there,' said Broadman.

'She's setting up the context for the riddle. The hidden message is in the next conversation when the Hatter talks about time as if it's a person. He calls time *him* instead of *it*. That's the hidden message.'

'It is?' Broadman leaned over the page and scratched at his massive black beard. 'I don't see it.'

'The HIM is printed in capitals.' Ali tapped the word. 'Why did Alice do that? Why draw our attention to it with capital letters?'

'We debated this years ago,' said Broadman. 'It denotes importance. Time is the master of everything and deserves a special status. Beyond that obvious interpretation, we have no idea,' the scholar grinned at Ali. 'You have a theory?'

'I do. Alice is using HIM as a simple acronym.'

'An interesting idea, certainly. And what do the letters stand for?'

'It's the ratio for how much faster time marches in the other worlds H I M stands for Hours In Minutes. One hour passes over there for every minute that passes here. Sixty to one. Sixty days pass over there, one day passes here. Sixty years over there, one year here.'

'An intriguing interpretation,' Broadman stopped scratching his beard. 'Very intriguing. No one has proposed this before.'

'What have we here?' The Chief Scholar appeared at the top of the stairs, he was not being carried, instead he was walking like a centipede on the dozens of tiny hands that grew from his sides. The effect was unnerving, and it took all Ali's resolve not to openly gag at the sight of it.

'Our young guest has provided us with a debate,' said Broadman.

'I mean, what have we here in the *gentlemen's* library?' Plato shook his head in a display of long-suffering graciousness. 'Your Majesty, I did make our position abundantly clear. This young lady can borrow and study as many of the books as she likes, but not in here and not at the expense of a scholar's valuable time.'

'Sorry.' Ali gave him what she hoped was an endearing smile. 'But what if I win our chess match?'

'I don't understand.'

'Our chess match,' said Ali. 'What is my prize if I win?'

'Win?' The Chief Scholar sounded confused. Clearly the idea hadn't entered his head. 'If you win? Well, in that event, you can demand whatever you like. For myself, I will demand a trip to the moon if pigs learn to fly. Broadman, kindly see our guests from the room, and then report to my table.'

'I wish to play you now,' said Ali. 'Here, in front of the Queen and Broadman and any others who wish to attend.'

'The challenger does not set the place. And as to time, I am far too busy to indulge you right now.'

'It won't take long,' said Ali. 'I only need ten minutes. I usually win in less than twenty moves.' She tried to sound matter of fact about it, not boastful.

'Do you indeed?' The giant caterpillar leaned forward and scrutinized her face, his own creasing into ripples around his eyes. 'It appears you believe this. Perhaps you played your mother and father, yes?'

'Yes.'

'Yes, lax parenting! Very lax. Allowing a child to win all the time might seem like a kindness. But it is not. It does wonders for their fledgling ego, and nothing for their humility. Then, one brutal day, life comes crashing in and a counterside to that coin emerges: humiliation.'

He gathered his body folds, pulling himself up to his full height. 'Very well, let the chessboard be the anvil, I will be its hammer. We will indulge you and beat some humility into you.'

Broadman hurried off to get the chess set.

'I must fetch the Hatter,' said the Queen. 'He will be vexed beyond measure if he misses this.'

A few minutes later, Broadman returned with a wooden box. Four scholars accompanied him and crowded around the table to help set out the game.

'It's very ornate,' said Ali. The chess pieces were wooden, carved from dark and pale woods. Ali realised she could identify the woods and sent a silent blessing to her Uncle Bertie. He loved every stick of furniture in their house, and knew from what trees each was made. At first, he had spared Ali any rambling lectures on the subject, but when he realised her enthusiasm was genuine, he took her through the entire house, extolling the virtues of every piece of furniture. She picked up two pawns, one white and one black.

'Ebony and oak?' she asked.

'Ebony, certainly,' said Broadman. 'The lighter wood might be elm. Who will play white?'

'What sort of question is that?' said Plato. 'The challenger always leads out. Now, can we get this underway with as little interjection as possible?' He waved one of his odd, tiny hands at his colleagues just as the door opened behind Ali and the Queen returned with the Hatter.

'Off we go then.' Ali moved her Queen's pawn forward one space. 'The sooner we finish, the sooner I can find a desk in here and start my studies.'

'An early finish it will be.' Plato couldn't hide the contempt in his voice. 'With that opening move, you are clearly planning to throw the game.'

Ali didn't reply; she just looked up and gave him the biggest, brightest smile she could manage. She had known all kind of bullies in her short life; some were complicated, damaged souls who were hard to read. Then there were bullies like her opponent at the table. These pompous, conceited creatures climbed their way up by pulling others down. They belittled them, filling them with shame and self-doubt, then kept them underfoot by making them feel worthless. Such bullies were easy to read and easy to attack. She didn't have to beat Plato at chess, she had to goad him into beating himself. Doubt was her weapon, and with her smile of radiant confidence she had planted the first seed. She didn't look down at the board, she looked at him, waiting for him to make his move. When he did, she countered immediately, with no hesitation, placing her knight, then smiling the confident smile of someone who was already thinking six moves ahead. She had used this approach before. Sometimes it had worked.

'Interesting.' The Chief Scholar glanced up at her, then back at the board. He took a full two minutes to make his next move. Ali took two seconds to make hers. Then the soft murmuring began; whispered commentary among the scholars. Ali glanced up at the Hatter and the Queen. Their faces gave little away, but one of the Queen's eyebrows was severely arched.

As Ali had predicted, the game was over in less than ten minutes. Plato's ego got the better of him, he simply couldn't handle the speed at which this young lady seemed to be reading the board and his mind. He couldn't handle the hushed whispers of amusement from his fellow scholars, or the steely-eyed silence of the Queen. He had felt compelled to show off, to make his decisions far more quickly, to appear to be seeing as many moves ahead as his opponent was. An unforced error became two, then three, and suddenly he was playing a defensive game that only had one possible outcome. He sighed and laid his king on its back.

'Congratulations,' he said.

'Accepted,' Ali replied.

'And your prize?' Broadman asked eagerly. 'You wish to study with us here in the library, yes?'

'Yes, I do, thank you Broadman, but only when I am freely invited to do so by a vote of hands.'

'Then what prize will you take?'

'I want to borrow this chess set and play my friend Jackie in the infirmary. I think it will give her some much-needed distraction.'

CHAPTER 18

BIRDBATHS AND BURROWS

———————

'That was entertaining,' said the Queen as she accompanied Ali back to her room. The Hatter had stayed in the library on the pretext of doing some research. In fact, he wanted to eavesdrop on the post-game gossip of the scholars.

'I nearly lost,' said Ali. 'Plato is a much better player.'

'Of chess, yes. Not of people. In that, my dear, you are clearly something of an expert. I stand forewarned. As to your request, Broadman will champion it and the Chief Scholar will fight it tooth and nail. I fear you went too hard on him; some men hold grievances to their graves.'

'I'm not sure Alice trusted him.'

'Is that so?'

'Yes. I think Alice saw what I see. Plato is good with words, I think it's how he maintains his status among the other scholars. He builds them up, then knocks them down to size. They want to seek his approval and avoid his sarcasm. It's the tools of a bully.'

'Interesting.' The Queen began drumming her fingers. 'What makes you think Alice shares this opinion of him?'

'That whole passage with the mushrooms in the first book. The caterpillar she meets is extremely rude to her; it ignores her, belittles her, then it offers Alice crumbs from the mushroom he's sitting on. Let's call those 'crumbs of advice'. They either make Alice grow big or they make her grow small.'

'They build up her self-esteem, or they belittle still further?'

'Exactly. It's one explanation, anyway.' Ali immediately regretted starting this discussion. She needed to get moving. If her theory on the time ratio was right, every minute she delayed was an hour back at the manor house. Now, a full day had passed, which meant two whole months had passed over there.

'Here we are,' the Queen opened the door to Ali's room. 'I trust Aphelia has told you who usually uses this room.'

'Yes. Alice.'

'Indeed. There's no doubt in my mind that you and Alice are related, the resemblance is striking. Which imperils you. The Jabberwocky will be after your blood. And I mean that literally. Did the Hatter alert you to this?'

'No, but he was going to great lengths to keep me safe from him.'

'I am not surprised. In his madness, the Jabberwocky has developed the notion that Alice is able to travel more easily between the worlds through some mutation in her biology, and that drinking her blood would bestow the same benefits on him.'

'Nice!'

'You must take this seriously.'

'I am, I really am. It's just that so much is happening so quickly, the idea of some mutant beetle wanting to drink my blood seems, I don't know, too unreal to take on board.'

'He will come for you, Ali, of that I have no doubt. We will do our best to keep you safe, but he will come when he has marshalled sufficient forces to storm the palace. I say that not to scare you but to arm you, and to request that you remain here within the palace walls. I want someone with you at all times.'

'Message received. And he's not the first person to think my family's blood might be interesting. Someone on the other side was also looking into it.'

'Theodore and the Hatter have shared a little of your story. We must put our heads together tonight and see where this woman, King, fits in. No one I have spoken to recalls her, which suggests her time here was spent in the fringes with the Wocky, or in some unknown community. I hope your research bears fruit today, and I look forward to your presentation in the Grand Hall tonight.'

'Presentation? Oh, right. The Telling.'

'Indeed. In the meantime, I wish you every success in your studies.' The Queen glanced around the room, nodded to herself and left. Ali closed the door and dropped full-length on her bed with the chess set. She took out the board and the playing pieces, then checked the empty box for hidden sleeves. Nothing. The board itself was a single panel of wood no thicker than a breadboard, its playing surface inlaid with squares of light and dark veneer.

Ali tapped it. The board sounded solid. The underside had a layer of green felt. Ali scratched one corner with a fingernail until it came free, then she peeled the felt from the base. No map. Frack!

She got up and paced the room. Was there another chess set somewhere in the palace? She had lost enough time already but without the map to navigate a safe route, she might wander into a time anomaly and spend days getting back.

Ali picked up the board and took it to the window. What was she missing?

She inspected the top more carefully, especially the squares for Q7, one black and one white. She held the board on end and looked across the surface like an ant. From this angle she could see the accumulated wear from its years of use, all the dents and marks in the polished surface. Most were meaningless scrapes and scuff marks, but on the white Q7 square there was a set of scratches that looked more deliberate, like crude hieroglyphics. Ali tried to pull the marks into focus, but they were too small, as if made by a needle. She badly needed a magnifying glass.

Ali propped the chessboard on the windowsill and searched the room for a drinking glass. There wasn't one, but on the other sill was a glass vase. Ali stood it in front of the chessboard, filled it with water from her vanity bowl, and peered through it. She had often done this as a child, seeing how distorted the world could look when magnified through water. She moved her head and the vase till she got a clear view through to the Q7 square. It was in mirror image of the real markings, but magnified enough that Ali could read them.

They were three pictograms, like the hallmarks of a silversmith: a spanner, a screwdriver and a hammer.

'Yes!' Ali jumped up and put the chess set back in its box. There might be any number of toolboxes in the palace, but there would definitely be one for the huge tank engine. It meant another trip to the kitchen, but she was planning to go there anyway to hide her journal before heading out with Theodore. She pulled her journal out and began to scribble furiously.

Dad – there's so much to tell you. So many questions. And not just figuring out the science behind all this, but basic questions like how do they survive? I see farming but no industry. People come stumbling through with their clothes and whatever stuff they're carrying, like I did with my backpack. But there's a traction engine here and a perfect copy of the Crystal Palace. Crazy! I could figure it out with enough time, but not while I'm here. If the time ratio really is sixty to one, then six months spent here will be thirty years over there for you!

So, next steps. I have to test my theory for safe passage. I won't write that up in here, in case the book is discovered. But I've thought of a different way to remember it. I hope.

Also, I'll bring one of Theodore's pocket watches with me to measure the exact difference in the passage of time over here. But I can't spend too long there on this first trip, no one on this side must know I've gone back, or they'll realise I can do it safely. Okay dad, that's the bones of it, I'll write more when I have time – got to go and hide this now.

She closed her journal, rolled onto her back and stared at the ceiling. The need to get back and find her father began rising like a silent panic, as if she were running late for a train, a train she *had* to catch or her whole world would come tumbling down. This was the first time she'd been alone that morning, alone with her thoughts. Keeping busy was the answer: action, momentum. Not this. She tried to ignore the feeling of panic, but it kept on coming. The room was large, but suddenly it felt small. A prison. Suffocating her.

'Shit!' Ali sat up and stumbled to the window. The latch was made of cast iron, delicate and a little rusty. She struggled to prise it open and failed. Air, she had to have air. Ali picked up the face bowl and was about to smash the window glass when Custard stepped into the room.

'Oh, wait!' the young attendant ran over and took the bowl from Ali, set it down and opened the window herself. 'Steady, steady. Lean out and take a deep breath. Come on.'

Ali did, her head pounding, her hands shaking. What was happening? Was this a panic attack? She took one more deep breath and held it in, waving Custard away. Every fibre of her body screamed for her to let her breath go, but she kept on holding it, letting the carbon dioxide build up, the scientist in her knowing what to do, even as her body wrestled against it. Slowly, very slowly, she felt the attack subside, and she released her breath.

'Thank you,' she whispered, as she let Custard guide her to a chair.

'We all get this at first.' Custard's voice was soft and encouraging. 'Nothing to be scared of. The Scholars have a very big word for it. They call it incarceration syndrome. The rest of us just call it the frights. Knowing we're trapped over here, it's like there's a big boulder on your chest, right?'

'Right.' Ali was half listening. Mostly she was focused on her breathing.

'I just came to give you something.' Custard went back to the door where she had dropped Ali's backpack. 'Here, I had the Queen's seamstress fix it up.' The bag was beautifully repaired, a little smaller and with a single strap. More shoulder bag now than backpack.

'This is brilliant, thank you. I'll keep my journal in it. I make notes and read them every day to remember myself. You keep a diary, right?'

'Everyone does,' said Custard. 'Mine's by my bed.'

Ali nodded, then put her journal into the shoulder bag. She glanced at Custard as she did so. There was no flicker of interest. Not that it mattered; if she was reporting to the Queen, let this bag be their focus of attention – but her journal wouldn't be in it.

'I'd like a bath, Custard. Is that okay?'

'Another one! So soon?' Custard looked surprised, then worried. 'Cook might be put out.'

'I'm sure she'll be fine with it. I have a puzzle to solve, remember?'

'The boys.'

'Exactly. I do my best thinking in the bath, so I need some serious bath time. Plus I need to wash that bite wound again.'

'Have you had a surgeon look at it?'

'No.'

'Why not?' Custard put her hands on her hips.

'I don't trust them.'

'You're letting them take care of your friend, Jackie.'

'Fair point. Yes, I am.'

'Let me see.'

'Okay,' Ali unbuttoned the top of her riding breeches and eased the waistband down over her hip.

'Oh dear,' Custard shook her head. 'That looks very unpleasant. I shall ask Cook if you can take a bath every day, but only if you agree to get this horrid bite properly dressed.'

'I will.'

'Good,' said Custard, and she set off for the kitchen. Ali closed her door and began searching for something she could seal her journal inside, anything that might afford it some protection if she hid it under a kitchen cupboard by the bath. She spotted a large flat box, opened it, and recoiled at the smell. Disgusting! Musty old cigars. How could anyone enjoy these things? They were grey with age and crumbled into flakes as Ali tipped them into the fire hearth. She tucked her journal into the box, dropped it into her bag and set off for the kitchens.

The big copper still sat where they'd set it the previous night, on the far side of the great kitchen between the heavy wooden cupboards. The screen was folded and leaning to one side. Custard had won the consent of the old cook and was already filling the bath with the help of Rupert.

'I wash my hands a lot,' Rupert offered, as if Ali had walked in on a debate.

'Good to know.'

'Here she is …' The cook Ali had met on her last visit was over by the large oven. 'Our scholar slayer.'

'News travels fast,' said Ali.

'I knew you were clever.' Rupert stopped helping Custard with the bath; he came over and parked himself next to Ali. 'Are you clever at everything?'

'No, I understand science and engineering, but I don't understand people very well.'

'That's not what we just heard,' said the cook. 'Word has it you understand our Chief Scholar a great deal better than he understands himself.'

'I was lucky,' said Ali. She pointed to the huge steam engine that was puffing and cranking by the west wall. 'Machines are more simple, more hard-working, and more reliable than people. Does Thomas ever break down?'

'No,' said Rupert. 'Not yet. Alfred makes sure of that, he's the scholar who tends him, but I help too, don't I, Cook?'

'You do, anything to save you doing your real work for me.'

'Let me guess,' Ali pointed to the large brass pistons that were hissing back and forth in their sleeves. 'You put grease on all these moving parts, yes?'

'Yes! And a great deal more besides. Do you want to see?'

'Yes please.' Ali followed the boy around the machine as he pointed out all the jobs that had to be done.

'That's a lot of work,' she said. 'Did Alfred give you the tools you need?'

'There's a whole toolbox up on the driver deck. Want to see them?'

'Enough!' the cook called out from her bench by the stove. 'You've shown the girl the engine, now go and get me the potatoes like I asked ten minutes past.'

'Going!' yelled Rupert. He grinned at Ali and hurried off.

'Three sacks, boy, and all to be peeled,' yelled the cook.

Ali clambered up three steel rungs to the steering deck. There it was, a battered tool box sitting beneath a wrought iron seat.

'Bath's ready,' Custard called out. 'Nice and hot, so best you come and enjoy it before it cools. I must get back to a few chores.'

'Be right there,' Ali called back. She opened the box, pulled out the tools and looked inside. The box was metal, but lined at the bottom with a piece of sacking. Ali peeled it up. Underneath was a thin book.

'You still hungry?' The top of the cook's head appeared beside the engine.

Ali leaned over and smiled at her. 'Always,' she said.

'Good. I've got porridge and sweetmeats. Proper food, not the sparrow seed the Queen eats. Hardly puts enough down to fill her fingernails, that one!'

'Thanks, I'll come right down.' Ali tucked the book in her waistband, pulled her shirt over it and repacked the tools.

'Smells delicious,' said Ali as she climbed down. She crossed to the bench just as the cook overturned a large baking tray. Hot muffins tumbled out.

'Whoa! Muffins!'

'Funny name,' laughed Rupert who had just arrived back, groaning under the weight of a huge sack of potatoes. 'We call them sweetmeats.'

'They smell brilliant, whatever they're called.' said Ali.

'Food can't be brilliant,' said Rupert. 'Scholars can be brilliant, sweetmeats can't be.'

'They're a great deal smarter than you, boy!' The cook tapped him softly with the back of her hand. 'Best make peace with yours when you next take a bite!'

'Talking of names,' Ali sat and smiled at the cook, 'I didn't catch yours.'

'Names aren't fish!' said Rupert.

'I'm sure I have one,' said the cook. 'No doubt I'll remember it one day. Most folk just call me Cook. Keeps it simple.'

Ali set about devouring four buttered muffins, each one bigger than her fist. The taste was almost too much; how could food be this good! She looked around as she ate, taking everything in. The morning sunlight slanting down from the high windows; pots on the crackling fire; the huge traction engine chugging patiently. With any luck, in a few hours, she would be back in her world and this would feel like a dream. A beautiful, terrifying dream. She ran her fingers over the tabletop, feeling the years of activity that had polished the wood into gentle grooves, the places elbows had rubbed, the hollows where dough had been pounded. So many years of daily life. All of it as real as her own. She wanted to imprint it onto her brain, an indelible engraving that could cheat the infliction of forgetting.

'Those were amazing, thank you.' Ali got up from the table, the muffins a delicious concrete in her stomach.

'Porridge?' asked Cook.

'I would burst, but thanks.' Ali went over to her bath and stepped behind the screen. She pulled the book from her waist band and flicked through it. Each page was covered in hand-drawn maps, all neatly marked with curving time gradients. Ali wanted to yell out in triumph and punch the air. Instead, she searched for a page that looked like the path to the bluebell clearing. She found it easily, Alice had given each map a name and there were small pictograms for things of note.

The path back to the bluebell clearing had simple drawings of a tower and a barn, one at each end of a narrow road. The map was empty of contour lines except for one tight circle of them in the middle of the road near the far end. In the middle of this circle was another pictogram of rocks or boulders. Ali took out her cigar box, put the book of maps in there with her journal, and slipped the box back into the shadows under the tall cupboard beside her.

For a moment, Ali felt overwhelmed by a mix of excitement and weariness. She stared down at the steaming water. It looked so inviting right now, but did she have time for this? Taking a bath had been a ruse to hide her journal and look for the map. To hell with it. Theodore could wait a few minutes. She stripped off and climbed in. The water was piping hot. Ali sat back, closed her eyes and let her mind drift.

'Watch them scamper!' Ali whispered. It was an expression a therapist had made up for her when helping Ali to manage her anger. The woman had co-opted Ali's love of science, encouraging her to observe the mechanics of her mind in the way a scientist might observe rats scampering through a new maze.

Observe the thoughts scampering around in your head, don't get attached to any of them, just observe them. Staying detached is the key. They are not yours; they are just things. Don't wander off with them. Watch them and note what they do.

As she watched, one thought kept returning and came to a standstill at the centre of the maze. One idea, one overpowering notion. Trapped. She pictured her fight with the critters and felt a surge of fear, not of being hurt, but of being stuck here and never going home. Of being hurt, and transforming, stuck here never to see her father again, or Martha and Bertie. Or Peter.

Peter? Where did that come from? Ali sat up. She had planted a kiss on his forehead when they'd left the church. He had been amazing, he had given her his complete, unquestioning support. No one outside her family had ever given that to her that before. And in return, he'd nearly died for it! When they'd survived the collapse of the church tower, she'd felt such a surge of relief and gratitude that kissing him had been spontaneous, an act that was out of character because the circumstances were out of the ordinary.

But now, looking back, she realised there might have been another factor. It had been safe. Safe because she might never see him again. She had already decided to save Waxstaff by bringing her through, and in so doing, she might get stuck here. So, a goodbye kiss. Safe.

Ali slipped back down into the water and sighed. Caring was always a mistake. Caring made you vulnerable.

Ali had arranged to meet Theodore on the front steps of the palace. She arrived still dressed in the borrowed riding tunic and breeches. Ali had asked for her own clothes back after her bath, but Custard wouldn't oblige.

'Not dry, sorry. They were washed and hung out this morning. They'll be good and dry by tonight for your Telling.' Custard had been assigned by the Queen to go with them and carry their refreshments.

'Late?' Theodore was pacing on the bottom step. 'Good morning. Aphelia, you can safely leave Miss Ali in my care. You are free to do as you please.'

'Yes,' said Ali. 'I shall tell the Queen you attended us dutifully all day.'

'A whole day on my own?' Custard handed over the picnic basket she was carrying. 'Whatever will I do with myself? I can't walk the grounds; people will see me and ask why I'm not attending you. I can't shut myself up in my little room – I should go quite mad to have the whole day in there.

'Take my room. You were looking with envy at all the books, well now you have a whole day to go through them.' Ali opened the basket and took out one of the carefully wrapped lunches. 'And you have your very own picnic too.'

'Oh goodness!' Custard took the lunch parcel. 'A whole day of reading all to myself. It has to be our secret.'

'Our secret,' Theodore agreed. 'Off you go. Not a word to anyone.'

He set off, with Ali trying to match his fast, bouncing gait. She followed him across the main lawn and through a set of formal gardens with gravel paths, box hedging and beds of miniature geraniums no bigger than buttercups. They passed a few other folk who dipped their heads to them but didn't approach.

'Here we are.' Theodore had led her to a small, secluded lawn right beside the perimeter wall. Four ancient and very gnarled olive trees dominated the space, one at each corner of the lawn, their branches reaching out to weave a low roof that gave dappled shade to the whole lawn. Ali had to duck her head as she followed Theodore inside. He spread their picnic blanket on the grass which was dotted with white and yellow daisies.

Ali dropped down onto the blanket, overwhelmed by a surge of melancholy. A lost memory had washed over her. A warm afternoon making daisy chains with her mother, their heads crowned in yellow and white.

'No time for this!' she whispered.

'Time for what?'

'Nothing …' Ali paused and looked up at the perimeter wall. 'So how do I get out of here? Not by climbing that!'

'No indeed.' Theodore pointed to a bird bath near a cluster of rose bushes. 'There is a burrow under that dreadful sculpture.'

'You dig burrows?'

'Not by choice, though I admit to having urges sometimes. The burrow was the Hatter's idea, our very own secret escape route under the wall.'

'Interesting. You have trust issues with the Queen.'

'No, it's the committee process we rail against. Every decision is made by consensus. Sometimes the Hatter and I like to exercise independent judgment without the burden of explaining ourselves.'

'Nicely put. Now then. How far to the bluebell clearing if I do it at a run?'

'Twenty minutes.'

'That's all?' Ali smacked the ground beside her. 'Twenty minutes from here to my barn? You lead us here in a twelve-hour circle yesterday!'

'Well, yes. Two reasons. Firstly, there is a sticky patch on this track where twenty minutes can become days. And secondly, the Critters were likely patrolling it.'

'Waiting for me to arrive through again?'

'Yes.'

'Might they still be there?'

'It's possible, but I don't think so. They saw Puddles come to your rescue. They know you're here. Safe at the palace.'

'Is the path covered in brambles?'

'It used to be, when the critters first patrolled it.'

'Chasing after my great-aunt?'

'Yes. The brambles grew so profusely they became an archway of thorns. The track is easy to walk now as almost nothing grows beneath them.'

'Ha!' Ali snorted a short laugh.

'What?'

'Nothing, it's not important.' The odd name Alice had written on her map for this path made sense now. She called it the Blackberry Tunnel.

'So ... you really are set on doing this ...' Theodore pulled his knees to his chest, hugged them tightly and let out a long sigh, 'this brainless adventure.'

'Yes.'

'Then will you, at least, share with me your theories on Ted and Ricky?'

'No. It's not right for you know before they do.'

'Is it right that they miss knowing their history if you fail to return?'

'No.' Ali conceded the point. 'But it will take too long to explain unless you can remember some English history. Can you?'

'Gone, all of it.'

'Then you have to wait. Do you have the two pocket watches?'

'Here.' Theodore took them from the hamper. 'How long do you need?'

'I shall be back in one hour exactly.' Ali got up and tucked the watches into the front pockets of her breeches. 'Twenty minutes to run to the bluebell clearing, and twenty minutes back. That gives me twenty minutes over on the other side, almost a full day if my sixty to one theory is right.'

'Very well,' Theodore got to his feet, went to the birdbath and tipped it on its side. Directly beneath was the opening to the burrow.

'Down there?' said Ali. 'A bit small, isn't it?

'It gets wider,' said Theodore. 'I'll put the birdbath back once you're through. You can call me from the other side, the tunnel is very short.'

'Okay,' Ali stepped down into the burrow. 'See you in one hour exactly. I hope you have a third pocket watch.'

'Yes.' Theodore gave the picnic basket a gentle shake. 'Three of them. I have developed a nervous obsession for being punctual thanks to your great-aunt.'

CHAPTER 19

WATCHING THE HORIZON

The tunnel was dark. The only light came from the narrow chimney Ali had dropped down. The floor angled steeply, so she sat and shuffled forward like a child testing out a playground slide. It flattened out a little and remained level for a dozen paces before it started to angle upwards again.

Ali emerged inside the stump of a hollow tree. It was only waist-high. She put her head up and looked around. The perimeter wall towered up behind her.

'I'm through!' she shouted back into the tunnel.

'Take care!' Theodore's voice was a thin echo.

All around were the remains of burnt trees. A battlefield or a forest fire? Ali climbed out and set off. Theodore had been very clear. *'Keep the wall directly to your back and you will come upon the path to the clearing in just a few minutes.'*

Ali couldn't see any guards patrolling up on the wall, but she moved from tree stump to tree stump, just in case, until the wall was far behind her. Then she broke into a steady sprint. There was no mistaking the path when Ali came across it. She had to squeeze through thorn bushes to get on it. The track ran left and right. Left towards the cultivated fields in front of the palace, and right to the bluebell clearing. Once through the wall of blackberry, the ground itself was clear of undergrowth. Tangled cables of thorns rose on either side like canyon walls, arching overhead, weaving together to become a curved ceiling.

'Bloody hell!' It was like sprinting down the nave of a ruined cathedral, its walls consumed by returning wilderness. Ali kept up a steady pace, the pain from the bite wound was still there, but a night's sleep and all Cook's incredible food had lifted her energy. The tunnel started opening up, widening from a lane to a road. The walls remained dense, but the tangled roof became patchy, full of holes where the sun streamed through, fingers of light angling down like laser beams.

Up ahead, one broad pillar of light fell on a tumble of rocks that stood in the centre of the road. Strands of yellow grass grew beside them where a spring bubbled up from the ground. This had to be the dense time anomaly Alice had marked on her map. Ali gave it a wide berth, jogging as close as she could to the left wall of thorns.

Then she saw them.

Three critters were pacing back and forth across the road ahead. They were growling at each other and stamping as if the ground was burning their feet. They reminded Ali of small children bursting to go to the toilet. Then they spotted her, and their wails turned into screams of glee.

'Shit!' Ali turned and broke into a run as the critters raced towards her. She circled back, placing the island of rocks between them. Did they know about the gravity well? They came on, screeching their pain and delight as they neared the tumble of rocks.

'Did ya miss us, girly?' The mutant hedgehog was in the lead, swinging a club as he ran. 'Hurt me last time, girly, time to pay. Going to do a bit of *breaking*.'

'Take you to Jabber in a sack!' screamed a large rat. 'Bundle you up, good and tight, all broken and bloody.'

The tumble of rocks shone like a pagan altar, an island of light transfixed in a beam of sunshine. The creatures came racing towards Ali, and directly into the time anomaly. Ali stopped running; her fear matched by fascination. The shrieks of her attackers dropped in pitch as they crossed the threshold into the gravity well, their cries becoming low growls, deepening with every step.

'Gotcha!' whispered Ali. The critters' movements slowed down. Ali had to rub her eyes. It was so weird to watch. The critters were running in super-slow motion. She picked up a small stone from the path and hurled it at the hedgehog. The stone slowed as it neared its target, Ali stared, witness to a phenomenon her father had described to her so many times. Everything she had been told about time, gravity and relativity was taking place in front of her, not on the threshold of a distant black hole, but here, just a few strides away. The slowly tumbling stone finally struck the chest of the hedgehog.

Ali wanted to stay and watch, stay and record every detail. But eventually the critters would pass through the centre and speed up again. Science would have to wait. She gave them a wave, and raced on.

The corridor of thorns started to thin out, the tangled vines replaced by forest, and Ali found herself back on the path to the bluebell clearing. She picked up her pace, sprinting to the silver birch tree with its ribbons and glass crystal. She leaned against the trunk to catch her breath for a moment, then pulled out the two pocket watches. She set them to the same time – 12 o'clock. The time itself didn't matter, they just needed to be synchronized.

A fallen branch lay half buried under the bluebells. Ali parted the flowers and wedged one watch under the branch. There were no clouds in the sky, no sign of rain, so there was no need to shield the watch from the weather, just from prying eyes. She winced as she stood back up. The waistband of her leather breeches had been rubbing the bite wound. She eased the waistband down. The swelling around the bite had grown, it was now a patch of inflamed tissue the size of her hand. She wondered if Potts' medical bag was still in the barn. Unlikely. Weeks would have passed over there.

She stepped around the tree to the spot where the barn stood, reached out and stroked the air. She could feel the resistance on her fingertips, the surface tension between the worlds. Cleaning the crystal had made the transition a lot easier, like pushing through a membrane of liquid.

When she'd been six or seven, a bad cold had turned to bronchitis, and then to pneumonia. Fluid had built up in her lungs, a soup of dead cells she'd struggled to cough up. The family doctor had taught her a breathing technique to squeeze her lungs like a sponge. Squeezing till there was nothing left, and then, before breathing in again, he had taught her to cough a series of small coughs that dislodged the last stubborn pockets of air, and with it, the sticky phlegm.

Ali breathed out, forcing out every drop of air. Then, without taking a breath, she made a series of small coughs, expelling the final trapped bubbles. The next step was the hardest. Holding her breath until she started to panic. The idea had come to her in the bath that morning. What better way to produce an adrenaline rush? Fat nicer than snorting chilli powder or cutting herself like Aunt Martha had done. It was working. She felt her pulse beginning to climb as she kept on holding her breath. Then, as her pulse climbed, the woodland around her began to fade.

Phasing, thought Ali. *I'm phasing.* The realisation was like a lightning bolt. There was no membrane to push through. No doorway at all. The worlds simply coincided here. To cross into her world, she just had to be in phase with it. *Was this all frequency entrainment?* Not just for the light, but for every cell in her body.

Slowly, gently, the barn materialised around her. There was a soft popping in her ears. *A pressure change?* She stood still and took in a long slow breath. There was no nausea. No stomach cramps. She felt a little dizzy, but that was all.

Then she heard the snoring.

Ali turned slowly and saw Potts. The nurse was sitting in a large, overstuffed armchair. She was snoring like a chainsaw, clearly asleep, and yet her eyes were open. Ali stood frozen to the spot, her mind switching to overdrive. She moved her head slowly, scanning the rest of the barn.

The mirror had been cleaned. It stood centre stage, but now it was protected inside a cube of glass as if it were a priceless sculpture in a museum. Equipment lined the walls, mostly lights and camera. They seemed positioned to cover every corner of the room. The floorboards were sprinkled in white flour. To register her footprints?

Potts stopped snoring. Ali froze, and stared at her. The woman's face and hands were a mess of scars, her white uniform had gone, replaced by military fatigues. And she was waking up.

Ali closed her eyes, slowed her breathing and listened for the birdsong of the woodland clearing until it was all she could hear. Then she opened her eyes. She was surrounded by bluebells, and the three critters were racing across the clearing towards her.

'There she is, grab her. Grab her!' The large mutant hedgehog was in the lead and began whooping with delight.

Ali looked down for a weapon. A stone or a branch. There was nothing. This wasn't a fight she could win; they would pull her to the ground in a matter of seconds. Ali set her feet apart, folded her arms, and waited.

'Hurry up,' she yelled. 'I've been waiting for you. I don't have all day.'

'Waiting?' A gigantic cane toad was right behind the hedgehog, keeping up by taking huge leaps. 'For what? What d'you want with us?'

'Doesn't matter what she wants,' the hedgehog said, slowing to a scuttling walk. The third critter, a large rat, did the same, and all three fanned out to surround her.'Only thing that matters is what the Wocky wants.' The hedgehog raised his front paws and wriggled his short fingers like an excited child. 'He wants to work his art on you.'

'Not the only thing, Mister Spikes,' the rat with the extended jaw said, pointing back over his shoulder. 'This girly ran past us like a poacher's arrow back there under the thorns. Ran like a blur, she did.'

'Yes, oh yes, Gutter, my dear friend. Just like the Alice girl,' the cane toad nodded to itself, as if dredging up a lost memory. 'Didn't she do that?'

'She did.' The hedgehog stopped and drummed its small fingers together. 'Now, girly, if you be as smart as I reckon you is, then you'll be wanting to share that little secret with us. Coz we might get all charitable on you and be sparing on the unpleasantries.'

'Break us a few ribs,' said the rat, Gutter. 'Chew off a few fingers, but leave the pretty face. What do you say, girly – fancy sharing your little secret with us?'

'No.' Ali forced herself to stay calm. 'I can give the Jabberwocky something far more valuable than that.'

'Trade? Don't think so.' The cane hopped forward, close enough to touch if Ali reached out. 'There's nothing else he wants.'

'I think there is. Something that will make him very proud of you. Now listen; one step closer and I'll disappear to the other side.'

'You won't!' Mister Spikes the hedgehog shook his head, the spines on its head rattling like dry sticks as they brushed together. 'Going back will kill you.'

'It won't, it makes me very sick, but I won't die. I can go back and forth all I want, like Alice. You can come with me if we hold hands.'

'With you!' Gutter laughed, but it was a nervous laugh. 'Why would we do that? Think we're stupid?'

'I think you want to make the Wocky very proud of you. I know where Alice hid the history of the Jabberwocky over there. You can bring it back for him. It's what he wants, isn't it? You three will be heroes.'

'We'd be dead heroes,' said Mister Spikes. 'On account of how we can't go through, we don't know the tricks.'

'But I do. You can come with me if we hold hands.' She had them. Ali could see the longing in their eyes, these wretched creatures had no memories left of the other world, but it haunted them. The urge to go back was a terrible longing, the desire etched on their disfigured faces.

'Can't be done,' the rat said softly.

'It can. You will be sick for a while, but you won't die. Not if you keep hold of my hands. What protects me will protect you.'

'Not me,' said the toad. 'I'm staying right here.'

'But if we could get the Wocky's history,' said Mister Spikes, 'the Wocky would love us *so much!*'

'Yes. You would be heroes,' Ali repeated.

'Not heroes', whispered Gutter. 'Free. We could be free of him.'

'Free of him?' Mister Spikes frowned, as if confused by such a subversive idea. 'Free of the Wocky?'

'No more of his torment,' whispered the rat. It looked around, eyes darting to every tree, as if the Jabberwocky was close by, listening to their treason.

'Yes,' said Ali. 'If you have his history, you will have power over him. Come on, let's go, quickly, it has to be now. Before I change my mind.'

She held out her hand like a parent preparing to walk children across a busy road. 'Come on, hold my hands and hold tight.'

To her surprise, two of them did. The large hedgehog and the deformed rat reached out and took her hands, they were trembling. Ali hoped their hearts would be racing too, it would make this a lot easier.

'Here we go ...' She didn't breathe out, didn't squeeze the air from her lungs. She didn't need to, not for this trip. Instead, she slapped herself very hard on her face, and waited for the two creatures to do the same. They did.

'Get ready,' said Ali, as the clearing started to dim around them. 'When we get through, you'll see a very large woman. She's got the Jabberwocky's history.'

The barn shimmered into reality around them. Ali let go of the critter's hands, forced herself to be calm, and felt herself phasing back. Then she was in the woodland clearing again, staring at a very confused toad.

'Where are they?' he stammered. 'What did you do?'

'Don't worry about them. Worry about yourself, you don't have teeth!' Ali launched herself at the toad. The creature leaped clear but Ali managed to grab one ankle. She held on as the toad thrashed and squirmed and yelled obscenities at her. She grabbed the other ankle, lifted the creature and started swinging it round in a circle. She was running on instinct, and stepped towards the tree. She had a picture in her head, a picture of slamming the toad against the tree trunk, of smashing its skull.

'Frack!' She let him go. Dropping him to the ground. Where had that come from, that urge to kill? The toad rolled to its feet and stared up at her, a mixture of anger and confusion in its eyes.

'Next time, I'll kill you,' Ali screamed. 'Go! Run!'

The creature did, leaping away in long, unsteady bounds. Ali dropped down onto the bluebells, closed her eyes and tried to imagine the scene unfolding in the barn. The creatures would be too sick to fight properly, but they would give Potts one hell of a fright.

Was it smart to go back now? Obviously not. Ali hammered the ground with her fists. Her return would be filmed. King was waiting for her, the woman must have taken over the house, which meant she controlled the gateway. The Queen had said there were other gateways, all in London, but would she tell Ali where? One day, perhaps, when Ali had built the trust which the Queen was demanding.

'*Frack!*' Ali punched the ground again. She couldn't wait. She had to go through now: she needed medical help, she needed information, she needed the map and, most of all, she needed to know what was happening to her family.

She sat up. Going right now, that was her best option. She had sown chaos and confusion by sending the critters though. How long had passed by over here? Two minutes? Which meant two hours had passed in the barn. With luck, the critters had wrecked the place. She set the two stopwatches back to twelve o'clock, and started to empty her lungs again.

CHAPTER 20

HOME

Ali stared at all the mess. The barn had been a battlefield. Cameras and lights lay toppled and broken. Potts' chair was on its side, and spatters of blood were everywhere. Sick or not, those two critters had put up a fight! No one was in the barn, but some of the cameras were still working, their tiny operating lights still blinking away. Someone, somewhere would be watching. If the monitors were up at the house, it would take less than a minute for one of King's Suits to come running out to the barn. Speed was her only option.

Ali made a dash for the door, then heard the whimpering. She stopped and looked around for the critters. They were huddled together under the sink in the far corner, hugging tight to each other and shivering, their fur and spikes matted with blood and vomit.

'You tricked us!' said Gutter the rat as Ali approached.

'I did, yes. I was protecting myself.' She reached down towards them. The rat curled back its upper lip.

'Keep away,' it wheezed faintly.

'I can take you back,' said Ali softly. 'You'll recover there.'

'He's over there,' said the hedgehog, its voice cracking. 'The Wocky doesn't forgive. We'll stay.' The creature pulled the rat tightly to it, like a little boy hugging its brother for comfort.

'Yes,' the Gutter nodded and closed its eyes. 'Back home now. Like we always wanted. We stay here now.'

Ali stood up, frozen by indecision. On the bench beside her were bowls and coffee mugs, a box of food, a kettle and a small fridge. Supplies for Potts and any Suits standing watch. She poured milk into two mugs and set them down beside the critters together with a plate of biscuits. It was all she could think to do. Then she ran outside.

The moon was rising into a dark evening sky. Ali couldn't believe how good she felt. No nausea. The only pain was from the wound on her hip. She had done it! Worked it out. It was residual air in the lungs that did the damage. Some small difference in the make-up of the gas elements? Going the other way didn't matter, it was just coming back. Why? At least it was a start; with a decent lab and her father's help they would get to the bottom of it. My god! She really did have the secret to passing safely between the two worlds.

Then she heard voices and people running from the direction of the house. She cut the other way, avoiding the orchard and the back lawn and setting off for the woodland path that followed the perimeter wall. She caught glimpses of the manor as she ran. Lights were coming on in every room and she could see the shadows of people racing about.

Ali shrank into the trees and raced along the path. *Get out of the grounds, get to the village, find Peter.* She whispered it like a mantra as she made her way round to the front gate. *Frack!* They were locked. Not just locked; they had been repaired and a guard house now stood to one side. Two men were on duty and both wore elegant black suits.

She watched from the shadow of the trees. The sight was disorientating. Her brain understood that a month had passed over here, but her body didn't. Her body clock knew she'd run through these gates two days ago, gates that had been rusted and broken. She turned and made her way back along the path, scanning for a tree close to the wall, one she could climb.

Then she saw the figure hunched in the shadows up ahead. She launched herself at the tree beside her, scrambling wildly for a branch just above her head. She got her hands around it and pulled. Arms grabbed her by her legs. Ali kicked out, lost her grip and fell backwards, her weight too much for her assailant who collapsed under her. Ali jabbed down with one elbow and rolled to the side.

'Stop it! It's me, Ali, it's me!'

'Peter?' Ali sprang to her feet, ready to fight, adrenaline pumping through every muscle.

'Yes,' Peter whispered. He crawled to a patch of moonlight so Ali could see his face. 'No talking, okay?'

'Okay.' Ali reached out and helped pull him to his feet, then threw her arms around him, relief flooding through her. 'I'm back,' she whispered. 'I'm really back.'

'Can't believe it,' Peter whispered, returning the hug. He took her hand and led her back down the path. He stopped and pointed to a tree growing four feet from the wall.

'There's a pipe behind that tree,' he whispered. 'It goes through the wall. Your uncle put it in years ago, for badgers. I can crawl through so you should be okay. Good to go?'

Ali nodded and followed him into the pipe. Bushes covered the exit on the far side. No one was about. Peter handed her a dark blue hoodie.

'Put this on, hood up. Your face is everywhere, missing person.'

Ali shrugged into the hoodie, which smelt of sweat and Peter. He held out his hand, Ali took it, and they set off for the village. He squeezed her hand and kept holding it. A young couple having an evening stroll. The road ran around the property, they crossed to the opposite side. Ali glanced back over her shoulder. No one was following.

'Nice trousers,' said Peter. 'Real leather?'

'Yes, someone's riding breeches. How long have I been gone?'

'Five weeks, give or take.'

'How did you know I was back?'

'I was watching a video feed from the barn. My cousin and I hired the barn off your folks. We set the cameras up.'

'Why?'

'For gaming. Just a legit way to have a lot of young people in the place so we could keep an eye out for you, day and night and make the house safer for the Greys. Turns out King owns the bank that swindled your uncle. She took over the manor house. We got kicked out , but her Suits wanted the camera system, so we sold it to them, but my cousin hacked it first and set up a feed so we can monitor the barn.'

'Tell me everything.'

'Me, tell you! Ali, you've been to another universe. Another universe! You're like an astronaut. Seen things I can't even imagine – and I have to go first?'

'Yes.'

'You're unbelievable.' Peter shook his head and laughed. They reached the main road. The village was to their right, it was only a short walk away but there was the occasional passing car. Ali looked up and down the road.

'The Suits will be out looking by now.'

'Sure to be. But they won't be looking for a couple, so we keep holding hands. If we split up, we meet behind the pub.'

'Right. Now tell me.'

'Okay, just the headlines. My cousin who set up all the cameras is Jeremy. He's a cop on Dovecot's team.'

'Dovecot. I liked her. Oh, heads down!' An elderly couple had just stepped out of their front drive with a dog on a lead. Ali dropped her head, but the couple were locked in a heated discussion and didn't pay them any attention as they walked by.

'So, tell me about Jeremy.'

'He's got a theory for why your dad went missing – that he was scamming the government for grant money, got busted, and did a runner.'

'Scamming the government? Your cousin is an idiot.'

'You said he looked cute.'

'That was him?' Ali laughed, remembering the look of complete shock on Jeremy's face when she appeared last time. 'He went white – nearly pissed his pants, I reckon!'

'Yes, he told me. Not an idiot, though. He's smart. He reckons your dad was getting the grant to build a wormhole between here and London.'

'Like I said. An idiot.'

'Kidding me, right? The girl who's stepping through a portal into another world is getting all sniffy about creating wormholes? Jeremy knows your dad's a big deal in physics. He thinks the research is going badly, so to stop the grants being axed, your dad set up a hoax in the barn with a trapdoor and fancy lighting.'

'A trick to buy time with the investors? Is Dovecot buying it?'

'No. She thinks there's another government in the mix.' He paused. Two cars came out a side road and turned towards them.

'Kiss me.' Ali reached up and pulled Peter's face down to hers. When the twin sets of headlights washed over them, she pressed her lips onto his. She felt his arms wrapping around her, and suddenly she felt trapped. Vulnerable.

'They're gone!' She pushed Peter away, took his elbow and started walking quickly. 'Okay, that was kind of weird.'

'Worked for me!''

'So, what does Jeremy think of the two critters coming through? Can't pass those off as a magic trick to impress the grant people.'

'He hasn't seen it. He was in London with Dovecot and your uncle, looking for your dad. He's on his way back, going to meet him soon.'

'And Aunt Martha?'

'Taking you to her now. She's at the pub. It's where I've been hiding out. So now it's your turn. Tell me everything that's happened to you.'

Ali did. She took his hand again and they walked in step, a regular young couple out on a date. By the time they reached the village the moon was sitting high above the ruined church and rain clouds were building out to the west.

'That's everything,' Ali said at last. Peter had stayed silent the whole time, just listening, no questions, giving his full attention. When she'd finished, he shook his head.

'That's so completely fucked up.' It was all could think to say.

The Traveller's Rest was an old pub, even by English standards. A two-storey building, it stood opposite the ruined church where it had served as a rest stop and watering hole for centuries. The young couple approached from the back, where old stable yards and a blacksmith's forge had been turned into beer gardens. There were no customers outside. The converted forge had three walls and a slate roof. Set into the back wall was a large barn door on runners. Peter hauled it open and led Ali into a storeroom full of dust and junk.

'Watch out for the glass,' Peter warned, pointing at the floor. Broken beer bottles lay strewn about between empty beer crates and stacks of white plastic chairs. Over at the far end there was an open hatch with a chute.

'Looks like a kid's slide,' said Ali.

'Kind of,' Peter climbed into it. 'And we're the kids. This is how they delivered beer barrels back in the day.' He launched himself down the chute. Ali followed. The wood was smooth as glass, polished by years of use. She slammed into Peter at the bottom, knocking him off the end of the chute.

'Thanks.'

'Too slow.' Ali looked around. The cellar was enormous, music was coming from speakers in the bar above. Peter crossed to a stack of beer crates – an entire wall of them, three crates thick. There was a concealed entrance where two rows of crates overlapped. It opened onto a small room holding a round table and chairs.

'The owner's little secret.' Peter dropped down into one of the chairs.

'Let me guess. The pub doesn't have a gambling licence.'

'Yep. Your uncle used to come here. Look at this.' There was a shoe box on the table. Peter overturned it and hundreds of old coins tumbled out. 'They use these: pennies, sixpences, farthings. When the police came busting in, all they'd find were these.' Peter grinned and spun one of the pennies on its edge. 'Your uncle's idea. He's been thick as thieves with the owner for years, it's their own after-hours drinking and poker club.'

'Uncle Bertie called in a favour? A place to hang out in secret?' Ali closed her eyes and rubbed them. Then burst into tears. Peter sat quietly, waiting, not saying anything.

'I brought all this on them,' said Ali. 'They've lost their house. Everything.'

'That's not how they see it. They're pissed off at themselves for not protecting you from that King woman.' Peter slapped the table and stood up. 'What do you want? Food or a hug?'

'Food. Do they do fish and chips?'

'Pretty sure.'

'Good, ... and leave me your phone. I need to check some history.'

'About what?'

'The Tower of London.'

Peter took his phone out, thumbed in his PIN and gave it to Ali. 'Heaps of data left, so go for it.' Ali watched him slip out through the wall of crates, then she sat back and started digging.

It was all here, everything she needed to know about the Tower of London, the official history anyway, and details of the prisoners jailed and executed inside its four walls. Then she saw an image of the central keep around which the Tower of London had been constructed. The keep was the first building to inhabit the site, erected centuries before the impressive outer walls and moat. It was modest by comparison: a square, five-storey keep sitting at the very centre of the site. It had been altered over the years, its walls pitted by centuries of weather, and yet Ali recognised it immediately. It was the palace she had just left behind on the other side. Identical in every way. How was such a thing possible?

She kept reading, scrolling down though the early history of the site, trying to separate fact from folk law. The story of the tower was steeped in legend, and those early builders had a clear purpose in mind. It was right here, in black and white.

Ali slumped back in her chair and gave in to her tears. She was here, but she wasn't safe. None of them were. The scale of what she had to do threatened to overwhelm her. She folded her arms on the table, closed her eyes and buried her face. Of all the images that rose up to haunt her, it was the picture of the rat and the hedgehog huddling together in misery that pierced her heart in a way she couldn't understand. Why that? Why them? Her tears turned to heaving sobs, and she felt as if she would cry forever.

Then the wall of crates began to rattle. Ali jumped up, wiped her eyes and peered through a gap. On the far side of the cellar a lift was coming down. Little more than a platform with chains and pulleys, it had no door and looked as old as the pub itself, an elevator for hauling stock up to the bar. Ali stayed hidden, then ran out when she saw the wheelchair.

'Aunt Martha!' she raced over, dropped onto her knees and wrapped her arms around Lady Grey.

'Careful dear. Old bones.' Her aunt beamed up at her, eyes as bright as a child's in their nests of wrinkled skin. Tears welled up, which set Ali off again, the two women weeping quietly as Ali pushed her aunt through to the gambling den.

'Your uncle is in London, with that lovely police inspector.'

'Dovecot?'

'Yes.'

'What have they found? Any word on Dad?'

'Not yet, dear. And all that matters right now is that you're back. Bertie and I can sleep properly tonight. It's been quite the ordeal.'

'And all my fault. I'm sorry.'

'Yours?' Lady Grey shook her head vigorously. 'No, dear child, you drop that burden this minute. A great many people are at fault in this, myself included. You are a victim of our foolishness. None of this can be laid at your door.' She patted the table as if calling the room to order. 'Enough of that. Tell me everything, and you can start with where you got your very fetching outfit. You look like old pictures of the royal children, Elizabeth and Margaret, when they went riding as teenagers.'

'Yes, fit for a queen. Funny that.'

Ali started from the beginning – her arrival in the bluebell forest with Waxstaff and the cost of her survival. Transformation.

'The dear woman survived. Thank goodness.'

'Because she chose transformation. If you're hurt, the body heals itself and decides what you heal into. If the transformation goes badly, they chop your head off to end your suffering.'

'How unthinkably brutal,' Martha closed her eyes. 'I thought this world was wretched enough.'

'It's not all bad over there. Some of it is so beautiful you want to just stop and stare at it forever. And the White Rabbit is ridiculously cute.'

'There really is a White Rabbit? Does he have a name?'

'Yes, it's … ' Ali frowned. 'His name is …'

'Never mind,' said Aunt Martha. 'It's not important. Tell me the rest.'

'Shit!' Ali jumped up. 'I didn't think it would happen this fast.'

'What? What is it?'

'The forgetting. Everyone starts to forget, so they keep notes, memory joggers. They read through them every day.'

'Oh yes,' Aunt Martha shook her head. 'Silly of me. Of course you forget, that's why I made my paintings of the bluebell woods, to remember my little visits. It would all become a fog very quickly when I came back.'

'I know!' Ali clicked her fingers. 'I told Peter everything as we walked here. He can be my diary.'

'My ears are burning.' Peter stepped through the wall of crates with a tray piled high with food. 'Fish and chips for two – your aunt has eaten.'

'What was the rabbit's name?' asked Ali.

'Theodore. Why?'

'Just making sure you were paying attention. Tell my aunt everything I told you, while I eat my way through this lot.'

'That's for both of us.'

'I'll leave you some. Talk.' Peter did, stealing a chip every now and then and dunking it in ketchup. Ali ate and listened carefully, waving him on whenever he paused to reach for a chip. Her memories returned, like a jigsaw puzzle where key pieces had been missing. Everything came back ... everything except for one critical piece she'd kept from Peter – the secret to safe passage. That she could remember easily enough. She had taken to reciting the lullaby the Duchess sang in the first book. As a memory jogger it worked almost too well, playing in her head like an ear worm.

Speak roughly to your little boy,
And beat him when he sneezes:
He only does it to annoy,
Because he knows it teases.

Ali pushed the tray to Peter, there was a piece of fish left and six chips.

'What do we do now?' asked Peter. 'Apart from getting some more food because Ali ate most of mine.'

'We all go to London,' said Martha. 'We get as far away from the house and King as possible, and we find your father.'

'Yes, London,' said Peter. 'Once we've smashed the mirror.'

'What?' Ali stared at him. 'No, why would we do that?'

'Why?' Peter shook his head. 'You're back. You're safe. We've been keeping our heads down, staying close by and watching the barn. Protecting the mirror as best we can, waiting and praying you'd come back. Now here you are. I think we do a midnight ninja mission. We smash the mirror and torch the barn. King will have no use for the house if we destroy the gateway.'

Ali could sense her aunt watching her closely. Watching for what? Signs of an addiction to the place? Peter leaned forward, clearly confused.

'What am I missing here? Is it your dad? King was only using him to get to you. If you smash the mirror—'

'Yes, I hear you!' Ali interrupted him, nodding as if she was running through the idea in her head and approving it. 'But smashing the mirror won't end it.'

'Explain.' Aunt Martha's eyes remained fixed on Ali.

'The mirror is an aid,' Ali explained. 'That spot in the barn seems to be a transition point. The membrane between the two worlds is weak there because the two realities are almost in phase. That glass in the mirror comes from the other side. And there are glass crystals hanging in a tree over there that come from our side. Light gets refracted back and forth and the frequency entrainment makes the phasing even stronger. King just has to find another piece of glass from the other side. What she wants is the secret to getting back safely – the secret Alice took pains to hide from her.'

'You're saying King won't stop?' Martha closed her eyes.

'After hundreds of years? No, this is merely a tiny setback for her.'

'Then we do nothing?' Aunt Martha still had her eyes closed, as if all this was exhausting her. 'Is that your suggestion, dear? We let that dreadful woman do as she pleases?'

'No. We have to assume she's seen the video of me coming back safely, so she knows I have the secret. She's going to hunt me down. None of us are safe.'

'Then what can we do?' Peter spread his arms.

'I don't know,' said Ali.

'Yes you do, dear,' Aunt Martha opened her eyes again and looked squarely at Ali. 'You are completely transparent. You are planning to kill her.'

'Not exactly, no.'

'Yes, very exactly. You can be very cold and calculating, young lady. That is a strength and a weakness. What good is any of this if, in the process, you dig an ever deeper bunker to hide in. There was a wall around your heart from the loss of your mother. I've watched you with admiration these last weeks. The way you have acknowledged it. The fearless love that has put you in this dreadful position. But ... murder, my dear? Cold-blooded, calculated murder? There will be no recovery from that. Your soul will be haunted forever.'

'I know, Auntie.' Ali found the warmth of Martha's love and concern almost unbearable. And she was right. She couldn't escape the image of the hedgehog and the rat huddled together, going through the unbearable torment of returning home, deformed and mutated and lost. She did that to them. She used them.

'You want to send King over there,' said Peter. 'That's your plan, isn't it? Without the secret to coming back, she'll be trapped there.'

'Something like that.' Ali wanted to hug him. 'She'll be no match for some of the people over there. She will be one more tragic soul trapped in their world.'

'That's not a plan at all,' Aunt Martha rolled her eyes. 'It has more holes than Swiss cheese. This organisation isn't just the King woman, is it? You have to pull the whole thing out by the roots. For that you need the support of the police and other agencies. Bertie and that superintendent are working their connections in London. Which is where we go. Right now!'

'Okay.' Peter held up his hands in surrender. 'One tiny problem. We have zero evidence for any of this. We will sound like idiots or dopeheads.'

'We need to find my dad. I think he knows about this, it's why King has taken him. His whole life he's had this obsession with gravity fluctuations and the multiverse. I never asked him why. Maybe Mum told him about her trip over there with Jackie; maybe she told him about it when they were students.'

'Not sure ...' Peter shrugged as if apologising. 'Sounds like wishful thinking.'

'I don't think it is. Look, Dad never let me read the Wonderland books, he even changed the subject if it came up on TV or when my friends wanted me to go to one of the films.'

'Okay. Your dad, your memories.'

'Ali dear,' said Martha, 'please heed what Peter is saying. You are pulling facts into a line to prove something because you want to justify your actions. Just as a drug addict would do.'

'What?'

'Don't play the indignant card, young lady. Listen, and be very honest as you do so. I cannot fault the logic of anything you said. I do, however, question its integrity. If you are half the scientist I think you are, then you must acknowledge the risk of unintentional bias in this grand thought experiment of yours.'

'Go on.'

'The unintentional bias is your subconscious desire to go back there, so I call it for what it is. An addiction. Now before you blow a fuse – your usual trick for avoidance – I ask you to look dispassionately at what I'm saying. Your assessment of what needs to be done might well be correct, but as we debate our next move, I ask you to please bring that critical thinking of yours to bear on the possibility of unintentional bias. Can you do that please?'

Peter let out a deep breath and was about to say something, but Lady Grey slapped a hand down on the card table, her eyes still locked on Ali. 'Quiet, Peter, not a peep. Well, Ali?' Ali said nothing; she just walked round the table, bent down and put her arms round her aunt.

'What would I do without you, Aunt Martha?' The woman was right. Ali felt no anger, no irritation. Once again, her aunt had nailed her to the wall. 'There has to be some bias in it, but I don't think it comes from addiction ... not exactly. Unless that's what happens to explorers. It's definitely intoxicating, seeing such different and exotic things. I think you said it once, Auntie, when you talked about your trips there as a child – how the place casts a spell on you. Well, it has definitely cast a spell on me too. But something else has happened to me over there. It's a bit uncomfortable, but it's happening.'

'Go on.'

'I've started to care about them. To worry about them.'

'Good. And you should. It is about time you let your shield down. But there is a cost. I care about all the dreadful suffering in every country of our own world. All the floods and famine and starvation. We all do what we can, and it is never enough, it never ends. But at the same time, we cannot turn away, can we?'

'No. And I want to make a difference. I want to bring them home.'

'How?' Peter reached up and combed his fingers through his hair. It was a gesture Ali had come to recognise, a sign that he was getting restless or irritated.

'I don't know yet.'

'But you feel compelled to try?' said Martha.

'Yes.'

'Good. Now look at me and look at me hard. Your mother felt compelled to help children all around the world who were suffering. She believed in it so much that she went to some ridiculously dangerous places and it got her killed.'

'Please don't—'

'No. This matters, child, so be brave and listen. The true cost to her, the sacrifice she made, was not losing *her* life, it was losing you. You stopped caring that day. You stopped loving. You have never forgiven her for leaving you because you didn't understand. You were a child, so how could you? But now you do. Forgive her now right now, Ali, because now you understand just how much that dear woman could love.'

'Auntie no, I ... please.' Ali dropped to her knees and put her hands over her head. Peter reached to help her but Lady Grey stopped him.

'No, Peter!'

'Mummy.' Ali toppled onto her side, curled into a ball and pulled her knees to her chest. Her crying became the whimpering of a child, an aching, endless cry of bereavement.

Aunt Martha stayed with her and sent Peter to call the others and to find out the time for the next train to London. A full hour passed before Ali surfaced from her cocoon of pain. She sat up at the table and said nothing for a long time. Her aunt didn't press her, just sat quietly waiting.

'Guess I needed that,' Ali said finally, her voice barely audible.

'Yes, dear. A long time coming. Now we can proceed as a team. Honesty and trust bring clarity, and clarity brings momentum. You cannot do this on your own. If we are to help those folk, we must gather a great deal of support. This will be a considerable enter-prise. Clearly King's organisation is a very selfish group who wish to own, control and exploit whatever opportunities the other world can provide. You, on the other hand, like your great-aunt Alice, just want to make it possible for those lost souls to return. Yes?'

'Yes.'

'Good. Then this is your mother's legacy, isn't it? To give help to others no matter the risk. Her passion has become your passion. Shall we begin?'

Ali did her best to smile; she felt dizzy from the tsunami of emotions that had swept over her. It was all she could do to stop shaking.

Then Peter arrived. 'I've called the others. We'll meet in London. The next train goes at 11.30.'

'Good,' said Ali. 'Need the loo, where is it?'

'Up the steps, turn left towards the front door,' said Peter. 'Don't go to the bar. Too many people in there. Your face was on the news and—'

'Prime suspect, yes, you told me.'

Ali climbed the steps, each one becoming a mission. She had to stop at the top, suddenly nauseous. What the hell! From climbing a few steps? She rolled down the waistband of her breeches. Her slide down that beer chute had rubbed the scabs from her wound. It was weeping a watery mess of blood and pus.

'Shit!' She needed painkillers and antiseptic. Most pubs carried a first aid kit behind the bar; alcohol and fighting were regular bedfellows. Ali toyed with the idea of going in there and asking for it. Safer to send Peter. She looked down the hallway. It was long and wide, the walls hung with sepia photographs, reminders of the pub's colourful history. Laughter spilled from the bar to her right. To her left was the main door of the pub and the toilets. Ali pulled up her hoodie and set off down the hall. The toilets were off to the side in a small alcove. She was stepping into the alcove just as two Suits came in through the front door. Ali opened the door to the ladies' room and ducked inside.

FRACK! She collapsed on the seat, dripping with sweat, almost passing out. *Not now, not now!* She pulled her hoodie back and bent forward, her head touching her knees till the dizziness passed. Had they recognised her? Peter's hoodie had covered some of her face, but they were out looking for her, so yes, of course they would have joined the dots. How many teenagers would be scurrying around this late at night in a village in the middle of nowhere! *FRACK!*

Ali pulled out the stopwatch. Thirty-seven minutes had passed since she'd stepped through. She cradled her head. *Not now. Not now.*

There was a tap on the door. Then a woman's voice.

'Will you be long in there? I'm bursting out here.' The voice was odd, the accent a poor attempt at a rustic Cornish and didn't fool Ali for a second. It was Nurse Potts.

CHAPTER 21

TICKING CLOCKS

————————

'Nearly done,' said Ali. She climbed on the toilet seat and peered out of a window set high in the wall. The two Suits were standing outside, looking directly up at her. Ali cursed silently, her adrenaline pumping, blood pounding in her ears. She turned and stared at the door. Could she surprise Potts – burst out and knock her aside? No, the door swung inward. What else could she do? One thing, perhaps. Play on the woman's weakness, her foul temper.

'Hurry up, dear,' said Potts. 'I can't hold on forever. Bladder's not what it was.'

'Hardly surprising. Dancing around wearing French doors can't be good for you.'

There was a brief pause, then Potts replied in her normal voice, 'Smart little shit, aren't you? I'm going to make you chew glass for what you did to me.'

'Not today, Potts. You and your little group don't want to draw attention, do you? I'm going to wait here till someone comes and queues up behind you.'

'Think you're so smart …' Potts snorted a short laugh. 'It's going to be fun showing you how little brains count in my business.' Ali saw the door rattle. The nurse was checking the strength of its hinges. 'Time to use my skills to prise a little secret out of you. After that, King said you're mine to play with.'

'Like my two little critter friends who played with your face?' Ali turned the lock back quietly, heard Potts taking a step away from the door. Then she climbed back on the toilet seat just as the door crashed open.

The giant nurse came sprawling through, carried by the force of her charge – a charge designed to meet the resistance of a locked door. Pott's broke her fall by reaching out and grabbing the bowl of the toilet. Ali jumped on her back, and leapt out into the hallway. She pictured Potts getting to her feet, estimating the time it would take her … three seconds? She ran down the hall and into the bar. Customers looked up from their drinks, one man shouting as Ali barged past him, spilling his beer.

'Sorry!' She imagined Potts stumbling out into the hall, the Suits running in through the front door. Another five seconds. A seven second lead, not enough to outrun them when she was feeling so sick!

The door to the garden bar stood open and she raced outside. It crossed her mind to go into the forge again and down the chute. Bad idea. She would be trapped in the cellar.

She raced headlong out into the street. Sick as she was, she might still be able to outrun Potts, but not the two Suits! A car came cruising by on the far side of the road, an old Morris Minor, more rust than metal. The driver saw her and stopped. His window was down. 'Ali?'

She recognised him instantly. The young policeman, Jeremy.

'Open the door,' Ali screamed as she raced across the road. The passenger door swung open and she dived in. The two Suits came racing into the street. Ali slammed her door and Jeremy stamped on the accelerator.

'Alison White.' He grinned across at her. 'Pleased to meet you properly.'

'And I you. Very pleased.' She reached over her shoulder for the seatbelt, dragged it down and clipped it. 'You can't outrun those people in this thing. They have a black sedan, expensive looking.'

'They do, a Daimler. My boss thinks it's government issue.'

'It's not, trust me.'

'And what do they want with you?'

'Information.'

'That all? My boss wants you for two assault charges, one missing person enquiry and the wanton destruction of a heritage building.'

'Not for scamming the government?' Ali slumped down in her seat. The nausea and dizziness were rushing back.

'No,' Jeremy chuckled. 'That was my idea. Dovecot doesn't believe a word of it, but it gives her an excuse to dig a bit higher up the food chain,' he paused. 'My god, you look terrible!'

'I think I'm going to puke.' Ali wound down her window, leaned out and threw up. Jeremy turned into a side road, killed his lights and parked up.

'Ali?' He leaned across and put a hand on her shoulder. Ali said nothing; she was unconscious. The nightmare was familiar. A sunlit beach, a perfect day. Ali was on a blue towel, her parents down at the water's edge smiling back at her. Behind them, the tide was rushing out to meet a growing wall of water. Ali was screaming to warn them, but her parents kept smiling and waving. Then her towel began to sink, the sand filling her mouth.

'Keep still, Alice, you're safe.' A gentle voice, one she recognised. Ali tried to focus, but the world was a chaotic fog of colours.

'Who is it?' Her voice cracked and her mouth felt like dry bread.

'Here, sip this.' She felt a straw between her lips. The water was warm and smelt of fluoride. 'You're in the clinic, Alice. A young constable brought you in.'

'Doctor Cherubic?' Ali felt a surge of relief.

'Yes, you're rather unwell I'm afraid. The constable has gone to the pub to fetch your aunt. Just rest up till they get here.'

'No, I can't stay.' Ali forced herself to sit up. Her vision was foggy, but it was coming back. She recognised her surroundings, a small recovery room at the village clinic. She was on a daybed.

'I'm sorry, young lady, you're not well enough to move. Please, lie back.'

'I think I fainted.'

'Passed out, yes.' The doctor's voice was gentle and reassuring, almost apologetic. 'We can talk about it when your aunt—'

'No, now!' Ali tried to shout, but the word came out as soft bark.

'I respectfully suggest we wait until—'

'*Please*,' she begged, looking up, squinting at the light and turning her head till she could see him. 'Please doctor, just tell me.'

'Very well.' The Doctor let out a sigh. 'You have a notifiable disease. Rather a serious one. I've contacted the health authorities and —'

'Notifiable? What, like a bird flu? Covid?'

'Rabies, Alice. You have rabies. I've given you an injection, the first of a series that can help fight the spread of the viral particles.'

'Rabies! Shit!' Ali sank back on the bed. That made sense, the bite on her hip! A memory from her childhood surfaced. A neighbour's kid had been feeding a stray fox. It had bitten her. The mother came running round for help. Ali's dad had called the ambulance and the whole scene had played out in Ali's kitchen.

'RIG?' said Ali. 'You've given me Rabies Immune Globulin, right?'

'Yes, I have. How would you know a thing like that?'

'A neighbour was bitten by a fox when I was a kid. Dad turned accidents into science projects, a way to distance me from the trauma. Facts stick to me.'

'Then I don't have to explain how serious this is?'

'No.'

'Very well. So, next steps: I've reported it, as required by law. The Infectious Disease Unit will have questions for you. Mostly about where this happened. They have to locate the animal and put it down. I assume from the size of the bite it was a dog. Was it local?'

'Ha!' Ali tried to not to laugh. 'Not local.'

'Okay, I'll leave the questions to them. Only one thing I need. Permission to access your medical history. I need to see if you had a rabies jab back then.'

'I'll trade you.' Ali closed her eyes. She felt utterly drained.

'For what?'

'A laptop. Twenty minutes on a laptop.'

'No, you need sleep, and besides, the clinic only has one and I need it.'

'Okay, ten minutes.'

'And let you into the clinic's data base and private medical records of other patients? I would be breaching every rule in the book. So, no. Sorry.'

'Your phone then. I need to do some research, you can set me up as a guest account. Then you can access my medical history. That's the deal.'

'Goodness.' The doctor smiled and opened his phone. 'Lady Grey was right. You are as stubborn as her. Show me how to set up a guest account?'

'Okay.' Ali opened his browser and set one up.

'I hope I don't regret this. Ten minutes only, then you get a sedative and more pain relief. Deal?'

'Deal,' Ali agreed. Doctor Cherubic left the room and scrolled to a medical info site that was jargon-free and basic.

Incubation is the time before symptoms appear. It can vary, depending on the number of viral particles involved. Initial symptoms are similar to the flu and include fever, headache and nausea. As the disease progresses, the patient can experience hallucinations, hydrophobia and paralysis. Symptoms vary greatly, but if not caught early and treated correctly, rabies is usually fatal.

Well, this was shit! If caught early? How early? The fight at the river had been a day ago. Was that too long? She kept reading. Doctor Cherubic seemed to be doing everything right, so she typed in 'The Great Exhibition.' Up came an image. She was right, the building was the same as the infirmary. Twin buildings, just like the keep at the centre of the Tower of London. Completely impossible, yet there had to be an explanation.

Ali had no tolerance for any concept not founded in rational science. All her life she had absorbed her parents' responses to soft, lazy thinking. They would roll their eyes and look at each other if anyone started talking nonsense about magic or the power of manifestation. For the most part they would ignore them, knowing rational argument couldn't change the opinion of anyone who chose to believe in a flat earth, creationism, alien abductions or astrology.

These twin buildings didn't arrive on magic carpets, they weren't conjured into existence by a sprinkling of fairy dust. A process made them, and behind that process would be fresh insights for how energy and matter might operate across the multiverse. In science, a problem was always an opportunity for learning.

Ali closed her eyes. Bloody hell. She realised the fever was taking hold, her mind was racing in overdrive. The nausea had gone and she just felt exhausted. Where were Martha and Peter?

She heard Doctor Cherubic come back in. 'The ambulance is on its way, Ali. The main hospital in Cambridge has been alerted and is ready for you.' He had a small tray with a syringe. He put it on the bed, and swabbed her arm. 'They want you to have a sedative. It slows the spread of the viral particles if we slow your metabolism. The hospital will start another round of the Immune Globulin as soon as you arrive.'

'Okay.'

'I've sent through your medical details; I imagine you'll be getting blood at some point.' He paused as he gave Ali the sedative. 'There we are. Speaking of blood, Chief Inspector Dovecot put me under a great deal of pressure to get those blood samples we took when you came in with Lady Grey. I haven't released them of course, and Lady Grey said she couldn't sign on your behalf, it would have to be your father.'

'Nice one, Aunt Martha,' Ali chuckled. 'She wants Dovecot to put more effort into finding him. Very smart.'

'Lady Grey is very intelligent, no doubt about that.'

'Must be where I get it from.' Ali felt the sedative taking effect.

'Well, that's a bit of a mystery. You are definitely related. You share the very same matriarchal markers in your DNA.'

'Well, duh! Of course we do – we're family.'

'No, that's my point, you see. You're not. Your mother was adopted.'

'What?'

'You have no genetic connection to the Greys at all. Absolutely none.'

'Your database must have that wrong.' Ali started to correct him, but sleep was rising up around her like a warm bath, and she gave herself over to it.

She remembered odd moments of the transfer to the hospital; being lifted from the clinic bed onto a gurney; the rattle of its wheels as she was pushed out to the ambulance; the rocking motion as they drove at speed; the rhythmic wash of flashing blue lights across the darkened windows; and finally, familiar hospital smells of disinfectant and flowers as she was settled into the ward. The journey was like a disjointed dream, interwoven with memories of the last few days. Her fight with the giant flies. Taking breakfast with a queen. The face of a large white rabbit. What was his name? Somehow that seemed important.

'Good morning.'

Ali opened her eyes. A cheerful young man in a white uniform was smiling down at her. There were curtains around the bed, but the high ceiling and the room beyond the curtains were bathed in warm sunlight.

'How long?' Ali mumbled. She felt really good, as if she'd slept for hours.

'How long have you been asleep? All night and most of the morning,' said the young man. 'I'm Nurse Fletcher, do you feel up for some visitors?'

'Definitely.' Ali tried pushing herself up as the nurse pulled back the green curtains. *What the fuck?* She couldn't move. Her hands were tied to the side rails of the bed.

'Surprise!' said Potts. The huge woman was standing at the foot of the bed. She was dressed in army fatigues and her face was one huge smile. 'Looks like we get to play together after all.'

'What?!' Peter was sitting in the back of Jeremy's car as he talked to Doctor Cherubic on his phone. Jeremy was driving, Lady Grey was in the passenger seat. 'Change of plan,' said Peter. 'Ali's being transferred to the hospital.'

'Cambridge?' asked Jeremy.

'Yes.' Peter closed his eyes. *What a mess!* Twenty minutes ago, he'd been at the pub, heading up the stairs to check on Ali. He'd heard the shouts from the bar and had raced through in time to see Ali running out into the beer garden with Potts in pursuit. Then Jeremy had called from the clinic and come to get them. Now this!

'How do we keep her safe in a hospital?' asked Peter.

'I called my Super,' said Jeremy. 'She's put in a request for a protection officer to be stationed outside her room.'

'Dovecot can do that?'

'Yes, but only by glamping up Ali's tag from "person of interest" to "key witness in possible homicide".'

'Good, she'll be safer locked up anyway.'

'Maybe. My Super is heading to the hospital by the way.'

'With Bertie?' asked Lady Grey

'Yes.'

'Good.' Peter felt a wave of relief. He didn't know how to help Ali. He was completely out of his depth and the added burden of watching Martha grow more frail with each piece of news was like being squeezed in a massive press. Lord Grey didn't have a handle on any of it either, but the man's fierce and unreserved love for his wife had to be seen to be believed. They had each other. They were stronger for it. Is this what was meant about the power of love, how it conquered all? Was that why he felt so inadequate? These feelings he had for Ali, they had started out as irritation, flipped to fascination, and then ... this. Was this what love felt like, this sick feeling of dread and concern for someone else?

The drive to the hospital seemed to take forever. Peter spent most of it on his phone, reading up on rabies. The more he read, the more anxious he became, and by the time they reached the hospital he was a wreck.

'Drop me at the main entrance,' he directed, unclipping his safety belt as they drove in through the gate. 'I'll find where she's been taken while you park.' He opened the door and jumped out before Jeremy had come to a complete stop. It was close to midnight and the large entrance hall was almost empty. There was one person on duty behind a long, curved reception desk. The woman looked up and smiled as Peter hurried over.

'If it's an emergency, the ER is the next block.'

'No, a transfer, Alice White. She should have arrived by ambulance. She's got rabies, look the police are on their way, but—'

'Alice White ...' The woman didn't look up, she was checking her computer monitor. 'Are you family?'

'No, they're outside parking the car. I'm a friend.'

'Well, take a seat, I'll need to speak to the family first.'

'Okay, but is she here? Just tell me that. Is she safe?' Peter leaned forward across the counter and tried to read the monitor.

'Excuse me! I know this can be distressing, but we have rules for a reason.' The receptionist angled her monitor away from Peter. 'For all I know, you might be the reason the young lady is in here.'

'Are you Peter?' A thickset man came striding down the hall.

'Yes, I'm a friend of …'

'Alice White, yes. Chief Superintendent Dovecot said you were on your way. You have that young constable with you?'

'Outside, parking the car. You're here to guard her, right?'

'Security detail, yes. Unfortunately, she hasn't turned up.'

'What?!'

'The ambulance was dispatched, it collected her from the village clinic, but then it's a no-show. We're checking the other hospitals now.'

Peter raced outside, straight into Jeremy who was getting the same news on his phone from Dovecot. They raced back to the Morris Minor and jumped in. Jeremy put his phone on speaker.

'There's no mix-up!' Peter yelled from the back seat. 'We're going to the house. She's been taken by King.'

'We have no evidence for that.' Dovecot's voice sounded shrill over the phone's small speaker. 'Stay at the hospital till we get there.'

'Not a chance! Jeremy, go now. Drive!'

'Constable Glover, explain to our young friend you can do no such thing without a search warrant. You wait for me. Are we clear?'

'Yes ma'am.' Jeremy turned to Martha. 'Sorry, Lady Grey. We sit tight till they get here.' He switched off his phone. 'Unless of course you ask me to drive you to the house for personal reasons. Did you leave some item behind?'

'Now that you mention it …' Lady Grey reached for her seatbelt.

'Hell yes!' Peter thumped the back of Jeremy's chair. 'Drop me off at the badger pipe. They won't let you in the at gate, but your arrival might get them running around like chickens.'

CHAPTER 22

KING

———————

'King is awake, and wants a little chat.' Potts was sitting on the end of the bed, looking down at Ali's feet. She began counting her toes. 'One, two three ... we will go see her shortly ... four, five six ... bring the chair would you, Fletcher ... seven, eight, nine, ten. Ten pretty pinkies.'

Ali glared at her, but said nothing. Conversation with Potts was pointless, no amount of pleading or debate would make a difference, and trying to appeal to her better nature would be a waste of breath. Potts didn't have one, she was a walking time bomb bent on payback!

'Not so full of yourself now, are you, Little Miss Pretty? But I reckon you'll be squeaking soon enough when these little pinkies come off. Snippety-snip. That's the good thing about toes. So many little nerve endings.' She counted them again, grabbing each toe in turn and pinching it. 'It will be twenty questions. First the nails, then the toes. Snippety-snip. I'm sure we won't need all twenty, you'll be super-chatty after one or two. But I'll keep going till I'm done. Count on that.'

Ignore her. Ali fought to keep calm. Potts was a foot soldier, nothing more.

Talking to King was all that mattered. King would trade anything for the secret to safe passage. Could she take them all though? Make that the deal? Tell them the secret if they all went together.

Fletcher arrived with a wheelchair. Ali didn't try to fight them as they untied her hands, transferred her into the chair and strapped her wrists to the armrests.

She studied the room. It wasn't one of the bedrooms she recognised, but most of the rooms had been mothballed by Lady Grey, the furniture and ornaments protected from time by drapes and bedsheets.

They wheeled her out onto the landing, and Ali got her bearings. They were three rooms down from the room that had been her aunt and uncle's bedroom. Potts carried on baiting her with tales of atrocities she'd performed on prisoners of war, and how they'd always talked in the end.

Ali let it wash over her like small talk on a crowded bus. Other people's business. Nothing to do with her life.

She heard them before she saw them, heard their quiet sobbing. The door to one of the bedrooms was open as Ali was pushed down the landing. She saw the two critters inside, strapped side by side on one bed. They were moaning as they wept, and didn't look her way as she passed.

King was in the master bedroom at the head of the stairs. Why the Greys' room? A sense of loss and despair threatened to overwhelm Ali as Potts wheeled her in. It had been only a few short days ago that she'd been in here talking to Aunt Martha. Yet weeks had gone by on this side, weeks that had rendered the room unrecognisable. The soft Edwardian furniture had been replaced by chrome and plastic medical equipment, computers and display screens.

King was sitting propped up by pillows on the room's one hospital bed. She looked close to death, her skin a waxy yellow. Large transformation boils were growing on her face and neck, bubbles of pus set to burst at the slightest touch, their skin stretched so tight it was translucent. King's glass eyes were gone, the empty sockets packed with medical swabs. Her head was uncovered, her long bat ears twitched slightly, and the hooked elbows of her wings protruded from under the bed sheet like disfigured shoulders.

'Here's your guest,' said Potts. She parked Ali by the top of the bed. 'Your prodigal fucking child returns.' She made no effort to hide her contempt for Ali. King might be her boss, but she was a weakened leader, reliant on the goodwill of her soldiers. Potts went around to the other side of the bed, folded her arms and grinned at Ali. It was a challenge. *Talk to King all you want, girl, but in the end, you'll be my little fly, and I'm going to pull your wings off.*

Ali did her best to look directly at King, pushing down her fear and disgust by dialling up her ability to be objective, to observe everything with the analytical eye of science. She had one chance to save herself from Potts. She had to prove herself valuable to King, and not just for the secret of safe passage, Potts would be able to prise that from her easily enough.

'Aah ...' King let out a long, crackling sigh. 'My thorn.' She rolled her head to the side. One of the medical swabs slipped from her eye socket onto the pillow. Ali stayed silent, her mind churning with a million questions. Then she saw King's glass eyeballs. They were in a drinking glass on a small unit on the far side of the bed. They were looking in different directions; the effect was chilling. Yet this was important. Somehow the eyes were important. Why?

'Look what you did to me, child,' said King. 'All my long years of suffering, all my work and pain and dedication, almost undone by a selfish little girl with no idea of what she's got herself into.' She paused. 'Nothing to say for yourself?'

'Lots,' said Ali. Her chaotic thoughts were suddenly silent. She felt again the strange serenity that had come over her a few times before. It was as if her mind had been a whiteboard covered with scribbled notes, and it had suddenly been wiped clean. A fresh, clear whiteboard open for a new idea. A mind map with a new image at the very centre; one from the first book. A glass key sitting on a glass table.

'Oh. Lots to say for yourself?' King sounded irritated. 'No doubt all of it is vacuous and self-centred. You have no concept of what's at stake, the scale of what I've been building all these years.'

'Tell me.'

'No, child. You squandered your opportunity to join this grand adventure when you rejected my offer at the well. Remember that? You could have been at the centre of this.'

'You lied to me.'

'I did not.' King sounded indignant, almost offended. 'I put a great deal of effort into you. I would have included you.'

'Not that. You said you needed the secret of safe passage so you could go back and finish your transformation and end your suffering.' Ali glanced across at Potts as she said it. 'That was the lie.'

'You think I want to stay like this?' King's irritation was growing. 'Of course, I want to go back and complete it.'

'Then go. You don't need my help. You only need the secret if you want to come back safely. You want to go back and forth as you like, just like my great-aunt Alice.'

'Do I now?'

'Yes. This is all about the two boys. This is about bringing them back here so you can dissect the hell out of those poor little kids. This is about unlocking the big secret and keeping it to yourself.'

King said nothing, rolled her head back and sighed. Ali looked up at Potts. The woman's body language had changed; her self-confidence replaced by a growing interest.

'I am weary of you,' King whispered softly. 'You understand nothing.'

'Is that right? Then tell Potts about your glass eyes. Tell her why you need them. Tell her where their glass came from and how they help you go across into Wonderland anytime you want to.'

Ali watched as Potts reached down and picked up the glass. 'That true?' Potts asked, and she swirled the eyeballs in the water like round ice cubes. 'These are made from glass that came from the other side?'

'They are,' sighed King, 'Now put them down before you drop them.'

'And Little Miss Smarty Pants figured this out?' Potts didn't put the glass down. She continued to swirl the eyeballs round in the water.

The door opened and two Suits came in, the same ones that had followed Ali from the pub. Neither spoke, they just entered the room and took up positions on either side of the door like sentinels. Potts took a deep breath, and put the drinking glass back on the bedside table.

'Very wise,' whispered King. 'A word in private, I think.'

'I meant no disrespect,' growled Potts.

'Well, of course you did. Young Ali here is playing you like a trumpet.' King rolled her head to face the Suits. 'You two – put our guest with the others while Potts and I have a private chat.'

'Of course,' said one. The other walked round behind Ali and wheeled her to the bedroom where the critters were strapped on a bed. The creatures turned their heads and watched as Ali was wheeled in. The Suits parked her wheelchair close to the bed and left.

'You too?' said Mister Spikes. His eyes were damp with tears, his mouth dry and cracked. 'Are they going to cut you up?'

'Like us?' sobbed the rat. 'Little pieces on the wall.' Ali looked at the wall opposite their bed. One of Gutter's small paws was pinned there like a butterfly, opened out, a detailed dissection revealing all the muscles, tendons and bone.

'Who did this? Potts?'

'Yes,' Gutter wheezed through gritted teeth, his eyes staring at the ceiling as if trying to escape the unrelenting pain. 'She did it for hurting her. Says she's going to cut us up piece by piece and all the bits will go up on her wall.'

Ali looked at the rat, one of its front legs ended in a bandaged stump. She rocked her chair, inching it forward to reach the side of the bed.

'You did this,' sobbed the hedgehog. 'You made us attack her.'

'I know.' Ali leant forward, dropping her head to the end of the leather strap that bound one of the hedgehog's wrists to the frame of the bed. It fastened like a belt buckle. Ali got the loop between her teeth and eased it up till the metal pin came free of the hole in the leather.

'That should be loose enough to wriggle your hand out. Then you can undo the other straps.'

'Now?'

'No, when Potts takes me to the barn to torture me. When you see her push me past your door, get loose and come down. I'll take you back through with me. If you want?'

'Wocky or Potts,' the rat whispered. 'Same pain.'

'They have a hospital at the palace. I'll keep you safe from the Wocky.' Ali heard the Suits coming. 'Be brave a little longer.'

The Suits came in and wheeled her back to King's room. King gestured for her to be parked close to the bed. Potts was on the other side, her head bowed.

'Are we clear?' King asked Potts.

'Clear,' said Potts, her face scowling with resentment.

'Then go and walk in the grounds, or dress your wounds, or do whatever it is you do when you get sullen and confused. You're already damaged goods – do your limited best not to diminish your value even further.'

Potts turned and left the room, but not before giving Ali a look of raw, cold hatred. The Two suits remained, silent sentinels framing the door.

'Do they talk?' Ali asked

'Only when required. The tall and very elegant gentleman is Mr Grimshaw, his partner, the attractive brunette, is Miss Drew.'

The two Suits dipped their heads to Ali.

'It has been fascinating to monitor you,' said Drew.

'Yes indeed,' said Grimshaw. 'Quite an adversary.'

'You were at my school, that first day.'

'They were', said King. 'All part of the considerable planning to bring you here and have you find your way through. All wasted, alas.'

'And the note I found from Alice ... that was you, wasn't it?'

'You know all this, child. So – enough! I am in a great deal of discomfort and in no mood to humour you further. Much as I admire your tenacity, it's time for us to say our goodbyes. The only thing I need from you is the secret of safe passage, and you can be sure Potts will extract that from you. The woman is desperate for you to suffer, and she wants to get back into my good books. The only question is how much suffering you wish to endure.'

'I'll trade,' Ali offered, pulling at her restraints. 'My father and Peter. My uncle and aunt. I'll trade for their safety.'

'I need your father anyway, but the others? No. You've told them too much, now they're stumbling around making all sorts of mess for me to clean up. So, no dear, thanks to you they will all be killed. You have nothing to trade, all I need is the secret to coming back safely, and Potts will relish the chance to extract that from you.'

Ali didn't see Grimshaw step up behind her until a silk scarf whipped round in front of her face. Her yelp of surprise was muffled as the Suit pulled the scarf tight across her open mouth.

'Forgive the gag, Miss White,' said Grimshaw. 'Sound travels on a still night like this. We don't want to distress the neighbors as we take you to the barn.'

The gag tightened, biting into the corners of her mouth and pressing her tongue back against her throat. She tried to scream, but the silk rubbed on her tongue and she struggled not to vomit. Grimshaw wheeled her down the landing past the open door of the critter's room. All she could see was Potts' back as the woman bent over the bed. One of the critters was screaming.

'Enough with them,' said Grimshaw. 'Time to work your craft on this one.'

'About time,' snapped Potts. 'I'll grab my bag of toys and be right down.'

Ali felt her whole body starting to shake. She had no control over it. Never in her life had she felt so weak and so vulnerable.

What Potts was doing to those creatures! What she was going to do to her!

Ali wanted so much to be brave. But she knew with absolute certainty that the moment Potts started to work on her, she would tell the woman anything to make it stop.

Grimshaw picked up the wheelchair and carried her down the stairs. The night air was warm and still. An ordinary night. Nothing special. Her last night? The gag was so tight she could only breath through her nose. The air wheezed in her nostrils as she struggled to draw enough in.

'Here we are.' Grimshaw opened the barn door and wheeled her inside. 'Let's get you settled.' He wheeled her over to the mirror in its protective cube of glass.

Potts came in behind them. 'Let the games begin! Grimshaw, you can take that gag off. I need to hear what she's got to say for herself. The noise won't travel far now we're in here.'

Grimshaw released the gag and Ali gasped, pulling in a deep breath, the fresh air washing through her. She took another, soaking it up like a sponge thirsty for water. With it came a brief moment of clarity, an idea born of desperation.

'Good.' Potts stepped up behind Grimshaw and put a massive hand on his shoulder. 'Now be a good puppy and scamper back to King. I can handle this one on my own.'

'And leave you to learn the secret on your lonesome?' Grimshaw chuckled softly and shook his head. 'I think not, Potts. I will stay and hear it for myself. We can't have you making yourself invaluable, can we?'

'Smug little puppy, aren't you, Grimshaw? Well, make yourself useful and hold her steady.' Potts opened her medical bag and took out a large syringe.

'You're going to drug me?' Ali almost felt relieved. She'd heard about such things – truth serums that could make someone give up their secrets.

'Heavens no. I want you wide awake for this. Nothing in the syringe, I use it as a probe to give you a little dental check.' She reached into her bag and took out a small wooden spoon. 'All right Grimshaw, put your arm round her head and tip it back till she's facing up.'

He did, and Potts pressed the handle of her spoon between Ali's teeth, wedging her mouth open. 'Storytime,' said Potts. 'I worked for a small black ops unit when I left the service. Got paid to do the work our government couldn't stomach.'

'*Ngaaa ...*' Ali tried to move her head. Potts leaned down, grinned, and began exploring Ali's gums with the needle of the syringe. Almost immediately she found a nerve. Ali's arched in her chair, her scream a muted gargle.

'There we are. That hit the spot, lots more fun to be had with this. Lots of jabbing around, lots of nerves to choose from.' She wriggled the tip of the needle under one of Ali's front teeth, burrowing and twisting the syringe as she hunted for another nerve.

'*Naaaaa ... stooo . . *' Ali roared with the pain, her eyes pleading for it to stop.

Peter edged towards the barn. Jeremy had dropped him by the badger's tunnel before driving Lady Grey on to the main gate. He had sprinted round the woodland track, his fear for Ali winning out over caution. He had been halfway around, with a clear view of the main house, when he'd seen Ali being wheeled out to the barn. He'd thought about calling Jeremy, but the light from his screen would be seen from the house. He'd hurried on, sprinting as quietly as he could till the track had brought him here, to the back of the barn.

He heard muffled voices coming from inside, and crept to a side window. The glass was streaked with years of dirt, but there were small gaps here and there. He stretched up and peered inside. The shock of what he saw was like a punch to his stomach. For a moment he stood there, transfixed by the horror of it. Then instinct kicked in.

'Oh, ready to share, are we?' Potts patted Ali on the cheek. 'Well, of course you are. But not just yet. This is much too much fun.' She jabbed at a new spot, just as the window behind her shattered and a rock tumbled onto the floor.

'Hold on, Ali. Help coming!'

Peter? Ali's head dropped forward as Grimshaw let go and ran to the barn door. Relief from the pain flooded through her, she gasped for breath and tried to clear her head. *Think. THINK!*

'That your little friend, was it?' Potts laughed. 'Being all macho and heroic, bless his little socks. King's been looking for him and now here he is, serving himself up on a plate. Not to worry, Grimshaw will catch him. No one gets to outrun Grimshaw.'

Ali's mouth was on fire. The prodding had stopped, but every nerve in her gums still echoed from the pain. Her tongue and lips felt thick and distant. She tried to speak, but all that came out was garbled nonsense.

'Ooh, cat lost its tongue?' Potts laughed and slapped Ali on the shoulder. 'Joke, get it? Now then, I can't hold your head still without Grimshaw, but not to worry. Needles are good, but they don't leave you with any mementos, nothing to remember me by. Not like all my bloody scars!'

Potts walked around the chair, stood in front of Ali and rolled up a sleeve. Her arm was a mess of ugly scars, dozens of them.

'My whole body is like that. All that glass you made me wade through! Only fair to give you some of the same memories. Let's pull a few of those pretty teeth, shall we?' She took a pair of pliers from her medical bag and held them up to Ali's face. 'Woodworking pliers, made for pulling nails. A bit rough and clumsy, but good enough for a few teeth.'

The barn door pushed open and Grimshaw came in with Peter slung over his shoulder like a sack. He dropped him to the floor. Ali craned her head round, trying to see Peter's face, but Potts tightened her grip, forced her pliers into Ali's mouth and took hold of a front tooth. Ali heard the tooth twisting round in its bed of gum, then felt a blinding white pain as the tooth gave up and was torn out.

'Oh look!' Potts laughed, holding up her pliers, the tooth dripping blood down its handles. 'No decay, nothing wrong with it. My mistake.' Ali looked up and spat blood in Potts' face. The huge woman paused, grinned, and raised the pliers to strike Ali.

'Enough!' King entered the barn, wheeled in by Drew. She was perched in the antique wheelchair Martha loved so much. The one her husband had bought the day she'd come back from hospital with her broken hip. The sight of the chair deepened Ali's despair. She looked down at Peter. His eyes were closed, but his chest was moving. He was alive.

'Push me over to her,' said King. Drew wheeled her forward, skirting round Peter's body. 'That's enough, Potts, this is bigger than your petty grievances. Alice here got the better of you. Deal with it.' King reached out, gripped Ali's chin and tilted her face up. 'Let's hear it, shall we, and put a stop to all this nonsense.'

'Air pressure,' Ali glared at King, staring her down, unblinking. Blood was filling her mouth and she wanted to spit it at the woman, instead she led it run over her chin as she spoke. 'Pressure in the lungs.'

'Explain.'

'You must take a deep breath and hold it before you come back.' Ali had to pause. It was hard to talk properly, her lips were numb and air whistled through the gap where her front tooth had been torn out. 'I don't understand the chemistry of it yet, I'm sure my dad will. The sickness is like the bends divers get when they come up too quickly. You must fill your lungs with air on the other side before you come back through. Something in that air must buffer your cells against the sudden change of atmosphere, or the mix of gases.'

'And you discovered this how?'

'A drawing,' Ali lied. 'Alice made a series of drawings on the wall of her room in the palace. A balloon, a submarine and a diver.'

'She does love her cryptic riddles, doesn't she?'

'At first, I guessed wrong. I held my breath when I came back through and I was sicker than ever. This last time I took a deep breath. It worked.'

'Well, there we are, all my hard work teasing you into this adventure really has paid off. Very well, we shall conduct a little experiment. You go back through right now and take Grimshaw with you. Clearly you can do that, you took Waxstaff didn't you?'

'Yes.' Ali said. She looked over at Grimshaw. The man was trying to hide it, but he was alight with excitement, like a child being told Christmas was early.

'How is Waxstaff?' asked King. 'Transforming, I imagine.'

'Yes.'

'To be expected, given how broken she was. So, take Grimshaw with you, and come straight back. And I mean immediately, Alice. Or Potts can pull out every last one of Peter's teeth. Understood?'

Ali looked down at Peter. He was very pale, and a bruise was starting to bloom on his forehead. Grimshaw must have knocked him out cold. She looked up at King and nodded.

'Yes,' she said. 'But there's a time difference. A few seconds over there is a lot longer here.'

'I know, dear,' she gestured for Grimshaw to untie Ali. 'My world had passed me by when I came back. It's disconcerting to discover all one's family and friends are in the ground, but surprisingly liberating too.'

Grimshaw pulled Ali to her feet. 'Now what?' he said. Ali could tell he was masking his excitement. 'What do I have to do?'

'You? Nothing,' said Ali. 'You're a passenger, hold my elbow.'

'Just remember, Miss Smarty Pants ...' Potts moved back to stand over Peter. She pointed at him and waved her pliers. 'Come back or I pull out all his teeth!'

Ali didn't reply. She had seen something the others had missed. Their eyes were on her. Not on Peter. He was still lying with his eyes closed, just as he'd be dropped. Except for the thumb of his right hand. It was extended. He was giving her the 'thumbs up' sign. He was conscious.

'Let's do this,' said Grimshaw.

Ali closed her eyes and slowed her breathing. The pain in her mouth and the trauma she'd endured made it hard to relax, but she could feel the pull from the other side already, it was like a hum she could feel but not hear. She pictured the bluebell clearing, and it began to emerge around her. She gave into it, and then, with no resistance at all, she was through.

She looked up at Grimshaw beside her. He was staring around, open-eyed in wonder, like a small child!

'It's real!' he whispered. 'I hoped it might be. Against all reason I dared to hope.' He let go of Ali's elbow, collapsed onto the bluebells and started to weep.

'No!' Ali reached down and gripped one elbow. 'Stand up, we have to go straight back!'

'A moment longer, *please*,' he beseeched her, like a child refusing to leave a birthday party.

'No! Right now,' she pulled him to his feet. 'Pay attention. We have to take a deep breath and hold it in. Like this.' Ali demonstrated, and Grimshaw did the same. 'Now close your eyes.' He did.

Grimshaw never saw Ali letting out her air, emptying her lungs slowly and quietly. But he did feel the full sting of her slap. Ali brought her free hand back and slapped him hard on the face with all the force her anger could deliver. She timed her cough with her slap, timed it so he didn't hear it, and would never hear it when he relived the moment again and again for King as she tried every means at her disposal to wrestle the details from him. He would never be able to reveal that the real secret of safe passage was to empty the lungs and then sneeze or cough to force out every last molecule of air.

The slap gave Grimshaw the adrenaline rush he needed to make it easy for Ali to escort him back. They emerged together, Ali gripping him by the elbow. She released him immediately. Grimshaw gasped, clutched at his stomach and fell to his knees vomiting.

'Peter, NOW!' screamed Ali. He had been ready, playing dead, waiting for her reappearance. Now he jumped to his feet.

'How tiresome,' sighed King. 'Grab him, Potts.' The huge woman tried. She slammed one fist down, aiming for his head, then roared in agony as something buried its teeth in her leg. The two critters had chewed through their bonds, then waited patiently in their room till they'd seen King being wheeled past their door. Then they'd crept to the barn, Gutter walking on his hind legs to spare himself more pain from the stump of his foreleg. They arrived as Grimshaw and Ali had emerged. The rat had reacted on instinct, throwing himself straight at the woman who had laughed while cutting his paw off. He sunk his teeth in her leg and kept them there, clamping his jaw.

Peter raced over to Ali.

'No!' roared King. 'Stop her.'

'To me!' Ali beckoned to the two critters. The hedgehog scampered to her, but the rat didn't hear, he was happy in his work, distracted, chewing his way into the scarred flesh of Pott's thigh. Potts stumbled screaming towards Ali. She almost made it, but tripped over Grimshaw who was writhing on the floor.

Ali threw her arms around Peter, hugging him as the hedgehog reached them. They picked him up, Ali closed her eyes, and immediately felt the bluebell clearing emerging around them. She was amazed at how easy this was becoming. Then she felt Potts' hand round her ankle. Ali stared down at the bluebells. Potts was lying there, the rat fastened to her leg. Ali dropped Mister Spikes, and the hedgehog into one of Potts' hands.

'Run,' Ali grabbed Peter by the wrist, but he was in shock, frozen to the spot, staring round at the silver birch trees.

'Going to rip you in half, girl!' screamed Potts. The woman was getting to her feet, stamping and swatting at the critters to shake them off.

Ali took Peter's face in her hands, drew him close and kissed him hard on the lips. He frowned, registering the kiss, his mind pulling itself together.

'This way!' Ali took his hand and led him to the far side of the tree where she'd hidden the second watch under a fallen branch. She took it out, noted the time difference and read them aloud to Peter.

'Three minutes and forty-five seconds. Four hours and ten seconds. Repeat it now, and remember it.' Peter did, his eyes wide with fear as he watched Potts stumbling and screaming her way towards the tree.

'Now we run,' said Ali. She took his hand, pulling him as she sprinted off. Peter ran, glancing back only once to see Potts losing her battle with the critters. She had fallen again, cursing and screaming, as the creatures overpowered her.

CHAPTER 23

LITTLE WHITE LIES

Jeremy got to his feet. He was still shaking and his legs felt like jelly, but he had to make it back to the car. What the hell had just happened? He stumbled into the trees, keeping to the shadows as best he could. An alarm was going off across the lawn at the manor house, and another further off to his right. The gatehouse?

He found the path again, paused, and leant against a tree as a fresh wave of nausea struck him. Jeremy closed his eyes and took a deep breath. Dovecot was wrong about him, he wasn't cut out for this job. He could handle almost anything a game threw at him. Cocooned in a VR headset with Dolby sound he had the courage of a ninja warrior. But this wasn't a game. What he'd just witnessed hadn't been built in Unreal by a bunch of talented nerds.

He stumbled on, almost passing the tree that concealed the badger pipe. He crawled through and crossed the road to his Morris Minor. Lady Grey was sitting patiently in the passenger seat. She turned to him as he climbed in.

'Is she there? What happened?'

'You wouldn't believe me.'

'On the contrary. Tell me everything – but as we drive. Your superior and Bertie will be at the police station by now.'

'Bad idea.' Jeremy folded his arms across the steering wheel and buried his face in them. 'This is big. No wonder my boss has been getting the run around. Someone high up must be looking out for these people, which means the station could be bugged.' He lifted his head, reached for his phone, and handed it to Lady Grey. 'Call your husband. We'll meet them at the pub.'

'This is all very clandestine!' said Dovecot.

They were packed into the gambling den under the pub: The Greys, Jeremy and Chief Superintendent Dovecot.

'Needs must,' said Lord Grey, 'but it has its perks. Anyone fancy a whisky?'

To his surprise, Dovecot accepted. 'Make it a double!' she said.

'I think you deserve it,' snorted Lord Grey. 'You've been off duty for hours. You've driven half the night listening to my prattle, and now this! Complicit in my illegal gambling cell.'

'Guilty as charged,' said Dovecot, as Lord Grey took glasses and a bottle of Bowmore single malt from one of the wall crates.

'Not for me,' said Martha, 'but one for young Jeremy, I think. After what he's just been through.' Dovecot raised an eyebrow but said nothing. Her constable was a sickly shade of white and had said nothing since arriving at the pub. This disturbed her a great deal more than their location. What had the silly boy gone and done? She looked at the glass being placed in front of her, took a sip, then levelled her gaze at Jeremy.

'So, why here? Why all the theatrics?'

'Because we're in over our head, Ma'am.' Jeremy looked up at Lord Grey, who was standing at his shoulder pouring him a finger of scotch. 'I think Lord and Lady Grey need to open up to us. Tell us the truth. They can't keep covering this shit up! If we don't know the full picture, we can't help them – and if we don't work together on this, I think we're fucked.'

'I agree.' Lord Grey put the bottle on the table, sat down and raised his glass. 'To transparency. It will make life a damned sight easier. I've spun such a castle of white lies I need a damned bibliography to keep up with myself!'

Dovecot looked round the table, trying to read each face. All she could see was stress and exhaustion. 'Very well, but not here. Not tonight. I need to do this by the book, that means recorded interviews tomorrow morning at the station.'

'At least see this first.' Jeremy put his phone on the table.

'See what?'

'Footage of Alice White.'

'Taken when?'

'Tonight, in the barn. From the cameras I rigged up. It's a 24-hour live feed that uploads to my drive in the Cloud. These are short clips I've pulled into my phone.'

He hit play and sat back.

Dovecot watched the footage in silence. She recognised the floor of the barn; the Victorian dresser and mirror stood off to one side. There was a circle of chalk painted on the bare floorboards. Close by was the trapdoor. Closed. Someone was sitting just out of frame, the toes of their polished boots visible in the shadows.

Then ... two puppets, strange animals straight out of some kids' movie, popped into view in the middle of the chalk circle. They stumbled, clutched at their stomachs, then launched themselves at the figure seated just out of shot. There was a lot of shrieking and yelling, then the camera tipped over and scene was framed from a different angle. A different camera.

'Potts?' Dovecot leaned in to the phone, cursing the size of the screen. Bloody hell! It really was the Potts woman. She was acting out a bizarre fight scene with the two animal puppets. The screen went blank.

'What the fuck, Glover? Did you make this with your gaming nerds?'

'No. Real footage, real creatures.'

'I see rubbish like this everyday! The internet is drowning in this crap. Aliens and faeries faked up as CC footage!' She pushed the phone back across the table and got up. 'Enough! I'm too tired to be angry right now. Tomorrow! My office!'

'One more, please. I saw this tonight – just the last bit anyway – through the barn window.'

'No! No fucking way!' Dovecot realised she was shouting. She grabbed her scotch, tipped it back in one gulp, and slammed the glass back on the table.

'Please Ma'am, you have to.' His hands were shaking as he took back his phone and scrolled to the next clip. 'They tortured Alice White, Ma'am.'

'What?!'

'Please…' He pushed the phone back. Dovecot stared at him. He was crying. Her bloody constable was crying! She looked at Lord and Lady Grey. They said nothing but their eyes spoke volumes. Apart from exhaustion, all she could see there was compassion, a depth of selfless compassion that was unnerving.

She sat down, took the phone and tapped the screen. She watched the whole thing in silence. Alice White being tortured by Potts. The blind woman dressed in a bizarre Halloween costume screaming instructions at everyone. Peter being dragged unconscious into the barn. And then those same two animal creatures again, coming to the aid of the Alice girl.

Dovecot put the phone down and closed her eyes. When she opened them again, she glared at Jeremy. The young man dropped his gaze, he'd never seen her look so angry, the corners of her eyes so pinched with rage.

'I should have gone in …' Jeremy's voice was a whisper, and he began to sob quietly, his thin chest heaving. 'I was at the window. I was so … scared, Ma'am.' Dovecot got to her feet, walked around the table and stood behind him. Then she cradled his head like a mother comforting a child.

'Pour them another drink, Bertie,' said Lady Grey. 'One for all of us, I think. We have a lot to discuss and a great deal of planning to do.'

Ali and Peter slowed to a walk as they reached the towering alley of thorns. Potts' screams had receded behind them and there was no need to run. Ali had come back a lot sooner than intended. She needed to time her arrival to the minute with Theodore, or risk being stuck in the burrow waiting for him to topple the birdbath.

Any more running would have been difficult anyway; they were in shock and a great deal of pain. Ali could see Peter was working hard to conceal his, but the bruise on his forehead spoke for itself, it had become a deep purple, the tissue swollen and tight with fluid.

Ali knew enough about head injuries to be worried, but not enough to know what to do.

Her own pain had become manageable. The nerves Potts had disturbed were beginning to settle down. The hole in her gum was throbbing with pain but the bleeding had stopped. Plugging the gap with the tip of her tongue kept the air from it and seemed to help a little.

'I have a thousand questions,' said Peter.

'Only a thousand?' Ali regretted her glib reply the moment she said it. Peter deserved better. 'Sorry, trying to keep it light. This is a bit overwhelming, isn't it?'

'Just a bit, yeah. And everything is so bright, so intense. I can almost taste the colours, or is that my concussion talking?'

'It might be. We need to get you checked when we get there. But all your senses will get swamped over here. Wait till you taste the food!'

'Cool ... what about touch?' He grinned at her. 'Is that, like, electric and tingly?'

'I've only touched a rabbit. So, no. Soft and furry doesn't tingle.'

'Just wondering,' he said.

'I haven't thanked you, have I?'

'That kiss was a good start.'

'I mean it, Peter.' She stopped, turned to face him and held out her hands. 'Hold my hands. Let's see if touch is special here too.'

'Okay.' He laughed again, but stopped and took her hands.

'This is interesting,' said Ali. 'I have to admit it's more electric than stroking a rabbit between the ears.'

'Good to know.'

'You? What do you feel? Electric tingles? Goosebumps, or just the scratches and sweat I've been collecting?'

'Can I close my eyes? Hard to concentrate.' He closed them without waiting for a reply. Ali closed hers too. She listened to his fingertips as he explored the skin of her hands and wrists. *Listened* ... that's what it felt like. How odd, as if she was listening intently with her skin.

'You waited for me all this time. Did your best to look after my folks. Did your best to keep the barn safe so I could make it back. You didn't have to do any of that. And now I've dragged you through here.'

'Didn't have a lot of options, did you?'

'No. But thank you. For all of it.' She opened her eyes. 'And I think we should stop touching now, it's a bit overwhelming.'

'But good, yes?'

'Yes. And I think I would kiss you again properly, except my lip hurts like shit and I don't think my mouth looks very attractive.' She gave him a huge grinning smile, her lips pulled back, her teeth extended.

'Kind of cute in a little-kid-losing-her-first-baby-tooth sort of way.' He leaned forward and lightly kissed her lower lip. 'We can make do with that for now.'

'For now? That's loaded with promises. Come on.' She let go of his hands and they carried on. 'Ask all the questions you want – you must be prepped for meeting the Queen, she's going to interrogate you.'

'Nice. In a Mistress Bondage kind of a way? Is she good-looking?'

'Very. Like a siren looks good to a sailor as she pulls him to the rocks.'

'Siren? That's a mermaid, right?'

'Kind of. Now, before I answer everything, you need to repeat back to me all the things I told you when we were walking to the pub last night.'

'Because of this thing about forgetting?'

'Yes, from now on we will be each other's journals. Every evening, we must recount the day to each other, and key memories of our lives back in our world. Writing everything down is okay, but people can find notes. This is safer.'

'Okay.' Peter took a deep breath, and tried his best to recount everything Ali had told him. By the time they reached the area of burnt trees by the palace wall Ali had done her best to answer all his questions and prepare him for what was to come. He looked up at the palace wall.

'So, you go back through the burrow. I go to the gate and just wander in?'

'Exactly. They welcome everyone. You tell them everything, the whole truth, except this last bit about me going back there. Say you came through looking for me. If the Queen knows I went back I'll lose all trust. We can't afford that.'

'Okay.' Peter hesitated. 'You'll have to act really pleased to see me.'

'It won't be an act.'

'I mean *really* pleased. You have to throw your arms round me.'

'No problem, now go.'

'Be convincing – smother me with like, a billion kisses, and refuse to let go of me and demand that we get to share our own room in the palace.'

'*Go!* That way.' She pushed him in the small of his back. 'If the guards on the wall see you, just wave and keep going round to the gate. Now help me up into this tree stump, the burrow starts in here.'

They were all exhausted. Only Jeremy had been able to sleep. He had folded his arms on the table, used them for a pillow, and within minutes his sobbing had turned to the muffled snoring of a distant chainsaw.

Dovecot sat and listened in silence as the Greys gave animated accounts of everything that had happened. When she heard people moving about above, and the welcome growl of a coffee machine grinding beans, she excused herself, went up to the public bar and sat alone over two cups of coffee and a bacon sandwich. She couldn't make sense of the footage, or the bizarre story Lord and Lady Grey had spun for her. Dovecot had interviewed enough witnesses over the years to be certain of one thing: the old couple believed every word of their explanation. But her constable? Why on earth would he go along with it? Had he made those videos with his tech friends? Was that why he'd broken into tears? Was it professional guilt at letting himself down?

Dovecot pulled out her phone, began searching, and discovered that there was such a thing as a shared psychotic disorder, a condition in which people in a relationship can share a delusion. Then she came upon 'folie à deux' – a syndrome where delusions are transmitted from a single person to a whole group. Young Ali perhaps?

She stopped searching. All this was all helpful, but it didn't give her any comfort for one very unsettling reason. If she embraced the possibility that this crazy story was true, then all the pieces of the jigsaw puzzle slipped seamlessly into place.

'Ah, bacon!' Lord Grey came into the bar pushing his wife in her chair. Jeremy appeared in their wake.

'You look terrible! All of you.' Dovecot got up and joined them at a larger table. Lord Grey parked his wife and went over to the breakfast buffet with Jeremy.

'You must come with us to the manor,' said Martha. 'You need to see Mrs King for yourself. Without her headscarf.'

'Not possible. I applied for a search warrant two days ago. I ticked all the boxes, I have reasonable grounds. But no. Someone high up the food chain is still blocking every step of this investigation.'

'Well, as it happens, we don't need one. Your Jeremy has found a way to get us inside, all above board.'

'Oh dear.' Dovecot closed her eyes and let out a long sigh. 'What's he done?'

'Nothing outrageous. Quite the contrary, something so mundane it won't have registered with your top brass. It concerns that dreadful new gatehouse. It was thrown up in a matter of weeks. Bertie couldn't see how they could have secured planning consent. Our home is a listed building with national heritage status.'

'So, Jeremy did some digging?'

'Yes. He has a young lady friend there, in county records. It appears that the building inspectors have been turned away three times.'

'Interesting. They can apply for a police escort.'

'Which they have. Jeremy helped them.' Martha looked up as Jeremy and Lord Grey arrived with trays of toast and cereal. 'No bacon and eggs?'

'Next course,' her husband kissed her lightly on the top of her head. 'Big day ahead of us. Need to fuel up.'

Two hours later, they were on their way. Dovecot and Jeremy used the police squad car, the Greys took their Bentley, and, sandwiched in between them was a council van with two building inspectors. The gates were closed when they pulled up, and no one came out from the gatehouse despite Lord Grey pounding on the Bentley's horn.

Jeremy stepped out and tested the gates. They creaked open a little. He turned and shrugged to the others. 'Not locked.' He squeezed through and went over to the gatehouse. Dovecot opened her door and yelled at him.

'Well done, you are now trespassing. Congratulations.'

'It's deserted,' said Jeremy, and he stepped into the gatehouse. Hidden motors engaged and the wrought iron gates swung open. Dovecot hesitated. The urge to drive in was incredible, but years of professional experience told her to stay out. One small error of process and any case she might build against King would be thrown out.

'Coming through!' Lord Grey held no such qualms. He drove his Bentley past the council van and pulled up beside the squad car. His wife wound down her passenger seat window and called across to Dovecot.

'Not to tell you your job, Chief Superintendent, but if keeping the peace and preventing acts of violence are part of your remit, you might want to follow Bertie and prevent an escalation of all this.' She turned to her husband. 'Foot down, my dear. Foot down.' He did, peppering the police vehicle with gravel.

'Get in!' Dovecot yelled as Jeremy emerged from the gatehouse. He jumped in beside her and started to mumble an apology. 'Not now!' Dovecot shut him down. They followed the Bentley up the long drive, and pulled up at the manor steps just as Bertie was climbing out.

'They've bunked it!' he growled. 'No sign of anyone!'

'Good!' Dovecot scrambled out. 'Constable Glover, check the barn. Touch nothing, understood?' Jeremy nodded and raced off across the lawn. Dovecot looked up at the house. There were no faces in any of the windows. What the hell was going on here?

'Here comes trouble,' said Lord Grey. Dovecot turned and looked back down the drive. A black sedan was approaching at speed. Lord Grey snorted, marched up the steps and opened the front door. Dovecot hurried after him.

'Listen up.' Lord Grey strode off down the hall. 'Search the damned house on the pretext of trying to find me. I shall set up camp in the pantry!' Dovecot didn't waste time arguing. She had two minutes at the most before her superiors pulled up outside. How the hell had they got here so fast. Had King called them? Were they cleaners? A cover-up team? She hit the stairs at a run, bounding up them two treads at a time. She raced from room to room. It was like a bloody hospital; high-tech equipment everywhere.

'What the hell?' Something caught her eye in one of the bedrooms. It was pinned to the wall. The severed paw of some small animal. Shouting broke out downstairs. The voice of her Chief Constable calling out to her.

'Up here!' she yelled back. She looked at the medical cart for something clean to bag the specimen in, pulled open a pack of disposable medical gloves, dropped the paw into one glove, tucked it in her pocket and strode from the room.

'What happened?' Theodore stared at Ali's mouth. 'How do we explain that? We are supposed to be having a quiet picnic while I help you do your research in these!' He waved the Wonderland books at her. 'Did we have a robust debate over one of her riddles?'

'No, I'll say I pulled my tooth out. All part of an experiment. Take me to the infirmary, I'll talk to one of the medical scholars there, explain it all to him. He'll confirm it to the Queen when she starts digging.'

'Which she will! Any more surprises I need to know about?'

'Just one. His name's Peter.' She did her best to explain what had happened, how Peter coming over was an accident of circumstance.

Theodore didn't bother to respond. He packed up their picnic and let his grumpy silence do the talking. They were halfway to the glass house before he spoke. 'I apologise. My silence isn't irritation. Well, it is in part, I confess. But you behave exactly like your great-aunt Alice. You are reckless, and I fear for you as I fear for her. You placed yourself at enormous risk and look what happened. Three critters attacked you and this dreadful Potts woman started pulling your teeth out! My disposition is not well suited to dealing with such distress.'

'I'm trying my best, Theodore. What else can I say?'

'Nothing. So, setting all these dramas aside, did you achieve your goals?'

'I did. The time speed ratio is sixty to one, or close enough. I spent four hours and ten seconds over there while only three minutes and forty-five seconds passed over here. Which means the precise ration is actually 66.6 to 1, which is a bit spooky because the number 666 carries all kind of symbolic baggage with it.'

'Should that concern us?'

'No. Numbers are just numbers. There's nothing supernatural about them. If you see a black cat with the number 13 written on its back, just find the nearest nut-job with a spray can and report him to animal welfare.'

'There you go again, more of your gobbledygook! Don't speak that way when you present your evidence on the boys to the scholars. And as to that – did you find the confirmation you needed for their true histories?'

'I did.'

'Oh, my whiskers! And what of the biggest secret of all? You are well, apart from the tooth, so can I presume you know the secret to safe passage?'

'I do. Keep that to yourself for now. We can sit down with the Queen and the Hatter and figure that one out together.'

They arrived at the infirmary. Theodore went to find a scholar and Ali hurried to see Waxstaff. Her transformation was well underway, and there was no doubt about the form she was taking. Waxstaff was becoming some kind of lizard, one with a row of spikes along the crest of its skull. Ricky and Ted were with her, curled up at the foot of the bed. All three were fast asleep.

Ali backed away. Waking them served no good purpose. She went to look for Theodore and found him leaving a small side room. He was carrying long-handled medical pliers and he was shaking his head.

'There's no understanding some people,' he said. 'I told the head apothecary in there that you intended pulling a tooth to see if it would regenerate. I expected an earnest rebuttal, but the man was positively enthusiastic and said I should be encouraging you in your studies!'

'I'll be sure to thank him,' Ali held out her hand for the pliers. 'Come on. I'll pretend to do it immediately.' She left the infirmary and started across the bridge. Stopping halfway.

'Here?' said Theodore.

'Yes, I can't show anyone the tooth so I need to pretend I dropped it, like, in the river.' Ali poked a fingernail into the gap in her gum. A blood clot had formed there, stopping the bleeding. She scratched it away, felt warm blood run out over her bottom lip, and rubbed the ends of the pliers with it.

'This is unsettling.' Theodore folded his arms.

'How easily I bleed?'

'No. How easily the theatrics of deceit come to you.'

'Call it imagination, it's more complimentary. Come on, we'll return these.' They went back to the side room in the infirmary. There were two scholars in there, intent on their studies.

Ali looked around and immediately felt at ease. It was a comforting mix of the familiar: work benches were covered in a bewildering array of glass pipettes, test tubes and distillation tubes; beakers stood bubbling on delicate tripods above the blue flames of small gas burners; and every inch of wall space was crammed with sample jars, tins and tiny boxes. All of it was dated, old-fashioned and yet familiar to Ali, as if she'd stepped into a dreamscape mash-up of her school chemistry lab with preservation rooms at the British History Museum and scenes from the Hammer Horror films she used to watch with her dad. The Head Apothecary looked up and beamed at Ali.

'Good show, young lady. That's the spirit of enquiry, right there. I doubt a new tooth will grow back as your body's not fighting to survive. That said, I have seen some gentlemen here sprout new hair on their balding pates.'

'I will share all my findings, erm, doctor?'

'Doctor of a kind, yes. I was a sawbones – are you familiar with the term?

'Is it what they called a ship's surgeon?'

'Exactly so. I use it as my appellation, serves to ground me. Head Apothecary is a little bloated, don't you think? So, please, I invite you to do as my colleagues do, and address me thus. Sawbones at your service.' He bowed and extended a hand.

Ali shook it. 'Delighted to meet you, Sawbones. As to the issue of 'surviving,' I might have a bit of a challenge there. I was bitten by a critter and I've contracted rabies.'

'Oh, gracious, child. Show me the bite immediately.' Ali did, rolling down the waistband of her breeches. The scholar frowned when he saw the modern gauze pad and medical tape Doctor Cherubic had used to dress the wound.

'Hmm, these are after my time, clearly.'

'I had a small medical pack with me,' Ali lied.

'Gracious, may I see?'

'I used it up, I'm afraid.'

Ali spent the next few minutes being examined and questioned, enduring the process by watching it with a dispassionate clinical eye.

From the questions, it was clear this man knew all about the symptoms of rabies, and the likely trajectory of the disease.

'Well, young lady, I fear you are correct. I will make you a poultice and you must return here every morning to have it dressed afresh.' He looked through the shelves behind him, taking down a variety of items.

'If it is rabies, will my body ... fight to survive?'

'Will you transform? Is that your question?'

'Yes.'

'I very much doubt it. I have had one case of rabies here. The patient made a complete recovery with no outward sign of change. Whatever biological miracles are at play over here in this odd world, transformation appears to be an act of last resort following extreme trauma to the body.' The physician mixed ingredients in a wooden bowl and set to work grinding a paste.

Ali left with her wound dressed and a small bottle of white liquid, a tonic for the pain should it get too troublesome. Ali suspected it was a crude form of unrefined morphine.

Theodore had taken himself outside, and was waiting patiently when she finally emerged. They carried on up the steep lawn to the palace and Ali could see right across to the front gate. There was no sign of Peter. Had he come through already? Unlikely. A crowd would have gathered and they would have remained there, speculating, even if the Queen had whisked Peter inside.

Ali and Theodore went directly to the palace kitchens. Ali was halfway down the steps when Rupert spotted her. The young man was peeling potatoes over at the workbench. He hurried over, his expression turning from joy to concern when he saw the blood on her chin and neck. Then Ali smiled and Rupert spotted the missing tooth.

'Who did this?' Rupert pointed a finger at Theodore. 'Did the rabbit do it?'

'Rabbit!' said Theodore. 'I can have my axe teach you some manners.'

'I did it to myself, Rupert,' said Ali. 'Now, if Cook will give you leave, would you fetch Custard for me please? I left her in my room.'

'Off you go, boy,' Cook called from over by the hearth where she was stirring the contents of large black pot. 'Then straight back here, or I'll have the potatoes peeling you.' She called Ali over. 'What fool-ishness have you done to yourself?'

'Just a little experiment.' Ali let Cook fuss over her for a while, cleaning her face and plugging the hole in her gum with a wad of chewed willow soaked in clove oil. Cook chastised her throughout.

Ali listened politely, apologising when Cook paused for breath. The kitchen was busy. Ali counted eight people, though it was hard to keep track with all the coming and going. None of them spoke, they were all listening intently to Cook's views of their guest's foolish behaviour. Good. Gossip would reach the Queen and spare Ali the need to repeat the lie.

'Wake up, Miss Ali.' Custard was gently stroking her shoulders. 'Wake up, the Queen wants to see you.'

'What?' Ali tried to open her eyes. The lids felt heavy as lead. She managed to open one of them.

Rupert was staring at her, one of his cheeks pressed to the table just inches from her own. 'You fell asleep,' he said.

'Gold star to you,' Ali mumbled.

'You're not quite as pretty when you sleep. You dribble.'

'Good to know.' Ali sat up, yawned, and extended a hand to Custard. 'Pull me up, would you?'

'Pardon me, Miss Ali, but I'm not a shire horse.' The Queen's atten-dant took a step back and folded her arms. 'Sleeping and suffering are not to be confused one with the other. So up you get, the Queen wishes to discuss the arrival of a comely young gentleman who came through not an hour past.'

They talked in hushed whispers as they bustled through the long palace corridors. Custard was ill at ease with the white lie Theodore and Ali had asked of her. She had spent the time in Ali's room, enjoying the novelty of doing nothing at all except reading books and staring out at the gardens. She wanted to get their story straight.

'Theodore has rehearsed me in what to say.' She held up one finger. 'First, I was with you both in the gardens by the south wall, sitting at a distance to give your studies privacy.' She held up two fingers. 'Second, when we set off to return to the palace, you told me to go on ahead so you could visit your friend Jackie in the infirmary. Theodore agreed with this and said he'd watch over you.'

'Good. Then that's what happened.'

'I shan't leave you alone again, Miss Ali. That stupidity with your tooth is exactly what the Queen wanted me to stop. People can do the strangest things when first they arrive. Do you really know who the boys are?'

'I do.'

'The Queen is beside herself with excitement.' Custard started wriggling her fingers in the air. 'She covers it well, but I can tell by her fingers, they get very agitated – like this. Tap-tap-tapping on anything they can find.'

'I noticed that,' whispered Ali. 'She drums them a lot, doesn't she?'

'Yes, I make a note of it and do my best not to irritate her.' Custard paused and put on her matronly expression. 'The sight of all your blood on her breeches and blouse will set her off no end, thank you very much.'

'Guess it will. Sorry about that.'

'I have your old clothes laid out in your chamber, all clean and pressed. Go and make yourself presentable. I will do my best to have her outfit made good.'

CHAPTER 24

A TALE OF TWO BOYS

———————

Ten minutes later Ali was dressed in her jeans and hoodie again. They were stiff with starch but they were clean, and the holes in her jeans had been darned. She grabbed her backpack and followed Custard to the Queen's chamber. The door was open, and Ali could see the Queen pacing back and forth inside.

'At last!' The Queen stepped out to greet them and stared at the gap in Ali's smile. 'We shall discuss that foolishness when time allows. Aphelia, please inform our learned scholars that our infuriating young guest will attend them shortly.' 'Right you are.' Custard hesitated. 'May I add "foolish and disfigured" to the description?'

'You may: infuriating, foolish and disfigured.'

'Thank you.' Custard glanced briefly at Ali, then bent her knee and hurried off down the corridor. Ali followed the Queen into her room and was surprised at how sparsely decorated it was. Except for the rugs. Every inch of the flooring was covered in them. The effect was like looking down on a patchwork quilt. The walls were covered, not with paintings or tapestries, but with hundreds of pages taken from books, newspapers and magazines, some going back hundreds of years. Ali was impressed. There was no ostentation on display here, only a genuine passion for information. Did the Queen read snippets from these every day? Was this part of her own diary system?

'Your room, I take it?' Ali asked the Queen as she scanned the walls.

'My drawing room, yes.'

Ali was familiar with this very English description. Lord Grey had corrected her understanding of the term when she'd asked him why there were no pens or paper in the drawing room at the manor. *'No pens, my dear, just brandy and a piano. It's where guests can be entertained after dinner. Back in the day it was called the 'Withdrawing Room', but that's a mouthful after a decent dinner and a few glasses of wine. So 'drawing room' it became.'*

She could almost hear his voice, the warmth in it, the gentle humour. It was so wonderful to have them in her life, and so bitter sweet to think how few years they had left.

'What happens to old people over here?'

'An odd question under the circumstances.' The Queen's manner changed instantly, her excitement and eagerness replaced by dismay.

'Why? What happens to them?'

'They die.' The Queen took a seat at one end of a worn sofa. The fabric was scuffed and faded, but it looked elegant and comfortable.

Ali resisted the impulse to sit next to her. On the far side of the room was a card table and four chairs. Ali brought a chair over, set it opposite the Queen, took off her pack, and sat down.

'I thought this place tried its best to keep everyone alive, so why don't old people transform?'

'This is what you want to discuss? This, of all things. Right now?'

'The question just occurred to me.' Ali noticed the Queen's fingers begin to drum on her knees. Why would this question be agitating her?

'Only a terrible injury or trauma triggers transformation. Ageing is neither, it is a slow and perfectly natural breakdown of our biological systems. However, this breakdown does take a distressingly long time over here, and with that comes the burden of all that prolonged distress.'

'Is being old harder over here?'

'For some, yes.'

'Why don't they force a transformation?'

'You mean, throw themselves off a balcony?' The Queen pointed to one of her windows. 'Fly like a stone and crack their head on the ground below?'

'Yes.'

'Now you venture from the inquiring to the morbid. It ill becomes you.' The Queen raised her voice. 'Can you begin to imagine that state of mind? Looking at the ground and picturing the impact that awaits you, the pain from shattered bones? No one of sound mind can do that to their body.'

Ali said nothing, she just smiled and pointed to the gap in her teeth.

'Yes, well that rather underscores my concerns about you. I said no one of sound mind. Yet it's true that some have done so. The result is a transformation with all the pain and distress of ageing still taking place in their new form. As a consequence, we have developed a leaving ceremony for anyone who decides that enough is enough.'

'You chop off their head.'

'Not me personally, but yes. It's called a departing ceremony, and its rather touching – until the chopping bit, there is no way to make that less gruesome.'

'Sedation?'

'Sedation?' The Queen was almost shouting. 'Why would anyone wish to miss their own goodbye? No one elects to have sedation. But we do our best with screens and music that make the event trium-phant rather than morbid.'

'But what if—'

'Enough! Enough of these distractions. What is the matter with you? We have far more urgent matters to discuss. Do we not?'

'My conclusions about the two boys?

'That, of course. But more urgently, a great deal more urgently – what in the name of nonsense is amiss regarding the young man who just came through?'

'Peter?' Ali felt her stomach turn to ice as she realised her mistake. No wonder the Queen was confused.

'Yes, of course Peter!' The Queen thumped her fist in the arm of the sofa. A small cloud of dust puffed out. 'How many other young men were you expecting? He purports to be a good friend of yours.'

'What's wrong? Is he hurt?' Ali scrambled to get her thoughts in order.

'What's wrong?' The Queen jumped up and glared at Ali. 'What's wrong is your lack of interest at his sudden appearance! Your complete lack of surprise! Instead of racing here and demanding to see him, you went sauntering off to your chambers to change your clothes. Now you come in here, ask nothing about him, and instead engage me in a spurious discussion about ageing. His arrival here is of no surprise to you at all. Was this all planned?'

'No!' Ali got up, she wanted to pace the room, to escape the scrutiny of the Queen's intelligent eyes. She wanted to think, but nothing came to her. The truth would spoil everything. No more trust, no more freedom to explore.

'Then what?' the Queen grabbed Ali's elbow. Holding it tight. Stopping her from turning her face away. 'Tell me right now or I will have the both of you locked in the dungeons.'

'I'm angry with him.'

'What?!'

'I didn't want him to come here. He was supposed to stay over there and take care of my aunt and uncle. He shouldn't be here!'

'And you're punishing him by showing no interest? By not rushing to greet him. No, you will have to do a great deal better than that.'

'He's going to be a distraction!'

'A distraction?' The Queen released Ali's elbow, her expression switching from anger to something else. Ali tried to read it. Contempt?

'How depressingly common of you, child. You *are* punishing him. I thought better of you.'

'I don't understand.' Ali stared back at her, genuinely confused. The Queen had drawn a line between dots that Ali couldn't see.

'Clearly you don't. Love really is most stupidly blind at your age!'

'Love? For Peter!'

'Oh, your face. How delightful. Yes, child. I may look like a piece of ancient granite to you, but I've been tossed around by my share of romantic storms. You're showing no concern for that young man because you have far too much concern for him! That's so ridiculously naïve, it's almost sweet.'

'There's nothing sweet about this!' Ali tried to hide her relief. The Queen was climbing up the wrong tree. Let her. It was a lie Ali could work with. 'What would you have me do – encourage him? Reward him for being stupid?'

'He came for love and you are spurning him for it. Love makes young men stupid, it's how these things work. Come and greet the poor boy. The scholars will be exhausting him with their endless questions, and we need to get on with the real business of the day.'

'The boys?'

'Yes. Have you settled on their true identities?'

'I have.'

'You have to be certain. If you're right, then telling them will bring it all back for them. That's no small thing.'

'Yes, but they have to know. You all do.' Ali tried to sum it up. 'If the boys are who I think they are, then either Aunt Alice was wrong about the speed that time passes in this world, or the boys are the most precious people in both worlds.'

'And you know this, how? From the two books?'

'Mostly, yes. Alice knows how important the boys are and she is doing everything in her power to keep them safe. She knows that a powerful group of people in the other world were searching for them.'

'Your Mrs King?'

'She's one of them. They call themselves the Order of the White Rose. They want the boys for themselves. So do you want to know who they are and why they are so valuable?'

'Of course I do.' The Queen stepped away and gestured at the hundreds of clips and cuttings that covered her walls. 'I long to under-stand everything about this wretched nightmare we're trapped in. Everyone here does, which is why I will hear what you have to say in the Great Hall, along with everyone else. Knowledge is power, as you know all too well, and should be shared. Don't you agree?'

'No.'

'Thus, it begins.' The Queen stepped back, spread her arms and mocked Ali with a small bow. 'Behold the arrogance and certainty of youth. You will choose, will you? You will decide who can know? You will decide because only you can be trusted with such choices? Alice had the same misconception. How alike you two are. There can be no doubt you're related.'

'All I want to do is keep everyone safe.' Ali raised her voice, matching the Queen in a rising shouting match. 'Would you tell the Jabberwocky? Or Mrs King and her White Roses?'

'I would tell the whole damned world, because everyone has the right to know everything. Only then can a consensus of the sane and rational face down the madness of a delusional and psychotic few.'

'Hypocrite!' Ali jabbed the Queen with a finger. 'You're keeping things from me. That's what you said to me at breakfast. Until you can trust me. Your words!'

'Can you blame me? You're unstable. Look at your mouth!'

'Don't change the subject! You want me to tell the scholars about the boys before you tell the boys. Which means you *do* decide who gets to know things!'

'The boys will be told. We will surround them with love and support and we will nurse them through the trauma that will overtake them when their memories come crashing back. Love demands that of us.'

'Then we're the same. I'm not keeping secrets because I want power over anyone. I'm keeping secrets because I don't trust you either. Not yet. You won't let me leave the palace and you won't tell me why.'

'Because you're young, willful and foolish and you need protecting.'

'From what? From you?'

'From yourself, child. From your reckless disregard for your own safety. You cannot be allowed to endanger yourself any further!'

'Allowed? *Allowed!* You do call the shots, after all.'

They were screaming at the top of their voices now. Circling like cats. Claws out, backs arched. Neither saw the door opening.

'Excuse me ...' said Custard.

Ali and the Queen spun around to face her, and with one voice screamed at the poor girl, yelling for her to leave. Custard backed out and shut the door. For a while, neither Ali or the Queen spoke. They sat back in their seats and glared at each other like sullen children.

Then the Queen burst into laughter. 'Yes,' she said at last. 'We are alike. Flawed creatures, struggling to do what we believe to be right. I should not be making decisions on your behalf.'

'You mean you are keeping something from me?'

'I am. Yes.'

'To protect me?' Ali leaned back in her chair.

'Yes, and I will continue to do so until I think you're ready. Now, I think we have left everyone waiting long enough.'

The Great Hall was full. Peter was already there, standing with Theodore in front of a half circle of scholars. Behind him, a jostling crowd of onlookers were listening intently to every word. Most were still human, a few had undergone a transformation. Apart from a row of desks and tables at which the scholars were sitting, the hall was bare of furniture. It reminded Ali of a Gothic chapel stripped of its pews and altar. Stone walls were lined with wooden panels and draped with tapestries; not the intricate tapestries she'd seen in stately homes, but roughly woven pieces, more craft than art.

'I know, it sounds weird, right?' Peter was apologising to the room. 'Best you ask Ali about the science of it. I think microwave radiation vibrates the molecules or something, and that heats them up.'

Heads turned as the Queen and Ali approached the scholars. Peter looked up, saw Ali and ran to greet her, his eyes alight with excitement. He opened his mouth to greet her and was rewarded with a sharp slap on his cheek. The crowd drew a collective breath of dismay. Then, before Peter had a chance to react, Ali pulled his head to hers and kissed him long and hard, her eyes open, holding his gaze. She pulled back an inch and whispered.

'Follow my lead. Say as little as possible. I'll explain later.' She pushed him away, slapped his face again, and yelled at him. 'I told you not to come here!'

'Sorry.'

'Not good enough! What were you thinking? No, don't answer that, we'll talk later. I've more important things to do.' She turned to the half-circle of scholars. There were eleven of them. Plato was at the centre, his body reclining as always on a richly padded chaise longue.

'Indeed, we have.' Plato turned his languid gaze on Ali. 'Your colleague has kept us entertained in your protracted absence. It is the convention here to invite all new arrivals to share the changing details of life on the other side while their memories of such things are still sharp.' He looked directly at the Queen, and Ali realised he was making a very public rebuke. 'Perhaps, young lady, you will grant us the same courtesy when your private tasks for the Queen are complete.'

A murmur rose from the crowd, a grumble of unhappiness. But for whom, Ali wondered – the Queen or the Chief Scholar?

'No private tasks,' said Ali. 'The Queen granted my request. I asked to finish my studies on the true histories of the boys. I was afraid I'd lose the thread if I get afflicted with any memory loss.' She scanned the faces of the scholars; most were nodding in agreement. At the end of the row sat Broadman, the man she'd met in the library. He stood and gestured for the Queen to take his seat.

'Thank you, Broadman. I fear I am too excited to sit still. It's all I can do to keep from pacing.' She walked over and stood behind him, resting her hands on the back of his chair. 'Are the two boys aware of our decision?'

'They are,' Sawbones answered. The Head Apothecary was sitting next to Broadman. 'They have elected to wait on our deliberations as to the merit of the young lady's theory.'

'Precisely so,' Plato looked up at Ali. 'Their circumstances are cruel enough without promises of false hope. My colleagues and I have studied the two books tirelessly. There is nothing in them to indicate Alice had discovered the identity of the two boys and left it there in riddles.'

'I respectfully disagree,' said Ali. 'The books contain a lot of references, but they are obscure and well hidden. Shall I unwrap it for you?'

'Unwrap?'

'It's a modern expression,' Peter interrupted. 'Like unwrapping a surprise to see what's inside.'

'Then we must allow the young lady to "unwrap" this puzzle for us,' said Broadman, his expression kind and supportive.

'Thank you.' Ali slipped the backpack off her shoulder and brought out the novels. 'The first clue is how much both the boys hate crows. Alice mentions it in the second book, twice.' Ali had placed blades of dry glass between the pages as markers. 'The first is when she meets Tweedledum and Tweedledee and recites a poem to them.'

Alice read it aloud for the entire hall to hear:

'Just then flew down a monstrous crow,
As black as a tar barrel;
Which frightened both the heroes so,
They quite forgot their quarrel.'

'Is that all?' asked Plato.

'No, there is second passage a few pages later.' Alt turned to her second page marker and carried on reading:

'It was getting dark so suddenly that Alice thought there must be a
thunderstorm coming on. "What a thick black cloud that is," she said.
"And how fast it comes! Why I do believe it's got wings!" "It's the crow!"
Tweedledum cried out in a shrill voice of alarm; and the two brothers
took to their heels and were out of sight in a moment.'

'So, then, a fear of crows.' The Chief Scholar wrinkled his brow. 'And are our two boys scared of crows?'

'They are.' A large Griffin stepped forward; he was standing in the crowd directly behind Peter. 'I have witnessed it myself on many occasions when flying in their vicinity. If my shadow passes over them, they drop to the ground and tremble like field mice.'

'Ted confirmed it,' said Ali. 'They both hate big crows, especially ravens.'

'Distressing for them, no doubt,' said Broadman. 'But how does this assist in identifying them?'

'It doesn't, not in itself,' said Ali. 'Its relevance becomes clear after you solve the other clues. It's like the last nail in the coffin.'

'Then hammer on and lay this mystery to rest,' said Plato.

'There are two main clues in the first book.' Ali flipped through the pages till she found the chapter set in the Royal Gardens. 'The Queen of Hearts will only allow red roses in her Royal Gardens, so the gardeners are painting the white ones red for fear of losing their heads.'

Ali read the passage aloud:

'A large rose-tree stood near the entrance of the garden. The roses growing on it were white, but there were three gardeners busily painting them red.'

'We have discussed that passage at length,' said a short scholar with large blue eyes and a mop of ginger hair. He didn't look up at Ali, instead he turned to either side and addressed his colleagues. 'May I elucidate for the child?'

'If you must,' the Chief Scholar sighed. 'Just the bones of it, Fortescue, not one of your tedious pontifications.'

'Certainly.' Fortescue got to his feet and addressed the crowd. He scanned their faces as he spoke, ignoring Ali completely. 'We long ago determined that this account relates to the process of transformation. The white roses represent our natural form, while the red roses represent our transformation into something far more exotic. Allow me to explain in more detail.'

'Allow me to save you the trouble,' said Ali.

'Excuse me?' Fortescue looked confused. He had taken hold of his lapels and puffed out his chest in readiness for making a big speech.

'The passage has nothing to do with transformation.' Ali wanted to walk across, pat the man on his bright ginger head, and congratulate him for his partial transformation into an exotic red rose. She restrained herself.

'Young lady, I have spent many years on this and—'

'Got it wrong? The passage is a reference to the Wars of the Roses,' said Ali.

'Oh, is it indeed?' Fortescue chuckled and shook his head.

'Yes. It's a period of English history my mum loved. She read me books about it when I was young, it was like a bizarre soap.'

'Soap? Cleaning soap?'

'No. A soap opera. Please sit down, Mr Fortescue.'

'Yes.' The Queen looked at the short scholar. 'With the greatest of respect, do please sit. We have come to learn, not to lecture. Continue, Miss Ali.'

'The period was known as the War of the Roses because roses were the symbols of the two great dynasties fighting for the throne of England – the houses of York and Lancaster. A white rose was the emblem for the House of York, it was on every flag and shield. A red rose was used by the House of Lancaster. Two young princes were in direct line to the throne. They were being protected in the Tower of London, and they disappeared. Most historians believe they were murdered, but the bodies were never found.'

The crowd, who had stayed quiet and respectful to this point, broke into a lively debate, a hundred voices all speculating at once. The Chief Scholar called for silence but no one paid him any heed. The Queen put a thumb and finger to her lips, drew a deep breath and startled the room with an ear-splitting whistle. 'Class act,' Peter whispered.

'Settle, everyone,' Plato cleared his throat. 'The interpretation has merit. I considered it myself many years ago but dismissed it because of an obvious flaw.'

'You mean the time difference?' said Ali.

'Quite so. Those events took place half a millennia ago in the time stream of the other world. That is five hundred years, child. Even allowing for the great discrepancy in the passage of time, our boys would be strapping young men. Your hypothesis and the facts are incompatible.'

A sigh of dismay passed through the crowd.

'I thought so too, at first,' said Ali. 'But today I finally solved the third and most telling clue. The riddle of the raven and the writing desk.'

'What? No! Enough of this!' Fortescue thumped a fist on the table in front of him. 'How much longer must we sit through this? We have graciously given the young lady the courtesy of a hearing, now we must get back to our studies.'

'My dear sir,' the Queen said, tipping her head to him, 'what is so urgent that you cannot afford a few more minutes with us? Solving this particular riddle has been your life's passion. Surely, you're intrigued to hear a new interpretation?'

'No, absolutely not! The riddle sits at the heart of the books. Alice held it to be of the utmost importance. It is not a parlour game. Solving it requires a solemn commitment to the principles of inquiry.'

'Forgive me, Fortescue,' Ali took care to pronounce his name correctly. The murmurs of dissent were growing in the crowd behind her.

'Surely, in the pursuit of knowledge, all that matters is the truth, not how that truth is arrived at, or who uncovers it. Science holds nothing to be sacred. We must kick holes in every box of thinking we build, even precious ideas we've spent years arguing for. They are the hardest boxes to pull apart, but we have to rip them open to embrace the light of new ideas.'

'Nice,' Peter whispered. 'That you or your dad?'

'Neither,' she whispered back, 'a TED talk.'

'I rest my case.' Fortescue smiled at his colleagues and started giving Ali a slow-hand clap. 'This young lady has proved my point, has she not? A woman's natural tendency to histrionics makes her ideal for life in a traveling theatre, not for life in a disciplined institute of learning.'

'Solve it yourselves, right now!' said Ali, raising her voice above the growing hubbub behind her. 'What is the difference between a raven and a writing desk? "Writing" is the difference. It is an adjective while raven and desk are nouns.' Ali stepped forward and walked the line of desks, eyeballing each scholar in turn. 'Take your pens, gentlemen. Make an anagram from those two nouns.' She looked up at the Queen, hoping for a sign of encouragement, but her expression was impossible to read.

'By heaven!' Broadman stared at his scribbled notes. Then he pushed back his chair, stood and beamed at Ali. 'You have done it, child!' He held up his paper, slapping it for effect. 'Right here! It has been in front of our sorry eyes the whole time. RED KNAVES. An exact fit, every letter. The anagram of RAVEN and DESK is RED KNAVES.'

'Yes,' Ali took the paper from Broadman and held it up to the crowd. 'The word KNAVE has two meanings. In a deck of cards, it is royal card, like the Knave of Hearts. It also means an urchin or a scoundrel. The two princes were called knaves by the Duke of Gloucester, the man who stole their throne. He called them scoundrels and pretenders to the throne, false princes and knaves.'

Ali turned back to the scholars, walked up to Fortescue and put the paper on his desk.

'And what colour rose was the emblem for the House of the two princes?'

'Red.' Fortescue spoke softly; he looked elated. Ali smiled at him, he was a man of learning after all, on fire with this revelation.

'Yes,' she whispered to him. 'The red rose for the House of Lancaster. And do you know what they called the chief jailer at the Tower of London?'

'No child, tell me.'

'He was called the Keeper of the Ravens. He was responsible for looking after the ravens, the giant black crows who lived in the Tower grounds. The large black crows the poor princes would have seen through their barred windows every day.'

'*Yes!*' Fortescue leapt up onto his desk and started dancing. 'Yes! There is no doubt. I live to see it. What a day!' He threw his arms in the air and shouted his delight to the crowd. 'The identity of our boys is proven to my satisfaction.' The crowd broke into applause and it was a while before the Chief Scholar could bring the hall to order.

'This is a remarkable theory,' he said at last. 'And our guest is to be given credit. However, let us take the time to discuss the two pressing questions that flounder in its wake.'

'The matter of their age?' said Ali.

'That, and why Alice felt the need for such a degree of secrecy.'

'Surely the nature of the boys' identity speaks to that,' said the Queen. 'The royal line was disrupted by their disappearance. Would not the country erupt into civil war if their survival was discovered?'

'No.' Peter shook his head, trying his best not to laugh at the idea. 'I don't think the general public, I mean the royal subjects of England, would care or even notice. No one but a few flag-waving zealots take the Royal Family seriously these days. The crown has no authority, all they do is sell mugs and flags to tourists.'

'I understood not one word of that, young man.'

'Peter means there would be no unrest,' said Ali. 'The Crown has no power these days. The reason Alice kept the boys' identity such a closely guarded secret was to protect them from a group in the other world. A society called the Order of the White Rose. But Alice failed. Those people have been trying to get here and get the boys. They want to study them and unlock their unique talent.'

'Which is?' The Chief Scholar was paying very close attention now, his eyes scrutinising Ali with an intensity she hadn't seen before.

Suddenly, she felt a surge of cold flooding her stomach, and in that instant she realised her mistake. *Plato was one of them.* The Chief Scholar was working for King and the White Roses.

'Well?' The Queen tipped her head to one side. 'Are you going to share this information with us.'

'No,' Ali said, keeping her voice flat and even, 'unless you can guarantee the boys are safe with you here in the palace, and guarantee that everyone here in this hall has the boys' best interests at heart?'

'I see.' The Queen smiled; outwardly she seemed calm and composed, but her fingers were drumming on the back of Broadman's chair, her agitation clear to all her who knew her. 'You are right, of course. Goodness, how like Alice you are. But tell me this – are the boys aware of this unique talent you speak of?'

'I don't think so,' Ali lied. 'Look, they desperately want to know their real identities, they have allowed you all to hear me first and decide if my theory is correct. Now you must take them aside and give them all the care and support you promised when you tell them who they really are.'

'And you?' The Chief Scholar hadn't taken his eyes off her. 'What do you intend to do I wonder?'

'I intend to take a bath,' said Ali. 'A very hot bath, and then I shall take Peter home.'

'No.' The Chief Scholar shook his head, sending ripples of movement down his long, caterpillar body. 'I won't allow it. Without the secret of safe passage you may die, this young man too. So let me speak plainly. We got off to a poor start, you and I, but you have proved me wrong. You are clearly a most accomplished scholar. I know I speak on behalf of my colleagues when I say you would be most welcome to study alongside us in the library.'

'More than welcome,' said Fortescue.

'Positively encouraged,' said Broadman. 'Please remain here and help us solve the secret of safe passage so that everyone gathered here in this hall can go home safely if they wish to.'

CHAPTER 25

PIES AND PROCRASTINATION

The two boys were waiting quietly for the decision, having elected to stay with Waxstaff during the deliberations in the Great Hall. They were sitting either side of her bed, holding her hands. They didn't jump up when they saw Ali coming down the main aisle. Ted got up slowly and went round the bed to Ricky. The two boys wrapped their arms around each other, almost cowering with fear.

Ali wondered which would be worse for them. The fear of disappointment if her theory was wrong, or the fear of discovering who they really were? Waxstaff reached out and stroked them tenderly. She was almost entirely lizard now, her skin an exquisite tapestry of golds, greens and yellows.

'Hello, beautiful,' said Ali.

'Thanks,' Waxstaff chuckled. 'The boys think it's an improvement too, don't you, kids?' She scrubbed their hair playfully. 'Which is more than I can say for you. What happened to the smile?'

'Potts.'

'She's still alive?'

'Possibly, but not in one piece. She grabbed onto my ankle and came through with me ... then she was taken by the critters.'

'Bloody hell. Come back and tell me everything – but first, these boys need to know. Were you right?'

'Yes,' Ali crouched down and took Ted's hand. Ricky held out one of his and she took that too, pressing them together between hers. 'Alice didn't break her promise to you. She found out who you were and tried to keep it a secret from everyone. Do you know why?'

The boys shook their heads.

'I think you do. You even told me. In fact, you kept telling me, but I was too lost in my own thoughts to understand what you were saying, *We don't change.* That's what you said to me. Well, Alice found out that you both came through here over six hundred years ago. That's how much time has gone by on the other side of the door. That's about ten years ago here in this world. Which means you should be young men in your twenties. But you're not, are you?'

The boys shrank back even further as they hugged each other.

'The truth is, you *do* transform. You transform every day. You transform to the exact same boys you were the day you stepped through.'

'We know,' Ted said quietly.

'People were starting to wonder,' said Ricky. 'Lots of whispering. Alice told us to stay hidden. She was going to help us.'

'Protect us,' said Ted.

'Which is why she hid your identities. If people knew them. they would know how old you should be. Your secret skill would be revealed.'

'To the bad people?' whispered Ricky.

'Yes. The bad people on the other side. But I think they found out anyway. I think they were coming to get you, but somehow Alice stopped them. She didn't desert you or break any promises. She went to stop them from getting through, from stealing you away.'

'Will she come back?

'I don't think so. She would have been back by now. She must have stayed and grown old back in the other world. She will be long dead by now.'

Ali looked up at Waxstaff. She was crying.

'So much suffering,' she said, her voice almost spitting, her long lizard tongue flicking out as she spoke. 'That King and her cronies, what cold, selfish creatures. All so they can live forever. They want to steal the boys, dissect them, take them apart cell by cell in a lab over there and sell the fountain of youth to a select few who will be the architects of a new age.'

'Something like that. I think Alice slowed them down big time.'

'Tell me later. The boys have waited long enough.'

'Yes,' Ali got to her feet, still holding tight to the boys' hands. 'Do you want to know? It's your decision, nobody will make you do this.'

'Do we?' Ted looked at Ricky.

'I think so,' Ricky nodded vigorously. 'Yes, we do. And if we don't like it, we can come back here and stop remembering it all over again.'

'Then Theodore is waiting for you outside to walk you up to the palace. The Queen wants to hold your remembering in the comfort of her private chamber, just the five of you. The Hatter, the Queen, Theodore and you. Unless you want me to be there.'

'No,' Ted said firmly. 'It will be too distressing for you.' And with that they set off towards the door. Ricky turned once, calling back to Waxstaff.

'Remember your promise, Jackie.'

'I will,' Waxstaff called back, her new voice cracking slightly. She looked at Ali and grinned. 'How the hell do I still sound like me when all the equipment is so different. Explain that science, girl.'

'It is different. Out here, anyway. Maybe in your head box it echoes around like your old voice. I think it's much nicer, there's a raspy little crackle and a hiss mixed in that makes it sound like you find everything a little bit amusing.'

'Maybe I do.'

'Is that why you decided to postpone forgetting? Clearly, you're still using the boys and the photos to remember everything.'

'For the moment, yes.'

'I'm glad. What changed your mind?'

'Those two. The boys. They said I had to remember everything because you were going to need my help when you found out.'

'Found out what?'

'They wouldn't say. But they were insistent I stick around, memory wise. That's the promise they just extracted from me.'

'Good, because there's another old friend wants to see you, I'll send him in if you're up for it.'

'Who?'

'Peter.'

'Good Lord, girl, that helpless little puppy – what the hell have you done? Yes, send him in, but tell him to bring snails. I'm starving.'

'I told him you'd say that. He's outside with Theodore hunting under every plant and stone.'

Ali and Waxstaff watched the two boys reach the door, wave and disappear outside. Peter walked in a moment later, spotted Ali and came hurrying down the central aisle.

'Eager little chap,' said Waxstaff. Ali ignored her, she could see Peter was doing his best to heed her advice. Walk fast, face the front, avoid looking closely at the beds.

'Hi,' said Peter.

'That's it?' Waxstaff stared at him with her new eyes, knowing full well how disturbing she must look. 'Last time we met, I wasn't a giant lizard.'

'Sorry,' said Peter. 'I hate hospitals, I never know what to say. I always end up saying the obvious – how are you? Then everyone stares down at the grapes and feels uncomfortable.'

'You brought grapes?'

'Not this time. Small and round though ...' Peter unwrapped a folded leaf the size of a napkin. 'Here you go – thirty-five snails. Where do you want them?'

'In my mouth. One at a time, you can feed me as we talk.'

'If you're doing your best to intimidate me, it's working, though compared with the mutated hedgehog we saw eating Pott's leg, you're a gentle pussycat.'

'Really?' Waxstaff turned to Ali and grinned. 'This boy will do. Now then, both of you, tell me everything, starting with the Greys – are they coping okay?'

They did their best to update her, tag-teaming their narration, interrupting each other if a detail was missed. Waxstaff interrupted sometimes, pushing for clarifications. When they were done, Ali and Peter stared at each other in silence, as if the retelling had made the events more real.

It was Ali who broke the silence. 'Something else I need to tell you. I didn't just Google the Tower of London while I was there. I looked into this place, too. It's the same building as the Great Exhibition hall, an exact copy.'

'Which isn't possible,' said Peter.

'Yet here it is. Have either of you heard of Entanglement?'

'Maybe,' said Peter, 'is it the thing Einstein called spooky?'

'Yes, Einstein actually called it – Spooky Action at a Distance.'

'Give the puppy a chocolate,' said Waxstaff

'And give the lizard a slap for being a smart-arse,' said Ali. 'Go on, Peter.'

'It's how something can happen in two places at once.' Peter paused and popped two more snails in Waxstaff's mouth. 'If stuff is entangled, you could take half of it to Paris and keep the other half in New York, then whatever you do with the lump in Paris, the same thing will happen to the lump in New York.'

'That's it,' said Ali. 'Even across huge distances, the changes happen at the same time, instantly, with no communication, no delay.'

'So,' Waxstaff shook her head slowly. 'You build with materials that have been entangled. Build something in Paris, and a copy happens in New York?'

'Yes. That's why Einstein called it "spooky action at a distance". It spooked him because it defies logic, but not his equations.'

'But it's just a theory, right?' Peter tipped the rest of the snails into Waxstaff's mouth. 'Just an idea on paper.'

'No, it works! Loads of experiments have proved it. Only in tiny amounts so far, and mostly using atoms of cesium, but it is a real thing. Maybe a process like that duplicated these buildings. Not entanglement exactly, but something like it.'

'My head hurts.' Waxstaff was struggling with the idea.

'Mine too,' said Ali.

'Well, I guess the three of us could be having this conversation in a psych ward somewhere,' said Peter.

'No, this is real.' Waxstaff took one of Peter's hands. 'See? Real lizard hand.'

'It's not cold,' Peter said, surprised. 'And it's lovely and soft.'

'I moisturise,' said Waxstaff.

'Forget entanglement,' said Peter. 'How the hell do you explain turning into rabbits and lizards?'

'Ask the girl genius.' Waxstaff lay back. She suddenly seemed tired.

'Do you want us to leave?'

'No. It's no fun being alone with myself right now.' She closed her eyes and sighed. 'Keep holding my hand, there's a good puppy, and listen to Ali.'

'Okay, the short version.' Ali smiled across at Peter. There was something very comfortable about him. Was this what real friendship felt like?

'Short and simple,' said Peter.

'Okay. Our cells contain genetic ghosts of every creature who came before us on our evolutionary journey. And we know stem cells can be switched on inside us that can repair and replace every damaged cell in every organ of our body. We can repair ourselves, theoretically, but we don't. Death of the individual and passing on our DNA is essential for evolution.'

'But it doesn't have to be that way? That's what you're saying?'

'Yes, we have all that historical DNA in our system, and the stem cells to differentiate into anything that we have ever been. Something in the environment over here switches that on. Clearly. Or you wouldn't be sitting here holding hands with a lizard woman.'

'What do we do now?' asked Peter.

'No idea,' said Ali. She looked at Waxstaff. 'Suggestions?'

'Too many, but you don't need me to tell you.' Waxstaff opened her lizard eyes and blinked at Ali. 'From your account just now, Lady Grey has already made that lecture. Look around you, girl, all these poor souls. Your great-aunt Alice gave everything to protect them. You made a good start with me. You carried me here to safety. Reckless and stupid, but not selfish. You came into that manor house a lost and angry girl. And look at you now – got yourself a job to do.'

'Guess so.'

'Now ... off with you both, I need my beauty sleep. Two more days and I'll be up and about like a newborn.'

They left her to sleep, and Ali took Peter to see Sawbones. The man had examined Peter's head injury when he'd first arrived and had pronounced it to be free of complications. No bleeding under the skull. No fracture. But Ali insisted on hearing all this for herself.

'Rest and hydration will do it,' said Sawbones. 'Sleep is the best tonic for a concussion. But you, my girl, you are a whole different set of challenges. Open your mouth and let me track your experiment.'

'No need, I can feel it with my tongue. It's growing back, there's a little tip poking through.'

'Excellent!' Sawbones was delighted, but insisted on looking for himself, and on changing the dressing to her wound.

He chatted excitedly the whole time, impressing on Ali just how much impact her arrival was having. 'Such excitement. Unlocking the writing desk riddle! Incredible. You bring hope, young lady. I do beseech you to stay and discover so much more. You have a rare mind. A rare mind.'

'That's one way to describe it,' said Peter.

'I'll try to help, Sawbones. I don't know how yet. But I'll try.'

'I know you will. I know it. Now, get this young man to bed immediately.'

'I'm sorry?' Ali glanced at Peter and saw the same surprise on his face.

'Sleep,' said Sawbones. 'He needs sleep, look at him. We questioned him for hours when he first arrived. Sleep.'

'And food,' said Peter. 'Can we please get some food? I'm famished. They gave me something but that was hours ago ... or maybe ten minutes. I can't really tell. Is that a thing here?'

'It is,' said Ali.

They left the infirmary and set off across the bridge. 'Our body clocks are all messed up,' she explained. 'I just use the sun. Look, it's about midday.'

They walked slowly, acknowledging the smiles and greetings from other folk out enjoying the gardens. Everyone was polite, even deferential, but it was clear from every gesture, every furtive glance, that there was a separation. Peter could see it. These people were in awe of Ali, even a little scared.

'Must be what it's like to be a celebrity,' said Peter.

'I guess.' Ali realised she was starting to relax a little. There was nothing she had to do right now except eat and sleep. It felt good. She had been making too many decisions, working on too many problems, all at once and for too long. 'I think I'm exhausted,' she said.

'You think?' Peter hooked an arm through hers. She didn't resist. They followed a path between terraces of hanging ferns and water fountains.

'I've been running on instinct since I got here. No one to talk to. No one that I can trust, anyway. Maybe Theodore.'

'And now there's me.'

'Now there's you.'

'Then talk. Start with King.' The ferns cast a dappled light over them, plates of shadow that moved across their faces. 'She's been trying to do all this in secret, right? Keeping it to herself. What's in it for her?

'Immortality, if she can figure out how the boys do it.'

'She's rich, right?' Peter paused, distracted by the scent from a row of giant oleander bushes with flowers the size of dinner plates. 'Like, filthy rich?'

'Must be. She owns the company my dad worked for, and the bank that cheated Uncle Bertie and took their house. God knows what else she owns.'

'Easy to make money if you can hang out over here for a while. One year here, sixty over there. Sixty years of compound interest on your investments.'

'I guess so.' Ali stopped. Sunlight was falling through a group of fountains to their left, the water vapour acting like a curtain, fracturing light into a rainbow of scattered colours. She hadn't thought about money before. Was that what King had been doing, again and again, for hundreds of years? Growing her wealth and putting it in trusts? Investing in businesses? Bequeathing everything to a string of fictitious heirs – new identities for herself.

'King must have known how to get back safely,' Ali mused as she watched the curtain of rainbows shiver as a breeze ruffled the screen of water vapour.

'Maybe she got injured,' said Peter. 'Had an accident, started to transform, went back to our world and tried to halt it. Then started forgetting things.'

'And got stuck over there till my great-aunt Alice comes on the scene and figures out the way to go back safely.'

'Why not? Got to start with a theory, right? That's as good as any.'

They reached the palace and stepped into the shade of the grand lobby. Two guards saluted them at the door.

'I'd love to meet Alice one day,' said Ali. 'To hear how she kept one step ahead of King.' She led them through the palace. Peter tried to follow the route, to map it in his head, but gave up. There were too many rooms and too many corridors.

'Here we are,' Ali stopped by a large oak door. 'The kitchens are in here. Be warned, you'll eat way too much.'

'What's that chugging noise?'

'Thomas.' Ali opened the door and led Peter down the flagstone steps onto the floor of the kitchen. Cook, Rupert and Custard were all there. They called out and Rupert came racing over, grabbing them by the hands and pulling them to the long table near the ovens. He was all smiles until Peter sat down right beside Ali.

'Do you want him to move, Miss Ali? He's far too close, isn't he? Plenty of room at the end of the table.'

'Leave them be, Rupert,' Cook scolded, flicking him with her wash-cloth. 'Help me set some food out. You too, Custard. The both of you can stare at them all you want while we're eating.' Ali watched Peter's face as food was set down in front of him, his eyes growing bigger with every item, his grin so wide and so genuine it was like watching a kid at a birthday party. There was a large pie, its crust a warm brown and shining with butter. There were loaves of bread, a block of fresh butter and wedges of a deep orange cheese. Then sausages arrived, and figs, bananas and tiny apples the size of grapes.

'Milk, lemonade or ale?' Cook came over and stood behind Peter. She put a hand on his shoulder, then bent and whispered in his ear. Peter laughed, spraying crumbs of pie onto the table.

'And?' Ali punched his arm and waited.

'Cook just asked me, very respectfully, if I'm available?'

'Oh, he's very available,' laughed Ali.

'Is that right?' Custard sat down opposite Peter. 'That's not how the Queen tells it. You're lovesick for our Miss Ali, followed her over to keep her safe.'

'Really?' Peter turned and grinned at Ali. 'Smart woman, that Queen.'

'I think it's romantic,' said Custard.

'I think it's stupid,' said Rupert, and he stomped off in a sulk.

An hour later they were in Ali's room, feeling stuffed, full of every-thing Cook had insisted on serving. Peter sat down on the bed and let out a long sigh, a mix of discomfort and satisfaction.

'So, do I sleep here?'

'Sleep, yes. Move over.' She sat next to him.

'That's a hell of a painting.' Peter pointed at the portrait of Theodore and the Hatter.

'Alice commissioned it. It's full of more riddles.'

'He's handsome, that Hatter. And young, I thought he'd be old and toothy like the pictures in the book.'

'He's scary handsome,' Ali agreed. 'Those black eyes look right into you.'

'You fancy him?'

'Too old. But the Queen does. She's completely nuts about him.' They sat in silence for a while, just staring at the picture.

'So,' said Peter, 'Lady Grey and Waxstaff think it's time to get serious about all this. Put some sort of plan together.'

'I don't know where to start.'

'Define the goal. Keep it simple. We have to get these folk home, don't we? We don't know how, not yet. But that's the goal.'

'Home to what though? Look how normal refugees get treated. We kill each other over every tiny difference there is. Imagine how we'll treat the transformed?'

'Like shit.'

'Like complete shit. We can't just wander back with them and expect a red carpet. And this is bigger than just these people being lost. This is as big as it gets – and dangerous! King is killing to keep it private.'

'Do others know?'

'I think so. There are people plugging the different gateways. The Tower of London was a castle built on the Thames to guard against attacks from invaders. Historians assume that meant invaders from across the sea. Vikings, Romans, the Spanish. But it wasn't built to keep armies out.'

'It was keeping them in.'

'Exactly.' Ali reached out and wrapped her hands part way around his head and tried to squeeze. 'Feel this? This is my head exploding. Someone, back in the day, realised the gate was a heap of trouble. They built the white tower on top of Tower Hill – a lid to stop the trouble from climbing out.'

'Then we stick to Martha's plan and we go to the government?'

'Yes. It's like exploring space. It needs an agency the size of NASA with billions of dollars and the best minds on the planet.'

'Maybe there is an agency,' Peter shrugged. 'Maybe there are scientists working at other gateways in other countries.'

'Like where? We'd hear about it. Secrets get out.'

'Roswell,' said Peter, trying to keep a straight face.

Ali didn't bite. She laughed. How did he manage to do that? To trigger her just enough to stop her spiralling too deep. A playful tweak that pulled her out of the whirlpool of her thoughts. A well-crafted safety rope.

'Frack you.' She reached out, grabbed a pillow and thumped it down on his head. Then thumped him again.

'Ow. My bruise. That hurt.'

'Well, defend yourself!'

He did, and within minutes the room was filled with goose down, the tiny feathers settling like snow over everything. The pillow fight quickly became a wrestling match. Ali got the upper hand, sitting on Peter and pinning him down. He tried to wriggle out, but one elbow jabbed into Ali's bite wound. She yelped and rolled off him.

'Sorry!'

They lay there, side by side, cradling each other, lost in their own confusing knots of thought, neither wanting to move.

'This is awkward ...' but Ali didn't try to pull his arm from around her waist.

'More good than awkward.' Peter rolled his head so he could look at her. 'Except for all this dandruff over everything. Sorry about the elbow.'

'You will be,' said Ali.

'You started it.'

'No, you did! You said Roswell.'

The door burst open and Custard rushed in. She took in the scene, stared at the snowdrift of feathers, and backed out, closing the door again.

'It's all right, Custard.' Ali sat up, brushing feathers from her clothes and hair 'Tell me what's happened.'

'It's the Hatter ...' Custard didn't open the door again. She called out the news from the other side. 'He's gone!'

CHAPTER 26

A RACE AGAINST TIME

The hunting party set off without fuss or fanfare. It was a small group of volunteers: Theodore for his persuasive common sense, Sir Stoke of Trent and his horse Henry in case the Hatter refused to come and needed to be wrapped in a saddle blanket, and Puddles the enormous dog, for security. The final two were Ali and Peter.

The Queen had strongly objected to Ali joining the group. 'No. You will slow them down, child. Speed is everything.'

'I know – that's why they need me.' Ali had disappeared to the kitchens and returned waving the time map. 'Can anyone else read it? No. So I'm going. With the map we can overtake the Hatter without breaking a sweat.'

'Then I'm coming too,' Peter had said. There had been no sense of panic; the Hatter had only been missing for an hour, and they were confident they would overtake him before he met with any trouble. If the Hatter's plan was to catch the critters and recover his stolen history, then he would be taking a track that could intersect with the critters' traditional route back to the Jabberwocky's lair.

'If it were me, I'd go through the Bamboo Forest,' said Stoke. 'It would take him directly to the road the critters use for the final stretch into the Fringes.'

Theodore agreed, lifting his ax and swinging it over his shoulder. 'And Alice mapped the Bamboo Forest. We spent days in there with our pocket watches. We have every opportunity of gaining time on the Hatter.' It was agreed. Stoke took the lead and the party crossed the lowland and open downs until they reached the start of the forest.

'Bloody hell!' Peter stared up at the massive canes towering into the sky in front of them. 'This is massive, like those redwood forests in Oregon.' The canes of bamboo grew in dense clumps, each clump the size of a village green. Paths weaved between them in a confusing lacework of trails. Some of the gaps were so narrow, the party was forced to walk single file for minutes at a time. Ali kept checking her map, trying to marry the different paths with the sketchy drawings.

'That's a map?' Peter stared at the page over Ali's shoulder. 'It looks like a kid's doodle of spaghetti.'

'Yes,' Ali laughed. 'It's crude but it's clear. There's only one distortion – right at the centre. We just have to avoid that.'

'Remarkable,' said Stoke. 'I usually march straight through there.'

'We must hope the Hatter has done the same,' said Theodore. They pushed on, and in less than an hour they were through the forest. It ended abruptly on a ridge. Lowland moors stretched out below them, an endless blanket of pink and brown. Ali could make out a road, its slate grey surface snaking a route between mounds of gorse and heather.

'He'll be down there somewhere,' said Theodore, 'picking his way towards that road. I mapped all this open heathland with Alice. Mapped it for days.'

'Why can't we see him?' Peter scanned the open ground. 'I've hiked across a few moors. You can see people from miles away.'

'Your eyes are playing tricks with you.' Stoke pointed to a single tree rising through the mounds of heather. 'Can you see that tree in the distance?'

'You mean that bush?'

'No, young man, that is a tree pushing its way up through the underbrush. The bracken and heather hereabouts grow twice your height. The Hatter will be pushing his way through there unseen.'

They set off into the heather. It formed a thin canopy above them and a carpet of dry petals beneath their feet. Ali took the lead, using the map to avoid a few patches of dense time.

'We must be closing on him,' said Henry. 'Puddles, have you got his scent?'

'No.' Puddles turned and glared at the horse. 'Have you?'

'I'm not a bloodhound!'

'Neither am I, Henry. I'm all teeth. I can rip and bite all you please. I can disembowel and dismember. But smell? No. Much more the rabbit's department.'

'He certainly passed through here,' said Theodore, his nose and whiskers twitching. 'And I believe his scent is a little stronger, so I assume we are closing the gap.'

'Will he oblige? That is our issue,' said Stoke. 'We don't want to dilly-dally here all day. If we can't persuade him immediately, I will secure him in the saddle blanket, and we will be on our way.'

'You plan to carry him yourself, do you?' asked Henry. 'Or are you making more promises on my behalf?'

'We are a team,' said Stoke.

'Really? I await your next display of team gallantry with interest.'

'Oh my goodness!' Theodore stopped. His ears popped up like periscopes and began rotating back and forth. 'Critters have been here.'

'I see no thorn bushes,' said Stoke.

'They haven't lingered. They came through at a pace.'

'How many?' Ali looked around and could see nothing but endless heather.

'Six at least,' Theodore put down his axe, dropped onto all fours and sniffed the ground. 'All trace of the Hatter's scent has gone.'

'Tarnation!' Stoke cursed quietly. 'He is off the ground. Most likely trussed up like a wild boar and hanging from shoulder poles.'

'Which will slow them down,' said Theodore. 'Come, we must overtake them. A few vermin will be no match for us.'

The party hurried on, but almost immediately, Theodore stopped again. 'Oh dear.' He looked to his left, then to his right. 'Two scent lines. Our prey has split up.'

'Why?' asked Peter.

'I have no idea,' said Theodore. 'Nor do I know which group has the Hatter.'

'I do,' Ali pointed along the track to their left. Fluttering on the ground was a short strip of ribbon, just like the ones with which the Hatter dressed his dreadlocks. 'Our friend is leaving a trail of breadcrumbs to follow.'

'Breadcrumbs?'

'Figure of speech,' said Peter. 'Let's go.'

The track was narrow, so they moved in single file, Theodore collecting the discarded ribbons and securing them in Stoke's saddle bag.

'There!' whispered Puddles from the front of the march. 'Come forward and keep your heads down.'

They had arrived at a small thicket of trees. Up ahead was a dome of high ground, a wide circle of granite free of undergrowth. Loose rocks and boulders had been cleared to the edge of the circle to form a wall. The wall was shoulder height and gave the clearing the appearance of a small hilltop fortress.

'This is one of their favourite camp sites,' said Stoke. 'With luck they will rest here a while. We can circle around ahead of them, choose a place of advantage and waylay them when they move on.'

'Respectfully, no,' Puddles shook his head. 'Remember that split in their company we saw earlier? We must presume they sent runners to the Wocky, boasting of their prize. He will come to claim the Hatter – and he'll bring a small army with him.'

'I agree,' said Theodore. 'We should move on them now while we have the numbers and the surprise.'

'Attack them?' Peter looked alarmed. 'Right now?'

'Not you, dear boy,' Stoke drew his sword. 'Leave the messy business to us. You free the Hatter. Bring him back to these trees.'

'We must use the advantage of surprise,' said Theodore. A narrow track wound its way to a gap in the wall. On either side of the track, the ground was covered in dense thickets of heather. 'We push through the heather. It will give us ample cover if we crawl our way to the top.'

'Not with my knees,' Sir Trent turned to his horse. 'Henry? Your opinion?'

'Your knees and my size preclude us from stealth. We will hold our position here in this grove. When the rest of you have crawled close enough to strike, we will break cover and gallop up the track directly to their camp. It will send them chasing their tails for a moment. You can use the surprise to rescue the Hatter.'

'Right,' Theodore nodded. 'Await my signal.' He pointed up at his ears and waggled them.

'The plan is good,' said Puddles. 'Use the axe to cut the Hatter free. I will put my teeth to work on his captors.'

Getting close to the wall was straightforward. The surrounding heather was shoulder high and they moved at a low crouch for most of the way, dropping to their hands and knees to crawl the final distance to the wall.

'Wait,' Theodore whispered. 'Something's wrong ... I can smell lavender.'

'Me too,' said Ali.

'But lavender doesn't grow here. The moors are just heather and gorse.'

'Maybe one is badly injured and transforming?' Ali whispered. 'Puddles tore the head from one and buried it, but he also injured others. They might have collected the lavender on the way.'

'Perhaps,' Theodore sniffed the air. 'But its more than lavender. Something doesn't sit right with my nose.' They pushed on, working their way along the outer face of the wall until they came to a section where a large rock had tumbled out. The gap it left was big enough to peer through.

There were only four critters in the enclosure. Three were pacing around, chattering quietly to themselves, the fourth was standing beside the Hatter. He was seated on the ground, his hands bound together, and he was strapped to a massive iron chain that spanned the breadth of the circle.

'How did that thing get here?' whispered Peter. Each link in the chain was bigger than his fist. 'That must weigh tons.'

'Indeed, it must,' Theodore whispered back. 'Can we attend to the matter at hand? When the others charge, the critters will scatter. I will cut the Hatter free, you get him back to the trees. Do *not* debate with him. Drag him there if you must. Are we agreed?'

'Yes,' Ali put her hand on Peter's shoulder. 'Don't try to fight them, okay? They're a sad bunch, they'll run when we jump them.'

'More servants than soldiers, you reckon?'

'I think so, but they might fight back if they're cornered, so all we do is chase them off and let them run.'

'Make ready, then.' Theodore pushed his head up through the thick canopy of heather and waggled his white ears. In the distance, Sir Trent bellowed out in response. Moments later they heard Henry's hooves thundering up the granite road towards them. Peter watched the critters through the gap in the wall. They began running in circles, screaming and wailing at the top of their voices, before backing into a huddled group at the far side of the enclosure.

'Now!' yelled Theodore, and he scampered up onto the wall. Puddles leapt it in a single bound. Ali and Peter followed, just as Henry and Stoke came charging through the entrance. The Hatter had been hunched over, a picture of resignation and misery. His head jerked up when he heard them and he seemed confused, then his whole face contorted with fear. 'No!' he screamed. *'Flee!'*

Ali and Peter kept on running towards him.

'Stop!' yelled Theodore. But his warning was too late. Critters were already leaping onto the wall, dozens of them, climbing up from their hiding places under the heather beyond the stones. They came swarming across the polished rock, a hideous collection of creatures, all deformed, all shrieking and laughing as they encircled the rescue party. They didn't attack, just gathered in a tight flank all around them, swinging clubs and stamping feet.

'Come on then!' yelled Theodore. 'What are you waiting for?'

'That would be me,' said a voice so deep it seemed to be rising from the earth itself. 'My little children are waiting for me.'

A dark shape rose up behind the wall, hundreds of sprigs of lavender falling from its body like water cascading from a rising leviathan. The rank and fetid smell of the Jabberwocky spread out across the clearing, an invisible mist of putrid air that overpowered the rescue team. Ali dropped to her knees, gasping for clean air and felt a dozen small hands dragging her across the ground. She saw the huge chain, and the Hatter tethered beside her. She tried to resist, kicking out as her arms were pulled behind her back.

'Peter!' she screamed out. She couldn't see him. She thrashed about as they bound her hands to a link in the chain. Air, she needed air. The putrid smell of the Jabberwocky was like a poisonous treacle clogging her lungs. Then she saw Peter being dragged over. He was unconscious, blood running from one cheek. They tied his ankles to the chain and left him lying face down beside her.

'I'm sorry,' she croaked. She wanted to shout but she couldn't breathe. She fought to stay awake, but the shrieking of the critters began to fade to a dull roar like surf on a distant beach. The last thing she saw was the clawed feet of the Jabberwocky as the shadow of his deformed body rippled across the ground towards her.

CHAPTER 27

A FESTIVAL OF BLIGHT

———————

'Is this not delightful?'

Ali opened her eyes. She had been lost in a confusion of dreams, old fairy tales and memories of childhood woven together into bizarre narratives with one common thread – an overwhelming sense of loss. The reality that greeted her was equally confusing. It was night. Dark shapes scampered about in front of her, their forms picked out in green light. None of it made sense. Then memory rushed into the vacuum like a savage punch to her sanity.

She wanted to scream, but instinct took over. She closed her eyes, feigning sleep, and focused on her body, testing muscle groups by clenching and releasing. She could feel bruises and scrapes everywhere, but nothing serious. Her fingers and hands were numb. She tried to move them, and pins and needles shot through her arms. The bonds around her wrists were too tight, cutting circulation. She began clenching and releasing her fists till blood and feeling returned.

There was one small mercy. The putrid stench of the Jabberwocky had all but gone. In its place was the pungent smell of lavender. Ali opened one eye just a fraction, and looked down over her shirt and jeans. A wreath of lavender had been placed across her shoulders.

'Ah, our salvation awakes.' There was no mistaking the deep, rattling voice of the Jabberwocky. He sounded close. Right in front of her. 'We have delayed our festivities for you. Disrespectful to start without you, when you are, after all, the main event.'

Ali steeled herself against the impact of seeing him, then she looked up. He was just as she remembered him. A nightmare on six legs. The Jabberwocky had the external skeleton of an insect, or perhaps a crustacean. It was hard to tell. Some mixture of the two, she thought. Except for the eyes. They were human, two large eyes the size of dinner plates. The irises were a hazel green, almost luminescent, the whites were a milky grey and rimmed with pink blood vessels. The lower lids drooped like sacks. Ali fixed her gaze on them, ignoring everything else.

'How old are you?' she asked.

'That is your question? When we have so much else to discuss?' Ali could feel his voice as much as hear it. The deep vibration drummed the air, the ground, and every cell of her body.

Questions. Her father's voice filled her head, firm and insistent. A conversation from long ago when she woke from a nightmare, too scared even to scream. *Questions, Newt. Keep asking questions. You can stare a nightmare down with questions; you can take control by asking questions.*

'You are so like her,' the Jabberwocky murmured, leaning in, examining her face. 'Yes indeed, a relative. No doubt. No doubt. My return is secured.'

Ali tried not to look at the creature's mouth, at the tiny limbs surrounding it like flagella, hundreds of them wiping and scraping scum and pus from his lips.

'How can you be this big?' She fought to keep her vice steady. 'When you transform, your body mass stays the same – you don't conjure new cells out of fresh air.'

'Listen to you!' The Jabberwocky put a claw under her chin and lifted her face to the light. 'You look like her. Now you sound like her. Always questioning, always interfering.'

Ali kept her eyes on his, but something was going on behind him. She could hear critters busying themselves at a task. Dozens of them were chatting, cursing and arguing. Even singing.

'So ... how? How did you get this big?'

'My children are good to me,' said the Jabberwocky. 'Any bits they don't need, they gift to me.'

'You eat the pieces you remove from them? The parts you cut off when you reduce them down to these small sad creatures?'

'Tokens of appreciation for the sanctuary I provide.' The Jabberwocky turned away. 'Enough chatter, time to celebrate this most momentous of days.'

He clapped two legs together, as if applauding himself, and scuttled to the centre of the enclosure where the critters had been at work. A bizarre throne now stood there. The seat was a stack of flat, broad stones, the back rest a wickerwork of sticks woven through branches. Hanging from the branches were a dozen glass jars that cast a shifting green light over the scene.

Ali shifted her weight, arching her back to ease the pressure on her arms and shoulders. She looked to her left. Her friends were all there, tied to the same chain, their hands bound, gags across their mouths. No one was struggling to get free. They all looked exhausted and dejected.

'Let the festivities begin!' cried the Jabberwocky. He ascended his throne, draping two of his crab limbs on the armrests and folding the others in a parody of crossed legs. 'We shall begin with a small feast. Bring the little hat man.'

Three critters scurried across, untied the Hatter, and dragged him over to the throne. Ali found it impossible to think clearly, fear was washing through her and stealing any chance at clarity. *Think, think!* She tried to stand, but her hands couldn't lift the chain she was tied to.

Then she heard Theodore whimpering. She looked over at him. He was trying to be brave. His head was up, his chin forward, as if he was forcing himself to watch his friend be mistreated.

'Read to my little children,' the Jabberwocky snapped the claws of one limb as if snapping his fingers. A critter stepped forward with a book and held it up to him. 'Not me. Give it to our little hatman, he's going to read it to us. Gather round that we may begin.' The critters shuffled in and settled at the Jabberwocky's feet. 'You may begin, hatman. Read us my story, the one Alice wrote for me.'

The Hatter took the book and began searching the pages. Even from this distance, Ali could see how badly his hands were shaking. He found the page, and in a low, faltering voice, began to read:

"Twas brillig, and the slithy toves, did gyre and gimble in the wabe.
All mimsy were the borogoves, and the mome raths outgrabe.
Beware the Jabberwock, my son, the jaws that bite, the claws
that catch.
Beware the Jubjub bird, and shun the frumious Bandersnatch!'

Ali tuned out. She closed her eyes and tried to focus on her breathing. A picture of the March Hare came drifting into her head, along with the image of a crystal ball. She knew her mind well enough, she knew it was trying to alert her to an idea that was chasing its tail just below the surface of her conscious mind. She watched and waited.

Over by the throne, the Hatter finished reading. He sighed, closed the book and waited with his head bowed. The critters began demanding more stories. The Jabberwocky held up a hand and they fell silent.

'More stories? Yes, my little ones; but not from that book. Stand our reader before me.'

Two of the critters took the Hatter by his elbows and pulled him to his feet. The Jabberwocky reached down to a scabbard strapped to one of his legs, drew a blade, and sliced off one of the Hatter's dreadlocks.

'Oooo, snakey!' He held it aloft and shook it, setting the memory ribbons to dance in the green light. Then he threw back his head and ate it.

'Mmmmm, delicious!' He made a great show of chewing and swallowing the braid. Then he cut another and ate that with the same theatrical gusto. Ali watched in silence, her mind swirling. Amid the chaos of her thoughts, the images of the March Hare and the crystal ball remained.

The Hatter's back was to her. He was enduring in silence, but Ali could see by the gentle heaving of his shoulders that he was weeping, a lost and tragic figure standing submissively as every one of his braids was cut from his head and eaten by the Jabberwocky.

'Think!' Ali cursed herself aloud. In one way, this creature was like the Chief Scholar. He had the same self-assured arrogance. Would he have the same blind spot? What did she know of him? Nothing but his name. Was his name another of her great-aunt's riddles – something as simple as an anagram?

A disturbance started up among the critters, a jostling out beyond the spill of green light. Faces turned to the source. Creatures stepped back to let new arrivals into the open circle by the throne. It was Mister Spikes and the small rat, Gutter. They were dragging a heavy load. Ali couldn't make it out at first, there were too many creatures stepping in the way. Finally, there was a gap, and she saw the terrified face of Potts. The critters were dragging her by her ankles.

Ignore it! Ali closed her eyes. *Concentrate. J-A-B-B-E-R-W-O-C-K-Y.*

'Well, well, who have we here?' The Jabberwocky sheathed his knife, sat back and smiled. 'My prodigal sons return – my dear Mister Spikes and his little companion, Gutter. I hear you went a-wandering, yes?'

'We have a gift,' said Spikes.

'And news to share,' the rat added, his voice trembling. 'Important news.'

'Then share.' The Jabberwocky patted what passed for his lap and Gutter and Mister Spikes scrambled up and settled there like puppies. The hedgehog turned and pointed at Ali as he started chattering softly to his master. Ali blocked it out. She didn't have to hear them to know what was being said. They had seen her go back to the barn. They knew she had the secret of safe passage.

Concentrate on the name. Nothing else.

'What a splendid day this is. Splendid.' The Jabberwocky patted the two critters on their heads. 'And what naughty children you are. But we will forgive, yes, we will. There will be a small forfeit. You will each choose a token, a gift of penitence.' He poked one of the rat's legs. 'This, perhaps? You choose – choose it and chop it, but all with smiles and happiness, no shrieking for my poor ears. One gift each and all will be forgiven.'

'Now?' said the rat, his voice failing him. He looked down at the stump of his missing hand. 'So soon?'

Concentrate. J-A-B-B-E-R-W-O-C-K-Y. Where to start? Rocky? Jab? A boxer? Where had he come through? The doorway in the barn, or the one in the Tower of London? She watched the letters swirl and dance, but nothing jumped out at her.

'As for this new plaything,' the Jabberwocky said, prodding Potts with the tip of one clawed leg, then leaning forward and smiling at her. 'You will be happy here with us, in time, when all your pain is behind you. This version of you will die in the white heat of that pain. You will become that which you hold yourself to be; your best and worst dreams made manifest. Choose well.'

He stood up, pushing the rat and the hedgehog from his lap. They grabbed hold of Potts' ankles and dragged her away.

Potts. The letters swirled again. People had often been named after their trades. *Potter, Thatcher, Miller. Was a trade hidden in the letters of Jabberwocky? Baker was in there. Even baker boy. Or jockey. Had he been a jockey in his former life? Had he resented being small?*

A stillness came over Ali, the odd serenity that had swept over her at the manor house. She felt herself detaching from the chaos around her, retreating into a memory. She was wandering a fairground with her mother. They entered a tent. Incense filled the air. A woman was sitting at a table behind a large crystal ball. *Watch how this works.* Her mother's voice. She had a finger to her lips. *Say nothing, just listen. You will see how she does it.*

'What next, my children?' the Jabberwocky slapped his armrest. 'How can I entertain you on this very special night?'

'Fight!' One critter yelled.

'Yes!' cried another. 'Fight!' Soon they were all stamping the ground and chanting with one voice: FIGHT! FIGHT! FIGHT!

Why that memory? Ali could see the psychic in her mind, the way she held the crystal ball. Her soft, theatrical voice. Why was this so important? All around her the air was ringing with the critters' chant. *Fight, fight, fight.*

'Enough!' The Jabberwocky got to his feet. 'My poor ears. A fight you shall have. Select your champion.'

'Me!' A deformed bear stepped forward. He seemed big for a critter, chest height, with broad shoulders and long arms. His fur was matted and dull and half his teeth were broken.

Listen to her questions. Her mother's voice. *She isn't using psychic powers. This is an old vaudeville act. She uses questions, nothing else, simple questions to tease out small details. Details she can use to build a picture.* Was this what the memory was telling her? How to use questions like darts, each one inching closer to a bullseye?

'Mister Scratcher.' The Jabberwocky patted the bear's head. 'I will allow it. You can honour us this day. Come, let us choose your opponent.' They walked over to the chain and inspected the captives as if selecting fruit at market. The bear stopped in front of Peter.

'This one,' he growled.

'Really?' the Jabberwocky pulled Peter to his feet. 'Rather scrawny. We'll give him two blades, Mister Scratcher. Only fair, you with all your fine claws.'

'As many blades as he likes,' said the bear. He slashed the ropes that bound Peter's ankles to the chain and started pushing him across to the throne. Peter turned to look back at Ali, his eyes wide with terror and confusion.

'Fool,' Ali said, as the Jabberwocky scuttled past her. 'Go ahead and waste more of your precious time.'

'Entertainment for my children is never a waste of time,' the Jabberwocky paused and smiled down at her. 'So much more to come.'

'Dull-witted, that's how the Queen described you. Now I see why.'

'I shall thank her slowly and painfully when we meet.' He shook his head like a disappointed parent. 'Enjoy the festivities. Last evening. Don't waste it.'

'You haven't asked why Peter's here,' she called out as he walked away. 'That is the measure of how stupid you are.'

'Enlighten me.'

'He came to warn me,' Ali lied. 'He came through here, risking his life, so I could go home before it closes.'

'Closes?' The Jabberwocky spun around. 'What closes?'

'The gate Alice uses. The one I've been using. It's kept open by a mirror on the other side. Peter came here to take me back. People on the other side plan to smash the mirror and seal the gate.'

'Liar!'

'To what end?'

'Mister Scratcher!' The Jabberwocky called out. 'A change to our schedule. Chain the boy back up and bring this one to me. It's time for my drink.' The bear growled under his breath but followed orders. Ali started flexing her fingers and hands the moment she was untied, clenching her fists and releasing them to get rid of the pins and needles. She was escorted to the centre and made to stand in front of the throne.

Still the serenity continued. She knew why. She was a deer confronting a lion, her body awash with flight chemicals. Subjective time was slowing down to a trickle. She lifted her head and looked up at the Jabberwocky, scrutinising him as if he were a bug on a glass slide, a curiosity for her microscope. He seemed to be a mix of crab and beetle, his body contorted by skin that had grown hard and thick like petrified leather. There were shreds of old clothing tied to his deformed limbs, and two daggers were strapped in sheaths to his hind legs. Ali could make out the source of the green light now. Fireflies were vibrating in the glass jars that hung from the throne like lanterns.

'I don't know the secret to getting back safely,' said Ali.

'I know. My wayward children told me how you tricked them. They fell ill, the poor things. It almost killed them. And you were sick too – oh yes, they told me.'

Ali said nothing. So, Mister Spikes and Gutter had lied to their master. She scanned the lines of critters, and there was the rat, watching her intently. Why didn't they tell him? Then, suddenly, she remembered her promise to them back at the house. To take them with her to the infirmary at the palace.

'You didn't die though, did you?' The Jabberwocky poked her with the sharp tip of one limb. 'You were sick, yes, but no death. Because, like our beloved Alice, you don't need the secret. You have your own special blood to take you safely through. So that's all I need from you. Not your clever words. Not the tasty terror in your eyes when the chopping starts. All I need is your delicious blood so I can go home.'

'If you take my blood, I'll die.'

'How does that inconvenience me?'

'I'm the only one who knows your true history.'

'Liar!' The Jabberwocky spat the word out. 'No one knows that! Even Alice couldn't find it.'

'But she did. She buried it in your name.' Ali paused, watching his eyes. 'Do you miss the smell of bread?'

'Bread?' The Jabberwocky looked irritated, even bored. 'I have bread and I smell it often enough.' Ali cursed silently. So, not a baker then. There were names in the anagram, too. Bob and Bobby. Jack, Jacky and Becky. Which one?

'Enough chatter.' The Jabberwocky turned to the critters behind him. 'Come, children, hang this windbag of fine wine from the back of my throne.'

Six of his deformed flock ran forward, eager to please. Ali didn't fight as they carried her to the back of the throne. She concentrated on the letters floating before her eyes. Then, all at once, she had it. The letters settled into two words. A name AND a trade. A perfect fit for every letter.

'Not like that!' the Jabberwocky slapped one of the critters aside. 'Has no one bled a deer before? We hang her feet up!' He reached down, grabbed Ali's ankles and hoisted her up against the back of the throne, holding her there as the critters strapped her ankles to the top of the backrest.

'Bring my drinking bowl. I want to get every last drop.'

A gigantic cockroach scurried forward, its tiny feet clicking on the stone ground, a large wooden bowl balanced on its back. It stopped inches from Ali's face, and in that moment the serenity deserted her. One moment she was in her own head, a quiet refuge in the eye of the storm, the next, she was engulfed by fear, the full impact of what was happening breaking over her like a tsunami of raw emotion.

All she could see in front of her was an upside-down patch of rocky ground, the leering face of the cockroach and the clawed feet of the Jabberwocky. She could hear the blood pulsing in her head. Her face felt bloated and there was a pressure building behind her eyes. The Jabberwocky's upturned face came into view and hovered above the ground, his eyes just inches from hers.

'Look, Roach,' he said. 'Look at the fat veins in her neck, all juicy now like pretty pink worms.'

'You're Jack.' It was a statement. She focused on his eyes as she said it, watching for any sign of a memory stirring.

'Who?' he grabbed Ali's head with one of his forelimbs. The end of it was covered in short hairs that tangled with Ali's own hair like Velcro.

'You pulled a cart,' Ali said, 'a wooden barrow.'

'Did not!' The Jabberwocky drew a blade and pressed it to Ali's neck. He was lying. Ali could see it in his eyes, confusion was blooming there. 'Not me. I was a king. Highborn.'

'You delivered beer.'

'Stop it! *Stop it!*' He dropped the dagger. 'We don't want to hear this.'

'In London. You pushed a barrow, you worked for a brewer.' Ali squeezed her eyes shut for a moment, they felt like they were going to burst from all the blood pooling in her face. She forced them open again.

'London ...' The Jabberwocky's own eyes were beginning to glaze over. 'What else, what else?'

'You were a brewer's boy. Jack. You delivered beer all around London.'

'Beer,' his voice dropped to a whisper. 'I remember the beer. Important people bought it. I went to important places.'

'You did. The Tower of London.'

'Yes.' His eyes turned inward, and he started to shake.

'You delivered your barrels to a storage room deep in the tower. One day you got lost or confused. You took a wrong turn.'

'I did. Lost, down in the dark.' The Jabberwocky dropped to his knees and began to sob. He pulled his forelimb from Ali's head. Some of her tangled hair tore free and she felt blood running across her scalp.

'You were a brewer's boy. Everyone called you BREWBOY JACK.'

'Poor me. Poor me.' The Jabberwocky tumbled to his side and clutched his belly. 'Mother, Father. I'm here. I'm here. Little sister Charity – come hold me, come hold your poor brother.' Then he was lost, travelling alone in a private nightmare of remembering, a pitiful figure curled up in a world of unimaginable grief. Critters gathered round his thrashing form, staring in confusion at their tormentor.

'Enjoy,' Ali whispered. She grabbed the Jabberwocky's fallen dagger and tried to curl upward to cut her ankles free. She couldn't get near them. She put the dagger between her teeth, and tried again, grabbing hold of the backrest to haul her weight up. Mister Spikes and Gutter beat her to it. They jumped onto the seat of the throne, reached up and chewed through her ropes. Ali dropped, rolled and sprang to her feet, the Jabberwocky's dagger still between her teeth.

'Take us with you,' yelled the rat, 'like you promised.'

'Can't stay here.' Mister Spikes jumped down next to Ali, stepping round the Jabberwocky who was rolling and wailing on the ground. Ali took the blade from between her teeth.

'Bring Potts,' she yelled, then ran off, weaving past the critters who were inching forward to see the thrashing body of their master.

'Ali!' screamed Peter when he saw her racing towards them. 'Behind you!'

Ali didn't stop to look round, she kept running, changing her line and making for Puddles, the giant black dog.

'Watch my back,' she screamed as she cut him fee. Six critters, including the cockroach, had shaken off their confusion and had come chasing after Ali. They hesitated when Puddles turned to face them. Mister Roach looked around, suddenly aware that none of their colleagues were backing them up.

'Hold on,' he growled to the others. 'Best we go back and await his orders.'

They hurried off, Puddles at their heels, barking encouragement as Ali cut free the rest of her friends. They huddled together for a moment, rubbing life and feeling back into their hands, hardly believing their sudden change in fortune. Sir Trent was the first to gather his wits.

'We can finish this now, while our foe is in disarray.'

'No,' the Hatter shook his head. 'This folly is all of my doing. These pathetic creatures should not pay for my foolishness.'

'Agreed.' Theodore stamped his feet. 'And a fast run will ease our cramped joints and get our blood moving again.'

'Is that the decision of our group?' asked Sir Trent. It was, everyone gave their nod. 'Very well. Let us be on our way and leave these unfortunates to dance about like headless fowl.'

They left by the gate, stepping out onto the roadway without a single challenge.

CHAPTER 28

RELIEF AND REVELATION

The return journey passed without incident. Once they were clear of the enclosure and its eerie green glow, they could see clearly by starlight. It was the first time either Ali or Peter had seen the night sky this far from the palace. Here, there were no flickering garden torches or light spilling from the palace windows. Out here on the open moorland, nothing competed with the light of the stars. The moon had yet to rise, but the shimmering starlight was enough to guide them safely across the lowlands of heather.

Little was said between them. At one point the Hatter started apologising for his foolishness, but Theodore quickly shut him down. Reprisals and apologies and all manner of explanations could wait till they were safely back at the palace.

'One thing I must know,' said Henry, 'for if you don't tell us, I will likely be inventing all kind of exhausting narratives the whole journey back. What in the name of madness did you do to the Jabberwocky?'

'I told him his true history.'

'You knew it?'

'No. I guessed that 'Jabberwocky' was an anagram with his real name or his trade hidden in it. I was solving it while he was eating all the ribbons.'

'Speaking of ribbons,' Theodore slapped the Hatter on the back. 'You will have to read the copies until your hair grows long enough to bear ribbons again.'

'Copies?' said the Hatter. 'I made no copies.'

'No, but the Queen did.'

'What?!' The Hatter's expression was hard to read in the starlight. Delight and irritation seemed to be in conflict. 'How? When?'

'A few ribbons every night when you were deeply asleep.' Theodore did his best to keep his voice neutral. The Hatter fell silent. They were halfway to the Bamboo Forest when Peter stopped and leaned his head back so all he could see was the extraordinary field of stars.

'Why are they so bright? Are they closer or something?'

'I don't know,' said Ali. 'These are not our stars.'

'Pretty stunning though, walking by starlight. Hand in hand.'

'We're not.'

'I'm working up to that. Stars are romantic.'

'Clumsy.' She pointed to a constellation. 'I'm not so great on astronomy, but that's Orion's Belt. So maybe most of it looks the same as our sky. We've stepped through to a copy of our universe, one that bifurcated off at some point, so some things will have evolved differently from that point.'

'Not quite the romantic angle I was going for.'

'Tough. Stop gawping and keep up.'

They reached the Bamboo Forest and set about making torches. Theodore found new shoots of bamboo thin enough to cut. Sir Trent had tinder, flints and tree gum in his saddle pack, and between them they made three flaming torches to light their way through the dense forest. They were almost through when they heard critters pattering in their wake. Sir Trent drew his sword to confront them, but Ali reassured him.

'I invited some old friends to join us.'

Mister Spikes and Gutter came shuffling into the light of the torches. They had brought Potts with them as instructed. She was unconscious, and they were still dragging her by her ankles.

'Henry,' Ali turned to the horse. 'Would you be able to carry this unfortunate woman back to the palace?'

'Now *that* is how to do it,' Henry eyeballed Sir Trent. 'No one is too old to learn a few manners.'

Peter helped the old knight wrap Potts in a saddle blanket. He tried not to look at the damage the critters had done to her. Dozens of cuts and bite marks covered her face and body. Every inch was a confusion of dried blood and dirt. Strips of clothing were meshed with strips of skin, all of it a grey brown colour, as if blood and soil had mixed with dry leaves to form a new skin.

They draped Potts' body, tightly wrapped up in the blanket, over Henry's saddle and set off again. A rising moon greeted them as they emerged from the forest, a glittering crescent moon, its craters clearly visible along the rim of the Earth's shadow line.

'It's starting,' whispered the rat. 'The hurting.'

'We knew. We agreed. Stay strong.' Mister Spikes put a hand on the rat's shoulder. They were still some miles from the palace. The Critters had walked in silence since joining the rescue party, but now their agitation and discomfort was making them whimper and curse.

'What is to be done with them?' Theodore was walking beside Ali and the Hatter. 'Your generous nature towards these creatures is to be commended, but their pain will only increase the closer we get to the palace. They will find no rest from their discomfort until they are back in the Fringes.'

'Yes, and why is that?' said Ali.

'No one knows.' Theodore shrugged his shoulders. 'The scholars have a number of theories. None have led to any practical way to help them.'

'Not that there has been a desire to do so,' said the Hatter. 'To cure your enemy from the one affliction that keeps them from your door? Surely such a focus of time and resources would be misplaced.'

'Look at them.' She gestured to the two critters who were now hopping as they walked, hopping and dancing as if the ground was burning their feet. 'Where would they rather live, out in the fringes with the monster who reduced them to be like this, or with us in the palace? If they were free of pain, they would choose the palace.'

'You would have us experiment on these two unfortunates?' Theodore shook his head. 'So is this compassion at work, or an overreaching pride?'

They arrived at the ridge overlooking the palace and were immediately spotted by a battlement guard. A small escort came racing up the slope to lend assistance. They hesitated when they saw the two critters, but Sir Trent vouched for them and the party moved into the palace grounds. Sir Trent, Theodore and Puddles went with the Hatter to see the Queen. Ali, Peter and Henry took the two critters and Potts down to the infirmary.

'Fascinating!' said Sawbones. Ali had gone straight to his office to seek his support. 'Where are they?'

'The injured woman is badly hurt; your staff are cleaning her wounds. Her transformation may be starting, no smell yet, but there's a boil on her neck.'

'And the two unfortunates?'

'Outside, running in circles to escape their pain. Henry is with them.'

'Your approach?'

'They need to acclimatise. The palace is the centre of a gravity well. I think the Fringes are the opposite, they lie beyond the effects of the gravity well.'

'You think the critters have adapted to living out there? Their physiology, their metabolics, all adjusted for life out in the Fringes?

'It might explain it.' Ali was relieved; she hadn't been sure the Head Apothecary would be sympathetic to the idea. 'When they venture out, every atom of their body is being very slightly compressed. They need time to adapt and acclimatise.'

'We can sedate them for a week or two. Wake them for an hour each day to assess their progress. Feed them poppy milk in their waking hours to ease their suffering.'

It was agreed, Ali hurried out to tell the critters and bumped straight into Waxstaff. She was walking on her hind legs, a glittering green and gold lizard as tall and slender as she had been in her human form. Ali screeched with delight and threw her arms round her mother's old friend.

'Look at you! You are magnificent!'

'I am, aren't I? Try not to hug me quite so hard, I'll lose my balance. Walking is hard to master on account of the tail.'

'You have to bend forward and lift it like a counterweight.'

'Oh, do I indeed?' Waxstaff's eyes glittered like gemstones. 'Done this a lot have you?'

'Long rainy afternoons in the Natural History Museum.'

'How sad,' she put her hands on Ali's shoulders. 'But now our little science nerd has found she has a heart too. Are you ready to do this?'

'We have to find a way, don't we? To help all of them?'

'We do. Now, enough with the hugging. Tell me everything. I just saw Potts being carried to a bed.'

'That okay?'

'Do I have a choice?'

'Of course you do. Theodore can lend you his axe. No one would stop you or condemn you. It might still come to that if the transformation goes badly.'

They found a quiet corner, and Ali gave Waxstaff a summary of the rescue trip. Then they helped Sawbones and his team settle Mister Spikes and Gutter into beds in the far corner of the infirmary. Ali held their small hands and reassured them as the sedation took effect.

'Now I have to keep my pledge to the boys,' said Waxstaff. 'They wanted to see you, remember? And I promised to be there for support.'

'Did I upset them or something?'

'It's hard to know. They're upset with your great-aunt Alice for deserting them. But with you? No, I don't believe so.'

'Are they recovered?'

'A little withdrawn,' said Waxstaff. 'What is that fancy new name they use for shell-shock?'

'Post-traumatic stress disorder.'

'That, yes.'

They left the infirmary, passing by Potts' bed to collect Peter. The sun was just lifting above the eastern wall of the grounds as they walked up the main lawn to the palace.

'I am so hungry!' said Peter. 'Can we go to the kitchen first?'

'No.' Waxstaff had turned a glittering crimson, the gold flecks in her skin reflecting the rising sun. 'The boys were insistent.'

'Okay,' Ali said, taking Peter's hand, 'we do this first, then I am going to soak in a very hot bath, then the three of us can sit over breakfast and plan our return.'

'Our?' Waxstaff shook her head. 'No.'

'I've thought about this. Our first step is to take back control of Grey Manor. Our beachhead. It's private and secluded, loads of bedrooms. If we go back with Sir Trent and Puddles and a few of the guards, we can take it.'

'And King?'

'We capture her.'

'Ha!'

'We can! She's paranoid about secrecy. Her team back at the manor house is a joke. Puddles will take them out in seconds. We capture King, take over the house and invite people like Dovecot to come and see what's really going on.'

'Yes!' Peter agreed. 'We've been letting King scare us and control us. If we are going to flip this, we need to go on the attack.' They reached the main steps and asked the duty guard where the boys could be found.

'The Queen's chambers,' said the guard. 'And if I may – bravo to you! Saving the Hatter as you did. We are all of us in your debt.'

Ali thanked him, and led the way through the palace. It was Waxstaff's first visit, and she hesitated when they came to one of the long hallways. Chandeliers hung from the ceiling and huge mirrors covered the walls.

'Must we go this way?' asked Waxstaff. 'I've looked down at my body for long enough, but I haven't braved a mirror yet.'

'Sorry, I wasn't thinking,' Ali spun round. 'I think there's a servant's passage we can take.'

'Oh, the fuck with it,' Waxstaff took a deep breath and walked over to the first of the mirrors. She stood completely still for a moment, staring at the strange reflection looking back at her. Then she closed her eyes and began to weep. Peter stepped up beside her and took one hand. Ali took the other. They didn't try to say anything. How could they understand what she was going through? They just stood with her, holding her hands until she was ready to move.

They arrived to find the door to the Queen's apartment wide open. Custard was hovering inside and was first to spot them. She ran out and embraced Ali.

'We should be holding a party to thank you – not this!'

'Now I really am worried.' Ali returned the embrace. 'What's so pressing it can't wait till I've had a hot bath?'

The two boys appeared in the doorway and held out their hands.

'Come with us, Miss Ali. Hold our hands if you please. We have something important to show you.' They took her hands and escorted her into the room. The Hatter was there with the Queen, Theodore and Stoke.

'My dear.' The Queen came forward, put her hands out to cradle Ali's head, and planted a kiss on her forehead. 'Words will never be enough to express my gratitude for what you did last night.'

'What's going on? Is this like some weird family intervention. Are you asking me to stay and help?'

'No. We ask nothing of you,' said the Hatter. 'We are here because Ricky and Ted have something to tell you. They asked us all to be here in support.'

'Then tell me,' Ali said, turning to the boys, 'and make it a short version of whatever it is. We've walked for miles, crawled through bracken and been splashed with the foul spittle of the Jabberwocky, and I intend to spend the rest of the morning in a steaming hot bath.'

'We can postpone this if you like,' said the Queen. 'Ali, you must decide. The boys want to show you a truth that might upset you. They guessed it some time ago. It's why they stuck like glue to Jackie.'

'All right then. Bloody hell. Just tell me.'

'We have to show you,' said Ricky.

'Then you'll understand', said Ted, 'because you're clever.'

'Now you really are making me nervous.'

'That's why we're holding your hands,' said Ricky.

'Both of us,' said Ted. They walked her across the room to a door on the far side. 'It's through here.'

'In her bedchamber,' said Ricky. They opened the door and led Ali through. On the wall was a painting, a portrait like the one in Ali's room. The same size. The same artist. Only the subject was different.

Standing by the tree in the painting was Alice, no more than fourteen years old. Except it wasn't Alice. It was Ali's mother.

'What the frack is this?' Ali whirled round. The others had all followed into the room. The Queen was holding something. She held it out to Ali.

'Your photographs. Jackie gave these into the boys' care.' Ali snatched the photos from her.

'You had this painted? From the photo? Why? What kind of sick present is this?' She turned back to the painting and poked it with a finger. The paint was dry. She looked more closely, and saw layers of dust on the ridges of oil paint.

No one spoke. Waxstaff came up beside her, reached up and touched the face in the painting. Her golden lizard fingers began to tremble.

'Frack you!' Ali felt a surge of pure rage, a blinding anger she couldn't control. She wanted to scream at them. To punch the looks of compassion from their faces. To rip and tear at their suffocating blanket of love and concern.

'NO! No fucking way!' She screamed and fell to her knees. Peter dropped down beside her and tried to hold her, but Ali shoved him away. He held her again, wrapping her as tightly as he could, while her body began to shake.

'Cruel!' One word. It was all Ali could see in the dark red of her anger. One word floating in the darkness behind her eyes. Cruel. She could feel Peter's arms around her like thick ropes of affection. Containing her, restricting her. A prison. Cruel. Then the word evaporated. It blew to pieces inside her, the shards cutting through her, ripping holes in everything she knew. Her eyes snapped open and she stared at Peter's face just inches from her own.

'It is her,' she whispered, her voice trembling, her eyes wide with emotions that Peter couldn't read. 'It fits. All of it. Alice is my mother.'

'We know why she never came back now,' said Ricky.

'Yes,' Ted nodded, 'We understand now. We can forgive her now. She stayed over there for you.'

AFTERWORD

They sat together on the lawn. Cook had made them a picnic break-fast and the Queen had asked everyone to leave them in peace for the day. Ali felt drained, more exhausted than at any time in her life. She felt adrift too, a boat with its moorings cut through. Her parents had lied to her every day of their lives. Peter and Waxstaff didn't press her to talk, they just sat with her, three refugees lost in their own thoughts, looking out over the palace grounds of another world.

'I have to find him,' Ali said at last. 'Find him and confront him.'

'Find him, certainly,' said Waxstaff. 'We find him, free him from wherever King is holding him, then we start. Nothing changes, girl. You will learn to grow and adapt to this news, as I must adapt to this.' She slapped one of her knees.

'Okay, just so I'm clear on this,' Peter glanced at Ali before pushing on, 'the Queen said Alice stayed here for over two years on her last visit. Which meant a hundred and twenty years or more had passed over on our side. She went back, but something had happened. And she forgot everything.'

'And my grandmother adopted her. Yes.'

'Fuck! Which means Alice is dead, right? Because your mum is dead.'

'Is she?' Ali pulled another muffin to pieces, but didn't take a bite.

'What do you mean?'

'Alice was a fighter. So was my mum, obviously. She never came back here once she had me. I love her for that, I guess. But she and Dad carried on figuring everything out, or trying to. All his research makes sense now, doesn't it? And they must have been keeping their heads down. Mum looked after me till I was school age, but then she started her work, traveling to war zones around the world with that children's charity.'

'And?'

'What if it was all a front and she was looking for the other gates, or for the people who are trying to plug the gates? What if the explosion was one big cover-up? We had a memorial, not a burial. What if she's not dead, Peter, but trapped on the other side of another gravity well? I think that's what Dad believes – it's what drives his work. I think he's been trying to find her.'

OTHER TITLES
IN THE SERIES

BOOK ONE

The Secret of Safe Passage

BOOK THREE

To Kill a Jabberwocky

due out late 2026

For up-to-date information about Martin's work
and links to his social media platforms, go to:
martinbaynton.com